Friends & Lovers

Friends & Lovers

June Francis

PIATKUS

First published in Great Britain in 1993 by
Judy Piatkus (Publishers) Ltd of
5 Windmill Street, London W1

**The moral right of the author
has been asserted**

*A catalogue record for this book is available
from the British Library*

ISBN 0–7499–0184–5

Set in 11/12 Linotron Times by
Phoenix Photosetting, Chatham, Kent
Printed and bound in Great Britain by
Butler & Tanner Ltd, Frome and London

Dedicated to
May Lilian and Irene May
with love

Acknowledgement

I would like to thank my Hawitt cousins Maureen, Majorie and Irene for their interest and willingness in helping me with my American research. It was much appreciated.

The secret sympathy,
The silver link, the silken tie,
Which heart to heart, and mind to mind,
In body and in soul can bind.

SIR WALTER SCOTT. *The Lay of the Last Minstrel.*

Prologue

'Hilda!'

Vivien Preston lifted her head and stared at the man in the bed. His face and neck were so wrinkled that he reminded her of a tortoise. 'Yes, Father,' she said, knowing it would only make her grandfather agitated if she said that she was not his elder daughter. Lucid moments were few and far between and most times Jack Preston had no idea who she was. Sometimes he was back in the previous century when he was a boy and believed Viv to be his sister, but today it seemed he thought she was his daughter.

She knelt by the side of the bed, her long red-gold hair veiling her face, and listened to Jack Preston's laboured breathing. The doctor had said she could put her grandfather in a home but she had known his feelings on that subject and had decided that, however difficult, she would continue to look after him so that he could die in his own bed.

An eyelid quivered and lifted. 'You'll look after your mother and little Flora now, Hilda girl? I won't be away long this trip.' The voice was thread-like.

'Yes, Father.'

'You know where the money is if you need it? Take one of the coins to the pawnbroker's.'

Involuntarily Viv glanced at her cousin George Cooke, standing by the window overlooking the street. His eyes were suspiciously bright and his hands clenched into fists. His grandfather's favourite, George had found it unbearably difficult to accept that the old man no longer recognised him

1

when he had finished his National Service and arrived back home in Liverpool.

'How many times has Grandfather asked that question about money? And I've still no idea where he kept it,' Viv whispered to him.

It seemed that George was about to say something but the old man spoke again, drawing her attention. 'You're not like your mother, girl!' His eyes, dredged of their once rich brown colour, were now pale and watery.

'What?' she said, startled.

'You're like *my* mother. She was a tough old bird. Nothing ever scared her.' He paused and seemed to be gathering his strength. 'Where are you, girl? You know Mam said you weren't to go wandering off!'

Viv's heart beat rapidly and tears suddenly prickled in her eyes' He was back to his boyhood again. 'I'm here, Jack,' she said.

'You mustn't go off. You know it worries Mam.' His voice was tremulous now and weak. 'You be a good girl and stay out of trouble.'

'Yes, Jack,' she whispered.

Silence fell. It went on and on and suddenly it seemed that Grandfather was hardly breathing.

George came over to the bed and knelt beside Viv. 'Do you reckon this is it?' His voice was unsteady.

She slipped her hand into his, unable to speak for the tightness in her throat. Once before they had seen a member of their family die and it had been a terrible moment. This was different, though. Rosie had been so young. Their grandfather was full of years and well past his three score and ten.

'Should I go for the doctor again?' whispered George.

'No, stay! What can the doctor do now?'

He nodded and a sigh escaped him as the pair of them continued to kneel side by side. They looked noticeably alike, the children of Jack Preston's two daughters, both now living in America. George's mother Flora lived on the west coast but Viv's mother Hilda had made her home in New Jersey on the east coast. It was eight years since Viv had seen her mother. She had been nine years old when Hilda had crossed the Atlantic alone, glad to leave behind a war-damaged

Liverpool. She still found it difficult to forgive her mother for that final leavetaking. Hilda was the black sheep of the family, having disgraced the family name by giving birth to Viv without the benefit of a husband and without naming the father of her child. Jack Preston had banished her from the house though now he had no memory of it, just as he had forgotten that he had so often called Viv 'Hilda's bastard'.

It was two years since she had volunteered to live with her grandfather, so enabling her aunt to go to California with her second husband Mike, an American ex-serviceman, and their three young children. Before senility had destroyed her grandfather's health and memory, his disapproval of Viv had been like a weapon he wielded to try and strip her of confidence. She had fought back, determined not to let him make her feel worthless. Yet still she found it hard to cope with the tasks that she had had to perform for Jack and which he obviously hated her doing. She had so wanted his affection, approval and appreciation. He had stubbornly refused to show anything of the sort and there had been times when she had come near to hating him.

But the earlier upbringing which her aunt had given her had stressed the importance of family. You should always be able to fall back on your family, whatever the sin, her aunt had dinned into her. Viv could only agree with her. After all, where would she have been if Aunt Flora had not taken her family responsibilities so seriously? She had been more of a mother to Viv than Hilda had ever been.

She still remembered the blazing row over a man that the sisters had had before her mother stormed out of Flora's house. Hilda had returned a year or two later but the incident and her desertion of Viv had left a wound that refused to heal with time. Hilda had married disastrously, only to be widowed, and then vanished once more from her daughter's life, emigrating to America. Since then Viv only heard from her mother at Christmas and occasionally on her birthday. She had remarried in America but not once had she asked her daughter to go and live with her. Many times Viv had yearned for such an invitation but it had never come.

'How much longer do you think?'

Viv gave her cousin a sidelong glance as he squeezed her hand. 'I don't know. But surely it can't be much longer? Perhaps if we prayed . . .'

'Prayed what? That he gets better!' hissed George, going a dull red. Any mention of God or religion was like a red rag to a bull since George's childhood sweetheart had thrown him over and become a nun.

'No, that he dies.'

Her cousin looked shocked but Viv did not care. Her life had been put on hold for the last two years. She stared down at her grandfather, praying that he would go peacefully, and hoped that God would forgive her. Enough was enough. It would be a blessing if this time he did not make a recovery. She and George needed to start living their own lives. Often of late her grandfather had made her think too much of the past and the part her mother had played in it. It was the future that interested Viv. Painful memories of her mother had no place in that.

Chapter One

The guests had finished the funeral feast and departed. Viv was kneeling in front of the large, old-fashioned blackleaded fireplace toasting a crumpet because she had been too busy and fraught to feel hungry earlier. She glanced up as George entered the room and saw that the sombrely dressed stranger of earlier in the day had vanished. He had changed out of his black suit into paint-stained cords and a checked shirt. It seemed that the old easygoing George, her hero of years gone by, was back.

He knelt behind her, slid his arms over her shoulders and nuzzled her neck.

'Don't, George.' She brushed away one of his hands which was too close to her breast. 'I'm not going to be a substitute for Kathleen Murphy so don't start messing about. You can butter this crumpet for us. I'm starving.'

'Me too. I couldn't eat before. I hated the whole shebang.' He straightened up rather unsteadily, having drunk a little too much on an empty stomach.

'You found it harder than I did.' It was a statement of fact. Viv reached for the butter dish which stood ready on the hearth.

'I wish I could have said goodbye properly to him. The man I'd known died while I was away.' George's expression was sombre.

Viv nodded. 'Still, he didn't suffer.' She moved to sit down in the old rocking chair.

George leaned one elbow on the mantleshelf. 'I kept wishing that mam could have been here – and your mam!'

Viv grimaced. 'Fat chance when she still hasn't got in touch! But at least Aunt Flo will be pleased when we tell her how many people turned up to give Grandfather a good Orange send off. Although I can't really be doing with all that Orange and Green stuff myself.'

'Mam'd be pleased about the anchor of flowers you had made up for him. It was just right. Grandad's weighed anchor and set sail for the blue yonder. He might be through the Pearly Gates right now.'

Viv smiled faintly. 'You're sounding quite poetic and religious. I thought you'd finished with religion since Kathleen?'

'You're daft if you think Kathleen means anything to me,' he said with a sudden spurt of anger. 'I'm over her.'

Viv stared at him but kept quiet and bit into the crumpet. Butter oozed out and she licked it up with her tongue. There was silence for a moment then George said, 'I wonder if your mam actually knows about Grandad yet? I mean, we phoned my mam and she said she'd let Aunt Hilda know, but she also said she hadn't heard from her for a while.'

'That's nothing unusual with my mother,' said Viv drily. And if she does find out, she won't care.'

'You're hard on her,' he said absently, gazing into the fire. 'Mam mentioned Rosie's grave. Did you remember . . .?'

'Flowers?' She nodded.

'Thanks, Viv.' He had a smile of singular charm which still occasionally had the power to turn her heart over in her breast. He was very good-looking. The spitting image of his father who had been killed in the war, so her aunt had said. Tawny hair, brown eyes, an aquiline nose – which sometimes he looked down rather haughtily at her – and a stubborn, square chin. The smile gave way to a more hesitant expression and he said, 'I haven't told you before but Grandad wrote to me while I was away. You'd told me that he was starting to go a bit funny so I didn't take what he had said seriously at the time. But thinking about it now, Viv, there might have been something in what he wrote in that letter.'

'What?' She was suddenly alert.

'You can't have forgotten the way he went on about the money and coins? He wrote me that he'd buried a box of gold sovereigns. I though he was going doolally. *Treasure Island*

6

and all that! But maybe there was something in it and he wasn't completely gone . . .'

Viv got to her feet. 'Well, where is it?' she demanded.

Suddenly George laughed and the sound seemed to banish the gloom that had enveloped them all day. 'Follow me!'

They filed out into the white-washed backyard. Next to the old pigeon hutch some slabs of sandstone had been taken up and in the summer the yard was bright with pansies, snapdragons and marigolds. There was also a soliltary little wooden cross set apart from the bedding plants.

'Fifteen men on a dead man's chest, yo-ho-ho!' sang George as he tossed the cross aside and plunged a trowel into the soil.

'I thought his favourite pigeon was buried there,' said Viv, glancing at the wall they shared with next-door and then up at the windows of the yellow brick houses in the next street which overlooked their yard, hoping that nobody was watching and thinking they'd gone crackers.

'X marks the spot, Viv.' George flung the trowel aside and she drew closer as he lifted out a soil-encrusted tin box.

They exchanged glances. 'It's real,' she said in an awe-filled whisper. It *is* like *Treasure Island*!'

Her cousin laughed loudly. 'Well, Grandad was an old sea dog!' He brushed soil from the box and wiped his hands on his trousers before turning the key in the lock. The lid fell back and off its rusting hinges to reveal a handful of gleaming gold coins and a couple of plaster figures.

Viv groaned. 'It's hardly a fortune, is it?' Trust her grandfather to disappoint them.

George stared dumbfounded at the figures he held in each hand. 'Do you see what these are? One's some bloody saint and the other's the Virgin Mary! Now who do we know that's Catholic?'

Viv was about to say 'Kathleen Murphy' and tell him that she had called while he was away and Viv herself had been out, but before she had a chance her cousin said, 'The bloody Kellys next-door!' And he was off, storming into the house.

She flew after him but did not catch him up until he was through the house and into the street. She seized his arm. 'George, I think you're wrong. Kathleen was here!'

He stared at her but barely paused. 'You've got Kathleen on the brain. You know the Kellys didn't like Grandad!'

'They put money in the street collection for a wreath for him,' Viv said staunchly. 'Mrs Dermot told me. That proves something, George.'

'Proves they've got guilty consciences,' he said stubbornly, wrenching his arm free and striding up to the blue and white painted door with its border of painted bricks to match. 'Bloody Evertonians,' he muttered, and banged the brightly polished brass door knocker several times.

Viv realised instantly that it was more than the money being missing and the drink that was affecting him. He'd been spoiling for some action ever since he came home. Kathleen throwing him over and then Grandad not knowing him had hurt him deeply. He was like a wounded animal wanting to hit out at someone. Anyone!

The door was opened by a young man wearing an open-necked shirt and trousers. 'Yep?' He rested a shoulder against the doorjamb. 'What can I do for yer, Cookie?'

'You can take this,' said George, and punched him on the nose, sending him tumbling backwards through the open vestibule door.

Viv rushed forward and bent over Joe while George, swaying slightly, blew on his knuckles. Unexpectedly a khaki handkerchief was thrust into her hand. She looked up at the figure that towered over her. He was dressed all in black. 'Darkly, devilishly attractive', her friend Dot would have said, because his hair was black also and the eyebrows that slanted up at the outer edges were sooty slashes. His eyes, though, were bright blue and appraised her briefly before he stepped past.

Instinctively she ducked as his arm swung back and his fist slammed into her cousin's midriff. Fury bubbled inside Viv and she hit the stranger in the chest. 'What the hell do you think you're doing, hitting my cousin?'

He seized her hand. 'What the hell is *he* doing hitting my mate without provocation?'

Some of her anger evaporated. 'OK,' she muttered. 'You've got a point there.'

'True.'

8

'He's quite drunk, you know,' she said placatingly. 'And we've had a hard day of it.'

'We all have hard days. That doesn't mean we go around taking it out on people.'

'You don't understand . . .'

'Try me.'

'I'd rather not.' Viv was thinking that he had a nice smile. She pulled herself together. 'It's none of your business, really, is it?'

'It's mine, though,' came Joe's muffled voice.

'It was a mistake,' said Viv, slanting a glance at him. 'You're not missing any holy figures in your house, are you, Joe?'

'How the hell should I know?' he cried, looking baffled. 'I've not been home five minutes from the army. Is it something to do with your grandad? Mam said he'd gone doolally!'

'I don't believe my grandad was doolally when he wrote me that letter,' gasped George, deciding to take part in the conversation.

'What letter?' said Joe. 'And what's holy figures to do with you hitting me?'

'Don't tell him, Viv,' said George hurriedly.

'I'm not going to,' she said, aware that the stranger still had hold of her hand. She attempted to free her fingers but he seemed reluctant to release her and she did not want to struggle in undignified way. She looked at her cousin. 'Let's go home, George. We should never have come. You wouldn't have if you weren't drunk.'

'I'm not drunk!' he said, flashing her an exasperated look while still clutching his midriff. 'Keep out of this, Viv. What are you trying to make me look like? A bloody fool?'

'You are a fool,' she snapped, suddenly losing her temper. 'Why don't you just say you're sorry?'

'Sorry?' yelled her cousin. 'Why should I? And it's me who should be getting an apology. Joe should fight his own battles.'

'You took me by surprise! Anyway, Brycie's a mate,' said Joe. 'He was sticking up for me, just like Viv's sticking up for you.'

'She's family. Who's this Brycie?' George glared at the

stranger. 'I think I've seen you before and I didn't like you then!'

'Oh, stop it,' said Viv, avoiding the stranger's amused glance as she finally released her fingers. 'If he says he's sorry you'll call it quits, won't you?'

'If that's what you want.' His voice held no trace of a Liverpudlian accent. 'What do you say, Joe?'

'Hey, hang on,' put in George. 'You did say Brycie? I used to know a Nick Bryce once.'

There was a brief silence.

'George Cooke,' said Nick, his voice expressionless. 'Well, who'd have believed it?'

'You know each other?' demanded Viv.

'From the old street.' George's tone held a wary note. 'We almost killed each other once.'

'You asked for it.' Nick's smile held a certain grimness.

There was silence before Viv murmured, 'A draw, was it, and neither of you willing to admit it?'

'You could say that,' murmured Nick. 'One of the neighbours threw a bucket of water over us. Nothing like the shock of cold water to stop you in your tracks.'

'It was you that started it,' said George, sticking out his chin, an implacable expression on his face.

'I disagree. It was you insulting my mother that caused it,' said Nick.

'I was only a kid,' said George, shifting uncomfortably.

Nick nodded. 'Cruel little swines, kids.'

There was another silence.

'It must have been a long time ago. Why don't you forget it?' said Viv, thinking this could go on all day with them getting nowhere. Men! 'Or are you going to make it a lifelong vendetta?'

A corner of Nick's mouth lifted and his blue eyes scanned her again. 'It's hardly a vendetta. But I'm prepared to let bygones be bygones.'

'George?'

Her cousin shrugged. 'Suits me.'

'Good!' She smiled. 'Well, if you two aren't going to kill each other, I'll leave you to catch up on what's been happening during the last few years.'

'Surely there's no rush for you to go?' There was no mistaking Nick's interest and Viv felt herself blushing. She thought, I bet he's used to girls falling all over him. Well, she wasn't going to. 'I've things to do,' she said firmly. 'We've just had a funeral.'

'Pity,' he murmured. 'I'd like to further our acquaintance.'

'Some other time,' she said, assuming a casual manner.

She went back to the house with a sigh of relief, wondering what had caused her to feel so wobbly about the knees.

She brought in the box from the yard to count the sovereigns. There were footsteps outside and George let himself in with the key on the string behind the front door. 'You were quick,' she said.

'Had to ask them to go for a pint later. Thought I should do something to make it up to Joe. They're both just out of the army.' He stood staring at her, humming tunelessly. 'How many sovereigns are there?'

'Thirty.'

'There should have been hundreds,' he said gloomily. 'I suppose Grandad was doolally.'

Viv said thoughtfully, 'I'm not so sure. At least what he wrote in the letter about burying the box with sovereigns was true. What if he was worried about someone seeing him and decided to divide the money and put some elsewhere?'

'You mean he could have done that and then forgotten where?'

She nodded.

'Where d'you suggest?'

'We could start with his bedroom?'

George's eyes brightened. 'Right, you're on!'

She rose and followed him upstairs. They began to search but found nothing.

Eventually George rested his back against the door and lit a cigarette. 'There's nothing here. I suppose we'll have to forget it.

Vivien sighed and went over to the window. She thought how great it would have been to have spare cash to buy some decent clothes and perhaps to go to America. Her aunt had suggested them doing so for Christmas.

She stared out of the window. It was getting dark. Her

grandfather had seemed to love watching the sky. In his lucid moments he had told her never to close his curtains and she had got into the habit of doing what he said. She had not washed them for an age. Now she tugged on the flower-printed fabric. It felt heavier than it should have. She fingered the hems, remembering her sailor grandfather had been skilful with a needle and thread. Her spirits soared.

'Scissors!' she cried.

'Six hundred sovereigns! I can't believe it!' George danced her round and round the kitchen, hugged and kissed her, then danced her round again. 'I can go off and paint! I can go to Paris! We'll have to have a party before I go!'

'What are you talking about?' gasped Viv, as excited as he was but forcing him to halt.

'About doing what I've always wanted! Painting! Ma told me that Dad always wanted to be a real artist but couldn't afford it. Now I can.'

Vivien stared into his eyes and smiled. 'And I can go to America. You should come to, George, really you should. Forget Paris. Paint in America. Your man would love to see you.'

His smile faded. 'Don't go on about America. Mam's living her own life and we've got ours. If you feel like travelling, then come to Paris with me. We'll have a great time. Or what about South of France? They say the light's magic there.' He hugged her and would have kissed her again but she averted her face.

'It's not on, George,' she said seriously. 'Your mam will be hurt if neither of us go. I can't go waltzing off to France with you.'

His arms dropped abruptly to his sides and he moved away from her to sit at the table. His fingers toyed with a fold in the brown chenille cloth. 'You know how I feel about America. If I go there Mike's family'll try and turn me into a Yank like they've done to Mam and the kids. You've read her letters, Viv,' he said earnestly. 'I'm British through and through, and proud of it! The Yanks think everything about their country is so great. It's bigger, it's better. You've heard the way the kids speak of the place in their letters.'

12

Viv said lightly, 'To them it probably is. They are half American. You wouldn't be getting so worked up if you hadn't drunk so much.'

'I hope Nick Bryce believed I was drunk because otherwise he'll think I'm an idiot after what I said to Joe about going round there.'

'Why? What did you say?'

He avoided her eyes. 'Told him I couldn't stand their house being painted blue and white anymore.'

'He'll think you're an idiot anyway,' she said drily.

A reluctant smile flashed across his face. 'You never have seen how important it is to support the right team, Viv. Your mam did,' he said. 'She was a keen Liverpool supporter when she was a girl. She told me so.'

'I don't want to know,' Viv said tonelessly'. 'But you do realise that if my mother knew about this money, she'd be over here quicker than you could say Jack Flash? She loved money did my mother, and she was a right skinflint. I remember her paying me a mouldy sixpence to help clean the flat when she was married to Kevin.'

'Sixpence was sixpence in the forties,' said George, smiling.

'Your mam didn't think so. She doubled it.' Viv got off the subject of the past quickly. 'Shouldn't you be getting ready if you're going out? But better not have more than one pint or you'll be falling down,' she added, remembering a terrifying time when Kevin, her stepfather, had been drunk.

'Don't be pert, young Viv,' her cousin said severely. 'I'll decide how much booze I can take. You just put the money away. I'll take it to Pryor's in London Road as soon as I get the chance.' He went whistling out of the room.

Viv swept the gold coins into the old tin box. Just as she closed it there was a loud knock on the window and she jumped. Joe stood outside, his face pressed against the glass. Quickly she placed the box under the table, feeling inexplicably furtive. Then she got up and went to open the door.

Nick Bryce entered behind Joe.

'George won't be long,' she said.

'What about you? Aren't you coming?'

The thought had not even entered her head and Nick's words surprised her. 'Isn't it boys only?'

'Not that I know of,' he said. 'Why don't you come?'

Before she could say anything George entered the room. He looked from his cousin to Nick Bryce and frowned. 'What's going on?'

'Nothing,' she said.

But Nick answered, 'I thought Viv might like to come with us.'

'She's not old enough,' said George abruptly'

'If she put on a bit of make-up she'd pass for eighteen,' said Nick softly. 'I thought she might be missing her grandad and need cheering up.'

'She was glad to see the old man go,' said George, zipping up his leather jacket.

Viv winced. 'Don't make it sound like I wished him dead!'

Nick leaned against the table and gazed at her. 'It's not so unusual to want someone dead, you know. Families can drive you mad at times. Mine often does. So I wouldn't feel guilty if I was you.'

'I don't know what I feel exactly,' she murmured, surprised by his words. 'He was old, senile, and I believe he's better out of it.' She smiled ruefully. 'He wasn't always lovable but maybe it's remembering those times when I wished him to kingdom come that makes me feel . . .' She shrugged. 'Oh, I don't know!' She stared at him. 'Do you have a grandfather?'

'No.' His smile came and went. 'But I have parents who made me feel guilty for years. They divorced and my family life before and since has been anything but normal.'

'I could tell her a few things about your family,' muttered George, impatiently opening the front door.

Nick's eyes glinted. 'Tell away. Sticks and stones may break my bones but names will never hurt me.'

'But that's not true!' said Viv with feeling. 'Being called names does hurt.'

'So I lied,' said Nick quietly. 'Are you sure you wouldn't like to go out? We could leave these two to go the pub and go somewhere else.'

Viv's heart suddenly bumped uncomfortably fast. She was aware of George staring at her, narrow-eyed, waiting for her answer. Suddenly she thought of the day she had had and realised that she could not take any more emotion. Peace and quiet and putting up her feet were all she needed. 'Thanks,' she said to Nick. 'But I'm worn out with the funeral and everything else.'

He showed no disappointment at her refusal. 'Another time perhaps?'

She nodded and her heartbeat slowed. 'Have a nice time, the three of you.' She turned away and picked up the evening paper.

The door closed and she wondered if after all Nick Bryce was just being polite. She considered what he had said about his family. His parents were divorced. There would have been gossip. Did he live with his mother or father? She found herself thinking of her own mother. Sticks and stones . . .

Learning about her own illegitimacy was something that had come late but Viv had always realised there was something about her that caused people to whisper as she passed by. Why couldn't you have been married to my father? she asked inwardly. I have no face to remember, no name to inherit. Inexplicably, she felt bereft because of not knowing. Never before had she felt it so strongly. She stared unseeingly at an advertisement in the newspaper then mentally shook herself. She was being stupid. What was the good of self-pity?

She read: 'Starlight glamour at C & A. Desert Song harem dress of brocade which whispers magic with every step'. It had a satin sash to enhance the high waistline, and a hooped underskirt. It was nine guineas, but what a dream of a dress! Viv's spirits lifted slightly. The dress could do wonders for her morale. Make her look older too. Not old enough to drink, George had said, clearly trying to put her among the young ones and out of Nick Bryce's reach. Nine guineas! She thought of the sovereigns and her spirits soared. She could afford it.

Viv turned several pages. Pinky and Perky were having a Christmas party at T.J. Hughes. Christmas was coming, the goose was getting fat, but where would she be for the holiday? America? Paris? Liverpool? It was nice to have a choice. She tried to concentrate on the newspaper, reading that Southport was reclaiming more land from the sea. That the

15

Cardinals in Rome were sending out smoke signals telling the world that they were having trouble choosing a new pope. That the son of a British soldier had been killed in Cyprus.

She put down the newspaper and stared into the fire, thinking of Nick Bryce. He had been tanned. Had he got that tan in Cyprus? Had he had to face death? She compared him with Pete of the Tony Curtis haircut whom she had gone out with what seemed ages ago now. Pete's creeping fingers had fiddled with the neck of her dress on the third row back in the pictures. She had slapped his hand, determined that no boy was going to consider her easy game. Next he had lifted the hem of her gingham skirt and hooped underskirt with his crepe-soled suede shoe, and rubbed her leg, laddering her nylons. How could he believe that did something to a girl? Perhaps he wasn't right in the head? He was only half a teddy boy after all with the shoes and a string tie and a jacket that wasn't draped right. He seemed so juvenile compared to Nick Bryce. He seemed like a man who had felt things, seen things, done things. How had she worked that out after knowing him just five minutes? She could be deceiving herself.

Viv's gaze wandered to the newspaper again and she stared at the sketch of the dress. It really would make her look older, but for what occasion would she wear it? Then she remembered that George had said something about a party. Who would he invite? Probably not Nick Bryce. Nine guineas! She wasn't used to spending so much money on herself and felt guilty. Then she thought of all she had done for her grandfather and made up her mind. To hell with being sensible. She would buy the dress and knock a few fellas dead!

Chapter Two

'You're not really serious about buying that?' demanded Dot Taylor, staring disbelievingly at the vision in apricot brocade. 'It would suit me better.' She was tall and slender with dark hair, whereas Viv was only five foot two and went in and out in the right places.

'You haven't got the money,' said Viv. 'So hard cheese.' She scrutinised her reflection with narrowed eyes. She felt really glam but was it the kind of dress for the party they planned? And was it right having a party so soon after Grandfather's death? She still had her doubts but had agreed with George that the old house could do with livening up. It had been in the doldrums for what seemed a hundred years. Her cousin had not mentioned Paris for a week and she hoped that he had changed his mind.

'Is it that John Hanson is going to be there and you want him to whisk you off to the nearest sandhill and smother you in kisses?' said Dot, taking the turquoise taffeta dress that Viv had also tried on and holding it against herself.

'Not at this time of year! Besides, he's too old for me.' Viv stroked the skirt of the frock, loving the feel of the brocade and the silky texture of the satin sash. She twirled round and hummed 'Some Day My Prince Will Come'.

You've a hope. There's no princes for sale in Liverpool,' Dot sighed. 'Put it back and let's go.'

'I'm buying it.'

'More fool you. It's not practical.'

'I'm fed up of being practical.' Viv's brown eyes were suddenly mutinous.

17

'You'll regret it. But hurry up, I want to go to NEMS and look at the records.'

As Viv struggled out of the dress she said, 'That reminds me – could you bring some of your records next Saturday? Some of those your Norm got off your cousin Billy.' Cousin Billy was a steward on a liner that went to New York and he brought back all the latest American hits before they reached the shops in England.

'Sure,' said Dot. 'Although are you sure you wouldn't prefer a live group? You know what a whizz our Norm is on the tea chest and two strings.' Her eyes met Viv's with an expression in them that said she knew her friend would enjoy the joke. 'Although you'll never believe this . . . he's bought himself a guitar from Hessey's on the never never and is teaching himself chords. I think he's deserting Lonnie and skiffle for Elvis and rock 'n' roll.'

'It's bound to be an improvement on thunk-thunk,' said Viv. 'But bring the records anyway. And Norm, unac-companied. One thing he can do, and that's jive!' And on that note she went to pay for the dress.

The day of the party was hectic for Viv. George had halfheartedly offered to help but once she got him to move some of the furniture upstairs to make room for dancing she told him to go to the football match. Paris had come up in conversation again that morning and she did not want him distracting her all afternoon by going on about the Louvre and Impressionist painters and the wonderful light in the South of France. She had told him that the light was just as good on a summer day over the Mersey and that she was going to California to get a suntan and watch the oranges grow. They had come near to quarrelling so she was glad to have him out of the way while she got on with making a trifle and several dozen sandwiches. Sausage rolls and meat pies were bought in.

That evening, as Viv prepared to go downstairs, she wondered which of George's friends would be there. She thought of Nick Bryce. Her cousin had not mentioned him since the day of the funeral and she figured that the past still rankled with him for all his fine words. She dismissed the

18

thought from her mind and worried instead about her catering, hoping that there would be enough food. She had heard the door open several times but had left it to her cousin to welcome their guests. She wanted to make a grand entrance.

She looked at herself in the mirror and dampened the wispy kiss curls on her forehead with spit before checking that her pony tail, which she had folded under and clipped, was secure. She used her mascara brush again and nearly blinded herself. Then she applied another coat of coral lipstick. Despite the freezing temperature in her grandfather's bedroom she had decided that a cardigan would spoil the effect of the dress. She straightened her back and took a deep breath, listening to the strains of the Everly Brothers' 'Wake Up, Little Susie'. Then she went downstairs.

Only Dot and her brother Norm seemed to notice Viv as she paused near the foot of the stairs to see who had arrived. Norm wolf whistled but it went unnoticed by most people there because of the music and conversation. George was dancing with a girl in a pink sweater, his expression animated for once. He did not look up.

As the record ended Norm called. 'Why not come wiz me to ze casbah and we will make mad passionate amour?' Dot hit him on the arm but several people looked up in Viv's direction.

She felt the blood rush to her face because she had already realised that Dot had been right and that she was overdressed for the occasion. Then she saw Joe come into the room, accompanied by Nick Bryce. Paul Anka started singing 'I'm so Young and You're So Old'.

How old was Nick Bryce? thought Viv. Twenty-four, twenty-five? She was seventeen. He seemed to vanish, only to materialise suddenly in front of her.

'I like the dress,' he said and, placing an arm round her waist, pulled her among the dancing couples.

'Thank you.' So what if she was overdressed? He liked the way she looked and it was her party. 'I didn't know you were coming. George never said,' she murmured.

His intense blue eyes gazed into hers. 'That's because he never asked me. I hope you don't mind, but when Joe told me you were throwing a party I couldn't resist gatecrashing. I wanted to see you again.'

She tried to prevent the colour rising in her cheeks. 'You could have knocked at the door any time.'

'George might have answered and I was warned off the other week. He doesn't think I'm good enough for you.'

Viv frowned. 'He has no say in the matter. It's up to me to decide whether you're good enough.'

'I'm glad to hear it.' His mouth quivered slightly. 'Has he told you anything about me, Viv?'

'Nothing. And I didn't ask. Your past is your past and nothing to do with me.'

'If we were to get to know each other better then surely you'd want to know more about me?'

'Like you'd want to know about me, I suppose?' she said lightly.

'I know some things about you. I can give you a few years and I've a good memory,' he said in a teasing voice.

Viv's look was questioning. 'I should remember you if we lived in the same street, shouldn't I? But I can't place you at the moment.'

'I moved when you were only four or five. I was at grammar school by then.' He twirled her round and when they faced each other again, added, 'I remember your Aunt Flora. I liked her. She was kind.'

'She was lovely,' agreed Viv, her eyes warm. 'I'm thinking of going to America soon to stay with her.'

'With her, not your mother?'

'My mother!' Viv's expression changed. 'You can't remember me as well as you claim to if you think I'd go and stay with her.' There was a tremor in her voice.

At that moment George made a sudden appearance, like the demon in a pantomime. 'What are you doing here?' he demanded of Nick. 'You weren't invited.'

'Don't fuss,' said Viv, glancing about them. 'What's one more? There's enough food, and it's nice to talk to someone from the old street.'

George's tawny eyebrows drew together in a ferocious frown and his whole body seemed to bristle. 'You still haven't remembered him, have you? The Bryces had a name in our street. *She* was notorious. There was nobody, but nobody, in our street who didn't know what she got up to!'

'That's enough, George,' said Nick, his expression furious. 'We're not kids now and I'd hate to have to shut your mouth.'

Viv's gaze travelled swiftly between them. Suddenly the atmosphere could have been sliced with a knife. 'You're making a show of us, George. Nick's our guest so will you let things go! We've got people here wanting to enjoy themselves. They're not going to if you start a fight.'

George glowered at her. 'He's got a reputation, Viv, and I don't want him messing you about. Just bear that in mind, and if he starts anything . . .'

'I'm hardly likely to start anything right here in this room,' snapped Nick, his eyes glinting. 'Use your commonsense, George!'

'That's right. He'd pick a quieter place,' Viv added in a coaxing voice, 'Now go away and leave me to look after myself. Enjoy the party! It was your idea after all.'

Before her cousin could say any more she pulled Nick's arm back round her and started to dance. 'Many a tear has to fall,' sang the singer. The music was pure smooch. She felt Nick's chin rub against her hair. 'Thanks,' he murmured. 'I haven't had a woman championing me for ages. My gran used to but she died and since then I've had to fight my own battles.'

'So has George,' said Viv quietly. 'I'm very fond of my cousin, Nick, so don't start thinking I'm on your side just because I stood up for myself. Whatever's between the pair of you from the past, I don't want to be involved.'

'I think you're what's between us now,' he said, smiling slightly. 'And the past isn't that easy to put behind you. It has a habit of spilling into the present. Memories can be hard to get rid off. Remember what I said about sticks and stones?'

'They hurt,' she said with feeling.

He pressed her closer to him. 'I remember being skitted at for all kinds of things . . . like the holes in my pants. I hated being a scruff. Then when I became a college kid and wore a blazer, I was called names for being smart. I couldn't win.'

'When I went to college I felt like that,' she murmured. '"College pud" I was called. It was as if I'd committed a crime, working-class girl passing the scholarship. I was an

21

outsider in the street *and* at school, amongst those with money who lived in Stoneycroft and Aigburth and places like that. And then there was my accent. They gave some of us elocution lessons.'

'How now, brown cow?' said Nick, rounding his vowels.

She grinned. 'Our teacher committed suicide. I always worried in case I was the cause of it. It was hard work polishing my vowels.' She heard him laugh softly but it was true that her teacher had committed suicide and Viv had believed for a while that it was her fault. 'It wasn't funny,' she said soberly.

'My gran made me work on mine.' His mouth brushed her ear and she shivered. 'No "yeahs" but "yes". She drove me mad and made life in the street even worse for me. I got into fights. In the end I developed an extra skin and kept my mouth shut. Then I got stones thrown at me.'

She felt enormous sympathy for him. As he lifted his head and gazed at her it was as if something electric passed between them. 'It is a hard life,' she said in droll tones to lighten what suddenly felt like a very serious moment.

'Yes.' He pulled her closer and they danced on in silence.

The record came to an end. 'Perhaps you'd like to dance with someone else?' she suggested politely.

'Not unless you want me to? I was thinking I'd like to get out of here so that we could talk properly.'

Her heart seemed to bump in her chest. 'I have the refreshments to see to.'

'How about a breath of fresh air afterwards?'

'Perhaps.' She was suddenly thinking about what her cousin had said. Had Nick really got a reputation?

At that moment Norm came over. 'Can I have this dance?' He looked belligerently at Nick.

'Of course,' said Viv immediately. 'You'll excuse me, Nick?' It would not do to have him think he was the only pebble on her beach.

'I'll see you later?'

She nodded and tried not to think about him as Norm chattered in her ear about his newfound prowess on the six-string guitar.

*　　*　　*

22

It was eleven o'clock and plates had been piled into the sink and washed. A few people had left, some still danced in the smoky kitchen but others had drifted into the other room and were gathered about the coal fire, smooching or swopping gossip. Viv was drying her hands on a tea towel when Nick came up to her.

'How about that fresh air? I'll have you back for the witching hour.'

'Okay.' It would be good to get out of the house.

Frost glistened on pavements and their breath turned to vapour in the light from a street lamp where some teenagers had gathered. 'Truth, dare, command or promise!' Viv heard one of them chant as they passed. She remembered the game from when she was younger. She huddled into the warmth of her cherry red winter coat and would have rammed both hands deep into her pockets but Nick took hold of one of them. 'Truth, dare, command or promise,' he said softly. 'The truth is that this is better than being in there or at home,' he said.

'You can't possibly dislike your family that much?' she said, flushing.

'Who says?' His eyes gleamed.

She was aware of the warmth of his arm against hers. 'What have they done?'

'What they're always doing when I'm around – involving me in their lives. Besides, Mam's turned all respectable while I've been away and it's exhausting watching her polish everything, including the aspidistra.'

She smiled but did not look at him. 'I'm not going to ask you what you mean by that.'

'Truth. I'll tell you anyway. She wasn't respectable before. Just like your mother was said not to be.'

Viv felt a sharp dart of pain pass through her, his mention of her mother had been so unexpected. She made to free her hand. 'I don't find that funny,' she said savagely.

'It wasn't meant to be.' He kept a tight hold on her hand and said with a hint of reminiscence, 'Truth. I think I was probably in love with your mother when I was ten. You could smell her scent from feet away. Californian Poppy it was. *You* wear Coty's L'Aimant. I reckoned she bathed in it. You're

23

more discreet.' He took her hand and sniffed her wrist before she could prevent him. She gave him a look that should have withered him but did not. 'I remember you being born,' he continued. 'All the women thought your mother would die. She should have gone into hospital, they said.'

'She didn't want me.' Viv's voice sounded like splintered glass and she was horrified that he had caused her to reveal how deeply she felt her mother's sin.

'There was a war on and she wasn't married,' he said in a comforting voice. 'It must have been terrible for her. Have a heart.'

'I have got a heart! But she shouldn't have messed around without a ring on her finger.' She was relieved to have control of her voice once more.

'Some messed around while they had rings,' he said, squeezing her hand. 'Don't you think that's worse?'

'You're defending my mother. Why? If you knew what I've had to cope with because of her, then . . .'

'Shush!' he interrupted ruthlessly. 'She had to carry the can. What about the man who got away with it?'

'You mean my father?' She paused and stared at him. 'Do you remember him?

He gazed back at her, unblinking. 'Don't you?'

I've never known who he was.' There was silence. Their footsteps rang on the pavement as Viv wondered about her father. A low sigh escaped her and she looked at Nick. 'What about your father? Do you miss him?'

His eyes glinted. 'Like two broken legs. Fathers aren't such a big deal in my estimation. Before the war he never bothered with me. During the war he was away fighting. When he came back he took me and my sister Mavis away from Mam. I ran away to Gran's but he took me back and knocked me black and blue with his leather belt. It had this big buckle on –' His voice broke off abruptly and she could feel his palm turn damp.

Viv was shocked. Even so she muttered, 'Not all fathers are like that. Dot's dad and Mike, Aunt Flo's husband, are lovely men.'

'Sure, there's nice dads around, but give me women any day.' He gazed into her face. 'At least my mother, for all her faults, knew how to show affection. She never hit me once. She knew what it was like to be beaten, you see. Not that I realised that until I was older.'

Viv returned his stare thoughtfully. 'My mother was never very good at showing affection where I was concerned,' she said quietly. 'She always made me feel a nuisance. Eventually she left me with aunt Flo and went off to America. The last words she said to me were: "Be a good girl and don't get yourself into trouble." No hug, no words of love . . .' Her voice tailed off.

'Don't let it get to you. Perhaps she found it difficult to part from you. When are you going to America?'

'For Christmas.' She squared her shoulders.

'I'd like to see you again before you go.'

'Okay.' She wasn't about to start being shy now. She wanted to see him but felt that she had to know something first. 'Is there anyone special in your life, Nick?'

He smiled. 'No one. I'd no intention of there being anyone for a long time. My parents' divorce put me off rushing into marriage.'

'I suppose that's understandable.' She cleared her throat and told a partial lie. 'I'm not keen on marriage either. I want to enjoy being free. I've never been able to do just what I want before. There was always grandfather to worry about.'

'What about George?'

She frowned. 'He isn't my keeper. We're close and I don't like upsetting him. He's been hurt and that's why he's over-protective. I don't think he wants me hurt because he knows what it's like.'

Nick was silent and she had a feeling that he did not agree with her. They walked without speaking for a while. It was a silence with undertones. Viv was trying to remember a boy called Nick with a sister called Mavis.

He said, 'Do you like jazz and skiffle?'

'I like Acker Bilk and Lonnie Donegan.'

'That's as good an answer as any. Perhaps you'd like to come out with me tomorrow evening? There's a session on at The Cavern. Afterwards we could go for a meal.'

'That sounds fine to me.'

'It's a date then.' He hesitated as he gazed down at her.

25

'Now I suppose we'd best get back or George will be waiting on the doorstep with a big stick.'

'I wouldn't be surprised,' she said with a sudden mischievous grin.

Nick was partly right. George stood on the doorstep, leaning against the doorjamb, smoking a cigarette. A scowl crossed his face at the sight of them. 'Where the hell have you been?' he rasped. 'D'you know what time it is?'

Nick glanced at his watch. 'It's the witching hour. Going to turn me into a toad, George?'

'Very funny. It's late, that's what I mean. Too late for Viv to be out alone with you.'

'Shut up, George! You sound like a mother hen.' She pulled a face at him. 'We've only been for a walk. I needed it after being in the house most of the day.'

His mouth tightened. 'I was worried about you. You didn't say where you were going. It was Dot who told me you'd gone with *him*.'

Viv slanted a look at Nick and he quirked an eyebrow. She smiled. 'He has a name. Didn't you enjoy the party, cousin dear? Didn't the girl in the pink sweater come up to expectations?'

George reddened. 'Barbara's very nice but that's beside the point. It was damn' rude you, leaving like that.'

'I suppose it was.' She sighed. 'Sorry.' She turned to Nick. 'Thanks for your company.'

'Thank *you*.' He kissed her lightly on the mouth before releasing her hand. 'See you tomorrow.'

She nodded.

'Bye, George,' said Nick.

He grunted something incomprehensible before seizing Viv's arm and propelling her inside the house, slamming the door behind them.

Viv wrenched her arm free and turned on him. 'Do you have to be so rude?'

'Rude? Me?' His face was set in moody lines. 'Do you know what his mother was?'

Viv kicked off her shoes and flung her coat on the back of a chair. She sat down. 'What's his mother got to do with anything? It's Nick I went walking with.'

'You mean you really don't remember his mother?'

She rested her head against the back of the chair. 'You tell me about her, George.'

'She lived next-door to Mam. She was a right tart! Entertained almost the whole of the United Nations. Yanks, Poles, Norwegians. You name them she had it off with them. Then her husband came home from the war.'

'I thought as much,' said Viv slowly. 'Nick's mother is *that* Mrs Bryce?'

'Yes. She's *that* Mrs Bryce.' His voice dropped as he sat in the chair opposite her. 'Now do you see what I mean about Nick?'

There was silence as they stared at one another. Then Viv said, 'I see what you mean me to see but Nick seems to have turned out all right *and* he's told me that his mother's turned respectable.'

'He told you that?'

Viv nodded. 'Yes. She has an aspidistra and polishes it.' A small smile played round her mouth.

George groaned. 'I don't believe it! You've fallen for him.'

'No, I haven't!' She was quite indignant. 'But I needn't judge him on who his mother is. I've lived in the shadow of what my mother did all my life. I'd say that gives Nick and me something in common.'

George shook his head. 'It's not just what his mother did. It's what *he* did. He got into trouble in his teens. Went round smashing windows and things.'

'What things?'

'I don't know for sure'. He lit up another cigarette. 'But there was talk. I knew a couple of lads who were at the Art School with him. He had a bad reputation. Girls and things.'

'"Things" again,' said Viv, staring intently at her fingernails.

'He came into lessons drunk several times. He was only fourteen.'

There was silence. Viv was trying to imagine what life had been like for Nick during the war, with his mother and her men, and after it when his father came home and beat him up. When had his parents divorced and when had he gone back to live with his mother? He had mentioned a grandmother several times. She felt angry with his parents, with George, and was surprisingly jealous of all those girls he had been with. 'What was it you and he fought over?' she murmured.

George hesitated. 'I called his mother a whore.'

She shivered at his callous use of the word and remembered years ago when her grandfather had occasionally used it of her mother. 'That must have made his day,' she said in a tight voice.

George drew on his cigarette and smoke trickled out of his nostrils. 'I'll never understand females. Mam was the same. She felt sorry for him. But he had a good time of it as far as I could see. Chewing gum, money, chocolate, comics . . .' He stood and gazed down at her. 'You women always think you can reform the bad guys. More fool you, Viv, if you're considering having a crack at Nick. Upbringing always tells. He's a hard nut.'

'Thanks for telling me.' And before he could say any more she picked up her shoes and walked out of the room, closing the door firmly behind her. If she had stayed she might have said things she would regret. They had both been under a strain in the last twelve months.

As Viv undressed she tried again to remember Nick as a boy but could only remember his sister Mavis who used to go to the park with her and Rosie occasionally. She thought of the way George had described the teenage Nick and was suddenly unsure of herself. Was she heading for trouble going out with him? Or had she found someone at last who would understand her feelings of inadequacy because of her birth? Who would provide her with approval and acceptance on her own merits?

A yawn escaped her and she flopped on to the camp bed that she had moved from the kitchen into her grandfather's room after having his smelly bed taken away. What was she worrying about? Hadn't she made up her mind to go to America? After tomorrow she might never see Nick Bryce again. The thought did not give her much joy.

Chapter Three

Viv was wakened by the clacking of a football rattle. She pulled a pillow over her head and put her fingers in her ears but the pillow was wrenched away. She moaned.

'D'you know what time it is?'

Viv forced her eyelids open and blinked at George. 'You're obsessed with time,' she muttered, remembering last night and Nick's answer to the same question.

He said mildly, 'I don't want to start on Nick Bryce now. I thought I'd better wake you up. You're going to be late for church. I'm off to the park. I've got a game.'

'Okay.' She seized hold of the pillow and put it over her face once more.

'Viv!' Her cousin lifted the pillow. 'I forgot to tell you, there was a letter from Ma yesterday. There's something in it about your mam. I thought you'd want to read it.' He placed a flimsy blue envelope under her chin then dropped the pillow back on her face. 'See you later.

Viv listened to his retreating footsteps and waited for the bedroom door to close before removing the pillow and taking hold of the envelope. She sat up, yawned, and began to read the letter. Immediately it was as if her Aunt Flora was standing at her shoulder and she experienced a warm feeling when the invitation to go to California for Christmas was mentioned once more. She continued reading and came to the part of the letter that mentioned her mother.

'A couple of weeks ago our Hilda turned up, crying poverty as usual– not that I believe she's penniless for one moment! She was wearing mink and looking a million dollars! Poor

Charlie died of a heart attack on the freeway and apparently she wasn't well herself afterwards. She was quite cheered when I told her about Father because she had been waiting for a third death and thought it might be hers. She'd had pleurisy so she said *and* she'd given up the ciggies. Miracle!

'Anyway she's gone off again without a word, which is infuriating but just like her. I wouldn't be surprised if she's waltzed off to Hollywood. It always was her dream to see the homes of the stars and in all the years over here she's never made the trip. Perhaps she'll come back to us? At Christmas maybe? You both really must come over and we'll have a lovely family time.'

Viv folded the letter slowly. It didn't look as though her aunt knew of George's plans to go to Europe and paint. Perhaps she could still have a got at making him change his mind? Had her mother really been ill or was it all an act? She'd always been a dab hand at making the most of a situation, and being newly widowed and ill was something she could milk to her heart's content. Unless she had really loved Charlie . . . But then Viv had never known her mother love anybody like she loved herself. It would have been interesting to have met Charlie and compared him with Kevin. He couldn't have been worse than the man who had attempted to sexually assault her when she was eight years old.

Viv shook off the memory and thought of her Aunt Flora and Uncle Mike. He had inherited money when his father had died and bought land in the Napa Valley where he had set about planting vines and learning about wine making rather than staying on the family farm with his older brother. She felt a spurt of excitement at the thought of visiting the American branch of the family. It would be a different world. She really must try and persuade George to go. The journey would be much more fun with him than going it alone.

George was in a good mood when he came in but that changed as soon as Viv mentioned his mother's letter.

'I'm not going,' he said shortly, lowering himself into the rocking chair.

'Aunt Flo'll be disappointed.' She placed a cup of tea on the hearth, handy for him.

He shrugged. 'It was her choice to go to America. She knew I never wanted to go.'

'Well, I'm going but it would be so much better if you came too,' murmured Viv, passing him a plate with four homemade macaroons on it, his favourite. Then she sat on the floor looking up at him.

He bit into a macaroon, eyes narrowing as he stared down at her. 'What about Nick Bryce?'

'What about him?'

'He said "See you tomorrow".'

Her eyebrows rose. 'One date! What's wrong with that? He's not going to carry me off to the casbah!'

He chewed thoughtfully. 'I want to go to Paris. I wish you'd come.'

'Why?' she said bluntly, 'Just to have me there handy in case things don't work out, to look after your physical needs? Once, George, I had a crush on you. I was deadly jealous of Kathleen Murphy. You were my big hero cousin and I thought you could conquer the world. I never thought you'd let a girl throwing you over get to you the way it has. I thought you had more guts and cared for the family more! But you're selfish. Even all that talk last night about Nick had more to do with your feelings than mine.'

'That's not true' He banged the plate down on the hearth and jumped to his feet. 'I care about you, Viv! What did he have to say about me?'

'Nothing much.' She picked up the cracked plate, removed the remaining macaroons and frowned as she got to her feet. 'Do you see what you've done to this plate? This was one of Grandmother's. It was years old. It had a lot of history.'

'Sod the plate,' said George, snatching it off her and dropping it on the floor. 'Did he touch you?'

Viv laughed. 'Of course he touched me! Did you expect us to walk miles apart.'

'You know what I mean.' He thrust his face close to hers.

She patted his cheek. 'You're a dog in the manger, George. You don't really want me. I'm just a substitute for Kathleen Murphy.'

He seized hold of her and pulled her closer. He kissed her with all the pent up passion which thoughts of Kathleen in a

31

convent evoked. Kathleen who had always been so willing. Kathleen who had once considered him the bee's knees. His hands slid up Viv's sweater and undid her bra. She struggled and stamped on his foot. He hardly felt it. Somewhere he heard a knocker banging and felt Viv tugging at his arm. 'For God's sake, let me go!' she said through gritted teeth, but he didn't want to listen. He was somewhere else with Kathleen Murphy. He forced Viv down on to the floor but it was a struggle to unzip her skirt because she would not keep still.

Unexpectedly the front door opened. 'Good God! What do you think you're doing?'

They both jumped out of their skins. Viv stared up at George and pushed him hard. He stumbled to his feet and smoothed back his hair.

It took Viv only seconds to tuck in her sweater and tug her skirt zip a couple of inches but it felt longer and her face burned. At last she looked closely at the woman in the well-cut black gaberdine suit – and her stomach turned over. The woman was only a shade plumper, her hair unnaturally blonde instead of the red-gold shade of Viv's. Make-up had skilfully been applied. Max Factor panstick, Viv thought irrelevantly as she recognised her mother, Hilda, the erstwhile black sheep of the family.

Nobody moved or said anything for several seconds. Then Hilda wrenched off black poplin gloves and flung them together with her handbag on to the table. She compressed poppy red lips, her eyes focused on George. 'Sweet Lord, you're like your father, George Cooke. What were you doing with this girl, writhing about on the floor? I'm thoroughly disgusted.'

He recovered quickly. Moving forward, he kissed his aunt on her scented cheek. 'How long has it been, Aunt Hilda? Eight – nine years? And you still remember the key being on the string behind the door.' His tone was light, without a trace of embarrassment. 'We never expected to see you here. Ma thought you were going to Hollywood. But, fancy, here you are. What an unexpected treat.'

Hilda smiled cynically. 'Yes, you *are* like your father. Good at the soft soap. Where's Viv?'

Without taking her eyes from her mother's face she sat

32

down in the rocking chair. 'Mother doesn't recognise daughter,' she said. 'Now isn't that a laugh?'

Hilda's face froze and it seemed to Viv that she paled beneath the panstick. Then the expressive eyebrows rose. 'You *have* changed! I hope the pair of you have gone no further than a kiss an' a cuddle? You are cousins, you know.'

'Tell us something we don't know.' Viv was suddenly angry. How dare her mother judge her actions after the way she had disgraced the family name?

George reached for his Woodbines and offered the packet to his aunt, who after the barest hesitation said, 'I've given them up. I nearly died from my chest.'

Viv and George exchanged disbelieving glances. 'You're still here, though,' said George. 'And looking great.'

'That's because I've learnt sense. You really shouldn't smoke. Think of the money!'

'I only smoke at weekends,' he said smoothly. 'Can't afford it any other time.'

Viv thought, she knows about the sovereigns. 'I remember you hardly ever being without a fag,' she murmured. 'You always knew how to burn money, all right, Mother. You were always puffing like a chimney.'

Hilda stared at her daughter. 'I worked for the money,' she said tersely. 'Still judging me, are you?'

Viv's smile was fixed. 'I don't know that I ever did. But if I'd have had a pair of socks for every packet of ciggies you got through, I wouldn't have had chilblains.'

Hilda's mouth tightened. 'So I'm to blame for your chilblains? Is that all you've got to say to me after I've come all this way? Aren't you even going to offer me a drink?'

Viv struggled with her finer feelings and lost. 'You're too late to do anything for Grandfather, and for his funeral! Just think, Mother, if you'd come earlier you could have had fun dancing on his coffin.' Unshed tears suddenly sparkled on her lashes. 'That would have been right up your street, wouldn't it?' To her shame, her voice wobbled. 'No love lost between you! I bet you're glad he's gone.'

'Those remarks aren't remotely funny.' Hilda's voice was frigid. 'Now make me a cup of coffee, and don't be giving cheek. I am your mother after all.'

'You've remembered?' Viv's laugh was bitter. 'You do surprise me.' And on that note she vanished into the kitchen.

'I believe the old man went peacefully,' said Hilda, draining the sweet Camp coffee in her cup.

'As peacefully as he did anything.' Viv's voice was carefully devoid of emotion.' At least he didn't know anything about it.'

'Senile, our Flo said.' Hilda grimaced. 'I suppose he didn't mention me?'

Viv exchanged glances with George, who laughed shortly. 'He'd forgotten you existed most of the time, and when he did remember it was only as a little girl that he recalled you.'

Hilda pressed her lips together and there was an expression in her eyes that puzzled Viv. Then it was gone and her mother shrugged. 'Perhaps that's not such a bad thing. Even in those days the sea was his mistress. I remember when Mother died –'

She did not finish but gazed at George and Vivien sitting side by side on the well-worn sofa. Her throat moved and it was several moments before she said, 'What are you going to do now he's dead? Have you thought of going to visit your mother, George?'

He hesitated briefly. 'I can't afford to go.'

'Come off it, laddie,' she said with a hint of mockery in her voice. 'There's no slates off my roof! Your grandad must have left some money.'

He stretched his arm along the back of the sofa and his fingers pressed Viv's shoulder, but she did not need his warning. 'We've been saving,' said Viv, fixing a smile on her face. 'But we haven't got enough to take us to California. Perhaps you could give us a loan? My stepfather died, I believe, and left you a rich widow.'

'Not that rich.' Hilda's smile wavered. '*You* haven't come in for a windfall?'

Involuntarily George glanced at Viv.

'No,' she said. 'But you obviously think we have.'

Hilda's smile was wary. 'Is that why you think I'm here? Because of Father's money?'

Viv shrugged. 'If it is you're unlucky. Does it look like he had any?' Her eyes roamed around the shabby room. 'Look at this place.'

Hilda said, 'I'm looking. It's obvious he hasn't bought anything in years. After Mam died he turned into a right tight-fisted old swine.' She leaned forward. 'Shall we stop playing games, children? I know he had some gold sovereigns. He started saving them years ago. He used to give me them to play with when I was a little girl and told me to use one if we ever got into difficulties while he was away. My mother was a hopeless manager. But then she had troubles enough after the rheumatic fever which affected her heart.'

'He must have spent them,' said Viv, determined not to be softened by this glimpse into her mother's past life.

George rose and went over to the fireplace. He picked up the poker and rattled it along the bars of the grate. Hilda looked at him. 'You've found them, haven't you, George? Tell the truth. You never could tell lies. You're like your mother in that respect. Her eyes always betrayed her.'

'They're ours! He left them to us.'

Viv groaned. 'Idiot! Now she'll expect a cut.'

Hilda's eyes gleamed. 'Too right! As for Father actually making a will leaving them to you, I don't believe it. He thought he'd live forever.' She leaned back in the rocking chair and laughed.

Viv got slowly to her feet. 'You never could miss an opportunity to get more money, could you, Mother?' she said, trying to control her temper. 'You always loved the stuff. Wasn't that why you married Kevin and Charlie? I doubt love ever came into it.'

Hilda stared at her, reached for her handbag, fiddled with the clasp. Then she dropped it abruptly, lifting one slender sheer nylon clad leg over the other. 'I was prepared to be generous – to split it three ways.' Her eyes swivelled away from her daughter to her nephew. 'It's rightfully mine and your mother's.'

George rammed the poker in to the fire. 'You did nothing for him. We bloody well worked hard for anything he left.'

'Don't you use that kind of language with me, George Cooke'. Hilda flushed. 'You're as cocky as ever your father was but only half the man.'

George's left hand curled into a fist. 'You can't hurt me by saying that. What have you got to be proud of? You deserted your daughter and left Ma to bring her up.'

'Thank God,' murmured Viv, watching her mother's expression. 'At least Aunt Flo cared about me. All you wanted was to live it up in America! You thought it was the Promised Land.'

'I didn't live it up! I never even got to Hollywood. New Jersey's thousands of miles away and Charlie wouldn't move. Freezing in winter and humid in summer. I felt like I couldn't breathe sometimes. Our Flo had the best of it marrying Mike.'

She reached for her handbag again, opened it, shut it, then pushed it away petulantly. Her expression was sulky. 'Damn! Why should I have cared about Father? He never cared for me when I most needed it. Our Flo was the one. I wish she hadn't been at times, but she was like Grandmother Preston so father said. That's why I left you with her. Don't you think I knew she'd care for you better than me?

'Anyway, that's all water under the bridge. When Flo said Father had died I though I'd better come home. I believed the pair of you might need a parent around and our Flo couldn't come, not with her brood. I thought you especially, Viv, needed a mother.'

'Me! Need you? That has to be the joke of the month,' she said, leaning against the table. 'I'm amazed you spared me a thought after all these years with hardly a word.'

'You're hard, Viv Preston,' said Hilda, her eyes glinting. 'You're not like your Aunt Flora. I was hoping that some of her ways would have rubbed off on you by now.'

Viv was deeply hurt. 'Perhaps I take after you then?' she said bitingly. 'You were always the hard one, never showing me any affection. Now you've come home all you can talk of is Grandfather's money. What are we supposed to think?'

There was silence. Hilda cleared her throat. 'Hasn't your mother mentioned the money, George?' she asked eventually.

'Never,' he said vehemently. 'If she thought about it she would want us to have it. And I tell you straight, Aunt Hilda, no way will you get your hands on my share. I have plans for it.'

'How much was there?'

'I'm not telling you.'

'I'll get a lawyer,' she said mildly. 'I've a legal right to some of it.'

'You've no bloody right,' George said explosively, his fists clenching and unclenching. 'It's not fair! And I'm not going to let you spoil things for me.' Without another word he strode out of the kitchen.

Viv stared at her mother. 'Are you happy now? No sooner do you come on the scene than there's trouble.'

'He'll calm down.' Hilda twiddled her thumbs. 'He's very like his father in some ways.'

'So Aunt Flo says. But why get him going in the first place? Why come back, Mother? I wish I could believe all that stuff about your wanting to be a mother to me, but I don't. I've managed quite happily without you and can carry on doing so. You don't belong here any more. So why don't you go back to where you *do* belong?' She walked from the room and ran upstairs, her heart pounding uncomfortably.

She found George putting his painting equipment into a rucksack. The lines of his face were taut. 'I'd forgotten just how grasping your mother was,' he muttered. 'I only remembered how she used to make things happen in the old days. There was never a dull moment.'

Viv sat on the bed, hardly able to believe what had just happened. 'What are you going to do?'

He looked at the paintbox in his hand. 'I'm going to Paris.'

'You don't mean right now?' Her voice was startled.

'Right now,' he said firmly. 'I'm not staying in this house a moment longer or your mother will wheedle some money out of me.'

Viv smiled. 'She can't do that unless you let her. We're not children any more, George.'

He grimaced. 'I'm glad you feel like that. She makes me feel ten years old.'

Viv shrugged. 'You're not, though. And she's got no proof that Grandfather didn't get rid of the sovereigns. I reckon she's having you on about going to see a lawyer.'

'Maybe. It makes no difference.' He shoved the box inside

the rucksack. 'What about you? Are you coming with me or staying here with her?'

'I told you, George, I'm going to America.'

'Even though your mother's here? You can't just walk out.'

She laughed. 'You're walking out!'

'It's different for me. She's not my mother.'

The laughter died in Viv's face. 'Your mother's in America and you don't seem to give a damn about her, George. You're a hypocrite. I'd have to be daft to go to Paris with you.'

He turned brick red. 'You don't understand, Viv! It's not the way you think. For men, sometimes the last person they need around is their mother. She'd smother me. She loves me too much. Besides, I'm doing this for my dad too. It was his dream to be an artist.' He hesitated. 'I'm sorry about earlier. You're right, I was using you as a substitute for Kathleen. But that doesn't mean I don't care for you in my own way.'

Viv's expression softened and she hugged him, suddenly close to tears. Then, without a word, she walked out of the room and downstairs, prepared to do battle with her mother once more.

Hilda glanced up from that day's newspaper which quivered in her hand. 'Well?' she said. 'Have you come back to insult me a bit more. Where's George? That lad's too like his father for his own good.'

'I wouldn't know anything about that,' said Viv, sitting down and gazing uncertainly at her mother. 'I don't remember ever seeing his father. Much as I never saw my own.'

'Hmmmph!' Her mother rustled the newspaper. 'I got a shock when I saw the pair of you rolling about on the floor. I believed you an innocent.'

'That is because I was a child when you left. But I'm still a virgin if that's what's worrying you. Although you're a right one to talk about morality! I'm illegitimate, remember?'

'You think I've ever forgotten?' said Hilda wryly. 'It was one of the worse moments of my life, finding out I was expecting you. This place has some unhappy memories. The worse was when Father threw me out.' She gazed about the small cramped room with its faded wallpaper and old-fashioned oak furniture, and a sigh escaped her. 'Still, I've some happy memories too. Mother used to lie on that sofa.'

Her expression was suddenly reminiscent. 'But we'll have to get rid of it. It's a disgrace. We'll keep the old rocking chair, though, and do it up.' Her face softened. 'I remember Mother sitting with me on her knee and rocking us both. I think we could make a nice little nest out of this place.'

'We?' Vivien could not believe her ears. 'You surely aren't stopping? We?' she repeated, feeling as if she had wandered into a play because everything seemed so incredible. 'Do you think I'd live here with you? Where were you when grandfather was incontinent and his sheets needed changing? When his long johns stank to high heaven and I had to peel them off him while he hung on to them? What right have you to be here now he's gone, talking about throwing out his furniture?'

'I was his eldest daughter and he never wanted me here,' murmured Hilda. 'If things were so terrible you should have put him in a home.'

The word triggered off old memories and Viv felt a surge of pain. 'Home!' The words came spilling out. 'That's what you wanted to do with me when you quarrelled with Aunt Flo, wasn't it?' she said furiously. 'You wanted to go to America and I was a handicap! If you didn't want me why didn't you have me adopted when I was a baby? Or was my father still on the scene and you believed he might marry you? Who was my father, by the way? You've never talked about him.'

'It was our Flo's fault I kept you,' said Hilda, her cheeks flaming. 'I thought I was going to die, and by the time I realised I wasn't it was too late. She said you were too beautiful to part with, and she was right. You were like a little doll – bewitching in a bonnet. Surprised, are you, that I had some feelings for you?' Her eyes lifted to her daughter's.

Viv took a deep breath. 'Yes. I didn't think you felt anything for anyone, but you still haven't told me who my father was.'

Hilda was silent for several seconds then drawled, 'Your father, honey, was no good.'

'What do you mean, no good? Was it that he didn't want to marry you?'

'He was a louse of the first order and I'd rather not talk about him. Now make me a cup of that awful coffee and tomorrow get some decent stuff.' She lifted the newspaper in front of her face, effectively shutting out her daughter.

But Viv was not going to be shut out. She pulled down the newspaper. 'It seems to me, Mother, that you're a lousy judge of character when it comes to men. Unless Charlie was all right?'

'He was all right,' said her mother, struggling with the newspaper. 'But I admit I should never have married Kevin.'

'Why was my father a louse? Didn't you love him at all?'

Hilda said sharply, 'Don't be so juvenile! What's love got to do with it? Are you thinking we swore eternal love and then he went off and got killed in the war? It wasn't like that.'

Viv stared at her, feeling as if all the air had been knocked out of her. When she had considered her conception she had romantically believed her mother had at least been in love with her father and that it had been just as she had said a few seconds ago, but now it seemed that it had not been like that at all. 'You . . . you mean it was . . . just sex?' she stammered.

'What's wrong with sex?' snapped Hilda. 'Even your Aunt Flo is a great believer in it.'

'When did it happen? Where did it happen?.

Her mother's face set stubbornly. 'Work it out for yourself. It was wartime. There was an air raid and a blackout.'

'You mean you couldn't see each other's faces?'

'I didn't want to see his face.' Hilda lifted the newspaper. 'I felt guilty enough as it was.'

Suddenly Viv could not bear listening to any more. She left the front room in a rush. It seemed her mother didn't even know who her father was! She had to get out, away from her. She ran upstairs and into George's room but he was not there and she realised he must have left by the back way while they had been talking.

She sank on to his bed. From downstairs came the sound of a radio playing. Her throat tightened with emotion. No way could she face her mother until she'd had time to pull herself together.

Then Viv remembered that she had a date with Nick Bryce. She glanced at her watch. It was still a few hours away but she could get ready now. Her spirits lifted a little. She could fill in a couple of hours at Dot's and apologise for not waving her out of the door last night.

She went into her grandfather's old bedroom and began to get ready. She donned a circular skirt with a hooped under-skirt, and a lacy sweater she had knitted, then took her time applying make-up. She felt better after that. She crept downstairs, pausing in the kitchen to listen for any sounds of movement from the front room but the only sound to be heard was Rosemary Clooney singing 'This Old House'. She paused. This house had been her home for the last few years. She had not always been happy in it but it seemed wrong to let her mother take it over. Her grandfather would turn in his grave. Suddenly it seemed to her that she would never be rid of his influence. Determinedly she crossed the kitchen to the back door and went out, resisting the temptation to slam it. Dot's first and then that date with Nick Bryce. Perhaps by the end of the evening she would know exactly what to say to her mother to get rid of her.

Chapter Four

'Mam asked if you had your monthlies. You look all pale,' said Dot, opening her bedroom door.

'I've got enough problems without periods thrown in,' said Viv, sitting on one of the beds.

'Tell Mother.' Dot sat crosslegged on the other twin bed in the room she had once shared with her sister. 'Have you and George had a row? He looked blue murder last night when he discovered you'd left with tall, dark and devilishly interesting-looking.'

Viv smiled but she had no intention of talking about Nick Bryce to Dot except to say, 'I've a date with him later. As for George, he's gone off to Paris so I don't have to worry about what he has to say any more.'

Dot's eyes bulged. 'You don't just up and go to Paris like that! Although I'd love to. It would be great!'

'He wanted me to go with him,' murmured Viv, toying with the cross on the chain round her neck. 'But I've other plans. And, besides, that isn't why I've come.'

'I knew you hadn't come just to say sorry because that could have waited till work in the morning. So give.' Dot leaned forward eagerly.

Viv took a deep breath. 'It's my mother. She's come home.'

Dot's jaw sagged. 'I thought your mother was dead,' she said in a stage whisper. 'You told me . . .'

'I lied! I didn't want to own up to her and that I'm illegitimate! My mother never wanted me. She dumped me on George's mother when I was little and I've hated her for it ever since.'

42

'Gol-ly!' Dot took a packet of Wrigley's spearmint chewing gum from a pocket of her skirt. 'Where's she been all this time then?'

'America! She always wanted to go there and I was in the way. She would have put me in a home but my Aunt Flo wouldn't let her. Now she's back and says she wants to be a mother to me. But what kind of mother is it, Dot, who tells her daughter that her father was no good and that she didn't even want to look at his face when they were making love?' She swallowed. 'Not that it was love. She said it was just sex and it happened in a blackout. I suppose now I'll never get to know who he was! And on top of everything she's given me a blinking headache. Have you got a couple of Aspro?'

'She said all that, did she?' Her wide-eyed friend handed her a strip of gum.

'I want Aspro not gum,' said Viv, unwrapping the strip. 'Can you imagine doing it with someone you didn't know really well?' She chewed absently.

'*The Devil's Daughter*,' said Dot unexpectedly. 'I read it in a book once. Except it wasn't the devil of course. It was some lord of the manor who had his wicked way on a dark stormy night.'

'Don't be daft!' Viv's glance was exasperated but slightly amused. 'You're always going on about something evil. My dad couldn't have been the devil. Although Mam could easily pass as one of his relations! A witch. Just like one of those hags in *Macbeth*. Although, if I'm honest, she's still too glam.'

'It was a good story,' said Dot, her expression dreamy. 'Exciting.'

'I bet it was. Enjoyed all that sex, did you?' said Viv dryly.

Dot grinned. 'What sex? There's never anything explicit. I wish there was. I might find out a few things.'

'And where would that lead you? Into trouble like my mother. It's no joke, Dot! Now get me some Aspro – please?'

Dot jumped up. 'Perhaps your mother's lying? Maybe your father's still alive and rich and famous and he's sent her money for years to keep quiet about him having an illegitimate child?'

'You're a fantasist,' said Viv, wondering why it mattered so much all of a sudden, knowing who her father was, when she had given him little thought in the past. 'Mam's got *it* still and seems to have no trouble hooking the fellas. Besides, he's dead.'

'Dead?' Dot paused, her hand on the door. 'How do you know that?'

Viv's nerves jolted and her fingers curled on a fold of her skirt. 'I don't know! Perhaps Mam told me years ago and it's been in my subconscious all this time.'

'It's amazing what you've got buried in your mind,' said Dot. 'I sometimes wonder if I've got my ancestors' thoughts as well as my own.'

'It could explain the odd things you say sometimes,' said Viv, her mouth curving slightly. 'She might have lied of course. Because if he's dead, why can't she talk about him to me?'

'Guilt!' said Dot positively. 'And she might just want to forget the past. Anyway, I'll get those Aspros.'

The silence after she left was as good as a pill and Viv stretched out on the bed as best she could with a hooped underskirt. She hoped Norm wouldn't come in suddenly because he'd see her knickers but while she could hear him practising his chords below she was safe. It was warm in the room because of the two-barred electric fire in the tiny cast iron and tiled fireplace. Guilt! Could it really be that which had brought her mother home? Viv found it difficult to accept. Her mother had never shown any sign of guilt before and had always gone her own sweet way, doing exactly what she liked. Viv remembered her dressing up for a night on the town. In her childish imagination Hilda had seemed like a fairy princess. How she had admired her in those early days before she had left without even a goodbye.

Dot came back into the room and handed Viv a drink and the Aspros. She took them with a word of thanks.

'Your father could have been a rich Yank,' said Dot, her eyes bright. 'Didn't your aunt marry a Yank?'

'Mike. Mam had her eye on him too but Aunt Flo beat her to him.'

'Your aunt might know who your father is.'

Viv stilled. It was a definite possibility. 'Aunt Flo wants me to go to America for Christmas,' she said slowly. 'I could ask her then!'

'You jammy thing!' Dot looked envious. 'Put me in your suitcase. I won't be any trouble. Just think of living in the same country as Elvis!'

Viv grinned. 'No problem. I'm sure they'll allow you to work your passage if you're discovered amongst my clothes.'

'What about your mother? Will she be staying here?'

Viv was silent. Would her mother stay in Liverpool if Viv went to California, or would she turn up at Aunt Flo's house for Christmas? It was a new thought. Her aunt had considered it a lovely idea, but was it? Viv needed to think some more.

'Well?' demanded Dot. 'What are you going to do about your mother?'

'I don't know.' She glanced at her watch and drained her cup. 'I'll have to be going. I'll sleep on it. Things always look different in the morning.'

'That's true,' said Dot, getting up. 'Dracula always has to go back in his coffin or the sunlight gets him.'

'Or Peter Cushing with a stake or crucifix. I wonder if I can get Dracula to take a bite out of Mam's jugular?' Viv grinned and rose from the bed. Dot saw her out, waving until she was out of sight.

Viv caught a bus in Tuebrook into town, hoping that she would not be late for her date with Nick. He had occupied her dreams but she had had little time to think about him since her mother's arrival on the scene. They had arranged to meet outside Boodle and Dunthorpe, the high class jeweller's, on the corner of Lord Street and North John Street in a part of the city that had been extensively rebuilt after being bombed during the war.

'I thought you might have changed your mind,' said Nick, taking Viv's hand and immediately beginning to walk up North John Street. He was dressed casually in a navy blue polo neck sweater and dark trousers, worn with a navy tweed jacket. His dark hair, which had been rather short back and sides when she first met him, had grown. He looked terribly attractive.

'I'm sorry I'm late but it's been a bit of a day.' Her voice was slightly breathless.

'George being awkward?'

'George has gone . . . off to Paris.'

Nick's eyes widened. 'He's what?'

'Gone to Paris. My mother came home and off he went. There was a big argument over Grandfather's money. Her causing trouble as usual.' Her voice wobbled. 'I wouldn't mind but she's newly widowed and rolling in it.' She stopped abruptly, surprised to be overcome by the intensity of her feelings.

Nick stared at her. 'Are you all right?'

'Damn!' she said, and scrubbed at tear-filled eyes. 'I don't know what I'm getting all worked up about.'

'Perhaps you're upset because George has gone?' suggested Nick, taking a handkerchief from a pocket.

'No! Yes!' Viv shook her head and a small laugh escaped her. 'I'm more upset about my mother turning up.'

Nick took hold of her chin. 'Keep still. You've messed up your mascara. You look like a panda that's been rained on.'

She stood motionless while he wiped her eyes, very aware of the strength in the fingers holding her chin.

'I take it she's come because of your grandfather's death?'

'Yes.'

'A natural thing to do, wouldn't you say? Especially if she's just been widowed. She's probably lonely. I take it there were no children of that marriage?' Viv shook her head.

Nick kissed the tip of her nose and smiled. 'My gran always said that death is a time when you look at life and wonder what it's all about. You think of what's gone before, and look at yourself, and ask: What now? Where do I go next?' He started to walk again and she had to quicken her natural pace to keep up with him.

'You think my mother has regrets about leaving me?' The thought made her feel churned up again but she did not let her emotions run away with her this time.

'Surely she must have?'

'She never showed it.' Viv's voice hardened. 'She was selfish, Nick. You remember her but you only saw the image she promoted to outsiders. Inside the family she was different. She could be charming, I'll give you that. And she's *still* glam. But if you're asking me to believe she's changed and become all loving and caring . . . well, I don't believe it, and I'm off to America as soon as I can!'

'I see. No second chance for your mother.'

Viv stared at him with an uncertain expression. 'I take it you gave your mother a second chance? But she was always there for you, Nick. You can't possible understand the way a mother mixes up a girl's emotions.'

He stopped and seized her upper arms with an unexpected, violent movement. 'Why is it *your* sex thinks they're the only ones who have trouble with their emotions? I tell you, Viv, there isn't anything you can tell me about mothers who turn your feelings inside out! Who drive you up the wall – who cause you so much shame that your insides feel so knotted up that you have to do something or you'll go crazy!' He smiled grimly. 'I busted a hundred prefab windows once because I felt so bad about what my mother was but it didn't do me any good. I still felt angry and wanted to hurt her. I did some stupid, crazy things.'

'I'm sorry,' stammered Viv.'It was a stupid thing for me to say.'

His voice quietened. 'I was sixteen when I finally lashed out at her and told her exactly what I thought of her. She broke her heart crying and kept saying she was sorry and that she wished a bomb had fallen on her in the war. It made my blood run cold because we'd both seen what a bomb could to do a body. Then she told me about my father. How she had been sixteen when he got her pregnant. He wanted her to have a back street abortion but she refused. So he married her but never forgave her for trapping him, as he called it.' Nick paused and his grip on her arms slackened. 'But you're right about one thing, Viv, she was always there for us – except for the time when Dad took us away from her. Eventually he rejoined the army and allowed us to live with Gran. Mam had met someone else by then and had a couple more kids. Even so she came to see us. Then the bloke went off and Gran got ill so Mam and the kids moved in with us and she looked after Gran till she died. Then we were back together and it was like that until Mavis married and emigrated to America and I did National Service.' His hands dropped away.

Viv rubbed her arms, thinking that she would have bruises there in the morning and trying not to show how affected she had been by his story. She cleared her throat. 'So you gave your mother a second chance and you feel OK about what she did now?'

'I'll never feel OK about that. And there've been other men while I've been away though they never lasted long. Now I'm back, Mam looks to me for financial help and to act as the man in the house to my half-brother and half-sister.' He added lightly, 'I happen to care about them.'

There was a silence which stretched. He had given Viv plenty to think about but it would have to wait. They had reached a narrow street made up of tall, blackened buildings. Mathew Street was just one such street of fruit warehouses existing not far from Liverpool's own Covent Garden where vegetable, fruit and flower traders set up in Queen Square behind St John's Market. The Cavern was a jazz club there which could only be reached by descending a flight of damp stairs into cellars which were dank, smoky, smelly and crowded. They had arrived a little late.

Nick produced a membership card for the man sitting at a table by the door and somehow he and Viv managed to squeeze their way in. The sound of a clarinet welcomed them, filling the cellars with noise. The place would have sent a claustrophobic mad.

Viv knew little about jazz and blues but was prepared to listen to the music and, think about what it was trying to say. 'Stranger on the Shore' always sent a quiver through her because the sound of the clarinet was so hauntingly evocative of the vastness of the sea and how small it made a person feel. Even so skiffle and folk music had been more to her taste before rock'n'roll had started to beat its way into the feet of the youth of Merseyside. She thought of music and the part it played in Liverpudlians' lives. Maybe it was because their city was a port situated within easy reach of America and the islands of the Caribbean, Ireland and Wales. So many people getting off boats or crossing borders went no further, and they brought with them the songs and rhythms of their own land. The Irish pennywhistle and fiddle could be heard in clubs, pubs and houses as could the sound of calypso, a Welsh tenor, folk songs, and sea shanties sung by sailors for generations. Most of them spoke to the heart and the spirit but did not satisfy the teenager's need to let off steam.

But live music was something else and it seemed to Viv that it was still echoing inside her head when she and Nick left the club. People vanished in different directions, some in search of alcohol at the nearby pub called The Vine because only soft drinks were served in The Cavern.

'Are you hungry?' asked Nick, gazing down at her as she shivered slightly in the cold air.

'Starving,' she said. 'I had no thought for food with Mam turning up.'

'Do you fancy a visit to Chinatown?'

'It sounds okay to me.' She slipped an arm through his as they began to walk and added in a warm voice. 'I've never gone for jazz that much but I enjoyed the music when I really listened to it, and it made me think that perhaps I should give Mam a second chance. Aunt Flo's in favour of a family Christmas in California. It wouldn't be so bad sharing a house with Mam if there wasn't just the two of us on our own – and I can ask Aunt Flo about my father.'

'What do you mean, ask your aunt about your father?' Nick's voice was unexpectedly sharp and she felt the muscle in his arm tense beneath her fingers.

'Ask her does she know who he is. Mam won't tell me. She got all uppity when I asked her,' explained Viv. 'She as good as said she didn't know who he was, but she was lying because she told me he was dead years ago . . . but then she could have been lying about that then, I suppose. She glanced up at him. 'Can you understand now, Nick, how difficult I find living with her? I never know where I am. She says and does things to suit herself, never mind whether it's right or wrong. *And* she wants me as a blinking skivvy. She treated Aunt Flo and me like slaves in the old days.'

'Maybe she's changed? You ought to listen to her, Viv. Give her a chance. Only by doing that will you get rid of that chip on your shoulder.'

'I haven't got a chip,' she said unconvincingly.

His smiling eyes met hers. 'Do the impossible, love. Our Mavis never could forgive Mam. They don't even write. I get the letters. It was me who knew first that she's having a baby. That news should have been for her mother.'

Viv murmured, 'You're too good, Nick.'

49

He scowled. 'Like hell I am!'

'I can't forgive my mother like you did.'

'Would you forgive your father?'

The words took her by surprise. 'Forgive him what?'

'Forgive him for doing the same thing as you accuse your mother of . . . deserting you. You see your father as some kind of hero because he was probably killed in battle, but what if he's still alive? As for your mother, you see her as a scarlet woman just because she couldn't cope with you on her own.'

She flushed. 'I don't see them as anything of the sort!'

'Don't you? Have you ever thought that she might have thrown herself into having a good time to forget? That she couldn't bear you near her after he had gone because you reminded her of him too much?'

'You're defending her again!' Viv's voice rose angrily. 'Perhaps you still fancy her? There are men who like older women.'

'Don't be daft!' He added softly, 'When I first saw you I thought, I like this one. She's got something. I still think that. Now shall we forget about your mother and mine and think of us? Tell me what you do for a living.'

Viv stared at him, her emotions in a turmoil. 'Just like that?' she said.

'Tell me,' he said quietly. 'All about yourself.'

'There's not much to tell,' she muttered. Even so, as they began to walk up Bold Street she told him how she had taken the first job the Employment had sent her to when she left school because she had needed the money. She worked in the Racing Department of Littlewood's, the pools firm, working out the odds. She had been reasonably content there because she liked the girls she worked with and one of them, Dot, had become her closest friend. At this time of year, though, they weren't very busy. The flat season was over and it was all national hunt race meetings. 'I'm not much a gambler myself,' she said ruefully. 'And now that Grandfather's dead I've been thinking about looking for something else. What do you do, Nick?'

They had neared the delicately carved stone structure of the bombed St Luke's church at the top of Bold Street and he

50

paused to look at it. 'I'm an architect. I finished my training before doing National Service. Look at the craftsmanship in this, Viv.'

'It's lovely.' She tried to hide her surprise at his answer. Working-class lads didn't often become architects. 'I have my lunch in the grounds sometimes in summer,' she added. Inside the shell of the building trees and grass had taken over from pews and pulpit and ivy had sent tendrils curling around empty window frames.

'Lucky you,' said Nick, smiling. 'And talking of food, we'll be there soon.'

They approached an area Viv did not know. It was brightly, almost garishly, lit by a string of restaurants.

Nick led her inside one of the smaller ones where paper lanterns hung from the ceiling and willowy oriental figures stared inscrutably from niches in the crimson and cream fabric-covered walls. Liverpool had the oldest Chinese community in Europe but Viv had never tasted Chinese food before.

She liked it, and by the time she had finished crispy Peking duck and illicitly drunk three glasses of white wine she decided that she did not want to go home and face her mother. 'Where else can we go?' she asked over coffee, not wanting to believe how late it might be or how the drink had gone to her head.

'Quiet or noisy?' murmured Nick, kissing her fingertips.

She giggled. 'Quiet, after all that jazz.'

'The local graveyard?' He smiled and she believed that he was joking. 'It's the nearest anywhere of quiet distinction you can get,' he added blandly.

'Take me,' she ordered, thinking she would have something to tell Dot when next she saw her.

The way was steep and the wind from the River Mersey whipped under Viv's coat, up her legs and beneath the swaying hooped underskirt, chilling the bare skin between stocking top and knickers. She was half frozen but was not going to admit it as he gazed up at the Anglican cathedral on St James Mount, looming above them in all its pseudo-Gothic glory. She should have guessed. She knew it well. Had been confirmed within its walls. 'You're crazy wanting to come

51

here at this time of night,' she said, shaking her head.

Nick put an arm round her and said, 'I love this building.' His tone was reverent. 'It was designed by a Roman Catholic, Gilbert Scott, when he was only twenty-one. The foundation stone was laid in 1904 and it's still not finished. It was bombed during the war but the work goes on. A job for life for some of the stonemasons, Viv. If I could design anything half as exciting . . .' He paused, shrugged, and she felt his change of mood. 'You couldn't get a job like this today. Now it's not beauty of form or outline that's important. Now we've got to give the ordinary people what they want and money's short and we've got to build quick. And it's drains! Bathrooms! Bigger kitchens with wide windows! That's what housewives want.'

Viv agreed but added, 'You're not responsible for those tower blocks going up, are you? They're ugly and so *high*!' She did not like heights.

'No, I'm not.' He smiled grimly. 'At the moment I'm working on specifications for a school. But lots of people live in skyscrapers in America. It seems to work there so why not here? It saves on land.' Once again he looked up at the cathedral. 'They didn't worry about that in the old days so much.' He hugged her to him. 'Now come and look at the graveyard.'

He led her round the building until they could see far below them a large elongated pit. There were mossy gravestones half concealed. Trees rattled twiggy fingers. Instinctively she snuggled closer to him. Both his arms went round her. 'There's a spring down there somewhere,' he whispered against her cold ear. 'It's supposed to have magical properties.'

'Perhaps it could turn you into a frog?' she said with a quiver in her voice.

'Or you into a princess.'

'Now you're being fanciful.' Her heartbeat, which had slowed down after the climb, had quickened again.

He kissed her ear and she thought what she wanted was respect from a man. A white frock on her wedding day that would really mean something. He licked the curve of her jaw.

'You're tickling,' she whispered.

52

'Well, look at me then.'

She looked at him and he kissed her, gently at first, then deeply as if he wanted to draw her inside out. She experienced such an upsurge of sensuality that it shocked her. She opened her eyes and attempted to disengage herself but although his grip slackened he did not release her. 'It's a beautiful night,' he said.

She looked up at the sky. It was beautiful. The wind was tearing the clouds apart and pale silver light spilled from the moon, lighting up the gravestones below and glistening on hoar-frosted grass. 'Don't say it,' she responded as calmly as she could. 'It's a night made for love.'

His lips twitched. 'I won't say it.' He pushed back the kiss curls from her forehead and pressed his lips against her eyelids. His fingers wandered down her cheek, stroked her neck. She caught hold of them before they reached her breast.

'I don't trust you, Nick Bryce,' she said with a hint of breathlessness.

'You can.' His eyes teased her and he pulled her arm around his waist. 'We only do what you want.'

'I want to go home,' she said.

He sighed. 'I knew you'd lie.'

Viv protested but he silenced her with another kiss, and another. Despite, or because of, their effect on her, she pushed him away in the end. 'Time to go home.'

'Yes,' he said quietly, 'I think it is.' And pulling her hand through his arm, he led her down the hill. It was when she was halfway down that she remembered her mother.

Chapter Five

Hilda woke as the strains of 'This Old House' died away. The voyage had been tiring. She yawned, switched off the wireless and stood listening to the silence. She had been born here. A grim smile played round her painted lips. A long time before those two wildcats. The cheek of George answering her back, and the way Viv had stood up to her! She remembered how, when Viv had been a child, she had tried to put down her own mother by ignoring her after she had been away for a year or so. It had made Hilda feel two inches tall but she had not let it show. It had been bad enough knowing that she had allowed her sister to fill her place in Viv's affections. And now – what chance had she of regaining that affection? She grimaced. Kids these days had no respect . . .

Kids? No! That was where she had made her mistake. Viv was a young woman and George a man. She had got the shock of her life when he had stood and faced her. She wondered how her sister would feel if she saw him now. Despite her marrying Mike the sight of him would surely bring back memories of Tom, her first husband, and how it had been in the thirties when they were all so young.

There had been times when Hilda had been so jealous and resentful of Flo that she could cheerfully have strangled her, but nearly dying a few weeks ago had given her pause for thought and she had realised in hospital just how important family was and had become aware of the need to sort out a few things. As soon as she had got out she had headed straight for her sister's home.

For a moment she thought of how happy Flora and Mike

were and how envious she had felt. She had done the right thing leaving them, of course she had. Resisting the urge to flirt with Mike would have been a strain on her newfound resolution to turn over a new leaf. But she had banked on Viv being pleased to see her.

What had happened to her coffee? Where was Viv? Good Lord, she should never have said that about her father being no good. A lie would have been better. She had intended telling the truth one day. The whole truth, so help me God truth, but it was so hard! And the little devil that seemed to ride on her shoulder instead of the guardian angel that Naomi Ruth had talked of, had caused her to protect her own interests. The whole truth would have done her no good at all.

Naomi Ruth would not have approved of her behaviour. Hilda remembered the elderly Pentecostal Christian she had met in hospital when she was feeling desperate. Death was leering at her from the end of the bed in the guise of a doctor in a white coat, and Hilda had been terrified out of her wits. Getting religion had suddenly seemed preferable to dying with no hope. But Naomi Ruth had prayed. Her whole church had prayed. Hilda had survived but Naomi Ruth had died. Even to Hilda that had seemed a little unfair, even granting that Naomi Ruth was eighty.

'Lord, where is that girl?' she said aloud. 'Not as pretty as me at her age but clever, so Flo said. Out to catch George, of course. Perhaps she's more like me than I thought?'

She opened the door and went in search of her daughter.

Hilda was annoyed. Where was Viv? And where was George? Had they gone together? She had left beautiful California without seeing Hollywood and the homes of the stars, and had paid a lot of money to come home to get to know her daughter because she had promised to do so to Naomi Ruth almost on her deathbed (some things even in Hilda's point of view were sacred), and now Viv had gone and vanished. It seemed unfair considering all the trouble she had gone to.

Perhaps they had only gone as far as next-door? The Kellys . . . did they still live next-door? A rare genuine smile lifted the corners of her mouth. It was years since she had thought of the Kellys. ' "There were seven in the bed and the little one

said, 'Roll over! Roll over'"' she sang softly. Did God mind
her finding some comfort in the memory?

Dominic Kelly had rolled right on top of her and she had
belted him. He had hit her back, not too hard, then kissed her
when she started crying. It had shut her up and she had not
minded when he held her close and explored beneath her
flannelette nightie. Her mother had just died and she could
not bear the pain of her own grief. How old had she been?
Ten – eleven? Over thirty years ago. Times had been difficult
and they had got worse when her father had gone back to sea
and Aunt Beattie had taken charge.

Hilda had never been her schoolmarm aunt's favourite and
in the early days her bare legs had often stung from the cane
she kept under the sideboard. Hilda's face tightened and her
hands curled into fists. Then she shrugged. Forgive and forget
it. All water under the bridge. At least there had been none of
that for her daughter. Was Viv next-door? There would be no
harm in finding out if the Kellys still lived there.

She did not bother with a top coat although a few
snowflakes fluttered on to her face. It was cold but it could not
compare with conditions in New Jersey in winter. As she
stood with her finger on the bell beside the partly glazed,
shiny blue and white painted front door, she could not help
comparing the two houses. Her father's door and window
frames were a dull green and paint was flaking off in places.
Obviously the landlord had got away with murder for years
and her father had been too mean to spend money having the
outside of the house done up.

The door opened and the young man standing there filled
the doorway. Her eyes devoured him. She had managed to
pack up the ciggies but the opposite sex was still a temptation.
His short hair was damp and tousled and there was a towel
around his bare neck. He wore tight black trousers and a
white sloppy joe. He looked twentyish, was a gorgeous
example of manhood, and was the spitting image of his father.
'Can I help you, missus?'

She switched on a smile. 'I'm Hilda Murray née Preston.
And you have to be one of the Kellys. Which one I couldn't
guess.'

'Joe.' His voice was interested. 'Gran used to talk about

you.' Hilda wondered what she had said. 'What is it yer after?' he asked.

'My daughter Viv. She isn't in your house, is she?'

'Nope. But I saw her walking up the back jigger from the bedroom window. Not long after George actually.'

Hilda did not let her annoyance show. 'Girls!' Her expression was rueful. 'My turning up gave her quite a shock.'

He was silent but a voice called from inside asking who was at the door. He shouted back, 'Hilda Preston, Dad.'

Several seconds passed and Hilda rubbed her arms. She was starting to feel the cold. The vestibule door opened and a man with thick straight greying hair loomed up behind Joe in the small space between the doors. He and Hilda stared at each other. He had been six foot at fourteen with the best shoulders she had ever seen. He still looked good.

'I don't believe it! The blinkin' prodigal's returned,' said Dominic. 'Bit late, aren't yer, girl? The funeral's been and gone.'

'I didn't know,' she said with a tremulous smile. 'How are you, Dom?'

'Fair to best.' He wore a cream Aran sweater which made his shoulders look even larger. 'How's yerself?'

She shrugged. 'Can't complain. Had a bit of a chest.' She placed a hand on her bust and coughed.

His dark eyes followed the movement. 'You'll have to look after it. Mam always said you were prone to be chesty.'

'We used to have such terrible fogs. Remember us getting lost?'

'I always knew my way about.'

A giggle escaped her and Dominic slanted a look at his son who was leaning against the doorjamb listening with obvious fascination. 'If you're going out you'd better hurry up, lad.'

Joe moved reluctantly.

'Nice-looking lad,' said Hilda.

Dominic shook his head. 'Too young for yer, girl,' he said in a teasing voice. 'Besides, he's not interested. Still prefers his mates, football and skiffle.'

'My husband liked jazz. He thought he could play the saxophone. I met him at a dance.'

'The second husband, I presume?'

57

'Yes.' She sighed. 'He died a few months ago.'

'So you're a widow.'

'Yes.' Her lips curved into a delightful smile. 'And not a very merry one at the moment. I need cheering up, Dom.'

'You haven't changed.'

She sighed. 'I'm older now.'

'Any wiser?'

'I hope so.' She thought of the fun they had had together. They had learnt a lot from each other. She felt nostalgic for those days and determined to keep the conversation going despite the fact that her feet were freezing in their patent leather high heels. 'You're still supporting the wrong team, I see.'

'Up the Blues,' he said dispassionately.

'Your house looks nice.

'You want to get George to paint yours now the old man's gone. Or aren't you stopping?'

'I'm stopping for a while if . . .' She shrugged. 'George has gone off somewhere and so has Viv. That's why I called.'

'Had a row did you? Money, I suppose,' said Dominic.

She wondered if he had heard the row through the walls. 'I was the eldest daughter,' she said with dignity.

He made no comment and her expression relaxed. 'Anyway, if I stay perhaps you could paint my door red and white?'

'It's the wrong time of the year,' he drawled. 'Besides the bristles would fall out of me brush with them colours. I wouldn't mind working inside if you've got any jobs? Get laid off on the building sometimes at this time of year.'

'Why don't you come in now and see what needs doing?' She smiled and said with a touch of satisfaction. 'I can pay, you know. I'm a rich widow.' They stared at each other in silence and she knew that the shiver she gave was not just due to the cold.

'Might as well,' he murmured. 'The wife's at her mother's for the weekend. She's crippled with rheumatism and the sisters take turns in staying with her.'

'Good!' Her smile dazzled. 'No time like the present.'

He closed the door behind him and followed her.

*   *   *

The house looked quiet and peaceful as Viv opened the front door. She had told Nick to leave her at the corner of the street in case her mother was waiting on the doorstep, saying that she wanted no noisy confrontations. It had only been partly true. If the truth were told, to her shame, she did not want him meeting her mother. Hilda was a damn sight too attractive still.

'What about America?' he had asked. 'Are you going or not?'

'I haven't decided. It depends on what happens when I get home.'

Well, she was home and there was no sign of her mother in the front room and the fire was almost out. She stood quietly, and caught the murmur of voices. She listened and recognised the deep tones of Mr Kelly from next-door. Her feet in their ballerina shoes made no sound as she walked across the room. She stopped when she reached the partially open door and heard her mother say in warm tones, 'You don't know what a comfort it was having you to turn to, Dom. I wanted to block out death and you helped me for a while.'

'It was my pleasure. Although if I'd thought on about how your father would react to your being in our house, I mightn't have been so reckless about letting myself go. We were lucky.'

'Yes! And so young. I had no idea where babies came from.'

'Do you think your Flora was aware of what was going on?'

'Probably. Your brother wasn't backward in coming forward and she was in bed with us, wasn't she?'

Viv was rooted to the spot. What had been going on? Her mother! Aunt Flo! Both in bed with Mr Kelly and his brother! The next words ensured she would continue eavesdropping.

'I don't think I could have survived without sneaking off with you,' said Hilda. 'They were awful days and Father was so *cold*. I couldn't get near him. He shut me out. Perhaps he blamed me for her dying?'

'Perhaps he blamed himself? He was always away and you were only a kid.'

'He expected me to cope, though. He had a high opinion of me then, Dom!' There was a pause and when Hilda resumed

59

speaking there was pain in her voice. 'Aunt Beattie ruined things between us completely by always complaining about me. He started to believe I was uncontrollable. That did something to me, Dom. I became what he believed I was. When I started with Viv that was it! He tore into me. I've never forgotten what he said.' She laughed. 'And there's Viv and George believing me the world's worst daughter because it seemed I didn't care about him! Perhaps I was? But if so I had cause. He rejected me more than once. Although I still believed he might come round in the end.'

There was a pause and then Dominic said, 'You should have let me know when he threw you out. I would have helped you.'

'You couldn't. You were in the navy and had a wife.'

'I've a wife now.'

'Pity,' said Hilda, a smile in her voice.

'I'd best be getting home.'

'Yes.'

There was silence and Viv just knew they were kissing. Part of the conversation she had overhead thudded dully in her head. 'You should have let me know . . . You had a wife.' Could Dominic Kelly be her father? Oh, no! She turned and fell over the cat which yowled. There was nothing for it but to walk into the kitchen and confront them. Her head was held high but she felt as taut as a violin string. 'I thought I'd come and ask you a few questions about my father again,' she said brightly. 'He couldn't be Mr Kelly by any chance, could he?'

Hilda opened her mouth, then closed it before smiling and saying, 'You shouldn't listen at keyholes.'

'I wasn't listening at keyholes.' Viv flushed. 'And if you wanted all that you said to be a secret, you should have locked the front door.'

'I was hoping you'd still be coming home despite the time. Didn't I say so, Dom?'

He did not answer her question but said quietly, 'I wish you were my daughter, girl. I always wanted one but the wife wouldn't have any more kids after the three lads.'

'Now that's sweet,' said Hilda, her expression hardening. 'If you'd kept quiet, Dom, we could have passed you off as her longlost daddy and then 'I wouldn't have her bringing the

60

subject up again. Now you'd better go. I want to have a heart to heart with my daughter.'

'That'll make a change,' said Viv, folding her arms over her breasts. 'You never wanted to talk to me in the past. Are you going to tell me a bedtime story? You were never there for Red Riding Hood and the big bad wolf in the past. You much preferred the human kind.'

'Hush.' Dominic placed his hand on her shoulder. 'A girl of your age needs a mother.' He picked up his jacket and left by the front door.

Mother and daughter eyed each other. 'When I think you made me feel dirty with George,' said Viv, her eyes glinting. 'And here's you alone with a married man at this time of night!'

'We're old friends,' said Hilda, frowning. 'And what's a kiss after all? It's hardly a full blown affair. And if we're talking about the time – where have you been? You're only seventeen. Who have you been with?'

'It's none of your business.' Viv's chin set determinedly. 'Don't think just because you've come home you're going to tell me what to do and what time I've got to be in. I had enough of that with Grandfather and George.'

'Fair comment,' said Hilda. 'Where is George, by the way?'

'He's gone to Paris to paint. It's what his father wanted to do and he never got the chance. That's why George wanted the money. So you see, Mother, why he took off without a goodbye.'

She shrugged. 'Sure I see. It was the easy way out. You're made of sterner stuff, Viv.'

'What's that supposed to mean?' She sat on the rocking chair.

'You lived here with your grandfather. It must have taken a lot of doing.' Hilda sat on the lumpy sofa. 'I admire you.'

There was a short silence then Viv smiled. 'Soft soap, Mother. You must want me to stay.'

'I do. I know things didn't work out for us in the past but there's no use crying over spilt milk. It's all water under the bridge. I'm the only mother you've got. Our Flo might have done my job for me in bringing you up but she's not here now.'

61

Viv took her gaze off her mother's lovely face and stared at the fireplace. Her heart was beating uncomfortably fast. Did Hilda really mean what she said?

'I've thought of going to America,' murmured Viv. 'Aunt Flo's asked me there for Christmas.'

'She's what?' Hilda sprang to her feet. 'Damn her! She's no right. You're *my* daughter. She has her own family. How long is it since we've had a Christmas together, Viv? You'll have to write back and tell her you're not going.'

She felt a spurt of anger. 'I'll what?' she cried. 'Aunt Flo wants me you never did! You never once invited me to stay with you in America!'

'You never once asked! I wish you had. It would have pleased Charlie. He thought you weren't interested in us.'

'I wonder where he got that idea?'

Hilda flushed. 'Okay, okay. So maybe I told him so. But I've changed since then. Since I nearly died . . .'

'Nearly died?' Viv laughed. 'You don't have to lay it on with a trowel, Mother.

'Since I nearly died,' said Hilda through gritted teeth, 'I've changed. I realise how many things I've done wrong and I want to make up to you for them. A girl needs a mother at your age. I only wish I'd had mine around. Things might have been different. In fact, I know they would.'

'In what way?'

'I mightn't have had to fight my own corner so much.'

'You mean *you'll* fight my battles for me?' Viv was amused. 'It's a bit late for that, Mam. I've had to do my own fighting for the last couple of years. Generally against grandfather.' She paused. 'Anything else you have on offer to make me stay?'

Hilda hesitated. 'Not to compare with what our Flo can provide in America.' She leaned forward and touched her daughter's knee. 'We're the only ones left in Liverpool, though, Viv, to keep the home fires burning if they ever return.'

Viv was strangely moved and said hesitantly, "I can't believe it's you saying that.'

Hilda smiled inwardly, remembering an American war film she had seen. 'You don't really know me, though, do you?

62

Give me a try,' she said persuasively. 'Our Flo would understand. She always wanted us to get together.'

Viv was silent, certain sure that she did not trust her mother
to be any different if she stayed. But Nick had given his
mother a chance and could she do any less? 'I'm not the
muttonhead I used to be, Mother,' she warned. 'I won't be
your skivvy.'

'Yes, Viv,' said Hilda meekly.

Viv slanted her a knowing look. 'Don't think I'm fooled by
that. Did you mean it about getting the house done up?'

'Of course I meant it!' Her mother's baby blue eyes
widened. 'Why do you think I had Mr Kelly in here? He was
measuring up the jobs that needed doing. He gets laid off for
days in winter.'

'Can I have a new bed? One of the latest divans.'

'You mean, spend extra money?' blurted Hilda.

Viv raised her eyebrows. 'There's my real mother speaking. Perhaps I'll go to America after all.'

Hilda bit back an angry retort. 'We'll buy the bed.'

'Jolly hockey sticks.' Viv beamed at her and got to her feet.
'You'd better take George's room. I'll be going up because
I've work in the morning. Perhaps you'd like me to give you
an early call?'

'No thanks,' said Hilda hastily. 'The voyage quite took it
out of me. The doctor said I have to have lots of rest.'

'I bet,' said Viv dryly and sauntered out of the room,
feeling that she had won the first round.

Chapter Six

Viv gazed at the board in front of her with Saturday's horse racing results and worked out the odds on two winning singles and a double before passing the green slip to Dot to check. Then she sat gazing into space, chewing on the end of her pencil.

'You'll get lead poisoning,' said Dot.

'I'm thinking.'

'Well, think afterwards,' said her friend. 'I'm waiting for more work from you.'

Viv nodded and got on with working out a Round Robin but part of her mind was taken up with thinking about her mother, who had still been in bed when Viv had left for work. Had she done the right thing by saying she would not go to America? Aunt Flo would be disappointed but there was no doubt she would be in favour of mother and daughter getting together. Who was her father? She was glad it wasn't Mr Kelly, but thinking about him and her mother together made her feel uneasy. Dominic Kelly was still a good-looking man despite being all of forty. She hoped her mother wouldn't get up to any of her old tricks. 'What's a kiss between old friends?' In her mind she still heard her mother's voice. What if she caused another scandal in the street? Viv wouldn't put it past her. Damn! Perhaps she should enquire about ships sailing to America but it would have to be done straightaway or Christmas would be here and gone. She pondered the matter off and on for most of the morning and was still undecided when twelve o'clock came.

When Viv came back from lunch she found Dot and several

of their workmates gathered round a desk. They were playing Ouija with letters, numbers and an upturned cup. 'One of these days,' murmured Viv, 'you'll get an answer and frighten yourselves to death.'

'It's only a bit of fun,' said Dot, grinning. 'I'm sure there's someone you'd like to get in touch with. Your dad for instance.'

'Not like that, thanks.' She shook her head, wondering if she was a fool still to want to know her father's identity after what her mother and Nick had said. Her heart gave a peculiar flip when she thought of Nick. He was the plus in staying home for Christmas, although when he had kissed her goodnight he had not said when he would see her again. He had told her that he had a lot of catching up to do in work and would be putting in extra hours.

When Viv arrived home that evening she found her mother clad in a dressing gown. She was seated in the rocking chair in front of the fire, reading a magazine. Her feet in fluffy nonsensical slippers rested on a pouffe. There were clothes on the backs of chairs and a glass on the floor.

'You can tell you're home,' said Viv, slamming the door. 'What a mess!' Her eyebrows rose. 'There's something missing!'

'It's the sofa.' Hilda's expression was wary. 'I couldn't bear the sight of it so I had Dom move it into the back yard. We'll need to get rid of it for when we get new.'

Viv shrugged off her coat and perched on the edge of a dining chair. 'You actually meant what you said last night?'

'What I said?'

'You know, about making a nice little nest of this place?'

'Of course I did. You didn't think I'd stay on as it is!' Her scarlet lips twisted in distaste. 'I'm used to better, you know.'

'So I gather,' said Viv dryly, getting up and going into the kitchen to put on the kettle.

The old-fashioned shallow stone sink was crowded with dirty dishes and cutlery. It looked like her mother had shared a meal of fish, chips and HP sauce with someone. Mr Kelly, she presumed. She felt her temper rising but kept control of it as she went into the front room. 'You're a lazy so and so, Mother. One of these days you'll catch some horrible germ and die.'

Hilda frowned. 'That's a nice way to speak to your mother. I haven't had time to think of doing the dishes. I've been busy, unpacking . . . shopping and things.'

'Did you think of getting something for my tea?' said Viv softly. 'Or did I do right by buying it myself?'

'I thought my first day home you'd know everything would be strange to me.' Hilda smiled sweetly. 'I was right, wasn't I? But I did buy you a cake. A jammy doughnut. If I remember rightly you used to love them.'

'It was lemon cheese tarts I loved but a jammy doughnut will do nicely,' said Viv, taking some mince, an onion and potatoes from her shopping bag.

Hilda's brow knitted. 'I could have sworn you liked jammy doughnuts.'

'*You* liked jammy doughnuts.' Viv went back out into the kitchen, followed by her mother.

'I take it our Flo taught you how to cook?'

'A bit. Necessity taught me most. Although luckily Grandfather wasn't fussy.'

'I remember.' Hilda's smile was gently reminiscent. 'He'd eat anything you put in front of him.'

Viv glanced up from peeling a potato. 'How was it you forgot how to cook? You must have done it when Grandmother was ill.'

Hilda's smile faded and she rested her back against the fablon-topped kitchen table. 'I never could cook properly. I muddled through, obeying my mother's orders. When she died and me and Flo went to live with old Beetroot – she was your Great-aunt Beattie, by the way – she wouldn't let me near her precious stove. She actually told me she couldn't have me wasting food by trying out recipes. I asked her how I was to learn and she hit me across the legs. Any backchat or anything she thought I was doing wrong and I would get a belt. When she found out I was seeing Dom Kelly she considered it disgraceful, me having anything to do with a Catholic. She hit me that hard my legs were red raw and bleeding. I hated her. I used to pray she'd die.' She paused to take a packet of Polo mints from the pocket of her dressing gown and jerkily undid the foil.

'It must have been awful,' said Viv, feeling sympathy for her.

66

'At least you never suffered like that,' muttered Hilda. 'I made sure you had a good home. There mightn't have been much there in the way of goodies but our Flo treated you like her own daughter.'

'I appreciate that you thought of all that before you left me with her,' said Viv gravely. 'But I wasn't her daughter, I was yours.'

Hilda grimaced. 'So you were.'

'When did you meet my father?' Viv's voice was gentle.

Her mother stared at her and laughed. 'You won't catch *me* by surprise. Forget him, Viv. You've got me and you don't need a father.' She popped a mint into her mouth and said vaguely, 'Talking of fathers – how much did mine leave?'

Viv's smile was fixed as she chopped a couple of potatoes and put them in a pan. 'You mean *your* father whom I looked after like a daughter? If he'd lived with you in America you'd have had to pay for someone to look after him, wouldn't you? Let's say that all the money he left is wages in lieu of the care I gave him in place of you hiring a nurse. Fair comment, don't you think?'

'I suppose so.' Hilda's expression was a little sulky. 'I haven't got that much money with me, you know. It takes time to transfer money from one country to another.'

'Crying poverty again? You shouldn't have thrown the sofa out because we might have problems buying a new one in that case. And you shouldn't have asked Mr Kelly to do jobs either, if you haven't got the money.'

'I didn't say I haven't the money,' snapped Hilda. 'Just that I haven't got it all right now! I've got some but not enough for all that needs doing. I thought you might like to chip in with some of Father's?'

Viv was silent as she placed the mince in a pan with water and lit the gas. Some of what her mother said about transferring money could be true. On the other hand she could still be just as tightfisted as she had been in the old days.

'I still plan to go to America sometime so I want my money,' murmured Viv. 'We could do the decorating ourselves, that would save.'

'I'm not going to be climbing ladders,' said Hilda firmly, straightening up as the kettle boiled and going to make the

67

tea. 'I've asked Dom to do it and that's that! I can't go back on it. Besides, I've already given him some money. He's starting with my bedroom and I've ordered myself a new bed. I can't be doing with George's. Yours can wait.'

'Just what I thought would happen,' drawled Viv. 'I hope you realise that if you're upstairs when Mr Kelly's there, Mrs McCoy over the road will soon know about it. She has a telescope in that bedroom of hers.'

'She always was a nosy faggot,' muttered Hilda.

'All you've got to do is behave yourself,' said Viv positively. 'I'll meet you halfway, Mam. I'll order and pay for my own bed and decorate my own room. I think I can afford that. Besides, I reckon this way I'll get what *I* want.'

'Okay.' That sounds fair enough. Although the furniture's a bit crummy in Father's room.'

'Let me worry about that,' said Viv, slicing an onion. 'Will you be getting a job if you're so hard up? Maggie might take you on. You have some experience working in a bakery, don't you?'

'I don't know why you're saying that about me being hard up.' Hilda's tone was irritable. 'I told you, it's just a matter of time. Besides, I wouldn't work in that bakery for a gold clock. When the money comes I'll get you a television to make up for not buying you the bed.'

Viv tried not to look disbelieving. 'We could rent one. Then if you change your mind about staying and I go to see Aunt Flo, we can just send it back.' She dropped the chopped onion in the mince and stirred the lot. 'By the way, I'll be writing to Aunt Flo. Is there anything you'd like me to say to her for you? I'd thought of asking her if she knows who my father was.'

'You what?' Hilda's whole body stiffened. 'What do you want to do that for?'

'Well, you won't tell me.' Viv smile was bland. 'But I thought there was a fair chance you might have told your sister.'

'I might have,' murmured Hilda, lowering her eyes and gazing at her fingernails. 'But then I mightn't have. She was like you, wanting to know who he was all the time. She was angry for me but I was daft in those days so I kept my peace.

Years later I think we might have talked about it again. I can't remember exactly.'

Viv's gaze was fixed on her mother's face and suddenly she remembered her expression of old. 'I think you're lying. I'm going to ask her anyway.'

Hilda threw up her arms. 'You do what you want! I'm not here to stop you doing anything! As long as you do me the same favour. But what good knowing about your father will do you, I don't know! He was no angel as I've told you.'

Viv flushed. 'I take it he wasn't completely evil either?'

'Men can be swines but he wasn't that bad,' said Hilda, her lovely mouth compressing. 'That's all I'm, saying, Viv.' With those words she poured tea into a cup and handed it to her daughter. 'Don't say I never do anything for you.' She forced a smile and went back into the front room.

Viv heard the click of the wireless going on and Lonnie Donegan's 'Rock Island Line' thrummed on the air. Damn you, Mother, she thought. If it wasn't that I need a visa to get into America and it's too late to get one now in time for Christmas, I'd leave you here and take off. Why can't you just be straight with me? But she had to accept that deviousness had often been her mother's way in the past and she had not really expected a miraculous change in her behaviour. Besides Aunt Flo was sure to give her the answer she wanted if she went by what her mother had just said.

At that moment there was a smell of burning and Viv had to act swiftly. She poured half of the tea in her cup into the pan of mince and lowered the gas. As she drank the first half she reflected that it might not be the first strange concoction she would be eating if her mother decided to take a hand in the cooking.

Over the next week or so Viv tried to accept Hilda for what she was but it was not easy. Mrs McCoy stopped Viv in the street and asked her point blank what Mr Kelly was doing in their house. According to her he was there some part of most days. An annoyed Viv told her to mind her own business and Mrs McCoy came back with: 'You're as bad as your mother!'

Viv wouldn't have lost her temper only she suspected that her mother *was* up to something with Mr Kelly. Every

69

evening when she came home Hilda was either in a state of déshabillé or dressed up as a cowgirl. Viv made a point of making no comment but was convinced that one day she would come in and find her mother being lassooed by Mr Kelly and dragged upstairs.

But that was not the only thing that exasperated her. She and her mother had agreed to share the work. Hilda had said that she would do the washing if Viv did the ironing. That seemed fair but her mother took the washing to the laundrette and sat watching it go round, gossiping and renewing old friendships. When Viv came home from a full day's work she was faced twice a week with a mound of ironing, most of it not hers.

Her mother's dinners generally consisted of fish and chips, tripe and onions in stewed milk, or meat pies from the bakery. She always apologised when placing these offerings on a table spread with a clean tablecloth, a candle and a glass of sherry for each of them, adding that she had had a cook when she lived with Charlie. Viv did not know if she was telling the truth or was just plain lazy.

There was also her mother's extravagance. For someone who was waiting for money to be transferred Hilda did a fair amount of shopping. Clothes, chocolates, magazines, bottles of sherry and gin, new cutlery, new curtains and bed covers! Then to top it all Viv came home one day to find Mr Kelly and her mother admiring the new bedroom suite in Hilda's room. As well as that there was a brand new television occupying a corner of the front room!

'Has your money come then?' demanded Viv, slamming the pork chops in the frying pan when Mr Kelly had gone.

'Not yet.' Hilda popped a mint into her mouth and said, 'I got them on the H.P., honey. Don't you worry, I'm not going to demand my rightful share of Father's money.'

'Rightful?' Viv's voice went up several octaves. Her mother knew just where to touch her on the raw. 'You've got no more moral right to it than the cat! And another thing – what's Mr Kelly doing here again? We aren't getting any more decorating done yet. You're getting yourself talked about, Mam. Before you know it Mrs Kelly will be banging on the door complaining.'

'No, she won't,' sniffed her mother. 'She's glad of the extra money for Christmas. I've given him more money and asked him to do something about the kitchen for me . . . get rid of that awful sink.'

'Doesn't that man ever go to work?' cried Viv.

She gave up trying to reason with Hilda and, slightly envious of her mother's transformation of George's old room, ordered some bedroom furniture for her own in light oak, consisting of a single wardrobe and a kidney-shaped dressing table with triple mirrors. It cheered her up because on top of having to cope with her mother's disruptive presence, Nick Bryce had not been in touch.

Sometimes she dreamed of him finding her on a moonlit beach in a rocky cove. He was dressed in Victorian clothes and swept her off her feet and tore the crinoline from her in order to kiss her passionately and make her his own.

She woke in her newly decorated bedroom with racing heart. It was crazy but her dream also reminded her of what Dot had said about *The Devil's Daughter*. It set her thinking about her father and she found herself doing something that had never occurred to her before when next she went Christmas shopping. She looked at older men's faces asking herself: Did my father look a bit like you? It was foolish and she soon stopped when a couple gave her the glad eye.

Christmas week arrived and there was still no answer to her letter from her aunt. Hilda made a comment about it but Viv said it was probably because it *was* Christmas time. She did not add that she had asked Flora to send the reply to her question to Dot's house. She did not quite trust her mother not to destroy a letter from Flo. A postcard came from George saying that he was in Paris and painting and was fine. It was a relief to hear from him because she had worried a little. She considered asking Joe Kelly for Nick's address. If she sent him a Christmas card then he would know that she had not gone to America and perhaps he would call and ask her out. But her pride got in the way and she left it. If he wanted to see her, he could do the chasing.

The day before Christmas Eve Dot asked Viv if she would like to go out for a meal with some of the girls from work and perhaps finish up in a club? Everything had been arranged weeks ago but a couple of the girls had dropped out. Viv had nothing else on and so she said yes.

Her mother was not pleased. 'I thought we'd be spending Christmas Eve together' she said irritably, ruffling the pages of the magazine she was reading. 'I'll be all on my own. Everyone's with their families.'

'Not everybody,' said Viv. 'And I'll be in just after midnight probably.' She hesitated. 'We could go down Breck Road together now if you like. I'm not going out till eight.' She glanced around the front room that had not enjoyed Mr Kelly's attentions yet. 'We should have put some decorations up. George and I always did, although Grandfather thought it a waste of time and he'd never countenance a tree.'

Hilda's expression brightened. 'We could get some mistletoe and balloons and we could do something about a tree! It's not too late!'

Viv was surprised by her mother's enthusiasm and it seemed to her that for a moment she looked much younger. Suddenly Viv felt lighthearted herself. It was the first time they had done such a thing together.

They meandered down Breck Road, looking in the brightly lit shop windows and stopping and buying when they saw what they wanted.

'Perhaps you should get some lights for the tree?' suggested Hilda. She had bought balloons, tinsel, mistletoe and holly. Viv had splashed out on the tree, a box of crackers, chocolate goodies and little knick knacks for the tree.

Viv was silent a moment. She had dipped into her grandfather's money for Christmas presents, a new skirt and jumper and the night out, and was reluctant to spend any more. But then a wave of nostalgia swept over her and she was remembering a Christmas at her aunt's when Mike and George had surprised them with a lit up tree in the front parlour. It was the first Christmas tree that Viv had ever seen and the magic of that moment had stayed with her. A sigh escaped her.

'You're right, Mam. We do need lights. A tree's nothing without lights. What if we go halfy halfy?'

Hilda hesitated then said with a grimace, 'What the hell? It's only Christmas once a year.' So they bought the lights and, loaded up, made their way home to decorate the front room.

Afterwards it was a mad dash for Viv to get ready to go out. As she closed the front door behind her leaving her mother watching the television she had to admit to a tiny suspicion of guilt. Nobody should be alone on Christmas Eve.

Chapter Seven

After Viv had gone, Hilda watched the television for a short while then switched it off. She changed into a satin nightdress and dressing gown in front of the fire, throwing her clothes over the back of a chair. She poured herself a gin and tonic before going over to the window. She lifted a corner of the net curtain and peered out at the dark street. Christmas Eve and no man to fill her stocking. She felt a deep regret that Charlie was no longer in the land of the living. Should she go to church in the morning at ten or should she try the Watch Night service on New Year's Eve? That was much more fun with drunks doing daft things . . . but there were people who went to confess a year of sin and cried halfway through the service.

Life was bloody queer. She could not understand how she had been saved by a lot of arm-waving Alleluia swingers. Why did some prayers get answered while others didn't? She felt depressed. This time last year she had been at a party with Charlie. You never knew. 'Death is just around the corner,' she muttered, experiencing a deep chill of fear as if a dark hole had opened up in front of her.'

'Shut up,' she told herself, and prayed aloud: 'God, help me not to think about worms boring holes in me. How about bright lights and music?' Her voice trembled to a halt. Lord, she was going off her nut. It must be her age. She'd be into the Change next!

She thought of Charlie and his saxophone. One of the kids in the house on the other side had a guitar while his brother played the washboard with bethimbled fingers. Sometimes the noise was enough to make the cat leave home. Vis said the brothers and their mates were behind the times. Skiffle was being taken over by rock'n'roll. Hilda pulled a face. Give her a good ballad and the sound of the big bands any day.

She frowned irritably. Dominic Kelly would be going to Midnight Mass with his family. The pleasure of his company was something she was going to have to do without for a couple of days. Perhaps it was just as well. She had been too weak-willed when it came to Dom. But then, it had been hard enough giving up the ciggies. She hoped her figure wouldn't go as round as the Polos she stuffed herself with trying to control the craving.

Hilda wandered over to the fire. It needed more coal. Damn! Dom had got into the habit of filling the scuttle and bringing it in from the yard for her. But not today. A shaky sigh escaped her. His wife would be keeping him on a close rein. Did she suspect anything? If so, it didn't show. There had been a Christmas card from the Kellys but none yet from her sister. Was Flo furious with her for keeping her daughter here? What would she tell Viv? Hilda had never thought that her daughter would be so interested in her father. She considered him for a moment. What a fool she had been over him! Could she tell Viv the truth? Earlier she had felt closer to her daughter than she had ever felt before. The truth might turn Viv completely against her. She shivered and slipped a coat round her shoulders before pulling a pair of old gloves over scarlet-tipped smooth white fingers.

She was halfway across the kitchen when the knocker sounded. Kids carol singing, was her first thought. Not on your nelly! She was almost broke. Out in the back yard she realised that there was no singing and whoever it was at the front door was heavy handed with the knocker. She dropped the scuttle and retraced her steps.

'Oh!' She stared at the tall dark-clad figure standing with one foot on the doorstep. 'I thought you were someone else.'

'Is Viv in?'

Hilda did not answer immediately. Young, attractive, smart in a suit . . . he was a bit of all right. Her expression brightened. 'What do you want her for?'

'To take her out.' He smiled. 'You're her mother, Hilda. I recognise you.'

'You do?' She scrutinised him more carefully. 'Should I know you?'

Probably not.' He held out a hand. 'I'm Nick Bryce. You won't remember me but I've never forgotten you. I'm pleased to met you again.'

She took his hand which was strong and firm. How she wished that she was young again! 'I'm sorry. I don't remember . . .'

'You might remember my mother, but we'll let that go.' He smiled without amusement. 'Viv hasn't gone to America after all, has she? Mr Kelly said . . .'

'No.' She sighed mournfully. 'But she's out. Do come in, though.'

Nick hesitated then stepped into the house and looked about him. The room was more untidy than he remembered and there had been a few changes. No sofa but a television and the room was decorated for Christmas with a lighted tree forming an oasis of colour in one corner.

Hilda smiled at him. 'You wouldn't like to bring the coal scuttle in for me, would you? I was in the yard filling it when you knocked and I'm not really dressed for outside.'

'No problem,' murmured Nick, and made for the kitchen.

'Don't fall over it,' she called.

As soon as he left the room Hilda darted around, grabbing stockings, corsets and knickers from the back of a chair and her sweater and a skirt from the sofa. She threw them behind the curtain that concealed the stairs in the kitchen before sweeping up a magazine and a newspaper and shoving them beneath a cushion. An empty chocolate box she threw on the fire. She cleared the crockery from the table and placed it in the sink. Finally the tablecloth was shaken in the direction of the fire, causing the slumbering coals to crackle and send out sparks. Then she spread the cloth over the table, rubbing at a sauce mark on the linen with a dampened finger. It would not shift and she gave up. Gasping with exertion and spluttering from an unexpected cough that tickled her throat, she picked up the bottle the chemist had made up for her and sank into a chair.

She was measuring out almost black medicine into a small glass when Nick, lugging the loaded scuttle, entered the room.

'For my cough,' she said. 'I sometimes get a bit of a chest at this time of year.' Her outspread fingers covered a breast.

Involuntarily Nick stared at it as he placed the scuttle by the fireplace. She had always been well endowed, just like Viv was now. He picked up the bottle and read the label. 'That won't do you much good,' he murmured.

'You're as bad as our Viv!' With an air of defiance Hilda licked the spoon. 'My father swore by it.'

'My mother swears by soap and sugar for drawing out splinters but it's never worked for me.'

'I can see you're a Smart Alec,' she muttered.

He grinned and began to make up the fire.

She was irritated. Who was he? Where was he from? 'How does Viv know you?' she asked.

He glanced over his shoulder. 'I take it she's never mentioned me?'

'No. But then, I don't tell her all *my* secrets.'

'I imagine you've got a few of them,' he said lightly. 'The pair of you getting on all right?'

'Shouldn't we?' A frown creased her forehead as she crossed one leg over the other, showing a couple of inches of thigh.

Nick made no answer but brushed coal dust from his fingers. 'Where has she gone?'

'Out for a meal with some of her mates.' Her eyes narrowed. 'Go and wash your hands before you mess up the place.'

He nodded and went into the kitchen, reappearing a couple of minutes later. He placed his back against a wall, dug his hands into his pockets and said in a friendly voice, 'You haven't got anybody coming?'

'Do I look like I'm dressed for visitors,' she said sarcastically, recrossing her legs and hoping the blue veins didn't show. 'I thought I'd have an early night.'

'On Christmas Eve? I would have thought you'd have had a line of old admirers queuing up outside the door.'

Hilda gave him a suspicious look. 'What do you mean by that?'

'You still look pretty good for your age.'

'For my age!' she spluttered. 'Thanks for nothing! I think it's time you were leaving.'

'It was a compliment!' He straightened. 'I suppose I'd best be going then if Viv's not here. Perhaps with that cough you're right to have an early night.'

'My cough's not that bad.' Suddenly she did not want him to go, and it was not just because she wondered why someone so assured and in their mid-twenties was interested in her seventeen-year-old daughter. She supposed it was youth and for a moment was jealous of her daughter and suffered a compelling urge to prove that she really was still attractive to men. Dom did not count. Their relationship owed as much to friendship as sexual expediency. She rose gracefully.

'I didn't really mean that about your leaving. I mean, where's my manners? Won't you have a cup of coffee? You haven't told me how you know Viv,' she gushed. 'Did she tell you I lived in New Jersey for eight years?' She smiled, giving it all she had.

'She told me that you'd come home,' he said abruptly. 'She didn't know what to make of it. You leaving her with Mrs Cooke might have seemed for the best at the time but you hurt her. A child feels rejection deeply.'

Hilda scowled. 'What's it got to do with you? Do you think I don't know all that now? I'm doing my best to make it up to her. We're getting on OK.'

'You haven't told her who her father is then?'

Her mouth fell open and several moments passed without either of them saying a word. Then Hilda said, 'You must be close to her if she's spoken to you about her father. Did you quarrel?'

Nick smiled. 'No. As for closeness – I hope we're on the way. I remember Viv being born, but like you she didn't remember me at first. We met on the day of her grandfather's funeral. Then later at a party.'

'You remember Viv being born?' Hilda latched on to that. 'So you must have lived close to our Flo's?'

He nodded, a slight gleam in his eyes. 'How about that coffee?'

'Righto.' As Hilda went out of the room she darted him another wondering glance.

Nick gazed into the fire. Had he gone too far? He thought of a conversation he had heard while lying reading on the

78

outside lavatory roof when his family had lived next-door to the Cookes. George's father had been home on leave from the army and he was whitewashing the back yard. He remembered it so clearly because their cat fell into the bucket of whitewash while George's dad had his back turned and Nick had gone down into the yard to rescue it . . .

He looked up as Hilda came back into the room with the coffee. She had dressed and put on fresh make-up and he could smell perfume. Boyish fantasies were recalled with a vengeance.

'Perhaps you'd like to go out for a drink?' he said impulsively.

Hilda's sober expression altered. 'Are you serious?'

Immediately he regretted the invitation. What was he thinking of? She was old enough to be his mother but he could not back off now or she would be hurt. 'Of course. Although most places will be crowded by now.'

Her baby blue eyes sparkled. 'I don't mind crowds,' she said with a touch of excitement. 'In fact, I used to prefer them.'

Nick thought swiftly. They would have to go somewhere where there would be music so that conversation was not important.

'I'm sure we'll find somewhere,' she said, forgetting completely the talk that had worried her. 'I'll go and get a coat.'

He watched her leave the room and took a swift gulp of the coffee. It was good. He drank the lot. He needed it.

Nick stopped questioning his actions when Hilda reappeared wearing a mink coat. She looked a million dollars and he decided that if he saw anybody he knew then he would tell them that she was his rich widowed aunt from America who had arrived unexpectedly and that he had been given the job of entertaining her for the night.

He took her to a pub for a couple of drinks and then on to a basement club in London Road. Smaller than The Cavern, it could take maybe forty at a sweaty best but it was cosy and the Christmas spirit was almost tangible there. Lonnie Donegan lovers and those who liked their folk songs jazzed up with a bit of Scouse humour thrown in were there in force. It went down well with Hilda which surprised Nick, as did the fact that she had a voice. 'I don't ever remember hearing you sing before,' he said against her ear.

'Didn't always have much to sing about in the past, kid.' She patted his knee and stared at him hard, puzzling again over his identity. 'But my Charlie liked his music – jazz – the blues. I liked all sorts. Burl Ives, Ivor Novello, Glen Miller, Noel Coward. "Mad Dogs and Englishmen"' You know the one?'

He nodded. 'How long has your husband been dead?'

'Five months.' She took out a gold cigarette case and lighter. 'He gave me these on our first wedding anniversary. I haven't used them for a while. But I thought earlier – it's Christmas, what the hell? Do you smoke?' She handed him the lighter and placed a cigarette between her lips.

'Used to.' He flicked the lighter and held the tiny flame towards her. 'But I gave it up when I was in the athletics team. Played havoc with my breathing.'

'Sensible lad.' She inhaled carefully.

'Not really. We all have vices.'

'Oh?' She blew smoke in his face and smiled. 'You've got me interested.'

Before Nick could respond the group launched themselves into another number, a Christmas song, 'I saw Three Ships Come Sailing In'. Hilda immediately began to sing along. He wondered what had made him say that about vices and smiled ruefully. Was it because Viv's mother was the kind of woman who made a man want to appear more devilish than he was? Viv, on the other hand, made him feel romantic, protective. He wondered where she was and hoped she would be there when he took her mother home.

She was not and he was disappointed and slightly annoyed at the same time. Hilda seemed to know just how he felt.

'You don't have to go yet.' She pressed his arm. 'Viv should be in soon.'

But it had gone midnight and although Nick was tempted to stay he reckoned that with several drinks down her Hilda might want more from him than he was prepared to give. Besides he had promised his mother that he would fill the role of Father Christmas for his half-brother. He made his excuses.

Hilda nodded slowly and then attempted to dazzle him with a smile. 'Why not come tomorrow? Viv'll be here. First Christmas we've had together for ages. Peace, goodwill to all men, *and* mothers.'

He accepted immediately and offered her his hand but she offered him her cheek.

'Thank you for taking pity on me. You really are a gentleman.'

He smiled slightly, pecked her cheek, squeezed her hand and walked up the street without a backward glance.

Slowly Hilda went back into the house, wondering about the relationship between him and her daughter. He was strong, had nice cheek bones and jaw, was romantic-looking in some ways. He reminded her of the hero in a film she had seen about the Russian Revolution. Lovely eyes! She only wished she could remember just who he was.

Chapter Eight

'You had a visitor last night.' Hilda yawned and gazed bleary-eyed at Viv across the table.

Her daughter said nothing, tossing back a couple of Aspros and draining a glass of water. She had got up too late for church and was annoyed with herself but at least the chicken was in the oven and the vegetables peeled. She had been a fool to make such a night of it but Dot arriving at the restaurant with the letter from Aunt Flora in her hand which Viv had swiftly read had made her feel like she was walking on air. She had thought about it but not really realised what a great difference it would make to her knowing who her father was. Maybe soon she would have a face to the name. Her mother must have kept some photographs of Jimmy but why had she lied to her?

'I said, you had a visitor last night,' repeated Hilda.

Viv shaded her eyes with a hand and stared at her mother. 'Who was that then?'

'We'll have to be getting ready.' Hilda yawned again. 'He said he'd be back.'

Viv sat up straight. 'Did he give a name?'

'I think so. But I can't remember what it was.'

Her mother poured another coffee. She had learnt how to make good coffee in America and had bought herself a grinder in Lewis's basement and purchased good quality coffee beans from Cooper's.

'Well?' demanded Viv. 'Was it Nick Bryce?'

'That was his name.' Hilda swallowed a couple of Phensic with her coffee. 'Do you know who he is?'

Viv smiled. 'Of course I know who he is. I've been out with him twice.'

'I didn't know him.'

'He knows you.'

'So he said.' Hilda yawned again. 'He seems to know our Flo, too.'

'Of course he does.' Viv was starting to feel better. She should never have been persuaded to have those two rum and blackcurrants. 'He lived next-door to her.'

'You mean in the shop?'

'No. Right next-door.'

Hilda forced her eyelids up further. 'What did I say his name was?'

'Nick. Nick Bryce. You probably wouldn't remember him. He was only a lad when last he saw you.'

'You don't mean his mother was Lena Bryce?' Hilda's hand paused halfway to her cigarette case. 'No, you can't mean her. I mean she was no good. She had a terrible reputation.'

Viv's fingers tightened on her cup. 'Nick said she's changed . . . become respectable. She even has an aspidistra.'

'An aspidistra? Hmmph!' Hilda took a cigarette from the gold case and placed it between her lips.

'I thought you'd given them up,' said Viv mildly. 'You'll be coughing your heart up next and wondering why. And what's wrong with Mrs Bryce having an aspidistra? She's more respectable than you are now with your fancy man next-door!'

Hilda puffed like an engine getting up steam, 'Dom Kelly and I are just good friends,' she snapped.

'That's what film stars say when they're carrying on,' retorted Viv, getting up. 'You've got no right to judge Nick's mother. She might have done wrong in the past but that's all behind her now.'

'Ha!' Hilda stubbed out the cigarette in a saucer. 'I see. You can say that about her but you weren't so quick in forgiving me, your own mother!'

Viv swallowed an angry retort and said patiently, 'It's Christmas Day. I don't want us to fall out. Peace and goodwill and all that. Let's just try and enjoy today. You said there's some good programmes on the telly. We've got food and drink and crackers to pull.'

'And presents to open. Although our Flo's haven't arrived yet.'

'We'll get them late.' Viv debated quickly whether this was the right time to bring her father into the conversation but decided against it. 'Aunt Flo probably thought I'd be there for Christmas so they'll be late. Now I'm going to get washed and changed. Did Nick say what time he was coming?'

Hilda shook her head, a slight frown still clouding her brow. 'I'll use the sink after you. I wish we had a blinking bathroom. When I lived with Charlie I had this lovely . . .'

'Oh, shut up, Mother,' groaned Viv. 'If everything was so marvellous in America, I don't know how you ever forced yourself to come home.' And she quickly walked out of the room. No, today definitely wasn't the day to bring up the subject of her father.

Mother and daughter were in their respective bedrooms when the knocker sounded. Viv peered out of the front window but could not see anyone from that angle. Swiftly she applied lipstick and gingerly touched the hair which she had piled up on top of her head to make her appear more sophisticated. Then she raced downstairs, the new pine green velvet skirt billowing up about her well-shaped thighs with the speed of her passing. She slowed down halfway across the front room, took several deep breaths and then opened the door.

Nick wore a burgundy sweater and dark plum-coloured trousers. His hair had grown even longer and was whipped into a Tony Curtis cowlick above his sooty eyebrows. Viv thought of moonlight and water and kisses. 'Hallo, stranger,' she said in what she hoped was a seductive voice.

He smiled. 'I came last night, hoping, but you were out gallivanting.'

'I couldn't get out of it. If I'd known . . .'

'It doesn't matter.'

Suddenly Hilda appeared at Viv's shoulder. 'He took me out instead of you,' she said.

'Oh!' Viv whirled round and looked daggers at her mother. She looked so different to the woman she had shared coffee with earlier. Somehow her mother had managed to squeeze herself into a too tight black skirt and walk downstairs in too high-heeled black shoes. Amber drops dangled from her ears and matching beads were a bright splash of colour against the black angora sweater that softened the swell of her bosom. Her hair was beautifully brushed and her make-up had been applied skilfully. Viv wished she could tear the jumper off her back and pour water over her.

'You didn't tell me that before,' she snapped, feeling a rush of jealousy.

'We didn't go anywhere special,' said Nick swiftly.

'No?' The single word fell from Viv's lips like an icicle. She was considering how he had not been in touch and what he had said about being in love with her mother when he was young. Some men liked older women. Perhaps he was one of them and may have already discovered just how sophisticated and experienced her mother was?

'Viv! Don't think it,' said Nick, his eyes challenging her to trust him.

'I thought it was very special.' Her mother tossed the words into the sudden silence and attempted to elbow her daughter aside. 'I really enjoyed myself. We were full of the Christmas spirit.'

'Gin, I presume,' muttered Viv, folding her arms across the rust-coloured sweater and refusing to budge.

'Don't be nasty, Viv,' retorted her mother. 'It's Christmas Day. Let the man in and let me give him a kiss.'

'Like hell I will,' said Viv. 'Go and check the chicken, Mother.'

Hilda sighed extravagantly. 'I don't know! Children these days have no respect, no sense of humour.' She went back inside and they heard the chink of a bottle.

'I suppose she kissed you,' said Viv roughly, staring at Nick.

'What do you think?' he drawled. 'How was your evening? Did you have a good time?'

'My friends and I do not need men around to enjoy ourselves,' she said, emphasising each word.

She had given him the answer he wanted and he smiled. 'Of course not. Are you going to ask me in?'

'If you want to come in. I can't offer you much in the way of sophisticated entertainment. You can have some dinner and a drink. Unless you've already eaten?'

'I've eaten but I can eat more.' His blue eyes glinted. 'Your mother is a very attractive woman, Viv, but my fancy is for someone younger. Made out of the same mould but a newer model.'

A small smile lifted the corners of her mouth. 'I'm sorry, but she gets me going sometimes.'

'Understandable.'

'Come in.'

Hilda was sitting in the rocking chair with a glass in one hand and a cigarette in the other. She stared at Nick and swigged at her gin and tonic. Viv waved him to the old easy chair. 'Would you like a beer? We have some in for Mr Kelly who's been doing some work for us.'

'Thanks.'

She poured out a pale ale, and a small sherry for herself. Then she raised her glass. 'Happy Christmas.'

'The same to you.' He leaned forward and kissed her where she stood under the mistletoe. Her mother made a noise in her throat and they drew apart.

'I'd better see to the dinner,' said Viv, singing inside herself. 'Sit down, Nick. I won't be long. I'm sure Mam can entertain you.' She cast a mischievous glance at her mother who was now gazing sulkily at the television.

A few minutes later Hilda followed her out. 'I don't know what you think you're playing at, Viv, but I don't like the idea of your going out with him.'

'What!' Viv stared at her. 'I hope you're not going to start on about his mother again, Mam, because you might as well save your breath. George might believe her behaviour brushed off on him, but I don't. Might as well accept what Mrs McCoy said about me being as bad as you. Do you think I am, Mother? Is it that you're worried I'll get into trouble like you?'

Two spots of colour darkened Hilda's cheeks. 'There's no war on now and I should hope you'd have more sense. It's just that I've remembered him. He was a quiet boy. If there was a game of cowboys and indians he was an indian. Soft-footed, Viv. Easy to forget he was around. Sneaky. You don't want someone like that, Viv. You need someone with lots of go in them. Someone who's got the push to go up in the world.'

'Oh, I think Nick's got plenty of push,' murmured Viv. 'He had a good granny. She saw to it that he had his chances. He's an architect, you know, Mam.' He'll go places.'

Hilda changed tack. 'Suit yourself! But ask what kind of man takes out a woman old enough to be his mother? Ask yourself that, Viv. I think he quite fancied me.'

Her eyes darkened. 'I don't know what you're playing at, Mother! I suppose you're missing Mr Kelly. He's just your style. Devious!'

Hilda bit back a swear word and left the room, closing the door firmly behind her.

Nick was standing by the fire. He looked up as she entered and said pleasantly, 'Changed your mind about me, now Hilda? You've placed me, haven't you?'

'You're Lena Bryce's son,' she said harshly. 'You can't blame me for wanting someone better for my daughter.'

A muscle tautened in his cheek. 'Are you sure it's only my being my mother's son that worries you? Nothing else?' The tone of his voice had changed.

Hilda reached for the gin bottle and topped up her glass. She gulped at her drink. 'What else could there be?' she muttered.

'Nothing if you say so.' He paused. 'I suffered a lot in the old days from malicious gossip. Lots of people with flapping ears, big mouths and very little heart couldn't wait to talk behind my back – some talked to my face. So is it any wonder I believe in keeping my mouth shut? Maybe one day you'll feel able to tell Viv the truth. Maybe not. One thing's for sure, she won't get it from me.'

'You're saying you know the truth?' she said in a brittle voice, hunching up her shoulders as if trying to get warm.

'I was there that day.'

'You could have been mistaken. You were only a boy. What did you understand of grown-up talk!'

Nick said softly, 'I'm my mother's son. I'd had years of it.'

Suddenly Hilda flared up: 'You had no right to be there in our Flo's yard!'

'No,' said Nick. 'But don't let's get on to what was right or wrong, Hilda.' A sharp laugh issued from him. 'Can I help myself to another beer? I feel like I need it.'

She nodded, watching him, a puzzled expression on her face. He turned and smiled, raised his glass. 'Happy Christmas, Hilda.

'How can you say that to me?' she said in a low voice.

'It's what I want for you and Viv. For all of us.' His eyes met hers over the rim of his glass. 'Smile, Hilda. Here she come with the dinner.'

It was a good meal and the conversation did not touch on anything referring to the past. Nick told them of his brother's reactions to his Christmas stocking and Viv talked of Dot's sister giving birth two days ago. 'She said having a new baby in the family makes this Christmas seem more special somehow.'

'Easy to see that,' said Hilda, keeping her eyes from Nick. 'It gives more meaning to the Christmas story.'

Viv looked at her in surprise. 'I never remember you taking much interest in Jesus's birth before.'

'I found God while I was in hospital,' said Hilda in such a way that Viv was unsure whether she was joking or not. Especially when she swiftly changed the subject to talk about the group they had listened to last night.

Viv did not want to hear about them. She wanted to be alone with Nick and wondered how she was going to get rid of her mother. It was Nick who manipulated things her way by suggesting that he and Viv went for a walk.

She jumped at the idea. 'I could do with some fresh air as well as the exercise,' she said, going for her coat before her mother could say anything against it.

'You won't be back late?' said Hilda, watching Viv wind a scarf which was at least six foot long round and round her neck.

'No. Why don't you go and visit Doris?' suggested Viv. 'It would cheer her up.'

Hilda grimaced. 'The house is so depressing and her mother doesn't like me.'

'Do it for Doris,' said Viv in a coaxing voice, grabbing Nick's arm and pushing him out of the door before her mother could say anything else.

For a while they walked without speaking. Viv was happy to be in Nick's company and happy thinking about her father.

Her aunt had said he was a hero and a bit of a charmer. In her mind she pictured him looking like actors from several war films . . . Richard Todd . . . John Mills . . . Dirk Bogarde. What had he looked like? Of course she remembered his brother, Stephen Martin. Her aunt had almost married him. Perhaps that was why her mother had been so secretive? But why lie? He was no stranger she had made love to in a blackout. They had known each other for years.

Nick broke the silence. 'What have you been doing the last few weeks? How has it been with you and your mother?'

Viv brought her mind back to the present. 'It could be worse. She drives me crazy at times but I think she's trying to be a mother.' She smiled up at him. 'I got a letter from Aunt Flo yesterday. She told me that my father was a soldier and that he was killed at El Alamein.'

Hell! thought Nick. Hilda will never believe me. 'My father fought at El Alamein,' he murmured.

'Some coincidence,' said Viv, sighing. 'His name was Jimmy Martin. I wonder if they ever met?'

'Who knows?' He took her hand and breathed easy again as they crossed Oakfield Road. 'Do you find it strange that we should meet after years of not seeing each other – of not really noticing each other much in the first place?' he said softly.

'It happens. It *has* happened to us.' She gazed in a shop window thinking how the tinsel-decorated gifts looked forlorn now that Christmas Day was nearly over.

'Perhaps we were meant to meet again?' he said.

She turned her head and looked at him, her brown eyes twinkling. 'You mean, fate brought us together for a purpose?'

'Kismet.' He leaned forward and kissed the corner of her mouth. 'For this purpose.'

Her eyes met his and her heart seemed to bump against her ribs. 'I think I do believe it's possible there's one person on earth especially meant for another person,' she said without drawing breath.

He touched her cheek with one finger. 'You believe that God pulls strings?'

She was pensive, very conscious of that finger. 'I suppose he can pull strings, but only if people are willing to let him.'

'Perhaps it's like some giant play?'

'You mean Shakespeare had something when he wrote "All the world's a stage and all the men and women merely players"?' He nodded and she added as they began to walk again, 'I suppose some people never get to meet because other people get in the way or else they don't obey the stage directions.'

'Do you think we've obeyed?' he said, and their breath mingled before his mouth came down over hers in a long kiss. She thought it was a good job that it was Christmas and the road pretty deserted. What if it was an ordinary day and Mrs McCoy out doing her shopping? A chuckle formed in her throat and when their lips parted she said, 'You know, Nick, you've got a way with words.'

He grinned. 'I'm glad you think so.'

'Do you read a lot of poetry?'

'Not really but I enjoy some. De la Mare . . . Tennyson. I like words. I like music. And well-spoken poetry can sound like music.'

Viv's senses were suddenly feather-edged with a lovely sense of well-being. 'I used to sing in the church choir till I went to live with Grandfather,' she said dreamily. 'Sometimes I felt like I was up there in the air with the sound reaching to Heaven.'

'Your mother can sing. You must take after her.'

Viv came down to earth. 'When did you hear her sing?'

'Last night. Remember the folk group she told you about? They had a singalong.'

She felt vexed all of a sudden. 'What made you take her out?'

'I felt sorry for her.' It was partially true. 'It was Christmas Eve and she looked lonely.'

Viv tried not to feel jealous but could not resist saying flippantly, 'She's the best, my mam, at working on people's sympathies.'

Nick said in what he thought were reasonable tones, 'But it's true that it's only months since she was widowed. She must miss her husband.'

'If she's missing him, then I'm a monkey's aunt.' Viv's voice was tart.

'What do you mean by that?'

She hesitated. 'It doesn't matter. Put it down to bitchiness. Mam brings out the worst in me sometimes.'

'I don't believe that,' said Nick, bringing her to a halt. 'You had something in mind.'

'Oh, all right then.' Viv took a deep breath. 'She's having an affair with Mr Kelly next-door and I don't know how to stop her.'

Nick's frowning eyes fixed on Viv's face. 'You know that for sure?' he rapped.

'Would I say so if I wasn't, with our background?' she said vehemently. 'They're old friends. Since my grandmother died and Mr Kelly's mother took her and Aunt Flo into his home because grandfather was away at sea. They might have been meant for each other, for all I know, if it hadn't been for him being a Catholic and Grandfather and Great-aunt Beattie being Orange.'

'She's a damn' fool,' said Nick. 'It's a good job you're there, Viv, you can get in their way. I'm sure you don't want Mr Kelly's marriage going bust.'

'No. But I don't see how my being there can prevent it. She takes no notice of what I say. You don't know my mother when she's made up her mind to have something. That's why it worried me when I discovered you'd taken her out.'

'I see. You believed I'd let myself be seduced?'

'No, of course not.' She flushed. 'But she's experienced, and knowing men . . .'

'Oh? You've known a lot of men, have you?' he said in a teasing voice.

'No! But boys . . . they try it on. Most of them are after one thing.'

'And you think I'm like that too?' The humour had vanished from his voice. 'What else did George tell you about me before he went off to Paris?'

Viv's colour deepened. 'This has nothing to do with what George said about you. A girl has to look out for herself, Nick. I mean to say . . .'

He interrupted, 'I know what you mean to say. You don't have to say any more. I'm not a rapist, Viv.'

She shot him a startled look. 'I never even thought that!'

'Then what are you worried about?'

'I'm not worried! I was just being honest with you. I thought you and me could be honest with each other. I mean, it can be so easy to get carried away by the mood of the moment . . . by words.'

'Like before?'

'Yes.'

'You could try trusting me.' His voice had deepened.

'I didn't even think about whether to trust you,' she said frankly. 'The streets might be quiet but it's not like up by the cathedral. Then I did think you'd taken me up there with ulterior motives in mind but you were only interested in the building.'

'That's not strictly true,' he said, smiling slightly.

'No. And that's when I started thinking about wedding dresses.'

'What?' It was his turn to be startled.

Viv bit her lip. 'I don't know how we got on to this subject. It's stupid.'

'Yes, it is. But then a lot of arguments wander from the point.'

'What *is* the point?'

'Do we really have to go into that?'

'It was over my mother and you taking her side.'

He raised his eyebrows. 'Was it?'

She smiled. 'Perhaps not. But we're not getting anywhere talking like this.'

'We could go for a walk in the park and kiss and make up?'

'We could,' she said, smiling.

He slipped an arm around her waist and she an arm around his and they made their way to Stanley Park.

Nick left Viv at her front door, saying that some aunt and uncle were expected and that he had better go and show his face.

The kettle was whistling as Viv let herself in. Her mother was dozing in the easy chair with the television on full blast. The kettle had almost boiled dry but there was enough water left to make a cup of tea.

Viv sat in the rocking chair and stretched her feet out

towards the fire. 'Wake up, Mam!' she called. 'I want to tell you something.'

'I wasn't asleep,' said Hilda, opening her eyes and stretching as delicately as a cat.

'Oh, no?' said Viv, smiling.

Hilda looked about her. 'He's gone then?'

'Well, he's not hiding behind the Christmas tree.' Viv reached for a chocolate from the large beribboned box with two fluffy cats on that Nick had given her. She offered the box to her mother who took two.

'What did you have to talk about away from me?' Hilda's voice was as casual as she could make it.

'This and that.' Viv reached for another chocolate. 'Kismet. Both our fathers, it seemed, were at El Alamein.'

Hilda choked on a Brazil nut. Viv got up quickly and banged her on the back. 'I thought that would shock you,' she said. 'I kept it quiet this morning but I was going to tell you I had a letter from Aunt Flo. I didn't trust you not to keep it from me so I had it sent to Dot's. At least Aunt Flo was willing to tell me what I wanted.' She left her mother and came back a couple of seconds later with a glass of water.

Hilda's face was red and her eyes streaming. 'There's no need to get upset,' said Viv gently. 'I'm not mad with you, Mam. I'm pleased that Jimmy Martin was my father. Perhaps you'll tell me why you lied about him? Aunt Flo said only nice things.'

Hilda was silent.

Viv hesitated then said, 'It is true, isn't it, Mam? Jimmy was my father?'

Her mother stared at her and put down the glass, a small smile curving her mouth. 'What are you going to do about it if it is?'

Viv's throat was suddenly tight. Why had she thought her mother had been about to deny it? 'I'm happy just to know about him, Mam,' she said in a rush. 'If you've a photograph I'd love to see it. Now I've a name, I'd like to put a face to it.'

'Sorry, honey, I haven't got one,' Hilda said, sounding sympathetic. 'I had one once, but with travelling about it just went missing.'

'Oh.' Viv swallowed her disappointment. 'Perhaps you could talk about him to me?'

'I'd rather not.' Hilda touched the back of her daughter's hand and looked mournful. 'As you said, it's been a bit of a shock. It still hurts thinking of those days. Maybe I'll be able to talk about it, eventually but don't ask me to do it now.'

She nodded, trying to understand her mother's feelings, but it was not easy.

That night when Viv went to bed she thought about Jimmy Martin and felt sad because they had never known each other and never would. She gazed across the room, not seeing the new curtains, and suddenly realised that she had known his brother. He was her uncle now, a real one, not just a courtesy one as he had been in the days when he had been courting her aunt. Stephen Martin had often taken Rosie, George and herself out with him and Aunt Flora, after Tom Cooke had been killed. Viv had liked him, although he and George had never really hit it off. She had felt sorry for him when Aunt Flo had broken things off to marry Mike – not that she wasn't very fond of her Uncle Mike.

Viv rolled over on to her side. Would Stephen be willing to talk to her? He must have been very hurt and angry when her aunt had called it all off. Perhaps she would go and see him? Not yet but soon she would visit him.

Surely he would remember her and maybe even be glad to see her?

Chapter Nine

The outside of Martin's Letterpress Printers and Stationers
had altered. It had expanded, taking over the shop next-door.
The rather tatty façade of drab brown that Viv remembered
had been replaced by daffodil yellow paint. No bell jangled
when she pushed open the door. Inside, the narrow lobby
which had always been cluttered with yesteryear's rubbish
had vanished, as had the reception area of stained glass and
polished wood. In their place was an open carpeted area with
plastic and metal chairs and a formica-topped counter with an
electric bell. She could hear and feel vibrations from the
printing machinery as her finger hovered over the bell for
several seconds before pressing it.

A youth in jeans and an ink-stained shirt came out of a
cream painted door. He gave her the once over and smiled.
'What can I do for yer, luv?'

'I want to see Mr Martin, please.'

'He's busy.' He leaned on the counter and leered at her.
'But if yer wanta wait, I'll keep yer company.'

'Just tell him that Vivien Preston is here.'

'Vivien? That's a posh name.'

'You think so?' She smiled. 'will you please tell him? I
haven't got all day.'

'Well, I'll tell yer now, he doesn't like the opposite sex. I do
though,' he said with another leer.

'Do me a favour,' said Viv sweetly.

'Please yerself.' He grinned and disappeared through a
door, only to reappear a few moments later. 'He sez yer to go
up. It's the door that says "De Boss".'

Viv thanked him, and following his directions went upstairs. Outside the door which bore the words 'Mr S. Martin. Please Knock' she paused to control her trepidation, aware of the curious stares of men working in the room to her left. She smoothed her checked skirt over her hips and flicked back her loosened hair before knocking on the door. A voice that she scarcely recognised told her to come in.

Stephen Martin was sitting at a desk, the chair slightly turned towards the window so that he presented her with his profile. He had dark curly hair going grey and his neck seemed thicker than she remembered. He wore a dark suit and the cuffs of his white shirt showed gold links. He stared at her without a hint of a smile. 'You're like your mother.'

Viv did not allow herself to be put out by that remark. 'I might look like her a little but we're different people.'

'You're saying you wouldn't behave like her?' he said, a mite derisively.

'In what way?'

He did not answer but scrutinised her carefully. Now she saw the scar that just missed his left eye. It had been caused by shrapnel wounds. 'What have you come here for?' he asked. 'What's so important?'

Viv cleared her throat. 'I thought there might be things you could tell me.'

'About what?'

'Your brother!' She leaned forward eagerly. 'Aunt Flo wrote to me telling me he was my father.'

'Don't mention her name here!' The words sliced through the air and Stephen picked up a ruler from the desk, rapping it on the desk to emphasise them. 'A cheap tart, that's what she was, and your mother was no different! She had a string of boyfriends. Your father could have been any one of them.'

'I don't believe that!' Viv's voice rose as her colour heightened. 'Nor was Aunt Flo a cheap tart! She was good and kind.'

'I'd expect you to defend her' His tones were no longer controlled but hot and angry. He tossed the ruler aside and got to his feet. 'She deceived me . . . rather have a no good Yank than a decent hardworking Englishman.'

'Aunt Flo loved Mike,' Viv said vehemently. 'And he'd

96

been asking her to marry him for ages.'

They think they won the bloody war.' He clasped his hands tightly together. 'All mouth and trousers, that's what they were.'

'He loved her,' she declared passionately. 'But she kept turning him down because she couldn't leave my grandfather!'

Stephen's mouth thinned. 'She left him, though. I heard she went to America.'

'*I* stayed with him. He's dead now.'

'She made me very unhappy.'

'It wasn't what she intended, I'm sure.'

His eyes darkened but he made no answer.

Viv said earnestly, 'Aunt Flo was the last person to wish anyone ill. She always spoke well of you and mentioned you had a tough time during the war. You were a hero, weren't you? I remember you promised George you'd show him your medals. Aunt Flo said Jimmy was a hero as well.'

He scowled. 'He's not your father. I won't believe it.'

'Why won't you?' Her brows puckered. 'I suppose it's because I'm illegitimate? Even so, I would have thought you'd be glad to have someone. Your mother and sisters died in the war, didn't they? It must have been awful for you, losing them and Jimmy.'

His face tightened. 'I don't need your sympathy,' he said roughly. 'Now will you get out? I've work to do.' He sat down and picked up the ruler again.

Viv fought back her disappointment but was not about to give up. 'Uncle Steve, are you sure about this? I know you have cause to be angry with my family but . . .'

'I'm not your uncle,' he muttered.

'I called you "uncle" years ago,' she said quietly, her eyes warm with remembrance. 'You didn't seem to mind then. You were kind to me. You took us out places.'

'It was different then. I was going to marry your aunt.' The ruler suddenly cracked between his hands. 'Get out,' he shouted. 'Get out!'

Viv stared at him, shocked at such a show of emotion from a man of his age, and terribly disappointed. With her voice barely under control she said, 'I feel sorry for you, *Mr* Martin.

What good does it do you, not being able to forgive Aunt Flora? It doesn't seem to have made you happy at all, just bitter, and that's really sad.' She marched out of the room, closing the door quietly. For a moment she stood with her hand on the handle, composing herself, then she ran downstairs.

As she walked along the road she kept telling herself that just because Stephen denied that Jimmy was her father didn't prove anything. He *was* her father. Aunt Flo had said so and she would never mislead Viv. As for her mother, she would have denied it if it was not true.

Viv had not told Hilda that she was going to see Stephen Martin. It was a couple of months now since she had found out about Jimmy but her mother was still reluctant to talk about him and inclined to act as if she had not heard her questions when Viv asked them, so she had made the decision on her own to go and visit Stephen. Perhaps she would mention it when she arrived home? Even so she was not ready to return yet. She was not far from Dot's house and would drop in on her friend and beg a cup of tea.

'You'll have to forgive the noise,' shouted Dot about the din coming from the front parlour as she opened the front door. 'But our Norm and his mates are practising. They're fixed up to play at Phil's. You know Phil who does most of the singing?' Dot went slightly pink as she mentioned his name. 'It's his brother's twenty-first and they're having a party in the Co-op Hall tonight.'

'Have you been invited?' Viv slipped out of her coat and hung it up on one of the hooks in the lobby.

Dot nodded. 'I won't know many people but I thought I'd go along and support the boys.'

'Your Norm's taught himself more than three chords now then?' Viv said teasingly.

'You may mock,' said Dot severely, 'but he's getting there. Do you want to go in and be encouraging while I make a cup of tea? Mam and Dad are out.'

'Understandable,' murmured Viv, turning the handle of the parlour door. Singing under her breath 'Putting on the Agony, Putting on the Style', she slipped inside the room as unobtrusively as possible and perched on the leatherette-clad

98

arm of a chair, prepared to say nice things to the four lads gathered there in the light of the leaded window, all wearing Western-type shirts and jeans.

The Lonnie Donegan number came to an end and Viv waved her arms in the air and shouted, 'More, more! Who are this fantastic group, about to dazzle Merseyside and the world?'

'Oh, shut up, Viv!' Norm grinned at her. 'It wasn't that good.'

'Of course it was. It was better than good. Your number two fan has spoken.' Her eyes danced. 'The thing is, can you do it again and again and again? Let's hear a Gene Vincent number, baybee!'

Norm adjusted the strap of his guitar, glanced across at Phil, who nodded, and they launched into 'Be Bop A Lula'.

Dot came into the room as the number finished. 'Now how about "You're Twenty-one Today"?' she said, putting down a tray on the floor. The four lads pulled faces.

'They'll expect it,' said Viv in a lively voice, taking a cup from the tray. 'You could jazz it up, though.'

'They might also want "Auld Lang Syne",' said Dot seriously, passing a cup of tea to Phil. 'I've been to tons of family parties where all the grown ups get soppy and have that played at the end.'

'What if they want "Knees up, Mother Brown",' said Viv, with her tongue in her cheek.

'We draw the line at "Mother Brown",' said Phil, who had brown hair, brown eyes, a dimpled chin, and a vocal pitch that ranged from the raucous to the romantic. 'This party is for the young ones. Our Dave's told me mam that he doesn't want all the old aunties there, but you know mothers.'

'They're a law unto themselves,' said Viv, smiling.

He smiled back and Dot nudged her arm. 'I think we'll leave you lot to it now. Me and Viv have things to say to each other.' She nudged her friend again.

'Perhaps you'd like to come to the party tonight?' called Phil as they were on their way out. 'You can keep Dot company while we're playing.'

'Thanks,' said Viv, refusing to be intimidated by Dot's scowl. 'I've got nowhere else to go tonight. Carry on playing,

99

fellas. Who knows? You might beat Cliff or Elvis to the top of the charts one day.'

As soon as they were out of the parlour, Dot said furiously, 'He's mine, Viv! Keep your hands off!'

She raised her eyes to the ceiling. 'I don't want him. I was just being encouraging like you told me. Besides, you're forgetting about Nick.'

Dot wrinkled her nose. 'That's because you haven't mentioned him for a couple of weeks.'

'Only because I haven't seen him,' Viv said lightly. 'There's so much rebuilding going on in Liverpool at the moment that's he's kept busy, but I'm not going to sit in waiting for him to call.'

'All right, I accept that.' Dot sighed. 'Love's awful, isn't it?'

'If it's that bad, I don't know why you're bothering with Phil.'

'It's just that I fancy him like crazy but I don't know if he really fancies me or is just being nice to me because I'm Norm's sister.'

'You underestimate your charms. You've got a lot going for you. I wish I was as tall as you.'

'I wish I had a bust,' sighed Dot as they sat down in the back kitchen. 'Anyway, what did you come for?'

Viv put down her cup and laced her fingers beneath her chin, resting her elbows on the kitchen table. 'I went to see my uncle today – only he wouldn't believe he was my uncle,' she said, her expression moody.

'Figures,' said Dot laconically.

Viv stared at her. 'What d'you mean, *figures*?'

'I bet you burst in on the poor man without warning and told him you were the result of a night of passion during the war.'

'A night of passion was not mentioned,' said Viv with dignity. 'I'm not that daft! But he seems to believe my father could be any of a number of men. He said Mam had strings of boyfriends.'

'I wonder how she did it,' said Dot pensively, toying with the spoon in the sugar bowl. 'We're having trouble with just keeping one. What's your mam look like, Viv? I still haven't set eyes on her.'

100

Viv grimaced. 'She's okay. Anyway, I don't think mentioning a night of passion would have gone down well with Uncle Steve. He's got his own business and he's very upright . . . but maybe you've got something about me breaking the news to him the way I did.'

'Give him time to think about it,' said Dot. 'Who knows? He might change his mind and decide he could be your uncle after all.'

Viv nodded and got to her feet. 'I'll have to go and buy a present.'

Dot stood up. 'You're really going to the party then?'

'Why not?' Viv slipped an arm around her. 'You did say you wouldn't know anyone there, honey chile. Well, now you'll know me. Come with us into town and I'll buy you a frothy coffee at the Kardomah.'

Dot agreed and they went to put on their coats. The last thing they heard as they closed the door was the lads playing Craig Douglas's one hit 'Only Sixteen'.

'You're never too young or too old to fall in love,' commented Dot with a heartfelt sigh. Viv said nothing but was thinking about her mother and a night of passion during the war.

'I'm going out tonight.' Viv frowned at the dust on the sideboard as she took an apple out of the glass dish kept there. Her mother had forgotten to polish again. With her free hand she wrote 'Vivien Martin' in the dust. When there was no comment from her mother, she said loudly, 'I went to see Stephen Martin today!'

Hilda looked up from the red-backed romantic novel she was reading, a startled expression on her face. 'Good God! What did he have to say?'

'He chased me!' said Viv with assumed brightness. 'He thought I looked like you, and said you had so many fellas in the old days that my father could have been any one of them.'

Hilda's laugh had a ring of irritation to it. 'Fellas I might have had but I wasn't one for distributing my favours freely, whatever he might like to believe. The trouble with Stephen was he was jealous of his brother – and of your Uncle Tom. They used to tease him because he was quiet and a few years

101

younger.' She shrugged. 'There were times when I felt sorry for him and wished he'd fight back, but he wouldn't.' She stared into space and murmured, 'But I'm not about to waffle on about those days. What else did he have to say to you?'

'He insulted Aunt Flo.'

'Not surprising. Your perfect aunt did almost leave him standing at the altar.'

'It was better than marrying the wrong man.' Viv's tone was defensive.

'True,' said Hilda. 'Even so, perhaps if I'd gone to see Steve things might have been different?'

A sharp laugh was torn from Viv. 'What could you have done to convince him when he doesn't have a good word to say about you? You've always believed yourself irresistible, Mother.'

'If that is true I've been proved wrong a couple of times,' said Hilda coolly. 'We'll, you might laugh, my girl, but if you handle some men right you can change their minds for them. Anyway there's no use crying over spilt milk. It's all water under the bridge. Forget the past and think of the future. Be glad that times have changed since I was young. The only career most working-class girls could have then was marriage. If I was young again today . .'

'You'd probably make just the same mistakes,' said Viv ruthlessly, irritated by her reluctance still to talk about Jimmy. Without another word she walked from the room. She was not about to give up on finding out more about her father. She would give Stephen Martin a while to consider and then she would go and visit him again, just to prove that she had *it* as much as her mother had ever done.

Chapter Ten

Hilda lay on the sofa, smoking and reading *True Confessions*. The things that women confessed to never failed to fascinate her. People get paid for writing these stories, she thought incredulously. How much?

Her money had come from America but it wasn't a fortune and would not last for ever. She imagined huge sums of money for writing her true-life confessions, considering those in the magazine pretty tame stuff compared to some of the things that had happened to her. She toyed with the idea of writing but putting pen to paper had never been one of her strong points. Perhaps she could nag Viv into doing it?

Viv! Cheeky little thing, telling her that she wasn't doing the housework properly and saying that she had all day and it was time she looked for a job. They'd had a tussle over keeping the place up and both refused to dust. Stupid! But it had turned into a kind of competition. But who would have thought that Viv would have changed so much over the years and would have had the guts to confront Stephen with her illegitimacy? How long ago was that now? Weeks. Easter was behind them but there was still a chill wind about.

Hilda raised her head and looked towards the window. Pity about the wind. She might have been tempted to go and call on Stephen Martin if it had been as warm as it looked outside. It would be interesting to see how he looked and not just have Viv's word for it. She thought she saw a shadow pass the window through the net curtains. The next moment there was a knock on the door.

She got to her feet, tightening the tie on her dressing gown.

She pushed her feet into their frippery slippers and went to answer it.

'Good God!' Hilda stared in amazement before placing a hand on a hip and pulling in her stomach. 'Think of the devil and he's sure to appear. Get blown here, did you, Steve?'

Stephen's jaw dropped, then clenched. 'I didn't expect to see you. I'll come back some other time.'

'No, don't do that,' she said quickly, pushing the door wide. 'Come in. You look chilled to the marrow.'

'No thanks.' He turned away then stopped and said harshly, 'Shouldn't you be dressed at this time of day?'

'I haven't been well.' It was not true but it sounded convincing and Hilda spoke with a calmness she was far from feeling. 'It's good to see you, Steve. You're not going to let a little thing like me not being dressed stop us from talking? I presume you've come about Viv?'

A pulse throbbed in his neck. 'Yes I was rude. She's not to blame for what Flora did. Nor is it her fault she's what she is. She really sounded like she cared.' His voice trailed off as his gaze wandered to the V where the neck of Hilda's dressing gown fell open, then down towards her exposed legs. His face reddened. 'I'd better go.'

She placed a hand on his arm. 'I won't eat you if you come inside,' she said gently. 'You could wait in the kitchen while I dress. Put the kettle on and we'll have a coffee.'

'I don't know. I didn't expect . . '

'Obviously.' She smiled up at him, pressing his hand. 'Come on in. It's ages since we've talked. It's so nice to see someone from the old days. A lot's happened to us since then. We've both loved and lost and suffered.'

'I suppose so,' he said dully.

She thought, Oh God, the things a woman has to do! 'You suppose right.' Her voice was jovial. 'Come in.' She slipped a hand through his arm and he allowed himself to be dragged inside. 'I'd forgotten you were so tall and strong. You make me feel all dainty and small.' She slammed the door shut with her free hand.

He cleared his throat. 'You'd better get dressed.'

'You've said that. Does it bother you?'

'I'm not used to seeing a woman . . . er . . .'

'Er? You and our Flo never . . . ?'

His expression stiffened. 'No.'

'There's been no one else?' He shook his head, tight-lipped. 'What a waste,' she murmured, stroking his arm. 'All this lovely muscle.'

'Hilda, don't!' He removed her hand and cleared his throat again.

'What have I done?' she murmured forlornly. 'I'm a widow again, you know. I'll get dressed.' She began to unbutton her dressing gown, revealing a peach satin nightdress beneath. He stared at her, then hurried into the kitchen.

I shouldn't really tease him, thought Hilda as she dressed, singing beneath her breath, 'One dream in my heart, one love to be living for . . .' She could see the young Jimmy in Stephen's scared expression. Hell! They'd had some good times. Pity about the scar on Stephen's face, but he had inherited the business and was not short of a bob or two . . . Fancy him having second thoughts about Viv! Perhaps he was going to own her after all? She put on black stockings, remembering the way Stephen had stared at her legs all those years ago when he had believed he would marry her sister. How to play him? She was fond of Dom but could not visualise him ever leaving his wife. 'One dream in my heart . . . money.'

'Viv came to me about Jimmy,' said Stephen, standing almost to attention in the middle of the kitchen. His hands gripped his cup tightly.

'I know.' Hilda crossed one leg over the other and hitched up her skirt slightly. 'It was quite a while ago.'

Involuntarily he stared at the expanse of thigh revealed by the movement before lifting his eyes. She was still attractive but had never possessed the dewy innocent beauty of her daughter. There had always seemed to be a hard edge to Hilda. 'It wasn't something I could rush,' he muttered.

'She was very hurt.' Hilda emphasised the 'hurt'. 'She's got a bee in a bonnet about her father and that's all she can think about. She said you weren't very nice about me.' She sighed. 'If I remember rightly, last time we met you weren't very nice about me either. I don't know what your Jimmy would have thought. He always spoke of you as having perfect manners.'

Our Steve's always putting on airs and graces, was what he'd actually said. 'He was very proud of you in a big brotherly way, even though he didn't show it often.'

'I don't want to talk about our Jimmy,' Stephen said coldly. He did but was afraid that his real feelings would show if she went on about how marvellously witty, funny and brave his brother had been. Too often his brother had been witty at his expense.

Her eyebrows arched. 'You surprise me. I would have thought that was why you were here? Don't you want me to give you some kind of proof to show that Viv is your brother's daughter? Well, I can do that.'

'You can?' She had completely flummoxed him.

'You heard me.' Hilda looked amused.

'How? I don't believe you.' He stumbled over the words.

'Why? Don't you want to believe me?' She stared at him intently but he was silent. She continued, 'He sent me letters when he was in Africa.' She paused to stub out a cigarette but her gaze did not move from his face. 'You've always thought the worst of me, haven't you, Steve? You never believed I truly loved your brother. Your judgement was right. I didn't love him but I was very fond of him and felt sorry for him. He was devastated over your mother's and sisters' deaths. I comforted him the only way a woman knows how that time he was home. It was a stupid thing to do and you don't know how many times I've regretted it, especially after he was killed.'

Her words rang true and matched what Stephen believed he knew of her. His shoulders sagged and he backed into a chair, unable to tear his gaze from hers. 'It's different to the undying love for him you swore last time I saw you.'

She came over to him. 'You were a different man then . . . an idealist . . . not so mature.' She crouched by the side of his chair, leaning her elbows on the edge of its arm so that they brushed against his sleeve. 'I think we can be honest with each other, can't we? You only wanted our Flo because she had belonged to Tom, and you'd always hated him because he teased you. It was your way of getting back at him.'

Stephen wanted to say that was only partly true but he remained silent, overwhelmingly conscious of her nearness. It was years since he had been with a woman. France 1950. He had got a little drunk at a mate's wedding in Caen and had woken up in the bride's aunt's bed. She had been forty-five to his thirty-one and had known all the tricks of the trade. He had felt ashamed afterwards but had learnt a lot during that lapse.

Hilda rested her hands on his arm and gazed up at him. 'It's a pity we never got together years ago but I fell for that pretty-faced first husband of mine. I was a fool! I should have gone for strength of character. I always admired you, Steve. Nobody could mess you around. If you thought something was right, you stuck to it. I was too easily deceived by a handsome face. I've learnt my lesson since.'

He cleared a throat that was suddenly too tight. 'Why are you telling me all this?'

Her eyes widened and he felt he was being drawn in. He had forgotten the irises were such an all over baby blue.

'Because of Viv, of course,' said Hilda. 'I've been such a terrible mother to her. Poor kid, she deserves all the help she can get. I don't think our Flo was thinking of her at all when she went off to America. She should have married you, Steve but I'm glad she didn't.'

There was a short silence. He did not want to discuss Flora and when he spoke his voice had hardened. 'I came to tell Viv that if she wants to visit me sometimes, she can. If we got to know each better then perhaps I might feel different about things. She might be in need of a job, and maybe in time I might accept Jimmy was her father.'

Hilda breathed easier. For a moment she had thought she had gone too far. 'That *is* good of you,' she gushed.

He shrugged. 'She's grown up well.'

'People say she looks like me.'

'Do they?' He eased his arm which was going dead.

Hilda lifted her chin and raised herself up a bit. Her knees cracked. A grimace twisted her mouth. 'Old age creeping up. Do you ever think about being old and alone, Steve?'

'No,' he lied, and got up out of the chair. 'I'd better get back.' He lifted his overcoat from the sideboard where Hilda had placed it and noticed the name written in the dust: Vivien Martin. An unfamiliar sensation washed over him and for a moment he suffered such a sense of loss that it was a physical ache.

Hilda was at his side, helping him on with his overcoat. 'You'll come again?' Her fingers were on the buttons, fastening them for him. He was reminded of when he was a little boy and his mother used to pat him on the shoulder and say, 'There, Stevie luv, all done.' Then she would kiss him before seeing him out of the house. He stared at Hilda and experienced such a craving for sexual comfort that it was like having stomach cramps. He thought of Vivien. Was she really his niece? He opened the door. 'You'll make my apologies,' he said roughly. 'And ask her to come and see me?'

'Of course.' She was all smiles. 'It's Viv's welfare we're both interested in.'

'I am,' he said bluntly. 'I don't know about you, Hilda. I never have. I still don't know whether to believe . . .'

Her mouth thinned and she moved suddenly, taking him by surprise. 'Believe what you like.' She shoved him out of the house, surprising him with her strength, and slammed the door catching the flap of his overcoat. She narrowly opened the door and freed it but before he could say anything she had slammed it again.

Hilda leaned against the door and stared unseeingly across the room. Damn him! Who did he think he was? He'd as good as called her a liar. She had a good mind not to give Viv his message. That would serve him right. He was interested in Viv that was obvious. What had he said? Her brow furrowed as she moved away, reaching for her cigarette packet. 'She's grown up well.' Not exactly a roaring compliment but Steve had never been able to get his tongue round a pretty phrase. She inhaled and coughed. There was a knock at the door and she went to answer it, still coughing.

'You should give them up, girl. They'll be the death of yer yet.' Dominic pushed past her into the house and seated himself on the sofa, stretching his long arms along the back. 'Who was that I saw just leaving?'

'Jealous, are you?'

'Curious,' he grunted, lighting up. 'Listen . . . do you want to give me some more money for paint and paper to finish this place? The missus is angling for an invite to come and see what I've been doing here and I can hardly take her upstairs.'

Hilda grimaced. 'Where is she now?'

'Gone to her mother's.' He smiled. 'D'you feel like a bit of fun?'

She sat on his knee. 'In a minute. That was Steve Martin.'

He pulled a face. 'The one that your Flo threw over for the Yank?'

'You've got a good memory.'

'What's he after? You now.'

'I'm not interested.'

'You mean he wasn't.'

She pouted and punched his chest. 'The trouble with you is that you know me too well.'

'People don't change that much from when they're kids. You always wanted everybody to pay you attention. You're insecure, girl. That's why you need me. Your memories of me are linked with being comforted.'

She laughed without amusement. 'You think you know it all, Dominic Kelly. I'd feel more secure if I didn't have to worry about your missus finding out about us.'

He hugged her to him. 'We can stop. Or you can give me some money and I'll pull out that grate and put in new and slap on some paint and paper. Then you can invite her round for scones and tea.'

'You've got a cheek. It would be Viv who would have to make the scones.' She kissed him several times before removing his sweater. 'Tell me, has your Joe seen Nick Bryce lately?'

Dominic nuzzled her neck. 'Not that I know of . . . but that doesn't mean anything. He doesn't tell me where he's going or who he's seeing.' He slid his hand up her skirt and undid her suspender button. 'What did that Martin bloke want?'

'Viv.' She unbuttoned his shirt, telling him what Stephen had said about her daughter. Her eyes darkened. Pass his message on! Like hell she would. She didn't want him taking her daughter away from her. Then she dug her hands down the back of Dom's trousers and dragged out his shirt tails. The room fell silent as he kissed her with enthusiasm and she clung to him as he rose from the chair and carried her upstairs. There was something to be said for meeting after so many years one's first uninhibited youthful lover.

*   *   *

Viv pushed open the front door and immediately the sound of her mother singing in the back kitchen assailed her ears. She grimaced, wondering which was worse – her mother her normal indolent, stubborn, trying self, with her refusal to talk about Jimmy and idiotic behaviour in carrying on with Mr Kelly, or else stirred by the mood of the moment when the unexpected could happen? Why was she singing? Maybe a visit from Mr Kelly? Viv groaned, sniffed and caught the faintest whiff of Brylcreem and something else. Mr Kelly didn't use aftershave. She forgot about closing the front door and walked through into the kitchen.

Her mother hovered near the cooker. She was wearing a frilly white organdie apron over a black dress and fishnet stockings. 'Hello, honey. Buy anything nice?'

Viv's eyebrows shot up. 'Mr Kelly must have been. You're all dressed up like a dog's dinner. Bit early in he day, wasn't he?'

'Now, Viv, don't be like that.' Hilda stared at her, noting the smoothness of her skin and the cheeks flushed a healthy pink with the wind. She looked so lovely and so young that Hilda experienced a terrible pang of envy. You could pain over the tiny wrinkles but no cream could smooth them away for good.

'Honest, you mean?' retorted Viv. 'It's just that besides disapproving of your making a fool of yourself and committing adultery, Mam, I don't want Mrs Kelly coming round here screaming blue murder.'

'If she does, I'll know where it's come from,' said Hilda, her expression clouding. 'Mrs McCoy. Nosy cow!'

'You should behave yourself,' said Viv, glancing over her mother's shoulder to see what was in the pan.

'You've got no right to judge me.' Hilda frowned. 'You don't know what it's like being a widow.'

'If your example's anything to go by then, then I'll have a gay old time. Have we had any other visitors?'

'Who were you expecting?' Hilda's voice was frosty.

Viv glimpsed a brown lumpy something in the pan and groaned inwardly. 'Nick. And I wouldn't put it past you to lie to me about him because I'm not daft. I can feel that you're still not happy about me seeing him.'

110

'Well, he hasn't been and that's the truth.' Hilda avoided her daughter's gaze and used a fish slice vigorously.

Viv stared at her. She was lying. She had that look on her face. 'Are you sure?'

'Certain sure.'

'You're fibbing, Mother.'

Hilda's mouth tightened. 'Our Flo would slap your face if she heard the way you speak to me. If you must know it was the man from the Pru. I thought I should get myself insured.'

Viv was not sure whether to believe her or not but decided to let it drop for the moment. 'What's in the pan?'

'Spam fritters. Our Flo used to make them in the war. They weren't half bad.'

'Aunt Flo could cook,' said Viv without thinking.

'I can cook some things.' Hilda's voice was suddenly harsh. 'You always think our Flo was the only one who could do anything right. I thought I'd surprise you! Give you a treat! But I can see I'm wasting my time.' She dropped the fish slice in the pan. 'You can do it yourself. I know when I'm not appreciated.'

'Stop getting on your high horse! I didn't say you couldn't cook.' Viv deftly slid the slice under the burning object and tossed it on to a plate that contained several thick slices of spam. She glanced at the bowl next to the willow pattern plate, saw that it contained lumpy batter mix and began to search for the whisk. She found it and whipped up the batter some more. Hilda had used a fork. 'How much did you insure yourself for? If it's worth having I could always cook you up some rhubarb leaves for lunch.'

'Are rhubarb leaves poisonous then?' asked Hilda, watching her daughter's deft movements.

'That's what I've been told.' Viv smiled. 'Who was he, Mam?'

Hilda hesitated, imagined her daughter enjoying herself in Stephen's company and was as jealous as hell. 'I don't know why you don't believe me. You'd think I was entertaining men all the time.'

'Not all the time, just some of it,' said Viv, dropping a couple of slices of spam in the batter.

Hilda's mouth tightened. 'Very seldom lately. Dom's been

working.' She gazed down at her fingernails. 'I've chipped a nail.'

'We'll have it with the fritters. Why should you suddenly decide to insure yourself? It's not like you to think about such things. Who was he? I mean, I'd be quite happy if you had someone else. At least I could stop having nightmares about Mrs Kelly throwing a brick through the window and painting "Scarlet Woman" on the front door.'

'Don't be silly, 'Hilda said crossly. 'I've told you, it was the insurance man. As for Dom Kelly – he's going to do the front room and I'll have her in from next-door to see what a good job he's made of everything. That'll lull her suspicions.'

Viv felt a deep disappointment. 'I'm ashamed of you, Mother. I don't know how you have the nerve to behave the way you do – sitting on your bum for most of the day, waiting for him to come. Don't you think it's time you stopped behaving like the cheap tart Stephen called you and act your age?' There was a loud sizzle as she dropped a couple of fritters into the pan.

Her mother whirled round and slapped her face. 'I am not cheap tart! You don't know what it's like at my age to feel like your charms are slipping away, to lose someone, to need love.'

Viv's hand went to her cheek and suddenly she wanted to hit out at her mother. 'I needed love when I was a child but you never cared about that! Nor did you care about my sense of loss when you went away! And what's the use, Mother, of trying to hang on to youth if you have to keep putting on the warpaint and applying the contents of the bleach bottle?' she said scathingly. 'You could try growing old gracefully.'

Old! That word again! A squeal warred with a roar in Hilda's throat and she swung her fist at Viv, who sidestepped so that the cooker caught the blow. 'Bitch, bitch,' moaned Hilda, nursing her hand. 'You'll get out of my house for that.'

'*Your* house? You want history repeating itself, do you? You were thrown out so you want me out – just because you can't accept that age is creeping up on you!'

'Out, out,' screamed Hilda, picking up the steaming frying pan. 'I'm not old! I'm barely forty and good for my age.'

There was a knock on the door and Viv hurriedly stepped

back. 'Okay, Mam, you're not old. We'll agree that you're a well-preserved thirty-nine.'

'Anybody at home?' called a voice which caused Viv's heart to jump in her breast. 'Mam, put the pan down, Nick's in the front room.'

'Who cares about him?' muttered Hilda between her teeth, swinging the frying pan as Nick came through the doorway. The scalding fat formed a skimpy glittering arc and one of the fritters flew out of the pan and hit him in the chest.

'What the hell's going on?' he asked.

Hilda glared at him. 'You shouldn't have got in the bloody way.'

'Say sorry, Mam,' said Viv, staring in fascination as the fritter slowly slid down Nick's jacket.

'Should I go out and come in again?' he said, flicking the fritter on to the floor.

'Just go out. Nobody told you to come in.' Hilda turned on her daughter. 'You should have shut the door. Now you've let the common rabble in.'

'It's you that's common,' said Viv, then found herself struggling not to explode into laughter. She shot a quick glance in Nick's direction. 'You're not burnt, are you?'

'No thanks to the cook.' He shrugged off his jacket. 'Isn't it a bit late for Pancake Tuesday?'

'Very funny,' said Viv, holding out a hand. 'Give me your jacket. I'll see what I can do. We need blotting paper and a hot iron.'

He handed the garment in question to her. 'Thanks. I did come to ask you out.'

'About time too,' she said dryly.'Where did you have in mind?' She forgave him quickly for not having been around and smiled. He returned her smile. Then they both jumped as Hilda dropped the frying pan on the floor, making a clanging noise. 'When you've finished twittering like a pair of love-birds,' she said in a seething voice, 'I want you to get out of my house, the pair of you! I've had enough! You're giving me a headache!'

'You're jealous because we're young, Mother,' murmured Viv, not looking at her. 'Why don't you admit it?'

'I admit nothing. Not even that I'm your mother,' she said,

and stepping over the mess on the floor, disappeared through the curtain at the bottom of the stairs.

'Marvellous exit,' said Nick, grinning at Viv.

'She should have gone to Hollywood.' She picked up the frying pan and placed it on the stove. 'If she'd had the breaks she would have made a marvellous Scarlett O'Hara. Instead she had to make do with naming me Vivien after the actress who played her.'

'And *you're* not like Miss Scarlett at all, of course?'

'I like to think not. I wouldn't have let Rhett Butler go.' She put up the ironing board and took an old exercise book from a drawer in the kitchen cabinet, tearing out the sheet of blotting paper at the front. 'Where were you thinking of going?' she asked.

Nick sat astride a kitchen chair, his arms resting on its back. 'Would you mind looking at another building?'

'Another cathedral?' She gave a mock groan.

'I was thinking of Speke Hall.'

'Now that's different.' Viv's pleasure showed on her face. 'I haven't been there since I was at school. I thought it interesting and romantic. I nearly fell over because I wandered round with my eyes shut half the time, trying to imagine all the people who had lived there.'

'You'd have to go back to the Tudors. Imagine Henry the Eighth! Of course it's hard to think of romance in connection with a man who chopped a couple of his wives' heads off but he did write "Greensleeves" which is a love song.'

'I bet those two warbled on the block "Alas, my love, you've done me wrong".' She smiled as she wiped bits of batter off the jacket and tested the iron.

'You'll come with me than?'

'As soon as I've done this.'

Overhead Hilda could be heard walking about. Nick raised his eyes ceilingward and said, 'What's up with her?'

'I told her to act her age. She's still carrying on with Mr Kelly. She said it was because she missed her husband and needed loving.'

'Don't we all?' murmured Nick.

Viv smiled and changed the subject. 'I remember Speke Hall has priestholes.'

It has some fine plasterwork, too,' said Nick, his eyes on her face.

She felt the heat rising in her cheeks. 'I wouldn't know the difference.' She handed the jacket to him before unplugging the iron. 'What about ghosts?'

'We can always find you one if that's what you want.' He shrugged on his jacket, a gleam still lurking at the back of his eyes.

'It'd be something to tell Dot,' she said, determinedly ignoring that look. She put away the ironing board and left the mess for her mother to clean up.

Nick found Viv a ghost in the Tapestry Room, otherwise known as the Haunted Chamber, where a lady of the Beauclerk family was said to have thrown her baby out the window before committing suicide in the Great Hall.

'Terribly sad,' murmured Viv, touching the Flemish cradle.

'Even the upper classes had their troubles,' said Nick, catching hold of her fingers. 'What do you think of the place? Would you like to live in a house like this?'

She wrinkled her nose. 'It doesn't feel like a home with all these rooms. Then there's the priestholes. Spooky. How would you know there wasn't anyone hiding inside them?' She shivered deliciously, 'Let's go outside.'

The remaining clouds had dispersed and the sun was shining from a clear blue sky. They viewed the house and Nick spoke of the Gothic Middle Ages layout and the influence of the Renaissance. Then he surprised her by saying, 'Why was your mother dressed like a French maid?'

Viv put a hand over her eyes. 'Do you have to ask? It used to be a cowgirl! I think she and Mr Kelly have these fantasies.' She found herself making excuses for her mother as she lowered her hand and gazed up at him. 'They met when they were kids and I think that's half the reason they're carrying on now. They feel comfortable with each other. I don't think each of them ever grew older in the other's mind.' She drew a deep breath. 'And I suppose Mrs Kelly doesn't go in for that kind of thing.'

Nick laughed. 'Can you imagine her dressing up like that?'

A smile hovered round Viv's mouth. 'I feel sorry for her,

115

but at the same time I wonder why Mr Kelly's doing what he's doing if the marriage is happy?'

'Is any marriage completely happy?' He paused. 'Perhaps Mrs Kelly has fantasies of her own but has never dared mention them? We all have dreams.'

Viv nodded. 'Especially in a place like this.'

'Agreed,' he said, and drew her beneath one of the enormous yew trees that occupied the courtyard. One was male, one female, and they were called Adam and Eve. He closed his eyes. 'I'm having a fantasy right now. I'm under this tree and a slave girl dressed in one of those eastern costumes comes along and asks if there's anything she can do for me.'

'I suppose you're on a silken couch and you'd like her to peel grapes for you and pop them in your mouth?' There was a hint of laughter in Viv's voice.

He opened his eyes. 'Amongst other things.'

She felt suddenly breathless. 'I wondered when we'd get round to other things. Slave girls are out. Do you want to know my fantasy? It's of knights in armour jousting for my favour.'

He drew her closer. 'Amour is definitely not on. Imagine how it would get in the way?'

'Perhaps that was the idea? Prevention being the better part of valour.' Her pulses were racing.

'I never thought of it being used for that kind of protection,' he murmured thoughtfully as he nuzzled her neck. 'Those days might seem romantic but I bet they weren't.'

'Perhaps romance is all in the mind?'

Her eyes closed as their lips met in a kiss that was as sensual as the feel of satin on skin. It deepened as his mouth moved hungrily over hers. She responded passionately and his hands slid slowly down her spine, pressing her against him. She was aware again of the extreme pleasure that being in his company gave her. If this was love, as the song went, she liked it.

His mouth lifted. 'Someone's coming,' he whispered.

Reluctantly they drew apart but there was a need within her still to touch him and she kept hold of his hand. They left the courtyard and walked through gardens past rhododendrons in bloom.

'How have things been with you?' asked Nick. 'I hope your

116

mother doesn't make a habit of throwing things at you?'

'No. And I think I provoked her. Most of the time we get along better than I ever thought we would. The only bugbear between us – besides Mr Kelly – is her refusal to talk about my father. I went to visit his brother a few weeks ago.'

'You never said anything about a brother.' He stopped and stared at her from questioning blue eyes.

'That's because I didn't think about him at first, and then I remembered his existence and how I used to like him.' She smiled warmly, her mind on the past, and did not notice Nick's frowning expression. 'He nearly married Aunt Flo. Unfortunately, that's probably why he refuses to believe his brother was my father. He told me to get out.' A sigh escaped her.

Nick squeezed her fingers and said seriously, 'You mightn't want to believe this, Viv, but it's probably for the best. You've lived without knowing who your father was for years. Now you know, why not just be content with that? Why rake up the past? It can sometimes lead to trouble. Let this uncle die a death.'

She was silent a moment, her brows knitting. 'I suppose you're right,' she said slowly. 'The only thing is that it's not that easy, Nick. I feel I need to know more about my father to understand my mother, and she won't talk about him.'

'She must have her reasons. Are you being fair to her, digging into what is really her past?'

There was a note in his voice that caused her to glance at him swiftly. 'Mine as well, Nick. I think I might write to Aunt Flo about my father again.'

'Is that wise?'

'What's wisdom got to do with it? I'm talking about a deep need inside me, Nick. I want to know my father even though we'll never meet.'

'Being reminded of the war can't be easy for your Aunt Flo,' he said roughly. 'But if that's what you want to do, you do it.'

She sighed. 'I don't expect you to understand. You never liked your own father.'

'That's got nothing to do with it,' he said, scowling.

'Of course it has, and I can understand that. But my case is

117

different, Nick. My father was charming and heroic.'

'So you've been told.'

Their gazes clashed.

'Are you saying that Aunt Flo lied to me?' Her voice was stiff.

'Did I say that?' he parried, his grip on her hand tightening. 'Let's drop this, Viv. What's the point of us falling out over something that happened years ago?'

'That's fine by me,' she murmured. 'Let's go somewhere and eat. I missed my lunch.'

'It didn't miss me,' he said in droll tones.

She laughed. 'Let's hope Mam's got over her bad temper or she mightn't let you in the house.'

'Does she still think I'm not good enough for you?'

Viv shrugged. 'I don't know what she thinks. She doesn't say that much about you. It's just a feeling I have when your name does come up.'

'Does it bother you?'

'Not really. It might make her have second thoughts about how I feel about her carrying on with Mr Kelly.' She hugged his arm and smiled up at him. 'Let's go and eat! I'm starving!'

Chapter Eleven

Hilda sucked furiously at a mint as she paced the small space in the front room that was not taken up with stepladder, bucket, pasteboard and rolls of paper. 'I'm really annoyed with her,' she said, not for the first time that morning. 'She's deliberately going against what I said.'

'She's at that age,' muttered Dominic, trying to keep his eye on what he was doing and wishing Hilda would stop pacing about. He had already messed up one length of wallpaper. Besides it was frustrating enough having Viv home from work with a cold without Hilda moaning on about Nick Bryce. Viv had just nipped upstairs for a book and would be down any minute and he had no wish to be caught talking about her.

'What's age got to do with it?' snapped Hilda. 'She's just determined to cock a snook at me because I'm seeing you.'

'I don't know what you've got against Nick,' whispered Dominic, thinking he heard footsteps. 'He'll make something of himself, that lad.'

'You know what I've got against him. His mother! I want better for my daughter.' The truth was, though, that every time she saw Nick she was reminded of her painful past and became more and more nervous, uncertain whether she could trust him to keep his mouth shut about Viv's father.

Hilda turned as her daughter entered the room. 'Did you hear me?' she shouted. 'I don't like his mother.'

'Control yourself, Mam,' murmured Viv. 'Admit you're just jealous because it's my turn to be going out evenings while you stay in.' She dragged the rocking chair closer to the new tiled fireplace, which had an electric fire in its grate, and opened her book. It was *Forever Amber*, and she would have enjoyed it more if she had not been determined to put a spoke in her mother's affairs by getting in her way. Mrs Kelly had been very snooty with her the other week when they met in Maggie's bakery and she wanted to allay her suspicions even more than her mother did.

'I am not jealous!' Hilda kicked the rocker. She was, of course. Every time Viv went out she felt like one of the ugly sisters left behind after Cinders had won her Prince Charming. 'And if you have the energy to answer me back and read a book, then you're well enough to get back to work,' she cried.

Viv said good-humouredly, 'I'm ill, Mam. Really ill. And I thought you'd be more sympathetic. I've had to listen to you coughing often enough. Thank God you've given up the ciggies again. I'll be going back soon enough so why don't you go out? I'll look after Mr Kelly. You mentioned earlier something about buying a new sofa?'

Hilda scowled. 'Perhaps I will go. There's nothing doing here.'

'No, nothing while I'm here.' Viv opened her book and pretended to read. She heard her mother whispering to Dominic and ten minutes later Hilda left the house.

Viv came in from the back kitchen with a try upon which was all the paraphernalia for making tea. There was also a plate of buttered homemade scones. Her feelings towards Dominic were mixed. Despite her disapproval of her mother's carryings-on with him she could not utterly dislike the man because he had always been kind to her. 'Teabreak.' She filled a cup and placed it on the cleared top of the sideboard.

He thanked her, put up the length of bright yellow and orange geometrical patterned wallpaper he had pasted, drank half the strong tea, and polished off two scones before saying, 'When will you be going back to work, girl?'

Viv shrugged and sat on the edge of the rocking chair. 'Monday, I suppose. Not that I'm particularly looking forward to it. The job can be boring.'

'Every job can be boring. I'm surprised you never went to

see that Stephen Martin after he came round. He's got his own business, hasn't he? Didn't your Aunt Flo work for him?'

Viv's heart gave a peculiar leap and *Forever Amber* slipped to the floor, unnoticed. 'What are you talking about?'

'You don't know?' He hesitated, scratched his head, and absently bit into another scone.

Her expression hardened. 'Come on, Mr Kelly, you can't stop now. You might as well tell me all of it. When did Stephen Martin come round?'

Dominic sighed heavily and finished the scone. 'A few weeks back. Said he'd had second thoughts about seeing you. Wanted you to call on him.'

Viv scrambled to her feet, a furious expression her face. 'I bet it was that day she said it was the man from the Pru! I bet it was! I knew someone had been! I knew she was lying! But why?'

'Jealousy,' said Dominic without thinking.

Viv laughed bitterly. 'That figures. She doesn't want anyone giving me attention. She wants it all for herself.'

Dominic said seriously, 'Have you ever thought why that should be, girl?'

'Ego! Conceit! Selfishness!' Viv paced the room, her arms folded across her breasts. 'How dare she not tell me he had called?'

Dominic shook his head. 'The pair of you are alike and neither of you can see it.'

'We're not a bit alike,' snapped Viv, her eyes glinting. 'I don't know how you can say that! Don't you be telling her that you've told me! I want to tell her myself and watch her expression and see what excuse she comes up with!'

'I'd rather cut me throat than tell her,' he muttered. 'She'll have me life.'

Viv's laugh had an edge to it. 'I don't know what you see in her, Mr Kelly. She's sneaky and conniving!' And on those words she stormed out of the room.

She washed and changed into a new Junior Miss dress she had bought in C & A. It was deep blue with full skirts and a bow under the bustline. She made up carefully and then hurried out of the house.

*   *   *

121

'I thought you would have been here sooner,' said Stephen, his eyes on her face as his strong fingers toyed with a pen, lifting the papers that littered the heavy mahogany desk.

'My mother didn't tell me that you'd called.' Viv could not conceal her anger but at least it had driven away any anxiety she might have felt about meeting him again. 'In fact, she doesn't even know I'm here.'

'Then how did you get to know?'

'Someone else told me. I could kill her for keeping it from me.'

He was silent, searching for the right words. 'It was probably partly my fault,' he said at last. 'We didn't part on the friendliest of terms. I'm being honest with you now, Viv. I told her that I still wasn't convinced that you're Jimmy's daughter. Having said that, I know it's possible that I'm just plain prejudiced against your mother because of the past. I suggest we get to know each other and then maybe I'll feel different. As you said the last time, I've no close family any more and I admit to being very lonely at times.'

Immediately Viv's anger receded and her natural sympathy was roused. She leaned forward and touched his hand. 'You don't know how happy your words make me. I'll be glad to visit you and to talk. I want to know all about your side of my family. There's no need for you to be lonely any more, Uncle Steve.'

His hand covered hers, sandwiching it between both of his. 'I had this idea that maybe you could come and work for me,' he said eagerly. 'I've been doing all the paper work myself since my aunt died but it's getting too much. I take it you can type?'

'Of course I can.' She did not add that she had only finished a course a short while ago and wasn't very fast.

'When your aunt threw me over, Viv, I thought the family line would die with me but if you are Jimmy's daughter then it will go on and if you have children . . .' His voice trailed off and his expression was dazed.

Viv had not really expected this and was almost dizzy with excitement and gratitude. She determined to go to night school and learn shorthand and business management. 'I'll work hard,' she said positively. 'I'll make you proud of me.'

'I'm sure you will. Perhaps there's something of my mother in you,' he said under her breath. 'Jimmy wasn't like her or me. He had the gift of the gab. He did a bit of this, a bit of that, never settled down to a proper day's work. He'd gad about on a motor bike, supposedly finding us work.'

She assumed a sympathetic air. 'Brothers and sisters are often different. I've noticed that.'

He smiled. 'When can you start?'

Her smooth white brow puckered. 'I'll have to give notice but I'll do that straightaway.'

'Good girl. I'm sure we'll get on.'

'So am I.' Her eyes shone with excitement and warmth. 'I really will give it all I've got.'

'I know you will, Viv.' He gazed down at their hands and said, 'It's not far off finishing time. Perhaps you'd like to have a meal with me?'

Her cheeks flushed delicately. 'I'd love that. Although I don't know whether I'm suitably dressed.'

'You look fine to me,' he said gruffly. 'You've grown into a proper young lady. I'd be proud if you were *my* daughter.'

'You're making me blush.' Her voice was unsteady.

He released her hand. 'Modesty becomes a woman, Viv. Just give me a few minutes while I have a word with the works manager then I'll be with you.'

She waited impatiently, thinking how well things had turned out and how proud she would be to be in his company. Despite being scarred there was a certain attractiveness to his face, especially when he smiled, and he had a good head of hair with just enough silver in it to give him a distinguished appearance. She wondered if her mother had noted all this and her eyes darkened with anger again.

Stephen took Viv to a restaurant in Dale Street and while they waited for their first course of prawn cocktail she wondered how to broach the subject of his brother without spoiling the rapport between them, then decided it might be wiser to leave that matter alone, just for now. She searched for something to say that might interest him and would sound intelligent. Unused to conversing with older men she was unsure what to choose. In the end she plunged in with, 'I was reading the letters in the *Echo* the other evening and someone

123

had written that Liverpool had missed a golden opportunity in planning the new city by not planting more trees. What do you think, Uncle Steve, should they have planned for more trees?'

'Trees cost money,' said Stephen seriously. 'And Liverpool has enough financial problems as it is without borrowing to countrify the place. Shipping is in a bad way and there's a fair amount of unemployment in the city. They're spending some money trying to improve the city's appearance. The Liver Building has been cleaned and they're doing something about all those blasted pigeons that are around. A health hazard, that's what they are, Viv.'

'Grandfather kept pigeons,' she murmured, toying with the stem of her glass. 'But he freed the last couple when he started to go funny. I suppose they helped to pollute the city, but he probably thought he was doing the right thing freeing them because he couldn't look after them any more and I didn't have the time.'

'Is that why your mother came home? For your grandfather's funeral?'

Viv could not resist a smile. 'Not according to her. She said she came home to be a mother to me, and that if she'd had her own mother around at my age then things might have turned out different for her.' She paused. 'A fine one she is when she didn't even tell me about your visit. She must have known how much it would mean to me.'

Stephen moved his knive a centimetre. 'She was very like you at your age, but not as sensible. She was wild and would do anything for a dare and would dare anyone.'

'Truth, dare, command or promise,' said Viv softly, remembering the game that had been in progress in the street that night she had gone for her first walk with Nick.

'That's right,' said Stephen, looking grim. 'She dared me to challenge Tom to a wrestling bout. I don't know why. He was older than I was and bigger.' He stared at Viv. 'That was your Uncle Tom, by the way. He married your Aunt Flora. Although he went out with your mother for a while before she went out with our Jimmy.' He hesitated. 'Hilda said something about having proof of your being Jimmy's daughter. Something about letters when he was away in Africa.'

124

'Letters!' Viv was startled. 'She's never mentioned any letters to me. All I get from her is that she finds it too hurtful to talk about him.'

He nodded. 'It could be true. There's things in my past that I find very difficult even to think about. You could ask her about the letters. It would do no harm.'

Viv nodded but had no time to say more because their prawn cocktails arrived.

Later, after a main course of Steak Diane and a dessert of apple pie and whipped cream, Stephen brought up the matter of the letters again. 'I'd appreciate it, Viv, if you could look into that without mentioning your coming to see me. I'd really rather not have your mother breathing down my neck, putting her spoke in. She always brings out the worst in me, I'm sorry to say.'

Viv hesitated. She had been looking forward to the confrontation with her mother but realised that maybe he was right. If her mother knew that she was going to work for Stephen or was having anything to do with him then she would want to get in on the act. She would not be able to resist interfering. If her mother had been honest with her about Steven's visit Viv would not have thought of keeping this from her, but Hilda had been devious and now it was her turn.

'I'll think up some way around it,' she murmured.

'I'm sure you will.' There was admiration in his eyes. 'Now how about another coffee?'

'Thank you.' They smiled at each other and she was warmed by his solicitude. Life had never felt so good.

During the next few days Viv tried to think of ways of broaching the subject of the letters to her mother but it was not until she was sitting in Dot's bedroom on Saturday that an idea came to her.

They had been to the pictures to see *The Blob*, and *I married a Monster from Outer Space* with Steve McQueen that afternoon and Viv had told her friend that she would be giving her notice in. Dot had been quite philosophical about it, saying she would miss having her around but was pleased that Stephen had come up trumps after all. It was then that Viv remembered that Dot's father had fought in the war. As she gazed at the far wall adorned with a framed photograph of a Swiss lake, she said abruptly, 'Dot, did your dad write to your mother during the war?'

'Sure he did.' She lifted her dark head from the *Valentine* magazine she was browsing through. 'Why do you ask?'

'Has your mother still got the letters?

Dot rubbed her chin. 'Quite a few of them, tied up in pink ribbon in the bottom of her wardrobe.'

'That's nice,' said Viv, smiling. 'Real romantic.' She stood up. 'I'll be going now. I'll see you Monday.'

'You're going already? I thought you'd stay for tea.'

'I've got something to do. I might see you again later.'

Dot shook her head again in bewilderment. 'You just said you'd see me Monday.'

'Sorry. I've got something on my mind. See you when I see you.' Without another word Viv hurried downstairs.

As she entered the house Hilda looked up. She was sitting on the new brown and beige cut moquette sofa with her bare feet up on the pouffe. There was an empty cup of coffee and an open box of Milk Tray on the floor near at hand. 'So you've come home at last,' she said crossly. 'I suppose you've been out with Nick?'

'No. He's away at a conference. I went to the pictures with Dot and then back to her house.' Viv sat in the rocking chair and then leaned forward, adopting a friendly attitude. 'We were talking about her father and mine, Mam. She said that her mother has a pile of letters from when her dad was away during the war. Did Jimmy ever write you any letters?' She waited, holding her breath as her mother's hand stilled before hovering over the box of chocolates. She picked one and bit into it.

'I love the nutty ones, don't you?' she murmured.

'Nuts for the nutty,' said Viv dryly. 'Did you hear what I said?'

'I heard.' Hilda ate the chocolate deliberately slowly.

'And?' Viv forced herself to control her impatience.

'I've got an awful dry throat.' Hilda smiled, ran a tongue round her teeth and trailed her fingers through the remaining chocolates. 'Perhaps you'd like to make me a coffee?'

Viv wanted to drop the chocolates on her mother's head but instead she made the coffee.

126

Hilda took it with a word of thanks. She swallowed several sips, then said. 'He wrote to me. But there are no letters now.'

'What?' Viv thought, She has to be lying. 'You're just saying that, Mam. Perhaps it's too painful to remember?' She could not help the sarcasm.

Hilda frowned. 'There's no need to be like that. There were letters but I got rid of them weeks ago.' She lifted her shoulders and then let them drop. 'I decided there was no point in keeping them,' she said mournfully. 'What was the use? He was gone.'

'But you must have known I'd have liked to read them?' Viv exploded. 'How could you get rid of them, Mam? If you love someone . . .'

'I once had a romantic little soul like you,' interrupted Hilda. 'But love doesn't always last for ever, Viv.'

'Then why do you always say that it hurts to talk about him? Sometimes I think you're playing some kind of game with me, Mother,' she lashed out in her disappointment. 'What the hell did you do with them?'

'I burnt them,' said Hilda coldly. 'I didn't want the binmen reading them. They were private. Besides, they were full of holes where bits had been cut out for security reasons.'

'They couldn't have been that private then,' responded Viv.

Hilda dropped her eyes. Taking a chocolate, she dipped it into her drink. 'He mentioned about my having a baby. I'd told him I was expecting.' She sucked melting chocolate from her fingers. 'He wasn't particularly pleased. There was his uncle, you see. He was very fond of Jimmy and thought him the bee's knees. Old-fashioned he was, and Jimmy knew that he wouldn't be pleased with such news. He told me to keep quiet about him being the father until he got home.' She sighed heavily. 'That was when I started wondering about eternal love. Of course, he never came home.'

Viv stared at her. Was this the truth at last? It would make some sense of her mother once having said that her father was no good. 'Honestly, Mam?' she said softly.

'Honest injun.' She wriggled slightly in her seat. 'It wasn't easy to accept, especially when your grandfather shook me till me teeth rattled because I wouldn't tell him who the father was.'

127

Viv smiled. 'You don't know how good this news makes me feel. I'm glad you came home after all. Do you remember what he wrote?'

'There were lots of "sweethearts" and "love you forevers" in most of the letters.' Hilda beamed at her. 'Once he got over the shock he wanted to marry me, of course. He didn't plan on casting me off like an old boot.'

'You wouldn't let him, would you, Mam? If nothing else you go after what you want. I'm glad you're like that.'

'You're like that too,' said Hilda, sighing slightly. 'That's what worries me sometimes. But as long as you feel better about it all now.'

'I do,' said Viv, sitting down. 'And I understand why you were so reluctant to talk about those times . . . but there must have been others when you were happy?'

'Of course there were.' Hilda shrugged her shoulders. 'But thinking of them makes me sad sometimes too.'

There was a silence, a long one, while each thought their own thoughts. It was on the tip of Viv's tongue to tell her mother about Stephen then but before she could her mother spoke.

'Dom didn't make a pass at you the other week, did he?'

Viv could barely believe her ears. 'Don't you trust him?'

Hilda laughed derisively. 'Do me a favour, Viv! He's cheating on his wife!'

'But he's been doing that since the first day! Could it be that you're starting to see sense, Mam?'

'I don't know about that,' said Hilda. 'He's an attractive man and you don't know what he has to put up with from that po-faced cow next-door.'

'So she's po-faced! But that's not her fault. She was born like that if you ask me. You were lucky, Mam, you came into the world beautiful, I bet.'

Her mother stared at her and smiled. 'What's this? The best softsoap?'

Viv grinned. 'Why not? you once told me I looked bewitching in a bonnet.'

'Aye. Me and our Flo had good-looking children.' Hilda hesitated then said, 'That time with George – if I hadn't come in, would you have let him make love to you?'

The grin faded from Viv's face. 'What's that got to do with the here and now? I don't get you, Mam.' She struggled to hold on to the warm feelings for her mother that she had had such a short moment ago but memories of the day of Hilda's return were suddenly with her. 'I told you, I'm a virgin! I'm saving myself for marriage.'

'Easier said than done,' muttered Hilda.

'I know that,' snapped Viv, remembering her last date with Nick.

'If Nick Bryce is anything like his mother then you've had it,' said Hilda.

The warm feelings vanished in a rush of anger. 'You won't leave his past alone will you? Why bring his mother into this? At least she's a reformed character which is more than can be said of you!'

Hilda's eyes flashed. 'Don't compare me with his mother. When I think that you want to marry her son it makes me feel sick!'

'Be sick, I don't care,' retorted Viv. 'I'll marry who I like and you won't stop me.'

'Oh, no?' said Hilda, biting into another chocolate. 'I'd do it for your own good, Viv,' she mumbled.

Viv leaned over her mother, resting a hand on the arm of the sofa, and said in a low voice. 'Mam, if you try and spoil things for me with Nick, I'll never forgive you.'

'Never is a long time,' said her mother, swallowing the chocolate and sitting upright. 'Have you met his mother?'

'Not yet but . . .'

'Then I don't know how you can compare me with her. I suppose you think you love Nick?'

'What's love?' said Viv in a mocking voice. 'According to you, the kind we read about in books and see in some marriages doesn't exist. All I know is that I believe if you love someone you don't set out deliberately to hurt their feelings. You consider them. You want the best for them and don't treat them like dirt.' She straightened.

Hilda's throat moved. 'You've got it bad, honey. If only it was as easy as that. But what if anybody comes between you? What then?' she said seriously.

Viv's senses were suddenly alert. There was something

129

here! 'Did someone do that at some time to you and Jimmy?' she said, thinking wildly of what Stephen had said about her mother. 'I believe you went out with Uncle Tom at one time. Did he try and come between you?'

Hilda went white. 'This is getting too personal!' Her voice was terse. 'Let's forget it all. Tell me about the film you saw. Do you think me and Doris would enjoy it?'

Viv hesitated. 'Mam, don't change the subject.'

'Enough!' Hilda got to her feet. 'Not another word will I say. The past is the past and is better left behind. What about that film?'

'You'll have a laugh,' said Viv slowly.

'Good! I need one,' muttered Hilda, and walked out of the room.

Chapter Twelve

'Viv!'

'Nick! You're back.' Her face lit up as he walked towards her from where he had been waiting on the corner of the street. It was a fine evening and children were playing out. It was top and whip time and several fancily chalked tops were whizzing along the street.

'I wanted to stop you before you reached home,' he said, smiling. 'I'm not in the frame of mind to put up with your mother.'

'Don't blame you. She's been in a right mood lately and getting worse by the minute. How was the conference?' Viv slipped a hand through his arm and hugged it tightly.

'Good. It stressed particularly that architects are no longer here for the favoured few who can afford follies and a couple of hundred bedrooms. We're in the business of providing what ordinary people need and want.'

'They surely can't want Creswell Mount or Everton Heights on St George's Hill?'

Nick smiled slightly. 'You get a fantastic view.'

'I hate heights.' She sighed. 'Probably because George made me climb a tree once and I got stuck.'

His smile faded. 'Have you heard from George?'

'Not since Christmas. I wish he would write more often. I worry about him.'

'George can look after himself,' said Nick grimly. 'I wouldn't be worrying about him.'

She frowned. 'Don't you worry about your family?'

'Sometimes. But . . .' He shrugged. 'OK. It's natural for

you to be concerned about George, but let's forget him for now. What's upset your mam that she's in a mood?'

'I said your mam was a reformed character, unlike her. Not the way to win her round to looking on you with more favour!' She pulled a face. 'She said something that made me think, though, Nick.'

His eyebrows shot up. 'And what's that?'

'I haven't met your mother or any of your family. Don't you think it's time I did or am I being presumptuous?'

'No.' He hesitated. 'It's just that I thought you weren't in any hurry to meet them.'

'For heavens sake, why not?' She stared at him in astonishment.

'Truth, Viv?' he said lightly. 'You haven't showed much interest.'

'Oh, heck.' She bit her lower lip. 'Sorry about that. I've been so wrapped up in my own affairs lately.'

He squeezed her hand against his side and smiled. 'And we haven't seen much of each other, which is my fault. Things aren't going to get any easier either. There's a competition coming up and I want to enter a design. It'll take most of my evenings.' He took a deep breath. 'If I win . . .'

'If you win?' she said softly.

'It would help me up the ladder.'

'Great!'

'I haven't won yet,' he said with a shrug. 'The competition's pretty hefty.'

'But you'll give it a damn' good try,' she said.

'Too right I will! It could make things happen so much quicker.'

They came to the main road.

'Where are we going?' asked Viv.

'You wanted to meet my family.' His eyes twinkled down into hers and she caught her breath. She really did love him. 'So I thought, why not now?'

'Like this?' She laughed, glancing down at the hand crocheted jumper she wore with a flared cotton skirt. 'I'm a mess!'

'You're a beautiful mess, Love.'

'To you, yes!' she said. 'But your mother and sister won't

think so. I wanted to look my best when I faced them.'

'You look fabulous,' he said. 'Honestly, Viv. Besides, if you're too dolled up they'll wonder why. They're just family, not royalty.'

'I should have gone home first,' she said mournfully.

'That would have meant me hanging round. And would you have told your mother you were going to meet mine?'

'I told you, she's in favour of me meeting your mother.'

'I bet it's so that she can say she's worn better,' said Nick dryly. 'They were always catty to each other.'

'Great! I don't stand a chance with your mother rightaway.'

'Neither did I with yours.'

'We're like Romeo and Juliet!' said Viv dramatically, putting a hand to her chest and striking a pose.

'Hardly,' said Nick, bringing her back to his side. 'You're not going to back out, are you?'

She tilted her chin. 'Of course not. If you can put up with my mother, I can put up with yours. She'll just have to take me as I am.'

'Just as you am will be fine,' he said, kissing the tip of her nose then her mouth and silencing her.

Viv gazed at the house. It was of red brick and had three storeys – much bigger than she had imagined. There was a gabled window in the slated roof and it had a large bay window on the ground floor where an aspidistra flourished. The net curtains were pristine white. Does she use Daz or Omo? wondered Viv inconsequently.

'Have you told your mother anything about me, Nick?'

'She knows who you are.'

'Perhaps I should wear a disguise?' she murmured.

'It wouldn't make any difference if you were dressed as the Queen of Sheba,' he murmured. 'She'd complain about any girl.'

The door opened and the bulky figure of a woman appeared. She carried a coat over her arm and her thickly lipsticked mouth was set in an uncompromising line. 'So this is her, is it?' she said, folding her arms across her massive bosom. 'I had a feeling I'd be meeting her soon.'

Viv squared her shoulders as if preparing for battle as she

surveyed the matronly figure in front of her dressed in a navy blue and white frock. The obviously dyed jet black hair was done in sausage-like curls and she suddenly remembered how Mrs Bryce's head had appeared to be permanently in metal curlers and swathed in a turban when she lived next-door to Aunt Flora. She held out a hand. 'How do you do, Mrs Bryce? I remember you well.' Immediately she realised that it was the wrong thing to say. Nick's mother turned brick red.

'Aye, well, I remember your mother too. A right flibbertigibbet she was!'

Viv's mouth half opened but Nick got in before her, 'Well, now we've got the pleasantries out of the way, Ma, perhaps we can come in?'

'You can do what you like,' said Lena Bryce, unsmiling. 'I'm going to work.' She nodded in Viv's direction. 'I suppose I'll be seeing you again?'

Viv smiled sweetly. 'You suppose right. And I can't wait for that pleasure.'

Lena cast her a dark look before brushing past them and treading heavily down the steps. She was soon out of sight.

'Nice friendly woman, your mother,' said Viv in a bright voice.

'You don't have to see a lot of each other.' Nick squeezed her hand and led her into the house and up the lobby. Their feet made little sound on the carpet runner which ran up the middle of the green and brown linoleum which was bordered by several aspidistras in brass pots. Ultra respectability, thought Viv counting them. There were six. Nick pushed open a door on the right at the far end and they entered a room lit by the evening sunlight.

A girl looked up from a magazine. Her hair was white-blonde and she had deep dimples in a chubby face. She was wearing Black Watch tartan trews and a green sweater. One hand lifted languidly and she gave Viv a long stare. 'So you're the girlfriend? Welcome to the madhouse.'

'Thanks,' said Viv, smiling. 'It can't be any madder than ours.

'You want to bet?' said the girl.

'This is my half-sister Ingrid,' said Nick. 'Only believe half she says, Viv.'

134

'Nice to meet you.' Viv nodded in her direction.

Ingrid grinned. 'She's not bad, Nick. Your luck must have changed.'

'Don't be cheeky.' He pulled her hair. 'Viv, your mam wasn't the only one who liked movie stars.'

Ingrid pulled down the corners of her mouth. 'Ma *loved* Ingrid Bergman. Says she was a real lady.'

Viv thought, Of course, Mrs Bryce would know the difference.

'Would you like a cup of tea?' asked Ingrid.

'That would be a good idea,' said Nick, putting an arm round Viv and bringing her against him.

Ingrid dropped her magazine on the floor and uncurling herself, said, 'Has he asked you to marry him yet?'

Viv shot a look at Nick. 'Not in so many words,' he said.

'I'm in no hurry,' murmured Viv.

'Why not?' said Ingrid, showing surprise. 'You'd be a fool to let him get away.'

'I don't think he's ready to be hooked yet.'

Ingrid grinned. 'She's got a sense of humour, Nick. Grab her. Mam won't like it, of course, but all the better. She's had enough out of you as it is. I don't know how you put up with it.'

'You know why I put up with it,' he said, and indicated the door with his head. 'Now make that cup of tea. 'Where's our Kenny?'

'He's in the yard, playing with those horrible frogs and newts of his.' She left the room.

'Come and meet my brother,' said Nick, and they went out into the yard.

A boy of about ten was ankle-deep in water in an old tin bath. He had Nick's dark hair and his eyes were blue as he glanced up at them. 'I think I've lost one of me frogs,' he said.

'I'm not surprised, the way they hop all over the place,' said Nick, squatting on his haunches. 'How are the tadpoles?'

'Some have got weeny legs,' said Kenny, gazing at the swimming blobs with pride.

Viv, trying to put to the back of her mind the mention made of marriage, was warmed by the sight of the two brothers together. Nick really seemed to care about Kenny. He would

135

make a good father. She crouched by the bath and looked inside at the rocks and weed and small amphibians half submerged in the water. 'You've got your own little nature reserve.'

'Do you like frogs?' Kenny's voice was eager. 'You can hold one if you like?'

Viv smiled at him. 'I'd like that.'

As she held out the palm of her hand to receive the frog, he said, 'We've got a budgie as well but Mam says she'd like to throttle it.'

'She doesn't mean it,' said Nick as Viv stared at him. 'It bit her once.'

Sensible bird, thought Viv, touching the frog's back. It immediately took off into the water. 'My mother curses our cat,' she said to Kenny, thinking how nice it would be to have a younger brother. 'She says it's getting too fat on cat food when it should be exercising catching mice. The thing is, there aren't the mice around that there used to be.'

'There aren't a lot of things around that there used to be.' Nick took her hand and pulled her away. 'Will you marry me, Viv?' he said softly.

'What?' Her face flooded with colour. 'Is it because of what Ingrid said?'

'Partly. But you must know I'm mad about you.'

She smiled. 'I'm mad about you, too. But it's a funny word to use in connection with love, isn't it? It's like saying you lose your senses when you fall in love.'

'You do love me then?' He dragged her further away from his brother.

'Didn't I as good as say so? But let's try and be sensible. We can't rush into anything.'

'Of course not,' he said blandly. 'We'll be very sensible and save up.'

'I mean it, Nick. I'd like us to have a house before we get married.'

'Naturally. I'll design us one.'

Her face glowed as she gazed up at him. 'That would be great. I am sounding sensible, aren't I? Mam would be proud of me. She thinks I've got a romantic little soul.'

'And have you?' he said, pulling her close.

Viv sighed heavily. 'What do you think?'

Nick laughed and swung her off her feet to whirl her round and round. 'Some enchanted evening,' he sang, before kissing her in mid air.

It was Ingrid calling that caused them to draw apart. 'Stop snogging, you two, or the tea'll get cold!'

'Come on,' said Nick, and under his breath added, 'Don't say anything.'

'I won't, I won't,' she whispered, having to run as he pulled her up the yard.

'I was going to take you out tonight,' said Nick as they bit into the cheese sandwiches that Ingrid had made.

'Where to?'

'I had thought of The Cavern.'

'Fine by me.' She would have been quite happy curled up in a cardboard box with him. 'Who's on?'

'Gin Mill. They sing folk as well as play skiffle.'

'Great!' She had no idea who they were but it did not matter as long as she and Nick were together.

The Cavern was fairly crowded but that meant they could cuddle closer and Viv thought dreamily that she would always remember the music that was played that evening, even though most of it did not go down particularly well with the younger crowd. 'John Peel' smacked too much of school music lessons even though the group had jazzed it up.

'It was a good rousing song,' said Nick, kissing the side of Viv's face as they came out into Mathew Street afterwards, discussing it. 'I remember it well. And "The Skye Boat Song".'

'We learnt "Who is Sylvia?" at school,' said Viv, her eyes sparkling. 'I still don't know who she is!'

He laughed, kissed her, and she wanted to bury herself in him. They walked on, very close together, and she was aware of the tug of sexuality between them. Control, that was what they had to have. She did not want her mother going on about that Nick Bryce ruining her daughter. She sought for something to take her mind off thoughts of sex. 'Dot's brother Norm is in a group. They just ape hit records.'

Nick glanced down at her. 'Wasn't he the one who danced with you at the party?'

'Yes. But it didn't mean anything. If we've nothing else to do Dot and I go and support the group wherever they're playing. We're getting to know the inside of that many church halls that Dot says her mother thinks we've caught religion.' She looked up at him with a teasing expression. 'Jealous?'

'Of course. I'd be jealous of any man that you spent time with instead of me.' His voice was controlled.

'There's no need. It's you I love, Nick. But we can't live in each other's pockets.'

'I know that,' he whispered, touching her cheek with an unsteady hand. 'You can't know how much I need your love, Viv. You're like no other girl I've ever met. You understand why I am the way I am and accept it.'

'And you understand me. So don't you go fancying any other girls.' She held up her face to be kissed.

They drew apart at last and he glanced at his watch and exclaimed, 'Hell! I'd better get you home! Your mam will be wondering what's happened to you.'

'She'd be having a blue fit if she knew I was with you!' Viv grimaced.

'You're not going to tell her anything yet?'

'No. I'll say I went straight to the pictures with Dot. The way she's been lately she might explode. I'll give it a couple of weeks and then see how she is.'

'And we'll see each other Sunday. I'll meet you at the Pierhead. Bring a picnic and we'll cross the river.'

Viv agreed to do just that.

It was not until she was in bed after a row with her mother over not telling her that she was going out straight from work that Viv realised she had not told Nick about Stephen. How would he react? He had not been in favour of her getting in touch with her uncle.

Jealousy was an awful thing. She thought of his face when he had spoken of George. For people with so much going for them she and Nick still possessed that awful sense of inadequacy that had dogged them both since childhood. How to get rid of it? It was a pity that George and Nick did not like each other. She wished they could because she loved them both. If wishes could come true, she would wish . . . would wish . . . A yawn escaped her.

I would wish that Nick and my mother would like each other. And Stephen and Nick. She was visiting her uncle's house on Saturday to tell him about the letters. She yawned again. She wished he would still like her, even though there were no letters, and would accept her as his niece. She wished that everything would turn out right. She fell asleep.

Chapter Thirteen

Viv stood outside the black-painted wrought iron gate of Stephen's house. She remembered her last visit as a little girl and how she had asked could the larger bedroom overlooking the back garden be hers? Stephen had said, 'No, it's for the boy.' Despite the boy being George and then clashing, no doubt because her cousin had resented Stephen trying to monopolise his mother. Jealousy again. Determined each to be top dog with Aunt Flora.

Unexpectedly Viv found herself remembering how as a boy George had chivvied her and his sister Rosie into dressing up in a couple of their mothers' old frocks, it being the only way they could have long dresses. They kept falling over the hems when they led the May procession of children from the street in their various versions of fancy dress. George had bullied them all the way to Lime Street, rattling an empty bean can to collect money. He had not bothered dressing up, of course! But it had been worth getting bossed around after all. They raised ten shillings and tuppence which had bought them ice creams and bottles of Full Swing lemonade. She smiled at the memory, opened the gate and walked up the path.

Stephen gazed at Viv across the oval table with its lace cloth and stainless steel cutlery. 'So there's no proof of your being Jimmy's daughter?'

'No.' Viv sipped her glass of sherry. 'I'm sorry. It seems mam must have destroyed the letters after you called. When she gets into a temper she goes a bit wild.'

'You don't have to tell me that!' Stephen cleared his throat.

'Does it make that much difference, Uncle Steve?' she said seriously. 'I so wanted to bring you some proof but Mam did say that Jimmy wasn't pleased at first about the baby because of your uncle.'

'Now that sounds real,' he said in a satisfied voice. 'My uncle would have gone bananas. Jimmy was his favourite. He wanted him to take over the business.' He smiled at her. 'I suppose gut feelings are more important than proof and I wouldn't have recognised Jimmy's handwriting if you'd brought the letters, anyway. My mother and sister used to write to me until they were killed but Jimmy and I seldom exchanged news. We did it through them.'

'I'm glad you feel like that. You don't know how I've missed having a male member of the family around,' said Viv, touching his hand, and gazing up at him. 'Have you any photographs of your family?' She thought saying 'family' was more tactful than saying Jimmy because of Stephen's feelings about his brother.

'I thought you might ask that.' He rose and took an album from a sideboard cupboard.

Viv grasped the book with impatient fingers and opened it. There were photographs of a woman who bore a strong resemblance to Stephen and then others of two girls who did not look a bit like each other. She turned a page and unexpectedly found her mother's youthful face staring up at her. It was almost like seeing herself and was quite a shock. Hurriedly she turned her attention to the three young men who were also in the snapshot. Two of them had a definite look of each other and she guessed that they were Stephen and Jimmy. Her father was certainly good-looking and there was a cockiness about the way he held his head. Plenty of confidence, by the look of it. 'How old was he when this was taken?' she asked.

'Eighteen.'

'You have a look of each other.'

'You think so?' Stephen scrutinised the photograph, lifting the album close to his face. 'Family likenesses are often in the expression, not in the colour of hair or eyes. Hard to believe now that was me.' He pointed a finger at the third young man. 'That's your Uncle Tom who broke my nose. He hit me with a

141

cricket bat because I was scoring more runs than him.'

'Could that be why you took against George?' The words were out before she could recall them.

'You noticed that, as young as you were?' He placed the album on the table and stared at her from thoughtful eyes. She wondered whether he was thinking about her Aunt Flora. 'I suppose that was part of the reason,' he said slowly. 'Where is George now?'

She told him.

'Best thing for him,' he said briskly. 'It'll make a man of him, fending for himself. Fancied his chances – just like his father, always liked the girls competing for his favours.'

Viv considered it wisest to keep quiet. Why did men always have to see each other as competitors in a game? She gazed down at the young faces again and tried to imagine what her life would have been like if Jimmy had lived. It was difficult to picture her mother behaving like an ordinary housewife. She had been even moodier than ever this morning and had not been pleased when Viv told her that she was going out that afternoon and would be out on Sunday too with Nick.

'I don't know why I bothered coming home from America,' Hilda had said tartly. 'We never do the things mothers and daughters do.' So Viv had suggested they went shopping together that morning. It had not been an overwhelming success as her mother had been brutally critical of Viv's choice in clothes and it had taken her all her time to keep her own opinions on her mother's taste to herself.

Stephen began to talk about work and Viv forced herself to concentrate, determined to prove to him that she would make a success of the job. He explained to her about ink and paper suppliers, about customers , and the different types of printing jobs. Her first task, though, would be to chase up the bad debtors. He had been waiting ten months for money from one customer and was just about ready to strangle him.

He fell silent at last and asked her whether she would like to listen to some music. She said yes but was not prepared for the blast of Beethoven that filled the room. He waved her to a studio couch and sat on a fireside chair after filling her sherry glass and pouring himself a whisky. Eyes half closed she watched his hands moving slightly in time to the music and thought how different it had been on Wednesday with Nick and on Thursday with Dot and Norm. Would this be how it would have been if Stephen had been her father? She supposed that in fact she would have had less to do with him. Dot said she seldom did anything with her father. Viv drank her sherry and dozed off, dreaming that she was by a stream, lying in the grass with Nick. As the music came to an end she stirred.

'I'm afraid it's not been very exciting for you,' said Stephen apologetically.

'I enjoyed it,' she said instantly, not wanting to hurt his feelings. 'It's just that I was tired.' She yawned delicately. 'I don't know much about classical music, I'm ashamed to say.'

'I suppose rock'n'roll is more your kind of thing,' he said gruffly. 'Perhaps you like comedy or a good play? We could go to the theatre sometimes. Do you like animals? I've never been to Chester zoo and it's said to be a good one. I know so little about your tastes.'

'I've never been to the zoo either,' said Viv, getting to her feet. 'My father and mother weren't around to take me. But I'd enjoy going with you,' she said with a twinkle.

'We'll go next Sunday then,' he said, looking pleased and fetching her jacket for her. 'But I'll see you before then. I'll see you at work.'

'Yes.' She slipped her arms into the sleeves, glad that he had not suggested this Sunday. She turned and kissed his cheek. 'Thank you for letting me see the photographs, and for the tea and the music and everything.'

'It's a pleasure, Viv. Perhaps you'd like one of the photographs?'

'I'd love one,' she said sincerely.

He gave her the one with her mother, Jimmy, himself and her Uncle Tom. She slid it into her handbag. Then he patted her shoulder and saw her out.

As Viv walked home, she knew that already her relationship with Stephen had moved further on and that he was eager to make her part of his life. It was something she wanted very much, too. In her mind he was already taking on the role of the father she had never had. She would tell Nick about him

143

giving her a job tomorrow but maybe it might be sensible if she did not tell him yet about visiting Stephen's house? Men could get such funny ideas about things and she did not want anything to come between her and Nick right now.

Chapter Fourteen

West Kirkby had once been a small fishing village situated at the mouth of the beautiful Dee estuary but now it was a large residential town which Nick and Viv had reached by ferry and bus.

'What d'you think of walking to one of the Hilbre Islands?' asked Nick, his eyes narrowing against the sun as he looked towards the crowded beach.

Vivien stared across the expanse of sand that the outgoing tide had left exposed. Somewhere far out on that expanse were three tiny islands that one could visit when the tide was out. On the far side of the estuary were the green hills of Wales.

'There and back before the tide comes in?' she murmured. 'We could get stranded. Do you fancy sitting on a lump of sandstone and grass with just a couple of thousand birds for company until the tide goes out again?'

'We could do more than sit,' he said, straight-faced.

'We don't have to walk far to do that.' She shook her head at him, a smile curving her lips. 'And I hate walking on sand.'

'Pity,' he said mournfully. 'Shall we go up on the moors then and walk to Mariner's Beacon?'

'If you like? Are you sure you don't want to look over the church?' she teased. 'I believe it's Norman.'

'No buildings,' he stressed, putting his arm round her. 'I just want to be alone with you. Let's to the hills!'

Only the lightest flurry of a breeze stirred the leaves of bushes and trees and soon they were hot from climbing. As they got higher the hillside, which was thick with gorse and

145

heather, gave off a somnolent sound caused by the humming of bees and insects. It seemed devoid of human life, a different world to the busy town which lay far below them. It was good to get away from people thought Viv. Away from her mother and everybody else and to be alone with Nick.

They came to the Beacon which was a tall stone column surmounted by a large ball. A windmill had originally occupied the site and had been a valuable landmark for sailors. Nick walked round it clockwise, while Viv went the other way. When they came face to face she clung to him. 'I didn't realise it would be so high!'

'You're not really scared?' he said.

'I'm not really scared,' she repeated, but wrapped both her arms round him.

He sang against her mouth, 'If you were the only girl in the world . . .'

'What would you do?'

'I'd make love to you right here.'

'But we're not married, she said. 'We can't be doing that.'

'Were Adam and Eve married?' Nick drew back a little and said seriously, 'Have you ever thought who instituted marriage?'

'I've always believed it was God.'

'Probably something to do with Him but did he make the rules or were they manmade.'

'You need rules,' said Viv firmly. 'For people's protection. Especially for children.'

'I agree, of course. Although I do believe, as you can guess, that some people should never have married. We'd both still be here.' He hugged her to him. 'Don't you think this is the perfect place and the perfect spot. It's like a little Eden.'

'We're not Adam and Eve.'

There was silence and for several seconds, with her cheek against his chest, Viv listened to Nick's heartbeat. It seemed louder than the birdsong all around them. Alive. Vital. Beating with the same urgency as her own.

'It's bloody difficult, isn't it, Viv?' He laughed harshly. 'If I could only win that award for my design! Then I'd feel better able to cope with all this.'

'With all what?' she said softly.

146

'Lust. I lust after you, Viv.' The passion in his voice seared her to the soul. 'I want your body.'

'Just my body? Thanks very much,' she said lightly. 'What about the rest of me? Is that all I am to you after all these months? A body worth having? Aren't I worth waiting for?'

'I don't know how you can ask me that,' he said, his eyes glinting. His hold slackened and he drew away from her again. 'A few days ago I asked you to marry me and told you that I loved you.'

'You've just talked of lust.'

'How do you separate love from lust? Your body is part of you and I want to be joined to it. For us to be one, Viv, now.'

There was a silence and she could feel her heart pounding. She freed herself and said, slightly breathless, 'I need to think and I can't do that when you're holding me.'

'So you feel something? A madness in the blood. It's summer beginning to burst all around us. Nature's going crazy.'

She made no answer but began to walk along the ridge, not caring that she scratched her arm on the yellow flowering gorse. She was as much aware as him of the effect the beauties of nature had on her senses.

He caught up with her and pulled her close, his hand passing over her hair which was loose about her shoulders and held back by an Alice band. 'Could you live happily ever after without me, Viv?'

'Don't ask daft questions. You know I couldn't.'

'Good.' His arms went around her and his mouth searched for hers.

It would have been impossible for her not to respond to his kisses, but the self-restraint she had always enforced on herself in his company was still in force. But how easy it would be just to slacken it and allow herself to surrender to the sensations that his touch aroused! They stretched out in the tall grass and the sun was warm on her skin as he buried his face against her neck. He slid the straps of her sun dress and bra from her shoulders and tickled her throat with his tongue before licking a wide swathe down to her breasts.

'You aren't going to eat me?' Viv's voice was barely audi-

147

ble, affected as she was by the sensations snaking down into the pit of her stomach.

'Fe-fo-fi-fum, I smell the blood of a damsel in distress,' he whispered.

'You're not going to get carried away by lust, are you, Nick?' The sun was painting patterns against her eyelids, orange and purple and black. She felt drunk on the scent of flowers and grass, and really terribly languid. His tongue drew circles on her stomach. She thought of butterflies fluttering above flowers, was aware of the hypnotic buzz of bees as they dived into buttercups and clover. Dive, dive, dive, she thought, into the heart of me. She felt as if she was expanding. A rose unfurling its dewy petals to the sun.

He stroked her thigh and she found herself reaching out for him, undoing the buttons of his shirt. As their lips met she rubbed her body against his in a gesture that was as old as time. He undid some buttons of his own and immediately she stiffened. She gazed up into his eyes, feeling her heart thudding against her ribs, and knew that she should protest. But all she could think of were the words: 'The lady dost protest too much, methinks.' So she just kept looking at him.

The next moment he had turned them both over so that she was uppermost. They both laughed. 'You're crazy, Nick. What do you think I'm going to do from up here?'

The corner of his mouth twitched. 'Take me! I'm yours.'

'Very funny. I'm not going to do that!'

'Aren't you curious about what it's like?'

'Of course I am but . . .'

'But what?'

'Someone could come up here.'

His eyes gleamed. 'If that's all you're worried about, I don't know what's stopping you. Nobody would see us, their eyes would be on the view.' He caressed her bare shoulder. 'Besides, this grass is good cover.'

'You've got all the answers, haven't you?'

Nick leaned up and kissed her breast. 'I love you,' he said.

Viv stilled, feeling unexpected tears in her throat. 'You're just saying that to get round me,' she said firmly. 'I'm not daft, you know.'

148

'Throw my love in my face then! But that doesn't mean it's not true.'

'Nick,' she said, touched again, 'don't say that. I'd never do that.' He kissed her and she found herself fighting an overwhelming urge to press down on him as his mouth started to move over her throat and her breasts. Then he looked up at her and her mouth searched for his blindly and she pressed down on him, allowing the waves of sensation to wash over her. Dear God! she thought. How did you think of it being done like this? Did you know what it would feel like? There was pain in it but not so much that it prevented her from obeying the compelling urge deep inside her.

'Stop, Viv!' Nick's tones were so urgent that she instantly obeyed him but inwardly she trembled at the enforced restraint.

Her eyelids flickered open. 'What's wrong?' she whispered.

'I need the control now,' he said indistinctly and carefully rolled her over. 'Now go with me, slowly at first.'

She nodded but then found that it was very hard to obey him. She switched off her mind and was aware only of that physical desire urging her to drive herself to a goal she had no conception of but knew she had to reach or be swallowed up in the attempt. Slowly a mild sunspot of pleasure rippled through her and she heard Nick sigh. Then he was obeying the pressure of her hands on his spine.

Afterwards Viv lay lazily stroking his bare chest. 'You made me do it,' she murmured. 'I didn't want to do it. I didn't want to do it. But you made me . . .'

He took her hand and kissed her fingers. 'Now you know why the birds do it, and bees.'

'Don't tell me about fleas,' she said. 'I can't imagine fleas doing it, even educated ones.'

'No fleas.' He smiled down at her. 'The right person, the right mood, the right place, Viv.'

She nodded. 'And now what? Do we just go on to have our picnic as if nothing had happened?'

'In a minute. If you get pregnant . . .' said Nick.

Her fingers tightened about his. 'After all I've said to my mother about sinning! Now I'm as bad as her. We should have waited, Nick.'

149

He frowned. 'I hate that word "sinning". Forget about whether it's wrong or right for the moment. I just want to say if you do get pregnant, I'll find us a flat. We'll get married immediately and take our chances on it working out.'

She sat up abruptly. 'Thank you, kind sir, but isn't that what happened with your mother and father? And I don't know if I like the way you doubt it will work out! If we love each other, really love each other, it will work.'

His frown disappeared. 'Of course it will. How stupid of me!'

'Yes. How stupid!' She wrapped her arms around her raised knees. 'We shouldn't have taken such a chance. It was a bit like Russian roulette. I won't be having another shot at it, Nick, until we're married.'

'We could take precautions.'

Her eyebrows lifted. 'I've heard about those things. They're not always one hundred percent safe.'

He smiled. 'Russian roulette, Viv.'

'You might be to good a shot, Nick,' she said quietly, shaking her head and reaching for the bag that contained the sandwiches. 'It's a game I don't think I want to play.'

'Let's wait and see.'

She was silent but had already made up her mind. If her mother guessed what she had done she would be convinced that she'd been right about Nick all along. Viv was suddenly uneasy. Her mother couldn't be right, could she?

Nick smiled at her and she thought, No. Then she began to hope and pray that she had not got herself pregnant in one careless afternoon.

Chapter Fifteen

'He's asked her to marry him.'

'What?' Dominic spluttered into his glass of beer.

'You heard me!' Hilda scowled at her gin and tonic. 'She hasn't said anything, of course, but something's happened. On Sunday she came in and there was a look on her face . . . Love's young dream!' She tapped a scarlet-painted fingernail against her teeth. 'She glowed. It was as if there was a lamp lit under her skin. I hope they haven't done anything.'

Dominic sighed. 'Well, you can't blame him, can you? She's a peach, is your Viv, and they have been going out with each other for a while.'

Hilda stared at him then kicked his shins under the table. He winced and glanced about the half empty lounge of the Gregson's Well pub to see if anyone had noticed.

'That's my daughter you're talking about,' she muttered. 'And I'm not having Nick Bryce messing her about. Thinks just because he knows things he can get away with doing what he likes. He's as bad as his mother.'

Dominic refrained from saying that some might say Viv was as bad as her mother but he need not have bothered, Hilda said it for him. 'I know I'm no Miss Pears. But I was looking forward to a white wedding for Viv with all the trimmings. I have my outfit planned.'

Dominic grinned. 'Who was she going to marry?'

'Some rich bloke. It can be done.' She nodded her head several times. 'I managed it twice. It could have been three times if I'd played my cards right but Stephen wasn't buying.'

'So that's what it was?'

151

'What what was?' She stared at him.

'You had your eye on him but he preferred Viv.'

'Did I say that?' Her voice was steely.

'Not in so many words. But he wanted her to visit him, not you.' There was a certain satisfaction in his tone. Sometimes Hilda's attitude was hurtful and on occasions he had felt that she was just using him without understanding just how much he had to lose by seeing her.

'Well, he didn't get what he wanted, did he?' she said, her eyes glinting.

'Didn't he?' Dominic drained his glass and stood up. 'D'you want another?'

'Yes. But – wait a minute. What do you mean: "Didn't he?"' She looked up at him. 'He hasn't been around again while I've been out, has he?' Her tone was suspicious.

Dominic had second thoughts about what he was going to say and vanished quickly in the direction of the bar.

When he came back Hilda grabbed hold of his sleeve. 'Now let's be having it, Dom. You haven't told our Viv that Stephen came looking for her, have you?' She fixed him with a rapier sharp stare.

'It sort of slipped out,' he muttered. 'It was when she was off sick and you went into town to buy a sofa.'

'That's a couple of weeks ago and she hasn't mentioned a word.' Her heart suddenly felt like stone inside her. 'You'll regret this, Dominic Kelly,' she said harshly. 'I trusted you to keep quiet.'

'So did she,' he muttered in resigned tones. 'Poor kid. What are you going to do?'

'Poor kid? Poor kid!' Her voice rose. 'She didn't swear you to secrecy, did she?'

He was silent.

Hilda downed both glasses of gin and tonic and said, 'We're finished, Dom.' She picked up her handbag and walked out.

It was when she was halfway home that she decided what she was going to do and retraced some of her journey to catch a different bus.

The wind tugged at Hilda's silk scarf as she stared up at Stephen's pebble-dashed semi with its leaded windows. It was one of those cold days that sometimes come in summer and she huddled inside her fur coat.

Not bad, she thought, but he could afford better. No wonder our Viv wanted to keep me away. What has she been up to? I bet she's visited him here more than once. Perhaps it's him she's been with and not Nick. She felt a burst of anger. It isn't right! A man of his age and a young girl. Viv needs protecting from herself and what Steve needs is a real woman to push him that little bit harder . . .

She thought of Viv out with Dot and was glad that she knew exactly where her daughter was because sometimes Viv had a temper to match her own. It would not do for them to come face to face on Stephen's doorstep. Not just yet. Without hesitating any further, Hilda walked up the step and rang the bell.

Stephen opened the door and did a doubletake. 'What the hell do you want?' he said, unsmiling.

Hilda threw back her head and laughed. 'No wonder you never won a sunshine badge – or our Flo's heart!'

He flushed. 'You're insulting. But you always did have a tongue sharp enough to cut yourself.'

She put a hand on his sleeve. 'I thought it was time we had a talk. My daughter's been visiting you, I believe? I don't know whether I like that. You're old enough to be her father. If you admitted to being her uncle, of course, it's possible I might feel different about her seeing you. Otherwise I think I might have to insist she has nothing further to do with you.'

'How did you find out?' he said quietly.

She looked him squarely in the face and smiled. 'You'd better ask me in and we'll talk about it.'

Stephen hesitated, then shrugged. 'I suppose you'd better come in. But don't think you're staying long.'

'What a gentleman you are, Steve.' As he stepped aside for her to enter she patted his cheek.

He grabbed her wrist, his eyes furious. 'Don't do that. I'm not your puppy dog.'

'Sorry.' She pressed against him so that his balance shifted and the front door banged against the wall as he was forced against it. Her lips touched his. 'So sorry.' It was a long time since she had played such games.

153

He dropped her wrist, pushed her into the house and slammed the door. 'You've been drinking.'

Hilda made no reply but walked up the hall and through the open doorway on the left. 'Nice,' she said, glancing about her as she pulled off her gloves. 'I like modern furniture. It's easier to clean around.' She slipped off her fur coat and held it out to him. He hesitated, then took it and hung it in the hall. She sat in the middle of the studio coach which was pulled up in front of a slumbering coal fire.

'Well?' Stephen stood to one side of the fireplace, scowling down at her.

'Well?' she responded with a glittering smile, smoothing down the tight black skirt before picking a non-existent thread from the swell of her breasts in a cream taffeta blouse. 'What have you to say for yourself? I hope you haven't been leading my little girl astray? She's got a romantic soul and sees you in the light of a fairy godfather. I hope you haven't disappointed her so far?'

'Why didn't you tell her I'd called?'

'I was angry. Don't you ever get angry when you've been rejected, Steve?' He remained silent, fiddling with the ear of a slender white porcelain cat on the mantleshelf.

'Who told you she was working for me?'

Her eyes narrowed. '*Working* for you! She's never said a word! I never thought she had it in her to be so sneaky.'

'She's not sneaky! I asked her not to tell you,' he said roughly. 'I didn't want you coming round here causing trouble.'

'Why should I cause trouble? What have you been up to?' Her tone was angry. 'She's pretty, isn't she, our Viv? does she ever remind you of our Flo?'

'No! She reminds me of you.' He looked away and removed the porcelain cat from the shelf with a violent movement.

'Don't break it,' cried Hilda, her heart leaping inside her with sudden surprise. So that was the way it was! She got up and took the cat from him. 'Me?' He made no answer. 'Guilt's a terrible thing, don't you think, Steve?' she said softly. 'Did you often wish them dead?'

'No!' His eyes glistened. She had not needed to cross ts or dot an i, he knew who she was talking about.

154

'Liar.' She stood so close to him now that her breath warmed his cheek and she could see how thickly his dark eyelashes curled. 'Did you put a curse on them?' she said in a mocking voice. 'Did you always want what Jimmy had because he wouldn't let you near it?' Still he remained silent. She goaded him a bit further. 'But he's not here now, is he, Steve? You can grab whatever you want if you only have the courage.'

'You're a bitch!' His voice was husky.

'You always knew that, but it didn't stop you fancying me.' She put a hand on his chest but he wrenched it away and, taking hold of her blouse by the shoulders, pulled it apart with a strength that shocked the life out of her. 'Steve, what are you doing?' she gasped. 'Take it easy, take it easy!' He dragged her against him and tore the button off her skirt. 'This skirt cost me a lot of money,' she cried. He ignored her words, pushing her on to the studio couch and dragging down the zip of her skirt. She tried to keep it up. 'Hang on, Steve. There's no need to behave like this.' He ignored her pleas, pinged her suspender button and rubbed her leg as he kissed her with an ardour that almost stopped her breathing.

He had utterly jolted her composure. Even so, she found it exciting. Dom had become just as predictable as Charlie. Always careful, always the same, never taking chances . . . not that she wanted to get pregnant. Now it was probably too late, even though she still had the odd period.

'Let's have a drink,' she whispered when Stephen lifted his mouth from hers.

'You've had enough to drink.' He nuzzled her throat, slid a hand between her breasts and down over her stomach. She began to tremble. It was so unexpected and the unscarred side of his face reminded her of Jimmy. Was this how it would have been if they had made love?

Stephen drew away and threw his trousers over the back of the couch. His underpants followed. She was shaking all over as without a word his body covered hers and slowly he entered her. Unexpectedly tears sprang into her eyes. She was thinking of when they were both young, remembering how he had stood on the sidelines watching her talking to Jimmy or Tom. Why hadn't she been kinder to him? Why had she always had to tease him unmercifully? Was it because she had known even then that of the three lads his intentions had always been good? Too good to think she was worth anything afterwards when everything went wrong. She only knew that now she felt sorry for the way she had treated him. Perhaps he sensed her feelings because suddenly he was being more considerate.

When it was over she was aware of him looking at her with an anxious expression. 'Did I hurt you?'

She shook her head and said huskily, 'Can I have a drink?'

'We'll both have a drink.' He went over to the cocktail cabinet and poured two whiskies. He topped hers up with ginger ale. 'I didn't mean for things to get out of hand but once I started I couldn't stop.'

She made no reply but sipped her drink. Eventually she said, 'I shouldn't accept your apology really . . . ripping my blouse off like that.' A smile curved her still beautiful mouth.

'I'm sorry. I'll buy you another.' He poured himself another whisky.

'Generous of you,' she said dryly, watching him drink and thinking, He's changed. Is that Viv's doing? She experienced a pang of jealousy. She needed to compose herself, to go to the toilet. 'Bathroom?'

'Upstairs.' He gazed at her in her underwear and she saw that the desire was still there and was suddenly thrilled because he wanted her.

She took her fur coat from the hook in the hall and put it on to go upstairs. It was a fully tiled bathroom with a good size bath. She used the toilet and then ran the hot tap, checking the temperature. She decided to have a bath.

She locked the door and gazed at herself in the mirror. 'He really fancies you, middle-aged and with all your faults,' she told her reflection, and pushed the thought of her daughter firmly aside. Her lips curved into a smile as she switched off the taps and slid into the Radoxed water.

When she came out of the bathroom, smelling of Old Spice talc and clad in just the fur coat, Stephen was sitting on the stairs with the bottle of whisky beside him. Its level had sunk a couple of inches. He glanced up at her. 'Can we go in the bedroom, please?' The words were slurred.

'How polite,' she said and held out her hand. He took it and she helped lever him to his feet. 'But a little less of the strong arm tactics if you don't mind, Steve.'

His dark brows drew together and he touched her arm again, stroking the fur. 'Nice. Soft.'

'You're the soft one,' she murmured, smiling. 'Now where's my drink?'

'In the bedroom,' he repeated, handing her the bottle. 'I've put glasses there.'

'Good lad.' Hand in hand, they entered the bedroom.

'Keep the coat on,' he whispered, rubbing the fur that curved over her breast as she poured them both a whisky.

'If that's what you want.' Hilda looked about her. Nice. New. She had seen something like that wardrobe in town. Sherry walnut shade, that's what it was, and it cost fifteen quid bar sixpence. The eiderdown was figured oyster satin and cool to the touch. He wanted her to lie on top of it and told her to take her coat off.

'Put it over us,' he whispered. 'Furry side down.'

'All right.' She swallowed a mouthful of whisky. 'Did you know there'd been a smash and grab in Bold Street a while ago? They stole three thousand pounds worth of furs. Imagine sleeping on that lot.'

'Comfy.' He took the whisky bottle and placed it on the floor and pulled her towards him. His head sank on to her breast and for quite a while nothing happened. Then he began to run his fingers up and down the fur covering her breasts. 'Mam always wanted a beaver lamb,' he said softly. 'What's this fur?'

'Mink.' Her voice was filled with pride. 'I bought it with some of the insurance money after my husband died. Feels lovely, doesn't it?'

'Lovely. I always wanted to buy Mam one.' His voice quivered. 'Did you know she died too?'

'Of course, silly. Sad for you.'

'And our Jimmy. But he had you to console him.' He frowned into her face, pushing back the peroxided hair. 'He often mentioned you but there were other women in his life. You were well rid of him, you know. You were well rid.' He kissed her mouth with a hunger that still made her want to

157

weep. She felt quite odd. She had guessed there might be depths to him but never suspected what was there. He kissed the soles of her feet and her bones felt as if they were melting. She let out a tiny squeal as he nuzzled where she did not expect. After that she stopped thinking altogether.

Later, after a cup of coffee, he saw her to the door. She smiled inwardly because as he handed over her fur coat he avoided looking straight at her. Was he ashamed now of what they had done? Probably. He had always been a very moral bloke. But she was not going to let him stop now.

'You won't tell Viv about any of this?' he said.

Hilda slid an arm into a sleeve and her eyes gleamed up at him. 'She wouldn't understand that at our time of life love can come round a second time.'

A slight laugh escaped him. 'I need to adjust. I need time to think.'

She stroked his cheek, ran a finger over his mouth, kissed him. 'I'll come again.'

'Yes.' He dug into a back pocket and brought out a wallet. He took out several banknotes. 'Buy something velvet. Black or red,' he said, his face colouring. 'I like you looking sexy. Come Saturday. Viv never comes then.'

She said against his mouth, 'I don't need your money, you know.'

'Take it.' He opened her hand and placed the money in it.

Hilda hesitated, then her fingers curled over the notes. 'Saturday. Viv goes to the pictures or dancing with her friend.'

'A girlfriend?' he said.

Hilda said carefully, 'Yes. But she does have a boyfriend. He's an architect.'

'She's never said.' He gnawed on a fingernail, frowning at her over the back of his hand.

Hilda felt jealous all over again. 'Why should she?' she said coldly. 'You're only her boss.'

'I'm more than that! I'm her uncle, aren't I?' he said earnestly. 'Or am I making another mistake, Hilda?'

Again she felt that odd sensation as he stared into her eyes. What was it? Fondness? Pity? Or was it something else? The love she had spoken of but had not really meant. She kissed his cheek. 'It was no mistake upstairs, Steve. I've never made love like that in my life. You won't take it out on Viv for not telling you about Nick? She's only young, and the young imagine themselves in love so often.'

'I don't know why she didn't tell me.'

'Does it matter?' She kissed his other cheek. 'I'll buy something really nice that you'll get pleasure from.' She kissed his mouth hard and his lips clung to hers, returning the pressure. Then she moved away from him. 'Tarrah for now,' she said. 'See you Saturday.'

'See you Saturday.' He opened the front door and watched her down the steps.

Hilda hurried up the lamplit road, her stiletto heels making enough noise to ensure that all the neighbours knew she was not staying the night. She wanted no gossip. She had some thinking to do.

Chapter Sixteen

'Only make-believe I love you . . .' sang Hilda.

'Do you have to?' murmured Viv, not looking up from the pile of newspapers. She had a day's holiday from work and would be meeting Nick later. 'A bit of hush would be nice.'

'That's a nice way to speak to your mother,' said Hilda, flicking a duster over the sideboard.

'I'm trying to read.'

'Read what?' She peered over Viv's shoulder and read aloud, '"New calls on Architects . . . a new social service rather than an art catering for an aristocratic minority. Urgent needs and rigid economy making new demands . . . measures its success in terms of efficiency rather than aesthetics."' She glanced sidelong at Viv. 'What's aesthetics?'

'It's something to do with appreciating beauty,' said Viv. 'Now go and sing somewhere else.'

'Are you in a mood? Has something upset you? You are all right, aren't you?' Hilda said anxiously.

'I'm all right. I've just got a bit of a headache, and you warbling around the place doesn't do it any good.'

'Are you sure that's all it is?' Hilda sat down abruptly. 'It's not something to do with Nick? He hasn't been coming it, has he?'

Viv looked up. 'Why don't you put it into words, Mam? You've got Mr Kelly in your life so why be so coy?'

'No, I haven't. I've given him up, like the ciggies,' said Hilda crossly. 'Have you and Nick been carrying on then?'

'You mean have we had sex?' Viv placed the scissors on the table and smiled at her, pleased by the news about Mr Kelly.

'Do you think I'd tell you if we had? As it is, I've got a headache because I've got my monthlies so you can breathe easy.'

'Thank God for that!' Hilda picked up the duster again but did not move from the chair. She sat staring at her daughter. 'Does Nick ever talk about when he was young?'

'What?' The question startled Viv. 'Why do you ask?'

'I just wondered. People often talk about their childhood.' She toyed with a fingernail, her head lowered so that Viv could not see the expression in her eyes.

'Nick doesn't. Mostly he wasn't happy. Especially when his father came home from the war and all hell broke loose.'

'I remember when Father used to come home. When I was small, before our Flo was born, I really looked forward to him coming back from sea.' Hilda's eyes wore a faraway expression. 'He'd bring me presents and tell me stories about the foreign countries he'd seen. I used to wish I could grow up to be a sailor.'

'You a sailor! I can just imagine it. We all know what sailors are,' said Viv, smiling, reminded of last week when Stephen had given her a gold wristwatch because the bad debtor had paid up at last. It had been wonderful being given an unexpected present. The only thing was that she would have to explain it to Nick and tell him about Stephen. It was something she was not really looking forward. There was also her mother. Should she tell Hilda about Stephen?

'That's enough of that about sailors!' Her mother wagged an admonitory finger. 'I wanted to see the world and they used to say : "Join the Navy and see the world". We all have daft ideas sometimes.'

'You can say that again!'

'Let's change the subject.' Hilda absently polished the cut moquette arm of the chair. 'Has he asked you to marry him yet?'

Viv stilled. 'Why do you ask?'

'I just wondered. I'd be against it, Viv.' Hilda shuddered. 'Imagine having his mother in the family. It doesn't bear thinking about.'

'She said you were a flibbertigibbet,' murmured Viv. 'Nick took me to meet his family a few weeks ago. You've worn

161

better than her. She's coarse. I'm glad you've given up Mr Kelly, by the way.'

'Glad I've done something to please you,' said Hilda dryly. 'Why didn't you tell me about seeing his mother?'

Viv closed her scrapbook. 'Do you tell me everything you do, Mam?'

'Nobody tells everything, even to their nearest and dearest. Did you ever mention going to see Stephen to Nick?'

Viv's fingers curled on the cover of the book, wondering if Mr Kelly had spilt the beans. 'What made you think of that right now?' she said casually.

'It just came into my head. Well, did you?'

'You mean when I went before Easter?'

'When else would I mean? Have you been since?'

Viv made up her mind quickly. 'No.'

Hilda smiled grimly. 'I bet Nick wouldn't be pleased if you did tell him. With his background he must be always worrying that you might betray him.'

'I should hope he knows me better than that,' murmured Viv, determined not to show that her mother's words had disturbed her.

'Jealousy is irrational, Viv. He might tell himself that you can be trusted but deep inside he won't have forgotten the kind of life his mother led and how she betrayed his father.'

'He hates his father,' said Viv, wanting to pooh-pooh her mother's reasoning. 'He reckons his father was as much to blame for the way his mother behaved as she was. They married too young and he regretted it and showed it.'

'There you are then, Viv. See a few other boys. Don't be tying yourself to just the one. How can you know he's Mr Right otherwise?'

'Gut feeling, Mother,' she said, getting up. 'I'm going out. I'm meeting Nick in town.'

Hilda stared at her and surprised Viv by saying, 'Bring him back. I don't want you thinking I don't like him for himself.' Viv gave her a look and went to get ready.

Viv and Nick met in the Coronation Gardens in Paradise Street. The sun had brought the crowds out and there was a band playing. She was wearing a new primrose duster coat over a sleeveless gingham dress and felt prepared for almost anything.

'You look as fresh as a daisy,' said Nick, slipping his hand into hers and smiling down at her. 'Real summery.'

'You don't look too bad yourself.'

He smile wryly, glancing down at his shantung shirt and light summer trousers. 'I'll be glad when fashion designers start coming up with more exiting clothes for men. During regency times it used to be us who were the peacocks.'

'Talking about design,' said Viv, 'how's yours going?'

'Finished it and I'm exhausted. I needed this day off.'

'Great.'

'What's your news?' His eyes were intent on her face.

'Everything's marvellous!' She squeezed his hand. 'And even Mam seems happier lately. And she's given up Mr Kelly.'

'I wonder what brought that miracle about?'

Viv shrugged. 'Perhaps she wants to be respectable for once.' She wondered how to broach the subject of Stephen.

'Any news from George?' he asked as they strolled past the floral clock.

She kept her voice dispassionate. 'He's in the South of France. Met up with this middle-aged English artist who lives in a windmill, would you believe, in some valley down there. George has gone to stay with him and says he's very encouraging about his painting.'

'Perhaps he'll stay there,' said Nick, and Viv sensed that he was pleased at the thought.

'Aunt Flo's still hoping that he'll go to America.'

Nick glanced at her. 'What about you and America? Are you still thinking of going to see your aunt?'

'I'd like to,' she said with a thoughtful air. 'If George doesn't go, I feel I should make the effort.'

'I might be going myself. You remember I told you that Mavis is having a baby? Well, she's talking about me being godfather when it arrives.'

'Perhaps we could go together?' This time she could not disguise her feelings of excitement and pleasure.

'It would depend on how work is but there shouldn't be any problem.' Nick grinned and squeezed her hand.

'I can't see any trouble either,' she said with a rush. 'Although – '

She was just about to explain about leaving her job and going to work for Stephen when he said, 'Let's get away from the band, Viv. I've got a surprise for you.' She stared at him and saw an excited gleam in his eyes. 'Don't ask what it is. Just be quiet and wait. I don't want anything spoiling this moment.'

'What is it? Where are we going?' she asked.

'Shush, woman. I told you, it's a surprise. Close your eyes.' He led her to a park bench where it was quieter and the smell of roses filled the air.

'Can I open my eyes yet?' She felt really excited.

'Yes. OK.'

Viv's eyelids lifted and she stared at the small box he held open in the palm of one hand. An emerald and diamond ring nestled in white velvet. 'It can't be real.' Her voice was hushed.

'Of course it's real. Do you think I'd give you glass and brass!' Solemnly he took the ring from its box and slipped it onto the third finger of her left hand. 'I just wanted you to know that my intentions really are honourable.'

'So you went out and bought a ring before you even knew I wasn't pregnant?' She gazed down at her hand and her vision blurred. 'I don't know what to say.' There was a catch in her voice.

'Not "This is so sudden", for God's sake,' he said with a hint of laughter in his voice.

'But it *is* unexpected.' Her voice firmed. 'I wonder what Mam will say?' She wiggled her fingers, watching shafts of light flash from the stones. The ring was only a teeny bit too big.

'Does it matter?'

Viv was silent a moment and then said, 'Mam told me to bring you back. I think she was trying to say that whatever she's said about you in the past, it's not that she doesn't like you for yourself.'

'Generous of her,' he said sarcastically. 'Do you want me to go back there with you and we can break the news together, after we've had a meal?'

'Yes!' Putting her arms around him, she kissed him. 'I really love the ring, Nick. And after we've seen Mam there's something I've got to tell you.'

'Is it important?'

'Not as important as you giving me this,' she said softly.

'Can't you tell me now then?'

She looked up at him and slipped her hand under his arm. 'Later. I don't want anything to intrude on this moment.'

'I wish you hadn't done this,' said Hilda switching off the television and facing Viv and Nick.

'Aren't you going to wish us well then, Mother?' said Viv, not too surprised.

'I told you what I thought earlier. You're too young to know your own mind, Viv.'

'I'm nearly eighteen!' Her voice was vexed. 'For God's sake, I'm not a child!'

'I know that!' Hilda waved her hand in the air. 'But you've had no life! At least Nick's seen something of the world.'

'Had you seen anything of the world at my age?' countered Viv, her eyes hardening. 'People don't have to go round the world to see life.'

Hilda stiffened. 'I know that. But I want more for you than I ever had. And if Nick cared for you, he'd say the same.'

'Thanks very much,' he interposed, glaring at Hilda. 'I'm wrong now, am I, for wanting to marry your daughter?'

She flushed. 'I'm not saying that.'

'Mother, I love him,' said Viv emphatically. 'I thought you understood that and hoped you wanted me to be happy.'

'Of course I want you to be happy,' she said tersely. 'I just want you to be happy with someone else. I'd be lying if I didn't say what I think.'

Viv was exasperated. 'Aren't you hearing me, Mother? I'd be unhappy with anyone else. I love Nick!'

'Love!' Hilda raised her eyebrows. 'I'm always hearing about love from you. I thought I knew about love at your age, but I didn't. I craved admiration and played games with people's feelings. Love hurts.' Her smile was twisted as she gazed at Nick. 'I'm sure you know that, laddie.'

165

'It doesn't have to,' he said vehemently. 'If you do things the right way.'

'Doesn't it?' She laughed shrilly. 'Oh, doesn't it! You think you know it all. So did I! I thought I could have my cake and eat it, and it didn't matter about anybody else. I thought I could cut other people's feelings off and harden my heart, fight back and grab what I wanted. But in the end I was the loser.'

Viv stared at her. 'You're talking about the past again. What's that got to do with us? It was because of the war that things went wrong for you and for so many other people. It's different now.'

'Is it?' Hilda's expression changed to one of amusement. 'Do you think love changes because it's peacetime? Do you think people's feelings are different? How do you think Stephen's going to feel about this?'

Shock jolted Viv's composure and she slanted a glance at Nick and then looked at her mother again. 'Stephen? What do you mean, Stephen?'

Hilda folded her arms. 'Don't pretend this isn't going to hurt him. He cares about you. He's given you a job with damn' good wages. He's taken you out and bought you presents. He sees you as his future.'

Viv forgot about Nick. 'How do you know all this?' she demanded of her mother.

'What's this about a Stephen?' asked Nick. 'What's all this about love and presents and taking you out, Viv?'

She eased her neck which was inexplicably aching. 'I told you about Uncle Steve. He's my father's brother, remember?'

He glanced quickly at Hilda and then back at Viv. 'You told me he didn't want to know.'

'He changed his mind so I went to see him,' she said impatiently, staring at her mother. 'How did you find out, Mam?'

Before Hilda could answer Nick spoke again. 'When?' His blue eyes glinted.

'Weeks ago. I didn't tell you because . . .'

'No more,' he said. He grabbed Viv's arm and pulled her towards the door.

Hilda moved suddenly. 'What are you doing? Where're you going with her?'

Nick flashed her a furious look. 'Keep out of this, Hilda. This is between me and Viv now. You've done your worst.'

'I don't know what you mean. Didn't you know?'

'As if you didn't know I didn't know,' he said in a silky voice. 'I don't understand how you could let this go on.' He opened the door and dragged Viv out.

'Nick, you're hurting me,' said Viv through clenched teeth. 'Will you let me go? I was going to tell you. Don't you remember I said I had something to tell you?'

'You should have told me before,' he said, pulling her along the street. 'Start explaining why you didn't – and it had better be good.'

'I'm not going to explain anything until you stop treating me like I've committed all the deadly sins,' she said, digging in her heels.

Nick stopped and stared at her. 'The truth, Viv.'

'I felt sorry for him. He was lonely and he'd had a tough life.'

'haven't we all?' said Nick sarcastically.

'You never lost your sisters and brother and mother in the war!' she said, flaring up. 'You don't have to make it sound like he was playing on my sympathy because he wasn't! But I could see that he needed me in his life. All his family are gone, Nick. I'm all that's left.'

He breathed deeply but several seconds passed before he said, 'So he gave you a job and lavished presents on you, took you out – and you never breathed a word to me! Was your mother in on this?'

'My mother? You're joking! She tried to keep us apart. But she must have found out that I knew he came looking for me from Mr Kelly. That's probably the miracle that caused them to break up.'

There was another silence before Nick said, 'Why didn't you tell me? Truth, Viv.'

'I kept forgetting.'

'Forgetting?' He laughed. 'Come off it. Something as important as that, and you forget to tell me?'

She frowned. 'Are you calling me a liar, Nick?'

167

'Too damn' right I am! Why can't you be honest with me and admit that you liked the attention? He's the father figure you think you need and you didn't want me saying anything to spoil your little fantasy. He's the sugar daddy who gives you all the sweeties you missed as a child.'

Suddenly Viv lost her temper. 'That's a lousy thing to say! You're just bloody jealous! It's not that you care about me being happy.'

'That's not true!'

'Isn't it? You just want to own me! To have me all to yourself.'

'And what's wrong with that?' yelled Nick. 'I love you!'

'A fine way you have of showing it if you can call Stephen my sugar daddy,' she snapped.

'You should have told me about him. I thought we were close. I thought we had something special.'

'So did I! But it appears I was wrong if you can't understand why I need Stephen. I don't think there's any future for us any more, Nick.'

'If you believe that then perhaps we'd better stop seeing each other?'

'That suits me fine.' She tugged at the emerald and diamond ring and held it out to him. 'You'd better have this back.'

His face paled but he laughed as he took it. 'It must be the shortest bloody engagement on record.'

'I'm glad you can laugh about it.' Her voice was icy.

Nick's expression hardened. 'Can't you see – don't you know – that if I didn't laugh, I'd bloody cry? And boys don't cry, Viv, even when their world falls apart. They just have to pick themselves up. I thought you trusted me but it seems I made a mistake.' Before she could answer he turned and walked away.

For several minutes she struggled with herself. Part of her wanted to run after Nick but the pain his words had inflicted kept her rooted to the spot. How could he believe that she wanted Stephen for a sugar daddy? How could he believe that she had deliberately not told him? How could he take back her ring? Her beautiful ring! Tears sparkled on her eyelashes. Her mother hadn't even admired it.

Her mother . . . This was all *her* fault. Had she done it deliberately? Viv turned on her heel and ran back up the street. She burst into the house.

Hilda was pouring gin into a glass and some spilt as the door was flung open. 'See what you've made me do,' she snapped dabbing her frock with a handkerchief.

'Serves you right,' said Viv in a harsh voice. 'I wish you'd drown in it.'

'I see,' said Hilda, her expression hardening. 'The two of you have quarrelled and you're blaming me?'

'It *is* your fault!' exploded Viv. 'You acted like Nick was a selfish swine and then threw Uncle Steve in his face. I suppose Mr Kelly told you I went to see him?'

Her mother's mouth tightened and her knuckles gleamed white as she nursed the glass to her bosom. 'I shouldn't have had to find out from *him* that my daughter was seeing an older man.'

'He couldn't have told you about the present and the job.' Viv paced the room, unable to keep still. 'You must have been to see Uncle Steve.'

Hilda gulped her drink. 'Of course I went to see him. What did you expect?'

'That's exactly what I expected,' said Viv, her eyes glinting. 'You can't bear anyone to take notice of me. You were jealous.'

'I was not!' Hilda took another gulp of gin. 'What have I got to be jealous of where you and Steve are concerned? He thinks you're just a child. He told me he'd taken you to the zoo.'

'So? Lots of grown ups go to the zoo! You never took me as a girl. In fact you never took me anywhere worth mentioning.'

'I could never afford it,' said Hilda crossly.

'You could afford to go dancing,' flashed Viv. 'When did you see him?'

Her mother shrugged. 'A week or so ago. I can't remember,' she lied. 'He was angry at first but eventually saw that I was only there in the role of your mother, because I cared. I didn't want you getting hurt like you were the first time you went to see him.'

169

'I don't believe you,' said Viv, her expression scornful. 'If you cared about me being hurt you would have been happy for me being engaged to Nick, but you only ever see your own point of view.'

Hilda placed the glass carefully on the table and said, 'So I have a different point of view from yours. What's wrong with that? What did Nick have to say about it all?'

'He said I should have trusted him.'

'Trusted him? That's a funny thing to say. I would have thought that he'd have said he didn't trust you any more.'

Viv stared at her. 'I see! All what's happened was intentional. You really did want to split up Nick and me. Well, you should be feeling very happy because I've given him back his ring. Are you satisfied now you've ruined my life?'

'Don't be so melodramatic,' Hilda said impatiently. 'If he's right for you, he'll be back.'

'No, not Nick,' said Viv, a break in her voice. 'We said too many things to hurt each other.'

'Then there'll be other boys,' said Hilda, draining her glass. 'You're only seventeen! I was secretly engaged at your age, and broke it off. I reckon now I had a lucky escape.'

'I'm not *you*, mother.' Viv forced the words through her teeth. 'Now I'm going upstairs to pack.'

'Pack?' Hilda was startled out of her assumed poise.

Viv paused in the doorway, her hand on the brass doorknob. 'Yes, packing. I remember George saying the day he left that he could only ever remember that things happened when you were around. He'd forgotten that they were generally trouble with a capital T!' She slammed the door and ran upstairs.

It did not take Viv long to pack and all the time she was expecting her mother to come upstairs to try and dissuade her. But Hilda did not come and even when Viv went downstairs her mother made no move to prevent her leaving, only staring tight-lipped at the television screen. Neither of them spoke as Viv opened the front door and closed it behind her.

Where should she go? It was only now that she had actually left that Viv considered where she could stay the night. Dot's?

No. Her friend would want to know everything and she wasn't up to explaining. She hurt deep inside. Where then?

Uncle Steve's house. The answer seemed to come from nowhere. It would be a slap in the face for her mother. That's if she let her mother know. She thought of Stephen again. She would have to tell him the truth about Nick. Would he understand? She could only hope so.

She caught the bus at the corner of the road and headed for Stephen's house.

Chapter Seventeen

'You've what?' Stephen stared down at Viv's wan face as she stood before him, suitcase in one hand, a smiling rag doll he had given her in the other.

'I've left home. I couldn't bear living with Mam any longer. I know she's visited you . . . interfering in my life! And now she's caused trouble between me and Nick. So I've come to ask, can I live with you? You are family, after all.'

For a moment he was struck dumb, fearing what Hilda had told her about the pair of them. Then he realised that she could not have told Viv anything or she would hardly be standing on his doorstep. 'Come in,' he said. 'You'd better explain everything.'

Relief flooded her face and he realised how unsure of her welcome she had been. 'I didn't think you'd let me down,' she said, and dropping her suitcase she hugged him right there on the doorstep.

Stephen shot a frantic look across the road and over the fence. Then, picking up her suitcase, he pulled her indoors. 'What's this trouble she's caused?'

Viv opened her mouth but he added hastily, 'No. Don't tell me yet. I'll make a cup of tea first.'

'Oh, good,' she sighed and leaned weakly against him. 'I haven't had a decent cup of tea all day and I feel shattered.'

He cast her an enquiring glance but remained silent, only ushering her into the lounge. 'Are you hungry?'

She shook her head. 'I don't think I could eat a thing at the moment. Too much has happened today. It's ruined my appetite.'

He felt sorry for her and eased her gently down into a chair. 'You just sit quiet, Viv.'

'You are a love, Uncle Steve,' she murmured, and blew him a kiss before closing her eyes.

He felt a catch in his throat. She looked so young and vulnerable. What had Hilda been doing to her? He felt annoyed with the woman he had unburdened himself to about a threatened printers' strike only a couple of days ago. She had been so prepared to listen, so soothing then. They had talked of how their life had been the last few years and then inevitably had made love. He'd known it was wrong but had been unable to resist her.

She had bought a red velvet full-length gown with a plunging halter neck and ever since he had seen her in it he'd had trouble concentrating on his work. He had begun to believe he had judged her too harshly in the past. The war made them all behave in ways they would never normally have done. But now Viv had arrived on his doorstep and he was wondering whether Hilda was the woman he believed after all. He felt miserable as he went and made the tea, placing some chocolate marshmallows on a plate.

It wasn't until Viv had drained her second cup of tea and eaten the last marshmallow that Stephen said, 'What's your mother done?'

Viv was silent a moment, her brown eyes fixed on his face as if determined to note his every reaction. 'I know she came to see you last week because someone told her about me visiting you. I think she's jealous of me having a life of my own and that's why she didn't want me to marry Nick.'

'Nick?' he said warily.

'My boyfriend,' she said quietly. 'Or ex-boyfriend, should I say, thanks to Mam.'

'What happened?'

She told him most of it.

'Why didn't you tell him about me?' He felt slightly envious of Nick, having Viv's love and an interesting job. At that age he had been in a hospital in the South of England, half out of his mind after being caught in an explosion in France.

Viv lowered her eyes and curled her feet beneath her. She could hardly tell him that she kept forgetting about him once

173

in Nick's company, so she improvised. 'I thought you belonged to different parts of my life. I wasn't sure you'd like each other so I just kept putting off talking to each of you about the other. I didn't want to lose the love you both gave me. I was happy just as things were.' Suddenly she realised as she spoke that some of what she was saying was true. 'It was stupid of me,' she said thoughtfully. 'Because I knew the way things were going with Nick, you'd have to meet. I really was intending to tell you both about each other. It was just choosing the right moment.' She cleared her throat. 'You see, I love you both but in different ways. You do understand, don't you, Uncle Steve?'

'Yes.' Stephen felt like laughing manically. Of course he understood the need to cling desperately to any chance of being loved. To be the important one in someone's life! That's why he was so touched by her words. 'The green-eyed monster causes a lot of trouble,' he murmured.

'My ring had an emerald in it.' The tears trickled slowly down her cheeks. 'Oh, Uncle Steve, I feel so hurt inside.'

He caught her to him, wanting to comfort her. She was warm and soft in his arms and his warning system flashed red for danger, but he could not reject her so stroked her hair as he would have soothed an animal in pain. 'Poor Viv. I'm honoured you came to me. But women are better at this kind of thing, you know. Tea and sympathy and soft words.'

She lifted her head. 'My mother's a woman and she is no good at tea and sympathy at all! You're much better. I knew I wasn't wrong about you.' She rested her head against his shoulder. 'But I don't want to cause you any trouble, Uncle Steve. If you don't want me to stay, say so. I don't want to be in your way.'

'Of course you can stay.' He put a tight lid on his misgivings. 'But what if your mother comes looking for you?'

'Looking for me?' She lifted her head and there was pain in her eyes. 'She won't.' Her voice was barely audible. 'She doesn't really care about me. But if she does come looking, don't tell her I'm staying here. And if she asks how I'm coping in work just tell her I'm OK. That I can get along fine without her.' She leaned forward and kissed him on the lips.

He released her hurriedly and stammered like an idiot, 'I'll show you where you can sleep, Viv. The room's in a bit of a mess and I'll have to find you some sheets and things but it'll do for now.'

'Anything'll do me!' She sprang to her feet, her expression much brighter. 'A floor would do me! Did you know I slept in an campbed in the back kitchen for months at Grandfather's?' She followed him upstairs, still talking. 'Is it the large back room? I always liked it. When you were going to marry Aunt Flo, I . . .' Her voice trailed off. 'I'm sorry. I didn't mean to remind you.'

'It's all right, Viv,' he said firmly. 'That's all water under the bridge now.' He held the door open for her to pass inside and pressed the light switch. 'It was something we were just drifting into really,' he added. 'Some people do, you know. They don't want to be alone.'

She looked about her and he did too, trying to visualise the room with its plain egg shell blue matt painted walls through her eyes. He thought, It isn't really suitable for a girl. Some of his books were piled in a corner along with old magazines and his coin collection. The furniture was dark and heavy. There was a stuffed falcon that had been his uncle's. Stephen had occupied the bedroom when he had come to live with *his* uncle after the war. Later he had been going to decorate it for George but had not bothered when his marriage plans had fallen apart. He watched Viv as she went over to the window.

'I love this view,' she said with a cheerfulness that he hoped was not assumed. 'I have a teeny patch of garden in our backyard but this is the real thing. A pity the apple blossom's over. It looks so beautiful. I suppose you've put all your plants in.' She paused. 'I bet Mam will forget to water mine.'

'I'll remind her if she comes,' he said quietly.

'Thanks.' She turned to face him with a smile fixed on her face. 'I really won't be any trouble. You'll hardly know I'm here.'

'I'm glad you are.' What else could he say? 'I'll go and get the sheets and things.' He left her staring out of the window over the darkening garden. The neighbours would talk but he would just have to grin and bear it. He had already told next-door that she was his niece. He squared his shoulders. Viv needed him and that was all that mattered.

What else mattered, though, was what Hilda would say if she found out Viv was staying here. What did he do when she arrived on his doorstep, as she surely would in a few days' time? 'You'll hardly know I'm here,' Viv had said. How wrong she was! Did she have any idea at all what a quiet life he had lived until she and Hilda had reappeared on his scene? It would get rather noisy if Hilda discovered he had taken Viv in but he was not about to betray her. She needed time to work things out. Somehow he had to do something about his Saturday night with Hilda.

Chapter Eighteen

Hilda came out of her blue and white painted front door and scowled at it. If she had been speaking to Dominic she would have had his life. How dare he paint her door those colours?

'You're all dressed up to the nines,' came a voice from next-door.

'Aren't I just?' Hilda's smile was forced as she gazed at Mrs Kelly. She was a big stocky woman a few years short of fifty but looking much older. She still dressed in the styles of the early post-war years. She wondered where Dom had found her. Perhaps he hadn't? Maybe it was his mother who had found her for him.

'Going somewhere special, are yer?' said Mrs Kelly, her eyes glacial.

'I'm seeing a manfriend.' Hilda knew it would get back to Dom and that was what she wanted.

'Oh?' Mrs Kelly's expression changed abruptly and she leaned on the handle of her sweeping brush. 'We haven't seen any men round. Been hiding him under a bushel, have yer? What's he like? Got money, has he?'

'He's got more than money,' said Hilda without batting an eyelash. 'He's got looks, style . . . everything a girl could ask for.'

Mrs Kelly tittered. 'You're hardly a girl these days . . . put a teeny bit of weight on . . . but that dress is nice.' She peered closer. 'Real lace, isn't it?'

'That's right.' Hilda's smile widened as she opened her handbag. 'Talking about money, I never did pay Dominic for painting my door. He did it the wrong colour, mind, but he still did the job.' She took a couple of pound notes from her purse and held them out to the other woman. 'Tell him thanks for all he's done but I won't be needing him any more.'

Mrs Kelly took the money and placed it in the pocket of her flowered pinafore. 'I'll do that for yer. How's your Viv? I thought I saw her leaving the other day with a suitcase.'

'That's right. Gone on holiday with a friend . . . be back in a week or two.' It did not matter if the old crow believed her or not. That was Hilda's tale and she was sticking to it. Viv would come home sooner or later, if for nothing more than to see if Nick had called. No doubt she was with that friend of hers but Hilda did not know where Dot lived. Even if she had she would not have gone running after her daughter. They both needed time to get over the upset.

'Well, I hope she has a nice time . . . and you too.' Mrs Kelly's smile was pure syrup. 'Maybe we'll be hearing wedding bells soon?'

'Oh, I'm not rushing into anything just yet. Footloose and fancy free, that's how I like it. Who wants to be tied to a broomstick? I mean a broom handle.' Her smile was just as syrupy as Mrs Kelly's as she waved her fingers before walking swiftly away, her white high-heeled sandals clicking on the pavement.

Stephen had the door open swiftly, effectively blocking her view into the house. He had a suit on. 'You look a treat,' he said, his blue eyes appreciative.

'Thanks.' Hilda's brightly painted lips titled upwards in a smile. Viv couldn't have said anything. She wondered what was the best thing to do. Pretend the row had never happened? That Viv was still living with her? 'I'm glad you like the dress. I bought it in that new shop that's opened in Church Street, Joan Barrie.'

'It's very feminine.' He took her arm. 'I thought you might like to go out? It's such a lovely evening. Maybe a meal at a little inn in the country? And if we don't feel like coming home, we could stay the night?'

The suggestion silenced her and it was half a minute before she was able to say with a total lack of her usual composure, 'I – I never thought you'd think of such a thing, Steve! I'd love to do that.' It would be good to get away from the house. The last few days it had felt so empty. As for the cat, it could fend for itself.

'Fine.' He closed the front door behind them. 'Let's go then.'

She could not take her eyes off him as he steered her down the path to the car parked at the kerb. 'This is a new Steve,' she said as he held the car door open for her. He made no reply, only walked to the other side of the car, humming jerkily under his breath. They shot away from the kerb faster than she expected, causing her to grab the seat swiftly. 'Good God, what's the rush?'

'Sorry. I got the clutch mixed up with the accelerator.'

'I wouldn't know the difference.' Her voice was good-humoured. 'That's more like you. You're not as confident as you sounded back there, planning a naughty weekend.'

'Perhaps not.' Dark colour suffused his face. 'But I got to thinking that it wasn't much fun for you, just coming to the house and listening to me talk.'

'We both talk.' She touched his knee before leaning back in her seat. 'Where are we going?'

'You name it.'

'I'm no good at names. The only places I know are towns and cities. I was never one for countryside.'

'You'd rather go to a town? Blackpool or somewhere?'

She grimaced and shifted uncomfortably. 'It's a long time since I've been to Blackpool, but I don't think so.' Fun place it might be but she had spent a honeymoon there and that marriage had been a disaster. She did not want any clouds on this silver lining that had turned up out of the blue. She continued, 'I quite like the idea of the country. As long as the food's good and the bed's comfortable, I'll leave it to you where we go.'

He seemed pleased about that. 'OK. You sit back and relax. Have a sleep if you like.'

'A sleep? You want me wide awake later, do you?' she said in a teasing voice.

Stephen flushed and his hands tightened on the steering wheel. 'I wasn't thinking of that. How has your week been?'

She stared at him. Was there any hidden meaning in that

question? 'A bit fraught,' she murmured. 'Nothing for you to worry about.' He nodded and she slowly stroked his thigh and noticed a muscle twitch in his cheek. She dropped her hand and closed her eyes. Later. For the first time in days she felt able to relax.

Hilda woke what seemed a short time later though it turned out to be hours. The car windows were open and she could smell air that was free of the taint of the city. 'Where are we?' she said drowsily.

'By Lake Windermere.' He smiled down at her. 'I just kept on driving while you kept on sleeping so we ended up here.'

She sat up and looked out of the window. The car had stopped outside a large grey stone building. There were trees, grass and flowers. She could identify the scarlet flowers as geraniums and the others as french marigolds. That was thanks to Viv. She felt an ache in the region of her heart. She had never known much about flora and fauna but her daughter had begun to teach her. In the near distance lay a sheet of muted grey silvery water. It was very quiet. 'What will we do about luggage?' she said abruptly.

Stephen groaned. 'I never thought of a suitcase.' Then he shrugged. 'I'm sure we're not the first to stop overnight on impulse.'

Hilda agreed, a tiny smile playing round her mouth as he helped her out of the car. She could scarcely believe the change in him since the day he had visited her in spring. It was her and Viv's doing, of course. They had brought him out of himself. Now Hilda wanted him to think he wouldn't be able to manage without them.

They went inside and signed the register as Mr and Mrs Martin and were shown upstairs to a room under the eaves. It had an excellent view of the lake and the bed when Hilda bounced on it was comfortable. She smiled up at Stephen. 'Not bad.'

'No.' He looked up from the sink in the corner. 'I haven't stayed here before.' He began to dry his hands. 'We'll have to move if we don't want to miss dinner.'

Hilda moved. She liked her food and there would be plenty of time later for bedtime frolics.

The food was plain but excellent. They both had a mixed grill, the full works containing fried bread, steak, chops, Cumberland sausage, black pudding and chips. A dessert was out of the question. They talked desultorily over their coffee and she toyed with the idea of asking how Viv was getting on at work but rejected it. He might wonder why she asked, having never done so before, and may be it would alter the mood of the evening. He would not want her daughter knowing about any of this. He was a strange mixture, she thought. He could be so passionate and yet often ended up guilt-ridden afterwards. She put it down to his upbringing and wondered when he would ask her to marry him. She hoped it would be soon.

Stephen suggested a walk and Hilda groaned. 'I doubt if I can even stand after all that food!'

He pulled her to her feet with a smile. 'All the more reason to have a walk or we'll both end up fat.'

She pulled a face. 'If you put it like that, honey, then I'll have to agree.'

He eyed her shoes and said resignedly. 'We won't go far.'

It was quiet except for a gentle lapping at the water's edge. Night was sweeping over a wishy-washy grey and peach-streaked sky. It was a time when confidences could have been shared but the atmosphere somehow seemed alien to Hilda, who had always lived in big cities. It was almost as if the mountains and lake had secret lives of their own. Hell! She was getting fanciful. 'I will lift up my eyes unto the hills from whence cometh my help.' What would God think of this lie she was living. She clung to Stephen's hand and said, 'Let's get back, I'm getting cold.' He took off his jacket and put it round her, and again she was left speechless by his thoughtfulness.

It wasn't until she was undressing in the costy chintzy room that her heart suddenly jolted wildly. She realised that in neither of them mentioning Viv there was something wrong. She should have said that she had to let her daughter know that she mightn't be home tonight and Stephen should have thought of it too! Her gaze fixed on him where he lay in bed, his shoulders naked above the covers. 'You know, don't you?' she said bluntly.

'Know what?' His voice was cautious.

'Don't pretend, Steve.' She tapped a comb against the palm of her hand. 'You know about me and Viv having a row.' She tried to make it sound as if it was not important. 'You've been too tactful not mentioning it at all, and I've been just plain stupid staying quiet. But I was happy being with you and didn't want to spoil things.'

He sat up and she could not tell if he was relieved or not. 'I must admit I was waiting for you to tell me.' There was a deep timbre to his voice and she knew that he was upset. 'She sits there, trying to work, but often she's staring into space. Thinking of him, no doubt.'

Hilda bit her bottom lip. 'I suppose she said I ruined her life?'

'Have you?'

She tossed back her hair. 'Of course not.'

His brows knitted together. 'What have you got against the engagement, besides her youth and his mother?'

'Aren't they enough?'

He looked down at his hands. 'They didn't plan on getting married straightaway, you know. He wants to build her a house.'

'He what?' There was a tragic expression on her face. 'You and she must have had a real heart to heart! I didn't think you were that close. As for him building her a house, I don't believe it! No man's ever wanted to build me a house. She folded her arms and stared fixedly at the opposite wall.

'Poor Hilda,' he said softly. 'Don't be jealous.'

'Jealous? Me?' She laughed. 'Do you know where she is?'

He was silent.

Her lips compressed. 'She didn't have to swear you to secrecy. I can guess where she is. At that friend of hers, Dot's!'

He smiled. 'She has mentioned the name several times and I know they're doing something together tonight.'

Hilda sighed heavily. 'Did she have anything nice to say about me at all?'

'She's in love and you hurt her.'

There was silence.

'Is this Nick that bad?' murmured Stephen.

'No.' Hilda sat on the bed in her flesh-coloured satin and lace underslip. She could not possible explain about Nick. Not yet. 'He's a Smart Alec, though. I don't want our Viv feeling inferior.'

Stephen stared at her in amazement. 'There's no reason for her to feel like that. Viv's not stupid!' Hilda made no answer so he changed tack. 'Do you miss her at all?'

Hilda shrugged. 'I'd got used to having her around. We were getting on. I know it's a bit late in the day to be saying this but I realised in America that she was the only daughter I was likely to have.'

'So what are you going to do to get her back?'

She hesitated. 'I'll wait,' she said at last. 'Sooner or later she'll come home.'

He looked astonished. 'You really believe that?'

She nodded and then smiled. 'We surely didn't come away to talk about Viv all the time, did we?'

'No.'

Without more ado Hilda pulled back the covers and flung herself at him. Instinctively he caught her to him and forgot Viv. He whipped off her slip. Breast to breast he and Hilda rolled over and over on the bed: kissing, hugging, caressing, arousing. Then they slid on to the floor and made love with the lack of control of seventeen-year-olds and an energy they'd last possessed in their twenties.

Hilda was singing as she pushed her key into the lock and stepped into the front room. She'd had a lovely weekend touring beauty spots: Rydal, Grasmere, the Langdale Valley. They'd had another night in a hotel in Keswick where they had shopped and Stephen had bought her a pendant made of silver and agate, not wildly expensive but pretty.

She bent and picked up the postcard and two envelopes on the mat, looking at the postcard first, squinting at the postmark. Frejus, France. She turned it over. It was from George and addressed to Viv. Her eyes scanned the lines quickly. He was enjoying himself by the look of it but had remembered Viv's birthday. Bit early but thoughtful of him. His father had been like that occasionally. She tapped the card against her teeth and then dropped it on the table and opened the blue envelope, a letter from her sister. Then she wished she hadn't. Flo wanted to know if Viv and she were still getting on okay? Hilda put the letter down with the card and picked up the other envelope.

It, too, was addressed to Viv. Again Hilda squinted at the postmark. (One of these days she was going to have to get reading glasses but not yet. She felt young, young, young, and there was still plenty of life in her yet.) The envelope had a Liverpool postmark and the writing was unfamiliar. She hesitated then slit it open with a finger. There was one folded sheet which she turned up and saw the signature. Nick. She had guessed right. Should she read it? Somehow she was reluctant to do so. People revealed themselves in letters in a way they didn't face to face and she was feeling guilty enough about Nick. He could have revealed the truth but it seemed he had kept quiet. She might start feeling really sorry for him and do something stupid.

Hilda tucked the letter back inside the envelope and put it behind the clock on the mantlepiece. Perhaps she would pass it on to Viv through Stephen, but not just yet. She made coffee and placed a fresh cream flaky pastry horn on a plate. She switched on the television and smiled as she remembered the weekend.

Chapter Nineteen

'I wish you'd hurry up,' said Viv impatiently as she waited for Dot to finish varnishing her fingernails pearly peach. 'Perhaps I should have stayed at Uncle Steve's? He looked a bit worried.'

He's probably glad to have you out of the way,' murmured Dot. 'It must take some getting used to for a bachelor, having a young nubile female in his pad. Although it was good of him the other week to let me stay a couple of nights while he was away on that business weekend.'

'It was good of him to pay for all the paint and wallpaper, with the printers' strike on . . . and to let us have a go at decorating the bedroom.'

Dot nodded. 'I hope you're not embarrassing him by leaving your smalls hanging all over the place?'

'Don't be daft!' Viv raised her eyes heavenwards. 'He had sisters! He knows what knickers are.'

Dot stretched out a hand and waggled her fingers in an attempt to hasten the drying process. 'I wonder what your mother would say if she knew where you were hiding?'

'I'm not hiding. And so far she hasn't come looking,' said Viv tersely.

'Temper, temper,' murmured Dot. 'You told me that your Uncle Steve said that she did get in touch but doesn't want to put pressure on you to go home. Maybe Nick'll call at your mother's tonight, it being your birthday, and everything will come right?'

'I doubt it.' Viv sighed heavily. 'He wouldn't want to see her, and he probably doesn't want to see me ever again.'

185

'Rubbish! A lovers' tiff. Haven't you heard that true love never runs smooth?'

'Yes, but . . . if he wanted to find me he'd have come looking for me by now,' murmured Viv, flicking her ponytail over her shoulder. Her hair was tied up with twisted black and white ribbons and had been tinted barley blonde. She had made an enormous effort to put on a good show. To make it appear that she didn't have a care in the world.

'You haven't gone looking. And maybe he has, but doesn't know where to find you.'

Viv stilled. 'Do you think so?'

'It's possible. Think about it, Viv. But for now try and enjoy your birthday.'

'I will, I will,' she said, and standing up pirouetted on white stiletto-heeled shoes that had black bows fastened to them. The black rose-patterned white skirts of the shirtwaister she wore flared up, revealing several layers of white net under-skirts trimmed with black bows to match those on her shoes. She wished desperately that Nick was there to see her.

'Very nice,' said Dot. 'You could audition for a talent show at the Empire.' She twisted the top back on the nail varnish so tightly that the plastic cracked. 'Just don't go making eyes at Phil tonight. He's mine, remember?' She hugged herself as she slid long narrow feet into a pair of orange slipperettes. 'I think I'm in love,' she sang, smoothing down her skirts which were patterned with large checks in yellow, orange and white. 'What do you think of the new name for the group?'

'The Swinging Spuds?'

Dot laughed. 'You're full of wit.' She pulled on shortie white gloves. 'You know it's Spades not Spuds. Let's be having you then. The Casbah Coffee Club opens at half-past seven.'

'It's me that's been waiting for you!'

It was the opening night of the club which was situated in the cellars of a large Victorian house in West Derby. The girls had heard of it through Norm who had signed himself up as a member as well as Dot and Viv. It had cost them half a crown each and they would have to pay a shilling at the door. Word had gone around that the Quarry Men, who had been disbanded, had been reformed and were playing that night.

'There must be hundreds here,' whispered Viv as they crowded into the cellars. She looked up at the black-painted ceiling. It had strange pot bellied figures painted on it. Ugly-looking things. Someone said that John Lennon, one of the Quarry Men, had done them. The music started. She looked over at the four members of the group who had arranged themselves in front of a juke box and determined to forget Nick and all her troubles and just enjoy the music.

'Long Tall Sally' set them all jigging. 'Sweet Little Sixteen' had Dot humming. 'Maggie May' had most of them joining lustily in the refrain. And 'Whole Lotta Shakin Goin' On' got them dancing. Viv was partnered by Norm. Fortunately he did not expect sizzling conversation from her but just loved to rock'n'roll. They danced on through Jerry Lee Lewis, Eddie Cochran, Carl Perkins. Then, after refreshing themselves with Coca-Cola, they listened to a vocal of 'Blue Moon of Kentucky' from Paul McCartney. Viv was almost beginning to enjoy herself when she noticed that she was being stared at. For a moment she did not recognise the fair-haired girl wearing too much mascara. then the stare became a glare and she realised that the girl was Nick's sister Ingrid. Her heart plummeted and she groaned.

'Did I stand on your toe?' asked Norm, stopping abruptly.

She shook her head and pulled at his hand. 'Carry on dancing. It's too late to hide now.'

'Hide? Who are we hiding from?'

'Nick's sister, but we're not.'

'Not?'

'No. And don't look.'

He did. 'Which one is she?'

Ingrid pulled a face at them.

'Guess,' said Viv mournfully.

'She looks like she's slipped with the mascara brush.' Norm's voice was amused. 'Interesting effect. She's got a good figure, though. but not as good as yours, Viv.' He gazed down into her face. 'Why don't you forget this Nick? You've got me.'

She smiled. 'Just don't let's talk about him, OK?'

'That's fine by me.' He held her closer as the music turned

187

smoochy and Viv felt like spitting nails. What chance of her and Nick ever making it up now? Ingrid would be sure to tell him that she had seen her out dancing with another bloke. She was glad when the evening was over and she could go home.

Stephen was out.

Viv wandered disconsolately into the kitchen, wondering where he could be. She made a drink of Ovaltine and switched on the television. An hour later he still had not come in and the National Anthem had signalled the end of transmission. She sat staring at the dot, willing it to fade. What would Ingrid tell Nick? Damn! She should have spoken to her and asked after him. But it was too late now. And where was Uncle Steve? She needed him to talk to. She went into the parlour and looked out of the window. Just then the car drew up. She had the door open in a flash.

Stephen came up the path, humming under his breath.

'You sound happy,' she said irritably.

He stopped in mid hum. 'I thought you'd be in bed. What's up? Did you have a good time?'

'Oh, great! What about you? Where've you been?'

He hesitated. 'Let's get inside, Viv. We don't want to be waking the neighbours.'

'I don't care about the neighbours,' she said crossly. 'Perhaps they need waking up!'

He stared at her before ushering her indoors and bolting the door. 'What's up?'

She leaned against him and buried her face against him then caught the faintest whiff of a familiar smell. 'Nick's sister was at the Casbah.'

'Oh.'

'She'll tell him I was dancing the night away with Norm.'

'I suppose she will.'

Viv lifted her head. 'Is that all you can say?'

He held her away from him and smiled. 'Let's go and sit down, Viv. I've something to tell you.'

She bit her lip. 'You don't want to listen to me moaning, do you?'

'Later, honey.' His arms dropped and he walked away up the lobby.

Viv followed him into the lounge. He waved her to a chair while he sat on the studio couch. 'Well?' she said.

He leaned forward, his hands clasped on his knees. 'Viv, I've been to see your mother.'

'You've what?' She sprang to her feet. 'Why? Did you tell her I was here? All she could think of was that he had seen her mother and come in humming. Humming! He should have been irritable, angry after being in Hilda's company.

'Sit down!' His voice was sharp and he was frowning now. 'Let me finish.' She sat down. 'It was because it was your birthday I went.' He delved into his jacket pocket. 'She gave me these.' He got to his feet. In his hand were several envelopes, a postcard and a small parcel. 'I'm going to bed. We can talk in the morning. Goodnight.'

'Goodnight,' she murmured, her attention fixed greedily on what she held. Her mother had not forgotten. The parcel first. It had a card attached to it in what was plainly her mother's handwriting. She tore the envelope open. 'To my dearest daughter Vivien . . . your loving mother Hilda'. She stared at it. Was this a peace offering? A kind of apology? She opened the parcel. Inside was a silver bracelet. She slipped it on to her wrist then turned over the envelopes, her pulses racing. She noted that one letter was from California, another from her mother's old friend Doris. The last one she put to one side with trembling fingers while she opened the others hurriedly and read George's postcard from Frejus. She toyed with a lock of her hair. He was enjoying himself all right. The elderly artist had a niece who had come to stay. She was called Jackie and had modelled for George. He wished her a happy day and sent his love.

She felt happy that he was happy, then picked up the last enveloped and turned it over. A frown creased her blow. The flap was stuck down but it definitely looked as if it had been tampered with. There was the tiniest rip in the paper. She slit it open and began to read . . .

Dear Viv,
Perhaps by now you have come down from the ceiling like I have? I am tied up at the moment with work but I should be free for your birthday. If you feel like talking,

meet me outside Lewis's at seven o'clock on the big day
and we can go for a meal.
Yours, Nick

Viv felt as if her heart stopped beating. For several seconds
she could not think, could not move. Then the words 'too late'
blazoned themselves on her mind and the letter shook
between her fingers. She felt sick. How long would he have
waited? Would he have been angry that she hadn't turned up?
Hurt? Disappointed? By now he would know just where she
had been. She eased her throat which ached with tears and
picked up the envelope. The postmark was over two weeks
old! Her mother must have read it and kept it from her.

Viv's hand tightened on the letter and she wished that
Hilda was there in front of her. In that moment she could have
clawed her eyes out. How could she do this? She must have
known how much it mattered. Did Uncle Steve know what
was in the letter? He had come in sounding happy. Maybe he
did. Perhaps all the time he had seemed so sympathetic to her
he had really been glad that there was no Nick on the scene.
Why had he really gone to see her mother? Was it truly
because of Viv's birthday? She just did not know. All she did
know was that she felt terrible.

Carefully Viv read the letter again. Then she folded the
paper and placed it in the envelope. After that she removed
the bracelet from her wrist and packed it up with its card.
'Return to Sender', that's what she would put on it. Then she
went to bed.

The next morning after a restless night Viv told Stephen
that she wanted him to take the present back to her mother.

'Why?' He looked startled and paused as he ladled a boiled
egg into an egg cup with a picture of Humpty Dumpty on it.

She told him about the letter. 'Mam must have read it and
kept it from me because she wanted to destroy any change I
might have had of getting back with Nick.'

Some emotion flickered across Stephen's face. He sat
down. 'You don't know that.'

'Don't I?' She smiled. 'I know my mother better than you do.'

He opened his mouth, was about to say something, then
shook his head.

What is it?' she said, frowning. 'Don't you agree with me? It's obvious what she's done, isn't it?'

'Why should she give the letter to me then? She could have just destroyed it.'

Viv stared at him, her expression uncertain. 'I suppose she could have. But . . .'

But what?'

'The letter *had* been opened. She'd know it would hurt more this way. Why couldn't she have got it to me sooner? And the cards? She couldn't have known you were going to call. She could have sent them into work.'

'You didn't want to see her, remember?'

Viv flared up. 'Why do you keep finding excuses for her? Did she turn all her charm on last night?'

Stephen picked up a teaspoon and hit the top of his egg a resounding crack with it. He did not look at her as he said, 'You admit your mother has charm then? I think it's a pity that the pair of you can't make up this quarrel. What's stopping you, anyway, from going round to Nick's house and explaining why you didn't meet him?'

'Because last night while he was waiting for me I was dancing with another bloke!' she yelled. 'He'll know that by now. His sister will have told him that we were all smoochy. He's not going to believe it was nothing and that I didn't get that letter till too late.'

He stared at her with a mixture of exasperation and sympathy. 'You could try telling him.'

'You don't understand,' she said roughly. 'His mother carried on during the war with all kinds of men. Her behaviour haunts him.'

'He must know you're not like that. Try, Viv!'

'I can't! I won't be able to bear it if he rejects me.' She shook her head and walked out of the room.

For the rest of the day the atmosphere was strained between them. Then, to top it all, that evening Stephen went out again.

Chapter Twenty

'I didn't read it,' said Hilda, her expression flinty as she placed the parcel on the small table next to her glass of gin and tonic.

'Viv reckons it had been opened,' said Stephen, his gaze piercing.

'Viv was right.' Hilda twisted her left foot round her right calf and avoided meeting his gaze. Instead she stared at the members of the Merseysippi Jazz Band, the resident group in The Temple, Dale Street, who were filling the place with music. 'It's a pity you didn't leave it until Monday. She wouldn't have reacted so badly then.'

Stephen scrubbed at the scar on his face and said, slightly impatiently, 'It was you who told me to take it round to Dot's! You wanted Viv getting her present as soon as possible, you said.'

'I shouldn't have bothered. Ungrateful, that's what she is.'

'I think at first she was pleased,' he said slowly. 'I caught a glimpse of her face as I went out of the door.'

'And she came round to yours later all steamed up about the letter! Huh!' Hilda took a large gulp of her drink. 'Why should I want to read a letter from Nick? I've got more important things to do.'

'Why did you open it then?' he said, exasperated. 'And look at me, Hilda, while we're talking.'

She looked at him and her expression softened. 'I didn't read it, honestly. I didn't know who it was from, that's why I opened it. As soon as I saw his signature I put it back in the envelope. I was curious but I thought it was private.' She took another drink. 'Then I put it behind the clock and forgot about it.' She shrugged scarlet-clad shoulders. 'It was wrong of me, but what can I do about it now?'

'You could make amends.' He covered her hand with his and grinned. 'Nothing difficult, Hilda. Just go and visit him and explain.'

'That's all?' she said sardonically. 'You have to be joking!'

'Viv being unhappy isn't a joke. If you cared about her, you'd go. You owe it to her.'

Hilda stared at him, a peculiar expression in her eyes. 'You care a lot about her, don't you?'

He nodded. 'I care about you too. Lots and lots.' He toyed with her fingers. 'How about it?'

She hesitated. 'I'll think about it. Now how about another drink?' He squeezed her fingers and went to the bar. Then they sat back and listened to the band, holding hands.

Hilda dithered for days about the visit to Nick. At last she made the decision that she would go – but she had to look her best. She opened the wardrobe door and rifled through the clothes that hung there. What should she wear? Something snazzy that would knock the Bryces' socks off or something terribly respectable? She had no doubt that she would have to face Lena as well as Nick. She took out the black flannelette suit she had worn that first day in Liverpool. With a cream blouse it would look quite smart. She tried it on, but the zip would not fasten. Blast and double blast! She'd have to go on a diet or take up the ciggies again. The trouble was that Steve had been full of praise for her giving them up. He believed that smoking was akin to burning money. Didn't realise how it had soothed her nerves.

She reached for a blue dress that she had bought a month ago. It was taffeta with a straight skirt, and buttoned at the front from the waist to the neck with its wide white collar. Steve had liked it. Said that she looked like a puritan in it. Then he had proceeded to undo the buttons. It had been fun that evening. A smile crossed her face. The dress would do.

Hilda pulled a face as she just managed to fasten the buttons. Her breasts had grown bigger. No more jelly babies or cream cakes. Now she was in the Change she would end up with middle-aged spread if she wasn't careful.

Her make-up took a little longer than usual and she paid

193

more attention to her hair, twisting curls round her little finger and lacquering them into place. Then at the last minute she decided to wear a hat, a nice little white number with a wisp of veiling. She stared at herself in the oval mirror on the chest of drawers, picked up her handbag, took a deep breath and sallied forth to face the Bryce family.

Hilda gazed up at the number just under the fanlight over the doorway and rang the bell again, hoping that she had got the number right. This time she kept her finger on the bell much longer.

There were footsteps and a voice complained: 'Hold your hurry, hold your hurry! What's the bloody fuss?' The door was dragged open to reveal a woman wearing a floral pinafore over her bulky figure. A turban concealed curlers in her hair.

'Hello, Lena.' Hilda was pleased that she had caught her at a disadvantage and awaited the moment of recognition.

Lena peered at her, then stuck out her chin pugnaciously. 'Well, if it isn't Hilda Preston, all dressed up like a dog's dinner. You've got a nerve coming here.'

She did not flinch. 'I'm looking for Nick.'

'Well, he's not in! And even if he was I wouldn't let him speak to yer.'

'You wouldn't?' Hilda's eyebrows shot up, disappearing completely under her veil. 'I thought he was a lad with a mind of his own. The last thing I thought him was a mammy's boy.'

Lena flushed. 'My son is nothing of the sort. He's a good lad, though. Sees me all right. Which is more than can be said for some children. No airs and graces about our Nick. Not like that daughter of yours. "How do you do, Mrs Bryce!"' She sniffed.

Hilda bristled. 'What's wrong with that? It's perfectly polite. My daughter's got manners – which is more than can be said for you!'

'She's snooty!'

'No she's not!'

'She's not good enough for him.'

Hilda's eyes glinted. 'My daughter can do better for herself than your son!'

Lena's double chin wobbled. 'My son could take his pick of

the cream of the girls in Liverpool. He's going places is our Nick.' Her voice took on a suspicious note. 'I suppose that's why you're here? Because yer've heard he's won that award.'

'What award?'

Lena folded her arms across her bosom. 'Your pretending yer don't know doesn't wash with me, Hilda Preston.'

'My name's Murray!' Hilda's voice was terse. 'And stop calling me a liar.'

'Yer are a liar. You knew all right. Big money prize and plenty of work coming his way.'

'What?' Hilda was taken aback. Then she rallied. 'Our Viv's not doing so bad either. Secretary. She could end up having shares in a business.'

Lena smiled haughtily. 'Easy for you to say that. She didn't look like no secretary the other Saturday when our Ingrid saw her.'

'What do you mean?'

'She never told you?' Lena smirked. 'Dancing she was, with another fella.'

'Oh, that! It was nothing. But I suppose your daughter told Nick about seeing Viv?'

'I did,' said Lena. 'He needed to know what she was really like. Smooching away. Two timing my son.'

'They'd split up,' said Hilda, almost grinding her teeth. 'What do you expect her to do? Become a nun? Anyway, that's beside the point. I just want Nick to know that Viv didn't know anything about his letter until late last night.'

'What letter?' asked Lena, her eyes bulging.

'You don't know?' Hilda flashed her a glittering smile. The score was even now. 'He wanted Viv to meet him on her birthday.'

'You're just saying it.' She looked really annoyed.

'Ask him when he comes in.' Hilda backed off the step. 'Ask him does he still love our Viv enough to build her that house?'

'Build her a house!' Lena's eyes nearly popped out of her head.

'Ask him,' repeated Hilda, giving a little wave as she walked away. She felt triumphant. She would go to Steve's and tell him she had done as he suggested. Now it was up to

Nick and Viv. At least she had done her best to make amends. The only trouble was she felt even worse about having Lena Bryce as part of the family. Still, Nick had won an award, and a cash prize was not to be sniffed at. She just hoped it wasn't all too late.

Chapter Twenty-One

Over the next few days Viv tortured herself thinking what might have been if she had received the letter in time, and having no idea of her mother's visit to Nick's home decided that maybe she was being a stubborn, stupid coward by not going to visit him as Stephen had suggested. So the following Sunday she made the excuse that she was going to church, not wanting to tell Stephen what she was really doing in case it went wrong. She did go to church, feeling the need for some spiritual help, and came away with the words of the third Collect for Grace ringing in her ears: 'Grant that this day we fall into no sin, neither run into any kind of danger; but that all our doings may be ordered by thy governance, to do always that which is righteous in thy sight; through Jesus Christ our Lord. Amen.'

There was a sharp breeze turning over bits of paper in the gutter in the street where Nick lived. A couple of girls were playing two balls against a wall and a small boy was riding a tricycle but there was nobody else in sight. Viv gazed up at the house, remembering the day Nick had brought her here. Her heart was beating painfully at the thought of seeing him. Taking a deep breath, she ran up the steps and pressed the doorbell.

It rang and rang inside the house but nobody came in response. She waited then rang again, keeping her finger on the bell a long time. Nothing. Her pulses settled to their normal rhythm but she was not about to give up yet. Perhaps someone was in the yard? It was a big house and they might not have heard the bell.

Viv walked to the end of the road and round to the wide entry that ran down the back of the houses. She went along, counting yard doors. When she thought she had the right one she tried the latch. It gave and in she slipped. Seeing the old tin bath which contained Kenny's collection of frogs and newts, she knew that it was the right yard but there was nobody there.

'Hello down there,' croaked a voice.

Viv started and looked about her.

'Up here.'

She looked up and her stomach turned over. Kenny was sitting on the windowsill of a first-floor window. His eyes were closed and he was gripping the side of the frame with one hand and the sill with the other. Behind him the sash window was half open. 'What are you doing up there?' she called.

'Me budgie flew out . . . and I got out . . . to try and catch him.'

'And I suppose he flew off before you could grab him?' Viv said as calmly as she could.

'He flew on to the roof. I've been here ages and I've shouted and shouted but nobody's heard me.'

'Where's your mam?'

'Gone to work.'

'Why don't you climb back in again?' she suggested but knew the answer before he gave it.

'I-I can't. I'm frightened to let go.'

Viv was silent, knowing just how he felt. Up that tree that George had persuaded her to climb she had been unable to let go. She took a deep breath. 'I take it nobody else is in?'

'Our Ingrid went out. She said she'd only be five minutes.'

Viv did not bother asking about Nick because he must be out, too. She felt a sharp ache of disappointment but it was no use worrying about that now. 'How long since Ingrid went?'

'Ages and ages.' Kenny ventured to open his eyes but quickly shut them again. 'Perhaps you can get the fire brigade?' he suggested tremulously.

Viv considered calling the fire brigade out a bit drastic. All she really had to do was go inside the house and pull him inside. It was not difficult. The only trouble was that when she tried the back door it would not open. 'Why is the back door locked?' she called.

''Cos our Ingrid said it was safer and I wasn't to let anyone in,' said Kenny. 'I've bin thinking. There's a ladder. You could climb up and rescue me.' He sounded happier but Viv's heart sank. Perhaps she should call out the fire brigade? Coward! she scolded herself. Find the ladder. She looked about her and saw it lying on the ground against the whitewashed wall. Somehow she managed to heave it upright and against the wall. 'Don't look down' was all she had to bear in mind. It wasn't so very high.

Viv placed a foot on the first rung and began to climb, trying to think of anything but the hard ground below. She imagined knights in armour. Had they ever really rescued damsels from turrets or was it all a fairy tale? They'd have needed long ladders, the ones used for scaling walls during sieges . . . the side of her head touched Kenny's shoe. 'Hi!' she said, smiling idiotically. 'What's it like being a pigeon?' She hoisted herself higher so that her head was level with his.

'How are you going to get me on the ladder?' he asked.

Viv stared into his scared blue eyes, noting their similarity to Nick's. 'I wasn't thinking of getting you on to the ladder. I was considering you giving me one of your hands and climbing inside.'

He gulped. 'I don't think I can.'

'Of course you can!' she exclaimed cheerfully. 'You'd have had to let go to come down the ladder. I'm frightened too, you know.'

'Are you?'

She wanted to nod her head vigorously but did not dare in case the movement disengaged the ladder. 'Just take my hand.' Her smile of encouragement felt as if it was glued to her face.

Kenny, keeping his eyes on her, slowly slackened his grip. She did not give herself time to think as she let go of the ladder to shove him through the window opening. Then, still keeping her mind blank, she gripped the frame and pulled herself inside to collapse on top of him on the floor.

For a moment they lay there, breathing heavily, and then Kenny sat up and cried, 'What about my budgie?'

Viv started to laugh. 'Forget it boyo! I'm not climbing on the roof. How about a cup of tea?'

'Okay!' He smiled, bounced to his feet and led the way out the bedroom.

It was when they were sitting down with their tea, and a jam buttie each that Kenny had made, that Viv asked him where Nick was.

'He's left,' he said with his mouth full. 'Gone to live somewhere else.'

Suddenly the bread she was chewing tasted like cardboard. 'Where?' she said.

'Don't know. Him and Mam had a big argument.' Kenny eyed her with interest. 'I've seen you before, haven't I? Nick brought you to see my frogs. Your name's Vivien. I'd never heard that name before, that's why I remember it. Mam said it several times when she was shouting at our Nick.'

So her name had come up in an argument? She gulped the tea. 'What was the row about?'

He shrugged. 'Dunno.' His expression changed, became alert. He got up. 'There's our Ingrid. I hope she won't belt me.'

Viv heard the key in the lock and stood up as Ingrid entered the room.

The girl stopped abruptly and frowned. 'What are you doing here?' Before Viv could answer she rounded on her brother. 'I thought I told you not to let anybody in!'

Kenny said defensively, 'I didn't! She came to my rescue. It was just like on the telly.'

'What d'you mean?'

'It was nothing,' murmured Viv.

'Yes, it was,' said Kenny, jutting out his chin. 'You said you were scared, so you were brave.' He began to tell his sister what had happened.

'You stupid idiot!' she muttered when he had finished. 'You shouldn't have taken the budgie out of its cage in the first place, never mind upstairs.' She toyed with the key in her hand and addressed Viv in an embarrassed voice. 'I suppose I've got to thank you. If he'd fallen Mam would have killed me and I'd have never forgiven myself. I only went to a friend's for a few minutes.'

200

'Forget it.' Viv smiled.

Ingrid cleared her throat. 'Why did you come?'

'I came to talk to Nick but Kenny told me he's left.'

'We don't know where he is!' exclaimed Ingrid, pressing the key against the palm of her hand. 'He'd been all quiet and withdrawn since he broke it off with you. He threw himself into his work. He's won an award, yer know?' A smile lit her face. 'That brightened him up a bit, but then he got all tight-faced again.'

'You told him about seeing me at the Casbah, I suppose?' said Viv quietly. 'There was nothing in it, you know.'

Ingrid shook her head. 'I told Mam. I didn't want to remind him about you. It was she who told him.'

'Is that why they argued?'

'I suspect it was partly that.' Ingrid shrugged off her coat. 'But the argument seemed to be more about some letter and him planning to built you a house. Mam didn't like that. Said why hadn't he ever thought of building her one? Stupid really, when we've got a house. But then mam always expected too much from our Nick. In the end he just had enough.' She stared at Viv. 'Why did you split up? You both seemed so happy.'

'It's a long story,' said Viv. 'Anyway, I'd better be going.'

Ingrid touched her arm. 'Listen, if Nick gets in touch, do you want me to tell him you called?'

Viv's mood lightened. 'If you would.' She rummaged in her bag and brought out a biro and scrap of paper. She hesitated before writing Stephen's address. 'He can get in touch with me there.'

Ingrid scrutinised the paper. 'I thought you lived Anfield football ground way?'

She smiled. 'I had Mother trouble too so I left home.'

Ingrid followed her out and on the doorstep thrust out a hand with a shy smile. 'Thanks for rescuing the little perisher.'

Viv squeezed her hand. 'Friends?'

Ingrid nodded, her eyes bright. 'See you again perhaps?'

'Sure.' Viv walked away, feeling little better than when she had come. But at least now she had friends in Nick's family. But where was he? And would she ever see him again?

Chapter Twenty-Two

Nick was up to his wellied ankles in reddish clay, overseeing the construction of his award-winning home which was to be the showhouse on a new housing estate the other side of the Mersey.

On the strength of his winning the design competition Tim Rushford, an architect with his own practice, had offered Nick the position of salaried assistant and the opportunity to become a junior partner in a couple of years. It was a break that he had never expected so soon in his career and he considered himself incredibly lucky in this part of his life if nowhere else. Advancement could be slow because architects were not allowed to advertise. It could take time to get your name known.

Tim and his wife had also offered Nick a room in their house near Eastham village until he found a place of his own. It was completely different to living at home. There was no mad scramble in the morning with Nick hammering on the door for Ingrid to get out of the bathroom. Nor did he have to worry about a frog fancying a swim in his cereal. Now it was grapefruit and toast in a proper rack on a checked tablecloth while watching thrushes and bluetits take food from the bird table in the garden. Conversation was different also. It was more to do with the state of Berlin and what the Russians would do next than whether his mother had washed Ingrid's new sweater in Lux as instructed.

If only Viv could see him now. It was a bittersweet moment for Nick, watching the foundations of his first house being dug. The working-class boy was on his way up. Hilda's words

'Not good enough' still haunted him. As he trudged towards the Land Rover parked at the edge of the site where Tim was waiting, he wondered if he had subconsciously started severing his links with his working-class background after the split with Viv or later after, the argument with his mother over the letter? Not for the first time he asked himself why Hilda had left it for three weeks before coming to say that Viv wanted no letters from him? Why had she bothered? He had got the message when Viv had not turned up on her birthday. Even so he still found it difficult to accept that he had been mistaken in Viv and that it was all over between them.

'Everything all right, Nick?' asked Tim. He was in his late-forties, a bit of a worrier and inclined to fuss.

Nick smiled. 'Fine.'

'We'll go into Birkenhead then before going home. Celia wants me to get some decent wine for dinner tonight.'

'It's good of you to include me,' said Nick, trying to sound enthusiastic. 'You don't have to, you know. I could have gone out.'

'Glad you're on the scene,' said Tim gruffily, starting the Land Rover. 'Between you and me, I hate these things my wife puts on but since the children have left home she seems to need to fill the house with people. I'd love a Saturday evening just lazing around but that's not Celia's way.' He sighed. 'Don't let on that's how I feel, though. She thinks I enjoy them.'

Nick said, 'How many people are coming?'

'Five. That's why you're a godsend. William and Joan's daughter Ursula has finished with college and just got back from hitchhiking on the Continent . . . dangerous thing to do in my opinion. But she's a bit of a rebel and very outspoken. Celia thought it polite to include her in the invitation once she knew she was back. Anyway you'll be able to talk to her and it'll be nice for her to see a young face.'

Nick smiled agreement but was thinking savagely: why is it that couples always feel they have to pair you off with somebody of the opposite sex? It's as if they believe the only state of bliss available is the married one. 'What subjects did she study?' he asked politely.

'She was at Art College, the same as you, but it's textiles she's interested in. Designs all her own clothes. It'll be interesting to see what she turns up in this evening. Probably make your eyes pop out.'

Nick thought sardonically that he couldn't wait.

Dinner was arranged for eight o'clock but the guests started arriving at half-past seven and Nick was given the task of pouring the drinks. The eye-catching Ursula and her parents were late and while Nick's eyes did not pop they definitely widened when a well-proportioned brunette of middle height paused in the doorway, obviously assessing the effect she was having on everyone. Her dress was all black and white but was printed so that the top half consisted of several dice, the piece from beneath her bust to her waist was made up of aces of spades, and the skirt patterned with oblong shapes of black and white stripes.

'I'm sorry we're late,' said her mother in a breathless voice. 'But she was still sewing until half an hour ago.'

'Very eye-catching,' said Celia, nodding her small blonde head vigorously. 'What do you think, Nick?'

Everyone looked at him including Ursula, whose eyes contained a lively curiosity.

'Gambling and licorice allsorts,' he said quietly. 'The sweet life in the South of France. Monte Carlo.'

Ursula's wide mouth eased into a grin and she clapped her hands. 'Clever! But actually I was just playing with the idea of black and white . . . contrasts . . . good and evil.' She came over to Nick. 'Pour me a drink, there's a good boy. I'll have a large sherry.'

'You'll have a small one and like it,' he said lightly, not enjoying being called a good boy. It sounded derogatory. 'We'll be going in for dinner any minute now.'

She pouted but accepted the glass he offered. 'I suppose they've seated us next to each other?'

'Do you mind?'

'Not at all.' Her violet eyes assessed him. 'I think that's why I was invited. Mummy said that Celia believes that you're suffering from unrequited love and I'm here to cheer you up. Is it true?'

Nick's hand paused a moment before putting the stopper in

the decanter. He smiled. 'Tell me, what was it like hitch hiking round Europe?'.

'Neatly turned!' She sounded pleased. 'It was interesting but tiring actually. It even got boring at times.' Her eyes twinkled. 'You know – fighting off the hordes of would-be rapists that Mummy was convinced we were going to encounter.'

'Weren't there any?'

'Mostly bottom pinchers. I had a near miss in some place beginning with an F founded by Julius Caesar. We were on our way to the St Aygalf Camp when – ' She paused. 'No, I don't think I'll tell you. Not unless you tell me who she is?'

Nick stared at her, his face expressionless. 'I told you, there isn't anyone. So you're quite safe to chase me yourself.'

'I thought it was the men who did the chasing.'

'Not in my experience. What if we chase each other?'

'The mind boggles! I have this picture of a snake eating its tail.'

'Do you consider that possible?'

She laughed and he was glad when at that moment their hostess signalled them to dinner. He hoped that would be the end of Ursula's curiosity but she was nothing if not determined. 'Was she pretty, witty, amusing?'

Nick laid his cutlery neatly on his empty plate. 'Would it satisfy you if I made something up?' His tone was caustic.

'Oh dear, I've annoyed you,' she said mournfully. 'But there's a look of Mr Rochester about you and it makes me very inquisitive.'

'Who?' he asked startled.

'*Jane Eyre*. The book. He had a wife hidden away and poor deluded Jane didn't find out until they were at the altar. You'd think it would be enough to turn you off a bloke but he had a good excuse. His wife was mad so what else could he do but lock her away and pretend she didn't exist?'

'I would have thought locking her away would make her madder.'

'Exactly!' She pounced on his words. 'Of course they looked at madness differently in those days.' There was a fulminating expression in her violet eyes. 'I'd love to see you all in black leather.'

'You're mad!'

She grinned. 'It's all the rage in Europe.' She drank half her wine. 'We're so insular in England and it's worse up here. London's not so bad.'

Nick's lips twitched. 'You'd like to see all northern men in black leather? What would the women wear – white satin pinnies?'

She laughed. 'We'll have to go out together while I'm home. It'll be fun. We can do that, can't we? Nothing serious.'

He hesitated, considering how he and Viv had said that they weren't going to get serious. The engagement ring was still in its box in a suitcase on top of the wardrobe in his bedroom. The memory of the day he had placed it on her finger still had the power to hurt.

'You don't have to if you don't want to,' said Ursula. 'But you're rousing my curiosity again.'

Nick forced a smile. 'Nothing serious?' he said.

'Goodie!' she exclaimed, and clapped her hands.

So began a period in Nick's life that occasionally seemed unreal. During weekdays he was on site or in the office. Several evenings and most weekends he went out with Ursula. Sometimes they went into Liverpool to The Jacaranda just round the corner from the Art College where they served the best bacon butties for hungry artists and musicians that he had ever tasted. He tried to feel some of Ursula's enthusiasm for the scruffy musicians but the music had gone out of his soul. They went to The Crack, crowded and smoky, to mingle with the arty crowd. Nothing seemed to have changed from his day. Everyone was still trying to get over their own point of view while some were trying to get in with those who had made their mark, however small. Because Ursula had made it clear to him that their relationship was not to be taken seriously Nick was relaxed in her company. She was a character and he found spending time with her a pleasant way to fill his empty hours.

Celia teased Nick about her, asking when the wedding would be. Ursula was well connected. Her father was an accountant and a member of the planning committee of a local council. Nick made a joke of it, saying that Ursula had her career to consider, but once the idea of marriage was in his head it would not go away. One evening he took out the small box with the engagement ring inside and the remembrance of Viv's face when he had put it on her finger was vivid in his mind. He sat there, staring down at the ring, thinking of her and Hilda.

Chapter Twenty-Three

'Cruising down the river on a Sunday afternoon,' warbled Dot that same evening as she and Viv rested their arms on the rails of the *Royal Iris*.

'You're out of date,' said Viv, fanning herself with her handbag. 'And it's not Sunday and it's not afternoon.' They were having a cruise on the River Mersey. Below deck music was playing and people were dancing.

'It's the only cruising song I can think of,' said Dot, easing her dress away from her skin. 'Isn't it incredible how much heat you can catch from people?'

Vivien stared out over the dark oily waters of the Mersey. 'It's the dancing that gets you hot, idiot . . . and getting steamed up over girls making goo-goo eyes at Phil. As well as the drink. How many Babychams have you had?'

'How many Babychams have I had?' Dot's voice rose. 'You've got a cheek! You've been tossing them down as if there was no tomorrow. Just because you're eighteen now there's no need to go mad.'

'I've had three. And you shouldn't be counting. I'm drowning my sorrows.'

Dot's expression changed. 'Why don't you go and see if Nick's come home?'

'He knows where to find me if he has,' Viv said quietly. Her fingers toyed with the clasp of her handbag. 'Uncle Steve said Mam was hurt when he gave the present back. He told me that she went to see Nick but he wasn't in so she spoke to his mother. He believes she was trying to make amends. All she did in the end was mess things up.'

Dot nodded sympathetically. 'I bet your mam finds Stephen attractive when he smiles. And he has that lovely curly hair and nice blue eyes.'

'Mam and Stephen? Oh, shut up, Dot! And don't talk about blue eyes. Nick has blue eyes.'

Her friend sighed. 'You're getting to be a real pain.'

Viv tossed back her hair. 'You don't have to stay with me. Go and find Phil. I'll be quite all right on my own.'

Dot raised her eyes to the star-sprinkled sky. 'We're mates, aren't we? Anyway, let's both go and see if we can find the boys.'

Viv did not move. She was in no mood to dance with Norm again. He got amorous when he drank too much. Yet she wanted to dance. She was feeling tense, restless, moody. If she did not let off steam somehow she would explode.

Dot let out a long breath and glanced along the shadowy deck. 'We really should get back to the dancing because there's a couple of those Norwegian sailors heading this way and I don't trust them.'

'Are there?' Viv twisted round. Suddenly bandying words with a couple of young sailors who had given them the glad eye during the dancing seemed the answer to her over-wrought emotions.

A fair Viking-like giant addressed Viv, his eyes carefully assessing her charms. 'You dance?'

'No,' answered Dot for her, pulling her arm. 'Our boyfriends have just gone to the toilet so you can scram.'

'Scram? What is this scram?' said the other sailor, who was shorter but tougher-looking.

'It's go away,' said Dot, clinging to Viv like the ivy in the song. 'We don't want you around.'

'You speak for yourself,' Viv said firmly.

The tall Viking smiled at her. 'You dance with me?'

'Yes,' she said, returning his smile.

'We dance up here,' he said, taking her arm. 'It is romantic with the sea and the stars, would you not say?'

'I might say so if you were someone else, but you're not,' replied Viv, amused by his turn of phrase. 'So it's downstairs, me laddo.'

''Tis all right. I will take care of you.' His hand slid down her arm and caught her fingers.

Dot hissed, 'Viv, what are you playing at? You'll get yourself into trouble.'

'Oh no I won't,' she said, flashing her a sparkling look. 'You go and dance with Phil.'

'We dance now.' The blond giant grinned and waltzed Viv along the deck. 'I like you.'

She sighed inwardly. Someone else had once said they loved her but he probably didn't any more. 'Let's head for the bright lights, if you don't mind,' she said. 'I could do with a drink.'

The Norwegian bought the drinks, draining his pint glass in a couple of seconds before seizing her hand and pulling her on to the dance floor. He was heavy on his feet, and loud – stamping and clapping, whirling her round with such vigour that her head spun. She determined to enjoy herself. There were more drinks and more dancing. There was smoochy music and the Norwegian held her close, sucking her earlobe and pulling on strands of her hair with his teeth. She wondered what he got out of it and if it tasted of Coty's L'Aimant. Her head was filling up with fluffy clouds and she wished it could stay that way. She was fed up of hurting. Another drink and the sailor talked of ships and ports. She needed a break and went to the toilet where she found Dot.

'I don't think I should speak to you,' said her friend, looking up scarlet-cheeked from straightening her seams. 'That other bloody Norwegian felt me all over before I managed to get away.'

'Sorry.' Viv squinted at herself in her compact mirror and jerkily powdered her nose.

Dot frowned. 'I wouldn't drink any more if I were you.'

'I'm having a good time.' Viv sang a snatch of a song.

'You want to be careful.'

She closed her compact with a snap and stared fixedly at Dot. 'I'm a big girl now, you know. And I wish people would let me run my life the way I want.' Her voice wavered slightly. 'I wish people would trust me. Nothing's fun any more.'

'All right, all right,' cried Dot, looking even more worried than before. 'Keep your hair on. I won't interfere. Don't forget, though, Mam wants us in at a reasonable hour.'

'Oh Lord, Cinderella!' Viv rolled her eyes. 'Watch Phil

210

doesn't turn into a pumpkin and you into a mouse.' She moved away.

Her partner found her, bought her another drink, and they danced again. But it was not so easy to dance now because Viv needed to hold on to him to prevent herself from floating away.

At last the ship docked and everybody started to head for the gangways. The cold air revived Viv as, surrounded by hundreds of other revellers on the Prince's landing stage, her eyes scanned the crowd for Dot, Phil and Norm. She felt a tug on her hand and looked up into the droopy grey eyes of the Norwegian. 'I see you home,' he said.

'No, I'm okay.' She blinked at him. 'I'm looking for my friend.'

'Please. You have been with me. It is manners that I see you home.'

Viv looked about her one more time and then accepted his offer. She took him in the direction of the bus stop, aware that he was more affected than her by drink. There was a long queue for the bus so he suggested a taxi. She accepted and without thinking gave Stephen's address.

As soon as the taxi left the kerb the Viking pinned her into a corner, sprawling on top of her. He breathed heavily and gave her several spanking kisses before biting her neck. She was more than annoyed, not only with him but with herself. She could just about breathe and kept trying to push him away but he always came back for more. The taxi driver was singing 'Hello, young lovers', and Viv felt like screaming.

At last the taxi rattled to a halt outside Stephen's house and the driver shouted, 'Let's be having yer, kids. Pay up and get out.' Viv stumbled out of the taxi but the Norwegian hung on to her, swaying on the pavement as he searched for money with his other hand.

It was a struggle but Viv managed to free herself and make her way to the front gate, her only thought being to get indoors. She had her key in her hand when she was grabbed from behind and shoved against the fence. The sailor's hot beery breath was on her cheek but his hands were pushing up her skirts.

Her heart jerked in her breast with sudden fear. 'What the

211

hell do you think you're doing?' she hissed.

'We make more love,' he whispered, and sucked her neck.

She ground her stiletto heel into his foot but except for his shaking his leg it didn't have the effect she'd hoped. He began to fumble with his trousers and she punched his hand hard. He gasped but straightened up. 'What is wrong with you? Why you play games with me? I not hurt you.' The words were slurred. 'It be goot. We make each other very happy.'

'No,' she gasped, struggling with him. 'You won't make me very happy. In fact, you'll make me bloody miserable.'

Light suddenly flooded out from the doorway and the next second Viv caught a swift glimpse of Stephen before being flung in the direction of the front door. A moment later and her partner was flat on the ground.

'What the hell's going on, Steve?'

When Viv heard her mother's voice she thought she was dreaming but on turning there she was silhouetted against the light, wearing Stephen's dressing gown. 'What's going on?' said Viv, blinking at her.

Hilda stared at her as if she could not believe her eyes. 'What are you doing here?'

Viv leaned against the doorjamb because her head was suddenly spinning.

'Get inside,' rasped Stephen. 'Don't let's be having a row on the doorstep.' He bent over the Norwegian. 'I'll have to get rid of him.'

'He's not dead, is he?' said Hilda.

'Don't be daft!' Stephen's voice held the slightest quiver. 'I knew exactly where to hit him.'

'You learnt it in the war, I suppose?' said Viv faintly.

'Will you two get in!' he ordered. 'I'm going to have to take him to the docks. Someone'll know which ship he's off.'

Hilda turned and walked into the lounge. Viv stumbled after her and collapsed in a chair while her mother poked the dying embers of the fire. Stephen pulled on a sweater and without a word to either of them went out to the car.

'Well?' said Hilda, putting down the poker and staring at her daughter.

'Well what?' Viv tried to sound defiant but felt too shaken.

'You know very well what. What are you doing here?'

'I live here.' Her eyes did not leave her mother's face. 'Perhaps you do too? Maybe he's had you locked up in the attic like the mad wife in *Jane Eyre*?'

Hilda threw down the poker, and the gauntlet with it. 'You sneaky, conniving little madam!' she cried. 'You've been staying here all along!'

'And what if I have?' Viv stood up. 'What the hell are you doing here wearing his dressing gown?'

Her mother flung back her head. 'We're lovers, that's what we are! Lovers! I bet he didn't tell you that when you came to live here.'

Viv felt as if her mother had hit her with the poker. 'I don't believe you,' she gasped. 'He wouldn't.'

'You think we're too old? We've been lovers for ages.'

'Ages?' repeated Viv stupidly, feeling as if her world had somersaulted and settled the wrong way up. 'But you didn't even like each other,' she cried.

'Well, it goes to show that people can change, doesn't it?' Hilda's eyes glittered. 'But don't think I'm not going to have a few words with Steve over this. What the hell was he thinking of, keeping your staying here a secret from me? It's not right! You shouldn't have been alone in this house with him.'

Viv's temper flared up. 'Why shouldn't I? I've got more right than you have! He's my uncle and he's been more sympathetic to me than some people I could mention. How could you keep that letter from me, Mother? You knew how much I loved Nick.'

'Loved Nick?' Hilda laughed scornfully. 'After what I've just seen outside? He'd love to hear about that, I don't think! Especially after the other little episode at a dance.'

Viv went white. 'It would be just like you to tell him about tonight, if you had the chance.'

Hilda's mouth tightened and there was a pause. 'You'll be getting yourself a reputation,' she said at last.

'It couldn't be as bad as yours,' snapped Viv. 'Does Uncle Steve know about Mr Kelly?'

'That's over.'

'So you say.'

'You wouldn't tell him?'

'Wouldn't I?' Viv laughed. 'I think I *should* tell him.

There've been enough secrets going the rounds.'

'If you're talking about Nick's letter again,' said Hilda in a seething voice, 'I didn't bloody read the thing and I tried to make things better for you.'

'Oh, aye? A right mess you made of it too. Mothers! Who needs them? How could you sleep with Uncle Steve behind my back? I've been a right fool not realising what was going on.'

'Me too! How was it I didn't think of your staying here?' Her mother's expression was grim. 'Well, you'll have to come home now. You can't stay here any longer.'

Viv's eyes glittered. 'You're going to stop me, are you?'

'Yes.'

'You won't! Don't be thinking just because you know I live here now it changes things.'

'It does,' said Hilda. 'Stephen's not your uncle. It wouldn't be right.'

The room suddenly seemed very still.

'That's not funny, Mother,' whispered Viv.

'It wasn't meant to be.'

They stared at each other.

'I don't believe you! You're just saying it to get me out.'

'I am. But it's the truth. Steve is not your uncle.'

Viv felt as if her throat was closing up. She swallowed. 'Who is my father then?'

'Don't start that again,' muttered Hilda. 'I never did tell you that Jimmy was your father.'

'But you told Aunt Flo.'

'I lied.'

Viv stared at her mother, hurting unbearably. 'You could still be lying.'

'I'm not,' whispered Hilda.

Viv believed her. She rubbed at the sudden dampness on her cheeks. 'Why is it, Mother, you get such pleasure out of hurting me?' she said in a low voice. 'I've tried so hard to love you but you've made it too difficult.'

Hilda stared at her, moistened her lips. Her throat moved but no words came out. Abruptly she turned and left the room.

Viv heard her slowly climbing the stairs. I'll have to leave, thought Viv. Now! This minute! I can't cope with any more right now.

She left the house and ran up the street. She was halfway down the main road when a car stopped beside her and the window was wound down. 'Viv, where are you going?' said Stephen.

'Does it matter?' She ran a hand through her hair and gazed unhappily at him. 'Ask my mother to explain. You might just get the truth from her.'

'Get in the car, Viv,' he said quietly. 'I know you're upset, but you can't go wandering around at this time of night. We can talk.'

'Not now.' She averted her face because it pained her, looking at him. 'Anyway, I'm not going to be wandering around. If you remember I was supposed to be staying the night at Dot's. Her mother's probably still waiting up for me, worrying herself sick.' She looked at him then, attempting a smile. 'I'm sorry I came home and spoilt your night.' She did not give him a chance to answer but walked away, knowing that by the time he managed to turn the car she would be out of sight.

Chapter Twenty-Four

Hilda was just leaving the house when Stephen drew up. He got out of the car and walked slowly towards her. 'Back inside.' His voice was low. 'You're not leaving till I've had a few words with you.'

'You can have them with Viv.' Her voice was brittle as she smoothed on a glove.

'Oh, I can, can I?' he said testily. 'I've just seen her halfway up the main road. She told me to speak to you. She's on her way to Dot's. So it's you and me who have to work this out.' He pushed her back inside the house and closed the door. He leant against it. 'Well?'

Hilda lifted her eyes to his face. 'She knows we're lovers and is upset. You've deceived us both, Stephen.'

He suddenly felt awfully tired. 'So she's left. And now you're leaving.'

'You knew I was worried about her all this time she's been away.'

'Not that worried.'

'Yes, I was!' Hilda's voice rose. 'I mightn't have shown it but I was. You should have told me that she'd run to you, if your really cared for me.'

'She didn't want me to tell you so I didn't,' he said harshly. 'I didn't find it easy deceiving either of you if that's any consolation to you.'

'Not really.' She stepped away from him with a jerky movement. 'I suppose that time we went away for the weekend it was to get me out of the way so you could keep your little secret?'

216

'Partly,' he said honestly. 'But does it matter? We both enjoyed it.'

Her eyes glistened. 'Oh, yes, we both enjoyed it. But soft me started believing that romance wasn't dead after all. At my age! Can you believe it?'

'Hilda!' He seized both her arms. 'I'm sorry I kept it from you, but no real harm's been done. We could get married. The three of us could live here together.'

She was suddenly very still, then a small laugh escaped her. 'Thanks, but I don't think it'll work out. Viv'll be back. She can't have taken any of her things from upstairs or I would have heard her. You have a talk with her. I think you'll feel different then about the three of us living here happily ever after.'

'Why? What can she tell me that you can't?'

'A fair bit, I shouldn't wonder.' Hilda swallowed and pulled back her shoulders. 'I think I'd like to go home now. I've said enough. If you can open the door, Steve?'

He stared down at her then let her pass. 'I'll take you home.'

'No. I think I'd like a walk.'

'At this time of night? Don't be daft!'

She turned on him. 'I'll go alone, I said,' she screamed. 'Now get to bed and get some sleep. I doubt you'll be getting any tomorrow!' She slammed the door and he heard her heels tap-tapping up the road.

Stephen did not sleep at all that night, and when Viv did not come back the following morning felt desolate. He went into her bedroom and fingered the new curtains and a skirt she had left flung over a chair. He looked at a photograph on the primrose-coloured wall and saw that it was of George and Flora. Something stirred at the back of his mind and then eluded him.

He skipped Sunday lunch. He did not go out for his customary walk in the park but waited. By teatime Viv still had not come so he went and had a couple of pints at the local pub. When he came back he realised how hungry he was and made himself a snack, wondering now about Hilda and whether they could get together again. He went to bed, hoping that Viv would turn up at work the following morning. The printers' strike was well over and there was plenty of work for them both.

She was standing outside the works entrance when he arrived, looking pale but composed. 'Hello, Stephen,' she said quietly.

He was instantly irritated. 'I waited in most of yesterday.' He slammed the car door shut.

Her eyes smouldered. 'I didn't think you'd expect me after what Mam had to say.'

'Your mother said a lot of things but nothing that can't be talked about.'

Viv's brows rose. 'Don't tell me she lied to you again?'

'What do you mean?'

'What did she say?'

'That you were upset because of what's between her and me.'

Viv laughed. 'Is that all?'

'No, but . . .' He hesitated. 'Shall we go inside and you can make us some coffee? Then you can tell me what else she should have said.' He unlocked the door and led the way in.

Stephen felt better after the coffee, and with Viv sitting at her desk in the office everything felt almost normal. Perhaps Saturday night had never happened? But he knew it had because he felt so awful inside.

'Well?' he asked at last, leaning back in his chair.

'You're not my uncle,' she said quietly. 'Mam told me last night.'

Stephen stared at her, hardly able to understand what she meant. He could hear the blood beating in his ears, then suddenly the words sunk in. 'What did she say exactly?' he said hoarsely. 'Think carefully. Could you have misheard her?'

Viv shook her head. 'I don't think so. She told me that you weren't my uncle.'

'And you believed her?' His tone was suddenly surprisingly incisive. 'She might have been lying because she was hurt by my deception.'

'Mam, hurt!' Viv's voice rose slightly then dropped. 'I thought she was lying at first to get me out of the house.'

He tapped his fingers on the desk. 'Now you don't think she was?'

'No. She was always reluctant to talk about Jimmy. She probably lied about the letters and there weren't any after all.' Viv traced patterns on a sheet of paper with a fingernail.

Stephen nodded. 'I suppose she didn't tell you who your father was?'

'No. And even if she had I don't known if I'd have believed her.'

He stared at her for a long time and it suddenly struck him just who her father might be. The thought made him feel sick.

Viv gazed back at him. Abruptly she got to her feet. 'What is it? Do you know?'

'Sit down,' he rasped, gripping the edge of the desk with both hands. 'How could I know? Your mother didn't tell me.'

She sat down again. 'I suppose you'll want my notice?'

'Did I say that?'

'No, but . . .'

'Does it really matter that my brother wasn't your father?' His voice was harsh. 'You never knew him while we've got to know each other. We have a working relationship and you know your job. We've lost enough working hours with the strike. I want you to stay, Viv. I need you.'

She was silent. Then she eased back her shoulders and met his look squarely. 'I'll stay.'

In that moment Stephen realised just how much there was of her mother in Viv, but whether that was a good or a bad thing for them both he was unsure. 'Do you think we can try and forget it all now?'

'I can if you can.' Her tone was positive.

He attempted a smile. 'Is there anything else you want to say?'

'I think enough's been said.'

Stephen picked up some papers. 'Take the cups out then. There's a good girl.'

Viv did as he ordered but as soon as she had gone Stephen's sank his head into his hands and for a long time did absolutely nothing.

219

Chapter Twenty-Five

'When are you going to make up your mind about your mam?' asked Dot.

Viv took her eyes off the wedding dress in Nanette's shop window. It was almost two months since the painful quarrel with her mother and her leaving Stephen's house and in all that time she had not seen her mother or Nick. 'Does your mam want me out of the way? If so I'll start looking for a bedsit,' she said.

'No! She's glad of the extra money.' Dot tucked her hand through Viv's arm. 'But what about *your* mam? Are you going to see her or not?'

'Not at the moment,' said Viv, her light tone at war with her feelings.

'What about knowing who your father is?'

'She's not going to tell me.'

'Perhaps he was married?'

'I have thought of that.'

'Well, if you're not going to ask your mam, maybe you could try getting in touch with him?'

'Are you being funny?'

Dot shook her head. 'Deadly serious. It might be worth a try getting in touch with the Other Side.'

'You sound like Maggie from the bakery. It's a load of baloney,' said Viv impatiently.

'You shouldn't knock something until you've tried it,' said Dot solemnly.

Viv tried not to smile. 'It's wrong to get in touch with the dead,' she said mildly. 'Look what happened to King Saul in

220

the Bible when he broke the rules. He was that frightened it resulted in his death.'

Dot came back quickly, 'But it does say in the New Testament that you should test the spirits.'

'What's that supposed to mean?' Viv frowned. 'That we ask who they are? Or does it just mean be on your guard against evil ones?'

Dot pulled on her arm and they began to walk towards Lime Street. 'There must be good spirits as well as bad.' Her face was animated. 'Maggie told me how this friend of hers went to see a medium in London before the war. Estelle somebody or other. Apparently she had a spiritual guide who was called Red Cloud. He was an American Indian and a man's voice came out of her mouth. He told the audience all sorts of helpful things from the spirit world.'

'What sort of helpful things?' Viv's voice was sceptical.

'If you're going to be like that, forget it,' said Dot indignantly.

Viv smiled. 'I wonder if they really do ask "Is there anyone there?"'

'Of course they do! It's a pity you don't take it seriously.'

'I do take it seriously,' said Viv in a reasonable voice. 'That's why I'm wary about such things. I believe in a spiritual world.'

'There you are then!' Dot's face brightened. 'All I'm saying, Viv, is if you get that way you can't stand not knowing any more, give it a go.'

'I'll bear it in mind.'

'Right. Now let's think what else I can do to cheer you up.'

'You could shut up about me needing cheering up,' murmured Viv.

'Okay, okay! I was only trying to help. Now how about NEMS? There's a new Alma Cogan record mam wants for her birthday. We can make that an excuse for listening to something more our kind of music.'

'That's fine by me,' replied Viv, despite its being the last thing she wanted to do, but the hours when she was not in work often dragged. She would be glad to get back to the office.

*   *   *

221

Viv stood, watching Stephen signing the letters she had just typed, wondering what he was thinking and whether he did know who her father was.

'What's wrong, Viv?'

'Why should there be anything wrong?'

'You're all fidgety. Have you seen your mother or something?'

'No.' Her eyes fixed on his face which had grown thinner and was more lined. She said abruptly, 'Uncle Steve, do you know who my father is?' He went pale and immediately she wished the words back but it was too late.

'Why don't you go and ask your mother?' he rasped. 'She's the only one who knows. Her and him! And he's dead, isn't he?' There was a harshness about his mouth that made her heart sink.

'You're sure he's dead?' she said slowly.

He nodded and lowered his gaze to the desk.

'Why don't *you* go and see Mam?' she blurted out, feeling more sorry for him than ever. 'Why don't you talk about him to her? Maybe she can give you some answers?'

'I think I know them.' His voice contained a note of bitterness.

She stiffened. 'You know who he is for certain?'

He hesitated. 'Not for certain. So I'm not about to mention names, Viv.'

'I see,' she said coolly, picking up the signed letters. 'It seems a bit unfair when it involves me.'

'But that's exactly it!' he burst out. 'It *wouldn't* be fair because I might be wrong and then you'd be hurt even more.'

'Why would I? Was he married?'

He hesitated. 'I think so. Listen, Viv, we've both taken a knock from your mother. Let's just carry on pretending we don't care and maybe eventually it'll be true.'

'Just like I'm pretending I don't care about Nick?' Her throat moved. 'His sister told me that he won an award for designing a house, you know.'

'Must have talent then,' said Stephen, lifting his eyes to her face.

She nodded. 'I should have told him about you earlier. I wished you'd met. I'd have valued your opinion of him, Uncle Steve.'

222

A line of colour appeared under his cheekbones. 'Thanks. But we're not likely to meet now, are we?'

'I suppose not,' murmured Viv. 'Dot liked him, though.'

'That says something,' he said dryly.

'She's not as daft as she sounds,' protested Viv. 'Although sometimes she comes up with some weird ideas. On Saturday she suggested I get in touch with my dead father.'

She half expected Stephen to bite her head off again but all he said was, 'You mean hold a seance?' She nodded. 'I suppose it would be interesting to see what results you'd get,' he said caustically. 'Not that I believe in such things.'

'Dot says you shouldn't knock things unless you've tried them. Perhaps it's worth a go?' she said with a hint of challenge in her voice.

He stared at her but all he said was, 'You'd better get these letters to the post. We've wasted enough time talking.'

That night Viv could not sleep. She thought back to the days when Stephen had been courting her aunt. Of things said and of the time her mother had come on the scene. Of the photographs Stephen had shown her that first time she had gone to his house and of the photograph he had given her. Suddenly she felt cold all over. Why hadn't she seen it? Could it be *him*? Oh God! She closed her eyes tightly as if she could rid her mind of the thought in such a way. No! No! No! She rolled over and pounded her pillow viciously before burying her hot face in it. It couldn't be true?

And yet so many things made sense if it was. Especially her mother's reluctance to tell her who her father was. Oh God, no! She thumped the pillow again.

'What's up with you?' muttered Dot from the next bed. 'Round and round, bang, bang.'

'I'm thinking about my father,' she said. 'Stephen as good as told me he was married.'

Dot sat up. 'Then he knows who he was?'

'I think so but he won't tell me.'

Her friend pulled a face. 'Why don't you have done with it and have a seance? We could ask Maggie to arrange it.'

'I'm not asking Maggie.' Viv felt she needed to know, though. Was it worth a try?

'If you don't fancy Maggie we could try a simple method

223

right now,' said Dot, switching on the bedside lamp and nearly knocking off the empty cup next to it. 'Like we used to do at work at lunchtime until they stopped us. Remember?'

'You mean play games with letters and a glass?' Viv's tone revealed that her mood was still sceptical.

'You can mock! Some weird and mysterious things happened to us playing that game.'

'You mean water suddenly appeared in the glass?'

'Very funny.' Dot slid out of bed. 'All we need is a board and some letters . . . numbers and a Yes and a No.'

'Is that all?' drawled Viv, trying to appear nonchalant by leaning back against her pillow, her hands clasped behind her head. 'What about a pointer?'

'The cup.'

Viv picked it up. 'There's no cocoa left for any thirsty spirits.'

'You're not taking this seriously,' said Dot, her tone severe, going over to a cupboard and taking out a draughts board. From a drawer she took a couple of pencils and a writing pad. She tore out several sheets of paper and handed a couple to Viv, as well as a pencil. 'Write down the letters of the alphabet in a way that we can cut them into decent size squares.'

'This is crazy,' said Viv, doing what she was told, nevertheless.

Dot's eyes gleamed. 'It's a very serious matter.' She sat crosslegged on top of the bed and with the tip of her tongue protruding, proceeded to write the numbers 0–9.

Fifteen minutes later she had removed the lamp from the bedside table, sending shadows dancing round the room, and had put the board in its place with the letters, etc, set in a circle around the upturned cup on the board. The table had been moved into a more central position between the beds. 'Now no messing,' said Dot firmly, glancing across at Viv. 'You've got to believe. Put your fingers on the cup and I'll ask it the first question.'

'"There are more things in heaven and earth, Horatio", and all that,' said Viv solemnly. 'Shouldn't we be in the dark to make it really spooky?'

'And how do we see where it points to?' said Dot in a long suffering manner.

'I thought the letters might glow in the dark.'

'Shhh! Don't you want to know who your father is?'

Viv was not sure any longer that she did. She hated the guess that she had come up with.

'Concentrate all your thoughts on him and he might get a message through,' said Dot.

'But how does he know I'm looking for him?' murmured Viv.

'Oh, shut up!' cried Dot. 'Now – is there anyone there?'

Viv fell silent and concentrated as best she could on a face in a photograph. It took some doing because she could not remember him clearly but in her thoughts the cup turned slowly and spelt out a name beginning with T. She opened her eyes and suddenly the cup did move to number one.

'What year? What year do you reckon he died?' whispered Dot.

'It would be nineteen forty something,' said Viv, her heart thumping even though she reckoned that Dot had pushed the cup. She tried to concentrate again but her mind began to wander and she found herself thinking of George and the evening her mother had returned from America to find them in a clinch.

The cup moved again.

'Nine, nine,' said Dot excitedly.

'This is the fire brigade,' murmured Viv. 'What is the emergency?'

'Don't mock,' said Dot, a tremor in her voice.

Viv closed her eyes and concentrated once more. Then suddenly in her mind's eye she could see George talking of his father's talent as an artist. The next moment the picture altered and her cousin was up to his neck in water. That was all down to his sister Rosie, she thought, but unexpectedly an icy finger of fear snaked down her spine. Seeing Rosie dying had been one of the worst moments in her young life. 'Rosie! I wasn't trying to reach you,' she cried silently. 'Get out of my mind!' But Rosie refused to go. She was filling Viv's thoughts with pictures of George. He was now up to his neck in water. He was in trouble and needed her help.

'Four, four,' cried Dot.

Viv opened her eyes. 'I think this has gone far enough,' she

225

cried, and swept the pieces of paper off the board.

Dot pouted. 'Spoilsport! Just when it was getting interesting. What happened in 1944?'

'The Normandy landings,' said Viv automatically. 'It's time we were in bed. There's work in the morning.'

Dot removed the board and cup and grinned. 'I got you going then, didn't I?'

Viv climbed into bed and snuggled beneath the bedclothes. 'I reckon my father did die in '44,' she said softly. 'So what have you got to say to that, Dot?'

Her mouth fell open but before she could ask any questions Viv pulled the covers over her head, effectively shutting her out.

'So you reckon you know who he is?' said Dot the following evening, flicking over a page of the *Echo*. It was raining so the pair of them had decided to stay in. They had the house to themselves.

'A guess,' murmured Viv. 'One that I'm not going to voice.'

'I reckon you're having *me* on now to get your own back.' She glanced up from the newspaper. 'What do you think of Marty Wilde marrying one of the Vernon Girls?'

Viv glanced over Dot's shoulder at the picture of the bride and her rock 'n' roll singer husband. 'Nice dress.'

Dot nodded. 'Phil and I are thinking of getting engaged.'

'Good for you.' Viv determined not to let it hurt. She stretched an arm over Dot's shoulder and turned a page. Suddenly she stiffened. 'Have you seen this?'

'Seen what?' said Dot.

Viv prodded the page and read aloud, ' "More than 300 people are feared to have died and many are still missing after a night of terror when a crushing wall of water from a burst dam in the Reynan River Valley 15 miles from Cannes on the French Riviera left a 4-mile path of destruction in its wake. The little holiday town of Frejus was where many of the victims lived . . ." ' Her voice tailed off. Frejus! Wasn't that where George had sent his postcard from? She read on, her fingernails digging into her clenched fists. Millions of tons of water had washed away farms and houses, uprooted trees and

226

telephone poles. The mortuary at the hospital, which fortunately was on high ground, was filled with bodies, most of them unidentified, while the hospital itself was jammed with the injured. The French Naval Air Base at Frejus Plage had been devastated and eight families were missing. The area was a well-known holiday destination for people from Merseyside and the North West.

Inside Viv began to quiver. She straightened and stared unseeingly at the television screen. *Highway Patrol* was just finishing.

'What is it? You've gone all pale,' said Dot.

'George,' said Viv, her voice trembling. 'Last time he wrote he was staying in that area.'

Dot blinked at her and said quickly, 'He's probably moved one.'

'I'll have to find out.'

'How will you do that? Have you got an address?'

'He never gave one or I would have written back,' said Viv, moistening her mouth. 'I'll go and see Stephen. He was in France during the war and has a mate who married a girl from Caen.' She hurried into the hall and took a coat from one of the hooks.

Dot said in a startled voice. 'You don't mean to go and see him now? It's gone nine o'clock and it's raining.'

'I'll take an umbrella.' Viv flashed a brief smile and without further ado left the house.

Stephen stared at Viv and said impatiently, 'George mightn't be anywhere near there now.'

'And he might!' Viv ran her fingers through her hair. This was more difficult than she had thought it would be. It was only on the way here that she'd remembered Stephen had had no time for George. 'I know it sounds daft,' she said quietly, 'but I couldn't stop thinking of him last night. I kept picturing him up to his neck in water after Dot and I messed around trying to get in touch with my father. Nothing happened but . . .'

'You daft pair!' exclaimed Stephen in an exasperated voice. 'What the hell were you playing at, frightening yourself to death? I suppose you're worried now in case George is dead?'

Viv gave a barely perceptible nod.

'What do you want me to do?' he rasped, going over to the cocktail cabinet and pouring himself a whisky. He also poured a sherry for Viv.

She accepted it gratefully. 'Phone your mate in Caen. I know it's miles away from Frejus but it's closer than here. It could be that George is just injured.'

He took a deep draught of the whisky before saying, 'I suppose I could do that. His wife has family in the South and they could put a call through and see what they can find out.'

'Yes please!' She seized his hand. 'Say at the least he's lost everything. He could have no passport, no money to get home . . .

'All right, Viv, calm down,' said Stephen. 'I get the message. I was there myself once in hospital, lost, alone, with no family.'

Her body sagged and she leaned against him. 'Thank you, thank you, Uncle Steve. You're so kind.'

He hugged her and sighed. 'I'll take you back to Dot's because it could take some time to get through.'

'Thanks. But I'll walk back. I don't want to waste the time you could be phoning.'

'All right. But don't expect to hear from me until the morning.'

The next day Viv was waiting outside the works, impatiently pacing up and down, when Stephen's car drew up.

'Well?' she demanded, as soon as he had the door open.

'Be patient, Viv.' He slammed the car door shut. 'Do you expect me to perform miracles? The lines have been down in the South of France and it's been raining there for five days apparently. There's flooding in several districts. Hopefully I'll get a return phone call by lunchtime. I gave the firm's number. Now get inside and make us some tea. It's cold out here.'

'But it's sunny,' she said, attempting to smile. 'Everywhere else in Britain there's terrible gales raging still but we only had a few hours' rain last night. Now we've blue skies.'

'I still need that cup of tea,' he said firmly, ushering her inside.

The call came at two o'clock. Viv had started to her feet

every time the telephone rang and this time was no exception. Stephen waved her back to her chair as he responded to the voice on the other end of the telephone but she stood listening as he spoke in French, recognising the words for 'thank you' and 'goodbye' before he put down the receiver and gazed at her.

'They've found him, haven't they?' Her mouth was dry.

'He was wedged in the fork of a tree, half unconscious, with blood from a head wound smeared all over his face. They don't know how he got there because he seems unable to speak.'

Viv sat down abruptly, feeling faint, and put her head between her knees.

Stephen came over and patted her shoulder. 'It's like history repeating itself, the way that lad gets into trouble. But he's like a cat, Viv. He's got nine lives.'

She lifted her head. 'How did they know it was him?'

'They were able to identify him from the passport in the back pocket of his trousers. It was damp but recognisable. Which probably means he wasn't in the water long.'

'I'll have to go and fetch him home,' she said.

Stephen nodded. 'I thought you'd say that. Family ties are strong with you, aren't they, Viv?'

'I'd do the same for you,' she murmured.

'I believe you would,' he said quietly, going back to his desk. 'Sam suggests that you fly out to Paris and he'll meet you at the airport. The pair of you can motor down. I said I'd ring him back with the time of the flight.'

Relief and gratitude flooded Viv and she got up and went over to him. 'You can't know how much I appreciate what you're doing for me.' She pressed her cheek against his. 'I wish you were my father, Uncle Steve.'

'You can't wish that more than I do,' he said. They smiled at each other, then he slapped her bottom. 'Enough of this, young lady! It's a good job it's nearly the weekend. Go and pack while I do some ringing about times and a ticket. I presume you have a passport?'

'Trip to Calais when I was at school.' And pausing only to pick up her handbag, she left the office.

*　　*　　*

229

The journey to Frejus had gone almost like clockwork. The only change of plan was in their having to take a boat to finish their journey. They discovered that a large part of the town was covered in a sea of brown mud and there was a faint smell of chlorine in the air. A gendarme told Sam Arkwright, Stephen's old comrade in arms, that soldiers had sprayed low-lying areas of the town to prevent an epidemic and that people were being injected against water-carried diseases and were having to queue for their drinking water from tankers. The French Navy from Toulon had moved an aircraft carrier to an anchorage off the resort and their helicopters were still active over the area affected by the flood waters. The Netherlands Red Cross had sent blankets and Pope John had sent a message of condolence to the town's bishop. The same gendarme pointed out to them the hospital, the school and the chapel, where some of the bodies of the dead still lay under the same roof as the homeless and injured.

It was a relief to Viv that Sam's French was so good because hers was only of the schoolgirl variety. He was a Lancashire man and very down to earth. He had a thatch of greying brown hair and a leathery skin which creased into a host of wrinkles when he smiled. Pale-faced but composed, Viv followed him into the school where he had been informed her cousin had been placed.

They found George in a classroom, wearing a pair of pyjamas too small for him and with a blanket about his shoulders. He looked battered and bruised, and showed no emotion when Viv knelt beside him.

'It's shock,' said Sam in a low voice. 'I saw Steve like this. He said he's Tom Cooke's son.'

'That's right,' murmured Viv, stiffening slightly. She shot him a glance. 'Did you know him?'

Sam nodded. 'The three of us ended up in the same unit after the D-Day landings. He has a look of his father.'

'So my aunt always said. What did you make of Tom Cooke? I don't remember him, you see.'

'He was an okay bloke except that he liked himself too much. Same as this lad, Steve reckons.'

Viv touched her cousin's arm. 'George, how are you?'

There was no response.

230

'Do you know who I am, George?' Her voice was quiet and gentle. 'I'm your cousin Viv. We've known each other all our lives. We were brought up together.'

Still nothing.

'He'll be hearing you,' said Sam. 'But it might take days or weeks or even months before he makes any sign of it or speaks.'

'I wonder what happened?' she whispered and addressed her cousin again. 'George, can you remember how you got caught up in the tree?' Silence. It was slightly unnerving. She looked at Sam. 'He will be better at home, won't he? I mean . . . familiar surroundings should trigger some memory that will make him want to talk?'

'I reckon so,' said Sam comfortingly. 'What he needs is to feel safe, and everybody feels better when they're with their family.'

Most of George's family is in America, thought Viv. But she was not going to worry about that now. Taking him back to Liverpool was the first hurdle to get over. 'Can you ask the nurse if we can take him with us?' she asked Sam.

'Sure, lass.' He straightened and went striding across the room among the makeshift beds. She felt confident that he would achieve what she had asked.

She took George's hand which felt boneless. She laced her fingers through his and held them firmly. 'You're not frightened, are you?' she asked. Then thought, that's a daft question to ask. Of course he's frightened, that's why he's like this. But at least he had not pulled away which meant that he might know her. She was unsure what to do. Should she keep on talking or sit quietly? It seemed unreal having George so quiet and unresponsive.

She decided to continue talking. 'Do you remember where you're from, George?' No answer. She answered for him.

'Liverpool. Remember Liverpool football club? You're a supporter. They've just got a new manager. His name's Bill Shankly. He wants to try and get the team out of the second division into the first. Everton are in the first division. They're Liverpool's rivals.' She paused and waited, gazing into his face.

His eyelids flickered slightly but that could just have been a

231

reaction to the close proximity of their faces.

'There's ships in Liverpool,' she said. 'Big ships. Some go to America. That's where your mother lives. In California.' She cleared her throat. 'They have a vinery where they grow grapes. Did you ever get to pick grapes over here, George?'

No response. 'What about your paintings?' Still no response. 'What about Kathleen Murphy?' No response. Viv fell silent, a huge lump in her throat.

Sam returned with some clothes over his arm. 'We can take him,' he said, smiling. 'They've got so many injured they're glad to be rid of him. They said to give him plenty of rest and quiet.'

Viv got to her feet and George rose with her, still holding her hand, which pleased her. Surely it must mean he trusted her? 'Is that it in the way of advice?' she asked Sam.

''Fraid so. They've got enough problems. He's alive and hardly injured compered to many. He'll start talking when he's ready.'

She said as cheerfully as she could, 'We might as well go then. Thanks, Mr Arkwright.'

'I'd better dress him first,' said Sam, grinning. 'He'll catch his death out there in just them jammies. If there's anything you want to do, lass . . .'

Viv took the hint and went to find a lavatory. When she returned George allowed her to take his hand and they left the school.

The journey was difficult. George became agitated several times, and they worked out it was when Viv was out of his sight. Yet he seemed to accept that Sam was friendly and only wanted to help him. The mind was a strange thing, thought Viv. How was it that George knew how to eat and drink and go to the toilet but was unable to speak and showed little emotion? What else could she do that would bring back his speech? Or was it just a matter of time, as Sam believed, and his voice would come back eventually.

She said goodbye to Sam in Paris. 'Steve'll meet you the other end,' he told her, shaking hands. 'It was nice meeting you, lass. I hope all goes well with the lad.'

'Thanks for all your help. It would have been so much more difficult without it.'

'Glad to help. Give Steve my best wishes.'

She said she would and with a last goodbye left him.

Stephen was there waiting at the airport as Sam had said. It was raining and George held on to Viv's arm in a grim kind of silence as they hurried to the car. Almost as if they had previously arranged it, Stephen asked no questions until they arrived home. Then, as he helped Viv off with her coat, he said, 'I take it you've given some thought to what you're going to do with him?'

'I thought I'd take him to America.' Before Stephen could come back with an answer she steered George into the sitting room and sat beside him on the studio couch.

Stephen followed them in, a frown on his face. 'You consider that a good idea, I take it? It'll be strange to him. He needs the familiar.'

'His family will be familiar,' murmured Viv, smiling at her cousin. 'You remember your mother, don't you, George?'

His gaze shifted from her for a moment to Stephen, then back again, but he said nothing.

'What about *your* mother?' said Stephen, still frowning.

'*My* mother?' Viv stared at him. 'You must be joking!'

'That house was his home. It would be familiar.'

'Not now it wouldn't,' said Viv positively. 'We've had it done up since George lived there. Besides, it would mean my going back to live there too and I've no intention of doing that.'

'She could look after him. They'd be company for each other,' insisted Stephen. 'He is her nephew. His mother took you in. Why shouldn't Hilda take George in?'

'Can you see Mam in a nurse's role?' she said with a sharp laugh. 'it takes her all her time to look after herself.'

'She can adopt a very sympathetic manner,' said Stephen. 'I've been on the receiving end, so I know.' He took a bottle of whisky out of the cocktail cabinet and poured himself a drink. 'She might show it towards George,' he added, after taking a sip. Then as an afterthought, 'I wasn't thinking. Would you like a sherry?'

'Yes please to the sherry but no thanks to Mam. I think it'll have to be America. I'll write to Aunt Flora and ask can she pay his fare. I've enough for my ticket.' Suddenly she thought

233

of Nick and said unsteadily, 'I always intended going to visit her one day.'

Stephen shrugged and drained his glass. 'If that's your decision then I'll have to go along with it. And in the meantime, what?'

'And in the meantime, can he stay here?' she said, unsure how he would take the syggestion.

'I wonder how I guessed that was coming?' said Stephen dispassionately, glancing at George. 'But I don't think he'll care for the idea unless you stay as well.'

Viv wrapped one leg round the other. 'I'll stay as well then,' she said, adopting a cheerful attitude. 'Although why you think he won't care for the idea, I don't know. He's made no sign of knowing who you are.'

Stephen handed her a sherry and took a mouthful of whisky, staring at the silent figure besides Viv. 'I think he knows me all right,' he murmured. 'Don't be deceived by outward appearances. Something's going on in that brain of his.'

'You think so?'

'I know so,' he said positively. 'I told you, the same sort of thing happened to me during the war – but I wasn't as lucky as him, having you. For months I stared at a wall.'

'Poor Uncle Steve.' Viv was extremely grateful for all he had done. She went over to him and slipped an arm around his waist. 'I really do appreciate all this.'

'I know.' He smiled down at her then glanced at George. There!' he exclaimed.

Viv jumped. 'What is it?'

Stephen's smile widened. 'He doesn't like you making a fuss of me. I saw it in his eyes.'

'Really?' Viv gazed at her cousin who gazed back with an unfathomable expression. 'I think you're imagining it,' she said.

Stephen laughed. 'He's just like his father! There's life there. I wonder what he's making of all this? He doesn't know anything at all about the wheres and whyfors of how we know each other so well?'

'No, he doesn't,' she said slowly. 'Unless Aunt Flo had his address and wrote to him.'

234

'Possible, I suppose,' murmured Stephen. 'You'll find out soon enough. Now how about some supper, then bed?'

She agreed and went to put the kettle on.

After the best night's sleep Viv had had for what seemed a long time she looked in upon George and found him lying on the campbed that Stephen had put up in the box room, staring at the ceiling. As soon as he saw her he sat up. The scratches on his face were now healing and the bruises had turned yellow. He badly needed a shave.

'I'll ask Uncle Steve for a razor for you,' she said, sitting on the bed. Suddenly both his arms went round her. She was so surprised that she stayed motionless for several seconds before managing to release herself, which was not easy though he was still weak.

She stood looking down at him, not sure how she felt about that demonstration of affection. 'Stay in bed,' she murmured. 'I'll bring breakfast to you.'

Downstairs she found Stephen reading the *Daily Mail* and eating cereal. 'I've been thinking,' she said.

Stephen glanced up, his expression was resigned. 'About George I take it, not about work? We could both do with going in this morning but if you're not able to I'm going to have to find someone temporary, Viv.'

She nodded, accepting that was how it had to be. 'I'm sorry to let you down. I'll be back as soon as I can.'

He folded his newspaper. 'I've been thinking too. Why don't you phone your Aunt Flora? She does have a phone, I take it?'

'Yes. But it'll cost a lot of money.'

'It'll be quicker, though,' said Stephen. 'I think I can stand the bill if it means getting George out of the house quicker. It would be best for both of us.' Before she could say more than a couple of words of thanks he had pulled on his overcoat and with a 'See you later', left the house.

Viv closed the door after him and rested her back against it a moment, her brows knitted. Then she went in search of her address book, picked up the telephone and asked the operator for her Aunt Flora's number in America.

Chapter Twenty-Six

Nick had read the report of the dam bursting in France. A week later he returned home. As he let himself into the house Ingrid peered out of the kitchen doorway and called, 'Who's that?'

'Your longlost brother,' he answered, feeling a flood of affection at the sight of her. 'Is the old battle axe in?'

'If you mean our mother, she's out,' said Ingrid, hurrying towards him. 'I'm just icing a cake for our Kenny's birthday tomorrow. I suppose that's why you're here.'

'Partly. But I did get to wondering how you were all surviving without me.' He hugged her and pecked her cheek. 'Are you all okay?

'Your money's been missed.' Her eyes narrowed. 'You don't look too bad. A bit thinner. Kenny hoped you'd come. In fact I think I can honestly say that he mentioned you in his prayers last night.'

Nick smiled. 'It must be the first time anyone's prayed for me for a long time.'

'It goes to show, doesn't it?' she said, smiling. 'There must be a God up there after all. Want a cup of tea?'

'Thanks. Where's Kenny?'

'Upstairs wondering whether he should collect birds eggs any more,' she drawled. 'He's suddenly worked out that if he didn't take them out of the nests there'd be more baby birds around.'

'Right,' said Nick. 'I'll go up and see him.'

Ingrid said, 'Ask him about the budgie.' Then she went back into the kitchen.

Budgie? thought Nick. Then he shrugged and took the stairs two at a time. He entered his brother's bedroom. The bed was covered in boxes containing birds' eggs cocooned in cotton wool. 'What a mess!' exclaimed Nick.

Kenny turned, his boyish face alight. 'I knew you'd come! What d'you think I should do with this ostrich egg? It's got the teeniest crack but d'you think I could still sell it?'

'It depends if anyone's desperate enough to buy,' said Nick, finding a space on the bed.

'I know someone who wants it but I don't think he will if I tell him it's cracked.' He sighed.

'Perhaps you could do a deal – lower your price?'

Kenny nodded and placed the egg carefully in its nest of cottonwool. He looked up at his brother, face alight with pleasure. 'Have you come back for good? I hope you have. Mam and our Ingrid argue more when you're not around.'

'Sorry, Ken.' He ruffled his brother's hair. 'Where I live now is nearer to the site I'm working on. At the moment the weather's put paid to work so things are dragging but when I get my own place you can come and stay with me.'

'OK,' said Kenny happily. 'Did you bring me a present? If you haven't, could you buy me a budgie?'

'A budgie?' Nick remembered what Ingrid had said. 'What happened to the one we had?'

Kenny shrugged his shoulders and looked uncomfortable. 'It flew away.'

There was silence.

'That's it?' said Nick, a small smile playing round his mouth.

His brother sat on the bed, avoiding his eyes. 'I did try and catch it but I got stuck on the windowsill outside. Didn't our Ingrid tell you?'

'No, she didn't. You tell me.' Nick's curiosity was truly roused now. What was so important about an escaped budgie that Ingrid thought he should know?

Kenny's eyes met Nick's. 'A girl came. You knew her. She got the ladder and rescued me.'

Nick stared at him. 'A girl?' he said carefully. 'I presume she had a name?'

He nodded. 'Vivien. She was scared as well. She told me.'

237

Nick felt a great leap at his heart while he tried to assimilate this unexpected information. 'When was this? Where was everybody else?'

'Ages ago. Mam and our Ingrid had gone out. Otherwise I wouldn't have let the budgie have a fly. Our Ingrid'll tell you. She and Vivien talked.'

Nick smiled and held out a parcel. 'Here's your present.' He took the stairs fast, picturing Viv up a ladder, guessing what it had taken for her to make such a climb.

Ingrid was coming out of the kitchen with a tray. 'I was just going to call you.'

He blurted out, 'Kenny said that Viv was here.'

'That's right.' She smiled. 'Came to see you, lover boy, but you weren't here.'

'When?' he demanded.

'Not long after you left. She gave me an address where you can get in touch with her. Apparently she left home too.'

'Have you still got it?'

'Somewhere. She said dancing with that bloke meant nothing.'

'That's all she said.'

'What else did you expect her to say to me? It was you she wanted to talk to! What are you going to do?'

'Find out what she wanted, of course.'

'I told you – you!'

Nick made for the door. Ingrid rushed after him. 'Aren't you going to wait for the address? And what about your cup of tea? And there's a letter for you from our Mavis.'

'Get us both while I drink the tea.'

She did as he asked and he stared a long time at the name and address on the paper before cramming it with Mavis's letter in his pocket and leaving.

Nick banged on the knocker then stepped back and looked up at the house. Pre-war and in good nick. He was trying his hardest to keep his feelings firmly under control but it was not easy. If Viv answered the door that would be best. He would ask if they could go somewhere to try and sort things out between them. The last thing he wanted at the moment was a confrontation with this Stephen. He heard heavy footsteps

238

and immediately knew that he was not going to get his wish. The door opened.

'Yes?' said the man standing in the doorway.

He was different from the person Nick had imagined, younger and tougher-looking and definitely no sugar daddy. 'Mr Martin? Stephen Martin?'

'That's right,' said Stephen, he eyes narrowing. 'What can I do for you?'

'I'm looking for Viv.' Nick held out his hand. 'I'm Nick Bryce. I don't know if she's mentioned me?'

Stephen's expression immediately showed interest. 'It would be a strange thing if she hadn't,' he said slowly. 'The pair of you were engaged once.'

'Briefly,' said Nick ruefully as they shook hands. 'Can I see her?'

Stephen hesitated then said, 'You'd best come in.'

'I didn't want to disturb you.'

'But you have.' Stephen smiled. 'And it'll be more comfortable talking inside.'

Nick followed him in, wondering if he was going to play the role of heavy uncle. They entered a back room but it was empty.

Stephen waved him to a chair. 'You might as well sit down. I'll tell you now Viv isn't here.' He hesitated. 'I don't know if you read about that dam bursting in France – '

'George was involved,' stated Nick, his hands balling into fists. He had wondered about that when he had read the report.

'He was injured and Viv went to bring him home.'

Nick took a deep breath. 'So she's in France?'

'No. She and George left on the *Sylvania* the other day for New York.' He opened a cupboard. 'Drink? Whisky?'

Nick felt like he'd been dealt a body blow.

Stephen stared at him. 'It's not what you think – George is in a state of shock. He can't talk so Viv's taking him to his mother."

'I see.' Nick breathed slightly easier.

'She didn't get that letter you sent in time to meet you, you know. Hilda put it behind the clock and forgot about it.'

Nick's mouth tightened. 'That wasn't what my mother told

me. Her tale was that Hilda said Viv didn't want any more to do with me.'

Stephen handed him his drink. 'Mothers! Jealous creatures when it comes to their young.' He raised his glass. 'Your health, Nick.'

He murmured something and downed the whisky in one go.

Stephen stared at him. 'Take it easy, lad. That's a waste of good whisky. I can give you Flora's address and you can write to Viv explaining what happened if you like. She'll listen.'

'You think so?' said Nick bitterly. 'She's with George and he'll make the most of his opportunities. He hates my guts.'

Stephen's hand paused halfway towards Nick's glass. 'And mine.'

'He's jealous over Viv,' muttered Nick, staring into the fire. 'And it's not right.'

Stephen took Nick's glass without his noticing and half filled it, adding ginger ale. He topped up his own as well. 'Are you saying that George feels more than cousinly towards her?'

'I've seen him kissing and hugging her.' Nick gulped his second whisky. 'I didn't like it. I don't think that – that cousins should come that close,' he said firmly. 'Anyway, you'll have had a chance to see what they're like together, surely?'

'Yes.' Stephen's hand curled tightly round his glass. 'What are you going to do?'

Nick stared at him. 'What do you mean, what am I going to do?'

'Well, you're not going to let him get away with it, are you? I mean . . . ' Stephen swallowed a mouthful of whisky. 'They'll have all those days on board ship alone – not that I think he could get up to anything at the moment – but Viv's in a vulnerable position. She's filled with pity and compassion for him because he's been through a bad time . . . covered in cuts and bruises and suffering from emotional trauma. I remember hearing a doctor say that about my state in the war.' He took another gulp of whisky. 'I'd lost all my family and then I was almost blown apart.' He laughed sharply. 'War's hell but love can be almost as bad.'

Nick remembered how Viv had sprung to Stephen's

defence. He's suffered, she had said, and he had shouted her down because of his anger and, yes, lack of understanding. He had never been able to relate to his own father so had not wanted to understand her need for a father figure. Now he considered Stephen's words about her being filled with pity and compassion towards George. She was a compassionate person. He had to do something before she made a terrible mistake.

Stephen said, 'Well?'

Nick lifted his head. 'There's regular flights across the Atlantic now, aren't there? My sister mentioned it in one of her letters. They started up last year.' He remembered the letter in his pocket and took it out. 'I've got a letter here from her.'

'Perhaps you can go and visit her? A plane would get you there quicker than a liner,' murmured Stephen. 'I can give you the name of the hotel Viv'll be staying at in New York for the night. George's stepfather is meeting them there.'

The men's eyes met. 'Why are you so keen on me doing something?' asked Nick softly.

Stephen said nothing as he took Nick's empty glass. Not until he had poured them refills, did he say, 'Like you, I don't believe in close blood relatives marrying.' He raised his glass. 'Here's to you and Viv.'

Nick smiled. 'And closer ties between us all.'

Chapter Twenty-Seven

Viv stood in Washington Square looking up Fifth Avenue, noticing the way the Empire State Building seemed to loom over everything from where she stood. Snowflakes pattered down on her upturned face as she murmured, 'I'm glad I'm not going up there.'

'Pity,' said her Uncle Mike. 'It's one of the wonders of the modern world and the view's fantastic.'

'There wouldn't be much of a view today,' said Viv, turning and smiling at him and considering that he had not changed much since she had waved him and his family off at the Prince's landing stage. Perhaps there were a few grey hairs among the sandy ones now, but his snub-nosed face was still as warm and friendly as it had been that first time she had set eyes on him on her aunt's doorstep more than ten years ago.

'It's the art galleries then,' he said resignedly.

'That's right,' she said in a teasing voice. 'We might get some reaction from George when he sees pictures. Art is the love of his life, after all.' She glanced sidelong at her cousin who still had not spoken a word.

George slipped a hand through her arm and she let it lie there. She felt more relaxed in his company now that Mike was with them. It had been a difficult voyage in many ways. George had been overtly possessive in his manner towards her in company, especially when they were on the receiving end of curious stares. She had explained the cause of his silence to a few people but some had acted as if being mentally ill was a contagious disease so she had stayed quiet after that and the two of them pretty much to themselves.

Mike had met them at the shipping terminal and taken George's silence in his stride, but then he had seemed always to accept things as they were.

Viv had expected to begin the long journey across America that morning but the weather had put paid to Mike's plan. A blizzard had raged, closing the main roads out of the city. It had abated somewhat now but the roads were still in a dangerous condition and Mike said they should give it one more day. Viv was quite happy about his decision to stay longer in New York as it meant that they could see something of the city so often featured in films such as *King Kong* and *The Bowery Boys*. The soaring skyscrapers really did take her breath away.

Mike roused her from her thoughts by saying, 'Which gallery first, that's the question? We've got America's finest right up Fifth. There's the Metropolitan Museum of Art and the Frick Collection housed in Henry Frick's original mansion. Now he was a rogue, but his pictures are worth seeing.'

'We'll visit the rogue's gallery,' she said, and linking her other arm in his, the three of them forged their way along snowy sidewalks that were busy with Christmas shoppers despite the weather. She paused to gaze at a pair of lions that sat outside the enormous bulk of the New York Public Library. 'They look more friendly than the ones outside St George's Hall in Liverpool,' she said, patting one on the head.

At last they came to the Frick Art Gallery. The building was airy and beautiful and gave Viv almost the same awed feeling she experienced in a cathedral. She thought of Nick and felt a familiar ache.

They began a slow wander, pausing when it felt right to spend more time viewing a picture. In the West Gallery where Rembrandt's *Polish Rider* was displayed Viv noticed a change in her cousin. He stepped back several paces as if to get a better viewpoint.

He stood there so long that Mike drawled, 'I'm going to take root if we don't get a move on.'

They entered the South Hall and Viv noticed that there were more people here. Mike led them over to El Greco's *Christ Driving the Money-Changers from the Temple*. The

243

Prince of Peace had a whip in his hand to chastise the polluters of the Temple. She exchanged looks with George. 'Do you remember Sunday School?'

He surprised her by nodding but before she could take it any further a voice spoke her name and she spun round, barely able to believe it.

'I flew out as soon as Stephen told me where to find you,' said Nick, his hands reaching out to her. 'It seemed the right thing to do, especially when I'd just received a letter from our Mavis saying to come over.'

'But how did you know where to find me?' stammered Viv incredulously.

'The receptionist at the hotel told me that you mentioned art galleries. Mavis suggested we try the Frick first because it's smaller. I'm glad we did.' His blue eyes were intense. 'We've got to talk, Viv.'

She could feel the controlled tension in him as his hands gripped hers firmly and her heart pounded with the strength of her own feelings. She had missed the sight of him so much! Her eyes searched his face hungrily. 'Yes! We have to talk,' she said.

He smiled. 'I made a helluva mess of everything.'

'So did I,' she said softly, oblivious to anyone but him. 'I should have been honest with you.'

They stared at each other silently, savouring the moment.

Mike cleared his throat and so did the woman at Nick's side, who also pulled on his sleeve. He said vaguely, 'Viv, this is my sister Mavis.'

Viv forced herself to tear her gaze from Nick's face to smile at the woman by his side who was carrotty-haired and freckle-faced. 'You were having a baby last I heard.'

'I had a boy.' Mavis grinned. 'Perhaps it'll be your turn next? Nick's going to be godfather tomorrow. You're welcome to come along if you can.'

'I'd love to,' said Viv in a dreamy voice.

'Not possible,' drawled Mike, touching her shoulder. 'What's going on, honey?'

Viv tried to pull herself together but it was Nick who answered for her. 'It's too long a story to tell now, sir. Viv can fill you in later. The pair of us have to talk, if you don't mind?'

Mike glanced at George. 'Sure. I get the picture. George and I will be fine.'

Viv had completely forgotten about her cousin. Now she turned to him to be greeted by a scowl that turned his handsome face ugly. Dear God, don't let him turn stroppy on me now, she pleaded inwardly. But she need not have worried. Mavis homed in on her cousin.

'Georgie Porgie, pudding and pie! Remember how you used to kiss the girls and make us cry!' She flung her arms around him and pressed him to her maternal bosom.

Viv and Nick exchanged glances and there was laughter in his voice as he pulled on her hand and said, 'Let's get out of here.'

'I'll meet you back at the hotel, Uncle Mike,' cried Viv, almost falling over Nick's feet in her rush to escape.

George looked like he was about to follow them but Mavis and Mike seized an arm each. 'Perhaps I can tag along with you and Georgie, Mike?' she beamed at the two men.

Viv did not worry any more about her cousin. It was taking her all her time to control the joy and excitement effervescing inside her. 'Where are we going?' she asked as they raced out of the gallery.

'Anywhere! You name it, we'll go there! I just had to get you away from them. I want nobody distracting us from saying what we've got to say to each other – and that means George especially.'

'You know what's wrong with him?' she whispered as an art lover gave them a frowning look.

'Emotional trauma, so Stephen said.'

She slowed her pace and scrutinised his features once more, her gaze lingering on his mouth which had a tender curve to it. 'What did you think of Stephen?'

'There's nothing sugary about him'. He flicked back a lock of dark hair that had fallen into his eyes. 'We could have spent the last few months together instead of in misery apart.'

She nodded. 'I was stupid. Even so, some of our misery is definitely down to my mother.'

'Not just yours, mine as well. Mam lied to me about Hilda's visit. She gave me the impression it was all over between us. At least your mother did try to make amends, so Stephen said.' He toyed with her fingers.

Viv was silent.

'What is it?' Nick's voice was concerned and he took her by the shoulders and shook her gently. 'Don't clam up on me now, love. You can say anything to me. We've got to be as honest as we can be with each other.'

Her mouth quivered. 'Mam and Stephen were lovers and I never knew it. When I found out I didn't want to have anything to do with her. I was so angry, Nick, I didn't want to believe or understand why they could feel and need each other in such a way.'

His uppermost emotion was relief because there was still a tiny part of him that felt insecure in regard to Viv's feelings towards Stephen, but he was determined to try and understand how she felt. 'I bet you were hurt?'

'Yes. But it wasn't just that.' She rested her head against his shoulder. 'It was a few things, one on top of the other. Mam not being pleased about us getting engaged – then it was her keeping the letter so long that it was too late to meet you. I felt terrible about that. And then on top of everything else she told me that Jimmy wasn't my father – which meant that Stephen wasn't my uncle.'

'What?' Nick held her off from him and his dark eyes blazed. 'She told you that herself! Did she tell you who was your father?'

'No. Although . . .' She bit her lip, then rubbed her cheek against his neck. 'I don't think I want to know any more. You were right, Nick. I should have left the past alone.'

There was a short silence before he murmured against her ear, 'Let's forget about your father then and just think of now. I want us to be alone so I can kiss you.'

'Me too.' Her voice was muffled against his shoulder.

They hugged each other then she lifted her head and smiled. 'Let's get out of here and you can tell me where you've been all this time.'

'Working on the Wirral.' He returned her smile as, hand in hand, they left the relative quiet of the Frick. Their feet made crunching noises in the snow as they made their way into the white wintery landscape of Central Park. He talked as they went and when he had finished, she said hesitantly, 'Now you're going up in the world, you won't let it change you too much, will you? I mean it won't change the "deep down" you? I know circumstances can change us all, make us stronger or weaker or more uncertain.'

'Stop worrying.' He drew her close and they wrapped their arms around each other. It was an extremely cold day and they were muffled up against the elements. 'It hasn't stopped me fantasising about you,' he murmured. 'Remember that conversation we had about armour?'

She threw back her head and laughed. 'If you think I'm going to strip off here, mate, you've got another think coming!'

He grinned. 'Somewhere else?'

'Behave yourself.' Her eyes sparkled and she pressed an icy cheek against his. 'We've only just met after yonks! But . . . I have a hotel room which is central heated. We could talk . . .'

'Talk?' He looked thoughtful. 'I have your ring with me. I could propose all over again. Go down on one knee if you like?'

'Having you at my feet is an offer too good to miss!' She kissed him and the moment was as sweet as the sun after a hailstorm as she thought of how many more kisses there were to come.

It did not take them long to get to the hotel where they took the elevator to the ninth floor. They peeled off their top clothes and Viv placed their footwear in the bathroom before padding back into the bedroom. Nick was gazing out of the window where a few snowflakes whirled lazily against the dark bulk of the building opposite.

'Not much of a view,' she said, standing at his shoulder.

'It makes me feel sleepy looking at snowflakes,' he murmured.

'Sleepy? You mean you're tired and want to go to bed?' There was a diffident note in her voice.

His eyes rested on her rosy face. 'Did I say that?'

'No, but . . .'

'No buts.' He led her over to the bed and kissed her ear. 'What about my ring?'

'I'll give it to you as long as you promise never to throw it at me again,' he said solemnly, getting down on one knee.

'I didn't throw it,' she protested. 'Anyway, I promise. If nothing else it's safer on my finger than in your pocket.'

'That's what I thought. It'll warn George off. He'll know you belong to me.'

She raised her eyebrows. 'What about you belonging to me? Perhaps a chain round your neck . . . who is this Ursula you mentioned a couple of times, by the way?'

His expression stilled. 'Nobody important. A friend. She sussed out that I was suffering from unrequited love and wanted to cheer me up.'

Viv's eyes narrowed and she tried to fathom if he was teasing her. 'I requited your love. What's she like, Nick?'

'Not as nice as you. Nor as pretty.'

'What colour eyes has she got?'

'Violet.'

'Violet!'

'She's just a friend.' His face was serious. 'I was in need of a friend. I believed I'd lost the best one I ever had. Weren't we that to each other, Viv? Friends as well as lovers?'

His words touched her heart and mutely she held out her left hand. He placed the ring on her finger and then sprang up and sat next to her. His arm slid round her waist and he kissed the hollow of her throat.

'You must have got awfully close to see the colour of her eyes,' murmured Viv.

'Not as close as I've been to you. Nor did I want to be.' Nick undid the top button of her blouse with his teeth. Then he lifted his head. 'What about Norman?'

'He meant nothing!' She seized Nick's head and pressed it against her breast. He smiled and managed to unfasten the next three buttons.

Viv swallowed and closed her eyes as he lowered her on to the bed. 'You won't be seeing her again, will you?' she said softly.

'Boxing Day. Same party. It's business really – and I've got to be home for Christmas. I promised our Kenny. Besides, I couldn't get any more time off to stay here longer.' He felt the sigh ripple through her.

'Don't kiss her under the mistletoe.'

'Don't you kiss George.' He loosened his tie and dragged it off. 'Let's forget them both. It's you and me now, Viv.' He touched her cheek with a gentle finger before dragging his shirt and T-shirt over his head. Then he lay beside her. 'Missing you was hell,' he said unsteadily.

Viv turned on her side and gazed at him. 'Hell,' she agreed, and went into his arms, her breasts brushing his chest.

He ran a finger down her spine and a tremor shivered through her. They kissed forcefully, passionately, and desire was a sweet flame that flared up inside them. They were both thinking of what had happened on the hills above West Kirkby.

'It's not safe,' she said.

'It would be nice, though,' he said languidly. The room was warm and all sound seemed muffled, outside and in. He landed several small kisses on her face that were as gentle as dew.

'I mean no, Nick,' she said, knowing that if he persisted she would soon be like putty beneath his touch.

'Trust me.' He laid the palm of his hand flat on her stomach.

Her flesh trembled but her mind was determined that her body would not respond to the sensations that swept over her. 'Nick, we've got to be sensible.'

He tickled her stomach with the tips of his fingers.

She closed her eyes and counted to ten. 'My mother said it was difficult. Perhaps I'm like her after all?' she said with a hint of self-mockery.

Nick sat up, his blue eyes dark. 'You've got a thing about behaving like your mother!'

She struggled upright. 'Is that surprising? You forget, I'm illegitimate. It still hurts at times, Nick.'

'OK!' He breathed deeply. 'But it's not important to me. But – just to prove that I'm not after your body, Viv, we'll call a halt right now. You're right. We have only just met after months. We should give it more time. Put your clothes back on.'

'You mean it?' Her voice was incredulous.

He frowned. 'Of course I bloody mean it! I've lived like a monk for months. I can carry on a bit longer. It's a struggle but – the battle is to the strong.'

'I think it's to the swift, isn't it? Or is that the race?' Viv's tone was doubtful and she sighed as she eased herself against him and put her arms around him. 'I know it won't be easy when you go back but you won't run off with Violet Eyes, will you?'

He pushed her away and said crossly, 'And you won't flirt with any Californian surfers while enjoying yourself in the sun?'

She kissed his bare shoulder and said mischievously, 'All the time, love.'

His frown faded. Taking one of her hands, he pressed a kiss on its palm. Longing ran through her veins like warmed syrup. 'Help me fasten my bra,' she said huskily, and knelt up on the bed with her back to him.

He picked up her bra but dropped it and cupped her breasts instead, holding her against him. 'I wonder if Delilah played your kind of tricks on Samson?' There was a deep tremor in his voice.

'I don't want to weaken you,' she whispered. 'I just want you to make an honest woman of me.'

'Damn!' he said savagely, and flopped on to the bed beside her. She kissed him ardently, saying against his mouth that she really did love him more than all the tea in China and adding that she madly wanted sex with him but that it was not on. Eventually they pushed each other away with desperate determination and slid off opposite sides of the bed.

'Are you still going to marry me?' said Viv with a slight smile.

He returned her smile and stretched out a hand. 'If that's the price I have to pay to have you.' And with that he pulled her flat on the bed again and began to kiss her all over again which was sweet torture.

'I think we should go shopping,' said Viv, a quarter of an hour later as she fastened her skirt. 'I haven't bought you a Christmas present.'

'Me and you both.' Nick slipped his tie under the collar of his shirt. 'I wish you could come home with me.'

'I wish we could both go swimming in the Pacific,' she said lightly before going into the bathroom for their footwear.

They walked back to Fifth Avenue, almost in silence. Nick commented on some of the buildings and added, 'I mightn't be able to build the house I want for us right away.'

250

'It doesn't matter.' She smiled up at him. 'We can both work towards it. I know we're going up in the world. Mam was wrong all the way about you.'

Nick hesitated before saying, 'When did you last see her?'

'Months ago.' Viv's brow furrowed as she stopped outside Tiffany's. 'Do you think I should buy her a Christmas present? If I do, will you take it to her for me?'

He squeezed her hand. 'You've made up your mind about her then, have you?'

'She tried to make things right between us as you said.' Viv stared at a glass bauble streaked at its heart with red and pink and green. It was a pretty piece of nonsense and somehow spoke to her of her mother. Red could be for danger or for warmth. Green was for go and growth. Had her mother been honest with her and Stephen about Jimmy? Perhaps she had lied because she was jealous? Viv wanted that to be true.

They went inside and the pretty piece of nonsense was more expensive than she had expected but she told herself that it was Christmas and her mother would probably be spending it alone. While she waited for her transaction to go through, a lengthy business in Tiffany's, Nick said that he would have a prowl round and meet her outside in half an hour or so. She guessed what he was up to and had a look around herself, coming to the irritating conclusion that there was nothing she liked that she could afford – so she spent money that she could ill afford but felt the better for it. Whether Nick would appreciate the thought behind the choice was a different matter.

As she emerged from Tiffany's she was humming 'I'm Dreaming of a White Christmas' but it had stopped snowing. Even so it was still Christmas inside her. Nick slipped his arm round her. 'After shopping in there all I can offer you is coffee and a doughnut,' he said with a smile.

'That'll do me.' In that moment she realised it was a very long time since she had felt so happy and she wanted to clutch the moment to her. All too soon Nick would be winging his way across the Atlantic while she headed West, following the trail of a hundred movies. Momentarily she felt afraid. What if anything happened to him which meant they would never see each other again? She shivered.

'What is it?' asked Nick. 'Cold?'

'Yes,' she said, and smiled up at him. No way was she going to spoil the next hours with irrational fears. Even so, she could not help remembering that where George was concerned, her fears had proved correct.

When the moment came for them to part Viv clung to Nick. 'It's not really goodbye, is it?' she said.

'No.' Just au revoir!' He hugged and kissed her one more time before handing her a small package. 'Don't open it till Christmas.'

She gave him his present and the one for her mother. 'I hope you agree with it,' she said softly. 'Wear it and think of me. And don't say anything soppy to Mam. I don't want her thinking I've gone soft.'

Viv ran up the steps of the hotel, determined not to cry. In the doorway she stopped and looked back. He lifted a hand, blew a kiss and was gone.

Chapter Twenty-Eight

Off and on across America Viv thought of Ursula's violet eyes. Stupid of her to worry, she told herself. Nick had not had to tell her about the girl. It was just an example of the honesty he wanted them to share with one another. So why hadn't she told him her suspicions about her father?

As they neared the California state border Viv's worry about her father's identity grew and she wondered if perhaps her mother might have written to her aunt about the cause of their quarrel? If she had not then Viv intended keeping quiet about Jimmy not being her father. Her aunt had enough worries with George, who had been sulky since the meeting with Nick.

At last they were in Napa country. Mike pointed out Mount St Helena a few miles away, and named trees and shrubs. Oaks mingled with redwood, laurel and pine. There were rivers and streams watering the land in plenty. As Viv looked about her at the green and beautiful paradise she wondered how her aunt, a city sparrow, had settled in such a place. They came to wide range of vineyards and orchards and Mike said with relief and excitement in his voice, 'Nearly there.'

They passed through a stone gateway and travelled up a drive lined with trees. 'Walnut,' informed Mike, who was looking tired after the week-long journey.

A house came into view. It was built of stone and wood and had a veranda running its length. There were lots of windows and the roof was graced by a high multi-windowed turret. Viv thought the view from there must be quite something. A hand slipped into hers and she glanced at George to see he was looking slightly apprehensive.

'Don't worry,' she whispered. 'Everything's going to be all right.' He nodded but kept a grip on her hand.

The car came to a halt on a wide gravelled space and Viv and George climbed out. A door opened and a woman came flying towards them. She halted a foot or so away. Her copper-coloured hair was streaked with grey and she wore it in a curling top knot; hazel eyes creased at the corners in a familiar smile in her sun-bronzed face. 'Aren't I going to get a hello or a kiss?' she said in a voice that quivered.

Viv would have flung herself at her aunt; George held her back. 'George, this is your mother,' she said quietly. 'You must remember her?'

His grip tightened and his throat convulsed but he did not speak.

Flora's smile faltered and tears brimmed in her eyes. For a moment she struggled for control and at last managed to say, 'It doesn't matter, Viv. All this must be so strange to him.' She moved towards them, hugging Viv but only touching her son's arm gently. 'Come into the house, George. You must be tired as well as hungry. I've made apple pies and there's steak and plenty of veggies. I could never fill you up in the old days. Remember we used to say you had hollow legs?'

He made no reply but walked beside them towards the house.

Mike caught up with his wife and said something in her ear. She nodded and said to Viv, 'Excuse me, love. I'll be with you in a second. The children are about somewhere. They'll have heard the car.'

Viv looked at her in concern but walked on with George to where there were several outbuildings surrounded by shrubbery and flower beds. Her aunt had always loved flowers but her garden in Liverpool had been tiny. Suddenly from round the corner of the nearest building raced three children. The boys reached them first and like their mother stopped a foot or so away. They were identical twins and stared from curious grey eyes. They were like Mike, thought Viv, except there was the slightest hint of ginger in the flaxen hair. A moment later their sister caught up with them, covering her face with her hands and peering through her fingers at them.

Viv crouched down so that her face was on a level with the girl's. 'Hi, Lizzie! Don't you recognise us? You were only three when you left Liverpool. How old are you now?'

The hands were removed, revealing a shy smile. 'Six. You're cousin Vivien and . . .' she pointed a chubby finger '*he's* my brother George.'

'That's right.' Viv smiled. 'Are you going to show us the house?'

Lizzie nodded and with an air of importance led the way. Her brothers trotted one either side. The one next to Viv said earnestly, 'I'm Peter and I'm nine. Can George really not talk?'

'Not yet. But he will,' she replied with a confidence she was suddenly far from feeling.

'What happened to him?' asked the other twin, Simon.

'We don't really know. When he can talk, he'll tell us.' She noticed that George was staring at Lizzie and felt a tingling down her spine. Had he spotted the likeness to his dead sister Rosie? Suddenly he loosened his grip on Viv's hand and walked towards his half-sister. Lizzie looked at him and smiled. A smile which was unexpectedly returned.

'Do you like wine?' asked Lizzie. George nodded. 'My pa makes wine. We'll show you after.' She took hold of his hand and led him towards the house.

Viv let out a long breath and followed with the boys. Her aunt was suddenly there beside her, still wearing a concerned expression. 'What's up, love? Is he all right? Are *you* all right?'

'I think so. He and Lizzie seem to have hit it off.'

The strained look on Flora's face relaxed. 'Lizzie's a cheery little soul and won't do him anything but good.' She squeezed Viv's arm. 'You must be shattered. Has he been terribly difficult?'

'Not really,' lied Viv, entering the house. 'I suppose you've been up the wall with worry?'

'Twice I was nearly on a plane but Mike told me not to be so mother hennish. That if you'd thought I needed to be in Liverpool, you would have said so.'

Viv smiled. 'I wouldn't have known where to put you, to be honest. That was one of the reasons I decided to bring George here. Mam and I have fallen out.'

'I know,' said Flora grimly. 'I received a Christmas card and a letter from her only the other day.'

'What did she have to say?'

Her aunt's smile came and went. 'We'll talk about it later.' She slipped a hand through Viv's arm and hugged it. 'It's so good to have both of you here. What do you think of my house? Its too far from the coast, of course, but we do have a beach house. We'll be going there on Boxing Day for a few days.'

'That sounds great,' said Viv, looking about her curiously. The room was as spacious as most rooms she had seen in America so far. This one, though, was more homelike. The sofas looke comfortable and there were hand embroidered cushions scattered about. A rocking chair rested near a window and there was a Welsh dresser against a wall. A log fire burned in the large open fireplace and on either side of it were shelves filled with books, records and ornaments. Tinsel garlands were strung along the mantleshelf; there was a decorated tree in one corner and a television in another.

George was sitting on one of the sofas next to Lizzie, an open book on his knee. Flora smiled at them before pulling Viv aside. 'You didn't keep anything from me, did you?' she whispered. 'This knock on his head – how serious was it?'

'Not very,' said Viv, eager to reassure her. 'Uncle Steve reckons his trouble is more to do with shock and is emotional. He thinks George will speak when he's ready. He just needs lots of loving care.'

Flora stared at her curiously. 'Has Stephen changed that much?'

Viv murmured. 'I think he's come to terms with losing his family and that's a good thing. He missed the mothering his mam and sisters used to give him.'

'You're very wise for your age, Viv,' said Flora, flushing. 'I didn't help him by breaking it off the way I did, though I'd tried to let him down gently first.' She hesitated. 'Come into the kitchen, love, and we can talk there. I've got to check on the dinner and we can make a cuppa.'

Viv followed her out and sat on a pine chair, wondering what was coming next. She gazed about her, considering how different this kitchen was from her aunt's in Liverpool. It had cupboards galore, a huge fridge and a view out of the window that would make doing the washing up almost a pleasure. She wondered whether to mention her mother again, part of her wanting her curiosity satisfied and the other not wanting to know if it was going to cause unhappiness to her aunt.

Flora set cups and saucers on a tray. 'Hilda's missing you. She sounds lonely.'

Viv looked at her fingernails. 'She brought it on herself.'

'I know that,' murmured Flora.

'What has she told you?'

Her aunt leaned against a cupboard. 'Let's say reading the letter was like reading one of those *True Confession* magazines.'

Viv lifted her head. 'You mean she told you the truth?'

'All about Dominic and Stephen.'

'I bet it was all melodrama.'

'Lots of sound and fury, signifying quite a lot. She said that I should never have told you that Jimmy was your father,' said Flora, her tone caustic. 'And that she wouldn't be as unhappy as she is now, if I'd kept my mouth shut.'

Viv sprang to her feet, unable to bear sitting still any longer. 'She's got a blinking nerve, Aunt Flo! When I think of the unhappiness *she* caused, and what she did to you! She doesn't deserve you to be concerned about her!'

Flora stared at her. 'What has she done to me that you're getting so worked up about?' she said softly. 'What do you know, Viv? or what is it that you think you know?'

She opened her mouth and then closed it firmly.

'That bad?' said Flora dryly.

'If you don't know,' said Viv, gazing at her fingernails again, 'then there's no need for me to tell you.'

'I see.' Flora took the kettle off. 'Hilda has no idea that you're here with George, you know.'

'Of course she hasn't,' said Viv. 'But she'll know soon enough because Nick's going to visit her. I almost wish he wasn't now but I had a moment of weakness in New York and bought her a Christmas present. He's going to take it to her.'

Flora smiled. 'At least that's good news. Mike told me of your meeting with Nick and your becoming engaged. I'm really glad about that, Viv.'

She clasped her hands in front of her and her face was pink with pleasure. 'I wasn't sure you would be. I mean, Mam went on and on about his mother's reputation.'

'None of us are perfect,' said Flora, placing the teapot on the tray. 'You'll be good for each other. You have similar backgrounds and you've both grown up in the hard school of life.'

'George doesn't like him.'

'He never did. Nick was that little bit older and wiser and George didn't like that. He's like his father, always wanting to be top dog.'

'Sam, Uncle Steve's mate, said he was like his father. He said Tom Cooke was an OK bloke though.'

'He was in lots of ways, but in others – ' She shrugged. 'I can see it all clearly now, looking back.' Flora's eyes met Viv's, reflecting her own feelings, and with a sense of shock she realised that her aunt either knew for certain who her father was or had guessed. 'George has always been like a brother to me,' she said with difficulty.

'Of course he has,' said Flora reassuringly. 'And his emotional dependency on you is due in part to your having been brought up together. As long as it doesn't go any deeper than that with him . . .'

'Now we're here things will change.' Viv tried to strike a confident note. 'Look how he's taken to Lizzie.'

Her aunt's brow knitted. 'That's a good sign, isn't it?'

'Yes,' said Viv, some of the tension seeping out of her. She decided to change the subject. 'How's that tea coming along, Aunt Flo? I'm absolutely parched.'

'All right, love. Enough's been said. But sooner or later you're going to have to consider your attitude to your mother. It seems to me that she has been trying to make amends for her past behaviour – if making a muck of it in the process.'

Viv grimaced. 'Too right. But don't let's spoil Christmas by thinking about her now.' With that she picked up the tray and carried it through into the living room.

Flora told Viv that she had decided they would stay at home

258

for Christmas Day instead of making their usual trip to Mike's mother's house. It would be too confusing for George with the whole rowdy Donovan clan gathered together. Viv was quite happy to fall in with whatever her aunt planned. It was good just to be with the family once more.

Christmas Day was peaceful but filled with simple pleasures. Viv opened her present from Nick alone in her bedroom. It was a silver heart-shaped locket and she immediately put it on. Mike and Flora gave George a large box of paints and for a moment Viv thought he would speak because his expression was one of sheer delight. But although he opened his mouth no words came, and then the smile faded and he put the box under the table and looked thoroughly miserable. It was a real disappointment and Viv found herself praying intensely that soon he would speak. Perhaps when they were all used to being together again, he would become himself again? Viv hoped so because she was convinced that until he did she would not feel free to go home.

The next day they travelled south and after a couple of days Viv felt she had been away from home for a month, not just a couple of weeks. She lay on a beach not far from Santa Barbara watching the surf roll in, toying with the locket around her neck. Already she had started a letter to Nick, describing the vinery with its wine cellar and distillery, and planned to write about this part of California with its Hispanic-styled architecture and lovely whitewashed missions.

She picked up a tin of Nivea and began to smooth cream on her arms. Her eyes narrowed against the sun as she watched her cousins splashing in the surf. Her aunt and uncle were further along the beach, their heads together in conversation. George was a foot or so away, part facing her as he pencilled something on a drawing pad. He looked up and she smiled at him. 'Is it going to be good, George?'

He shrugged and then gave his attention once more to his drawing. For a while Viv lay sunbathing but as the sun grew really hot, decided to cool off.

'Are you thinking of going in for a swim?' she asked her cousin. He shook his head and not for the first time she wondered if his experience in France had bred in him a fear of water that had not been there before.

There was a breeze off the sea and the water was deliciously cool. The surf was boisterous and swimming difficult so that she did not seem to get far for all her effort. She envied the surfers their skills on their boards and soon gave up swimming to do as the children did and jump into the waves.

It was exhilarating when a wave rolled in that was higher than the preceding ones. Where had she heard that every seventh wave was a whopper?

She glanced sidelong to check that Lizzie and the twins were all right but they were no longer there. Anxiously she looked about her and saw thankfully that they had joined their parents on the sand and were making a castle. Suddenly that whopper she had been watching for came sweeping in when she was not looking. She had no time to fill her lungs with air and was caught up in a churning mass of water and sand that tossed her over and over so that for a brief time she had no idea where was the surface and where the bottom. Water went up her nose and she needed desperately to get rid of it. To breathe! To cough! Her lungs were hurting, bursting! God, where was the surface?

Then there was a wrench on her swimsuit and she was being dragged along. Her heart was pounding. She had heard about sharks but her skin told her what had grabbed her was not teeth. Suddenly her head burst above the surface of the water at the same time as her knees scraped bottom. Coughing and retching, she was heaved out of reach of the waves to collapse on the sand with her rescuer beside her.

Instantly Flora and Mike with the children were crowding round them. 'Hell's bells, Viv, one minute you were there, the next you'd vanished,' said Mike. 'It was a good thing George had his eye on you.'

Still gasping, Viv lifted her head and stared from sore red eyes at her cousin.

'Thought you'd die,' he said in a jerky voice. 'Couldn't bear it. Saw . . . saw Jackie die . . . and Rosie. Didn't . . . want . . . you . . . to die.'

Viv looked up at her aunt but it was Lizzie who expressed their deepest feelings. 'George talked,' she cried, jumping up and down in her excitement. 'George talked, he talked, he talked!'

Flora and Viv could not speak. Tears rolled down their cheeks. It was left to Mike to say, 'Hey, come on, girls! This is good news! Let's have a drink to celebrate.'

'It'll have to be champagne,' sniffed Flora, gazing at her son. 'There'll be no stopping you now, George.'

He said nothing, most of his attention still seemed to be for Viv. 'You are all right?'

She nodded, scrubbing away at her face, not knowing which was saltwater and which was tears. She went towards him on her knees and put her arms round him. He returned her hug and for several seconds they stayed like that. Then she said in a muffled voice, 'Jackie was that artist friend's niece, wasn't she? Do you want to talk about it?'

George drew away from her and was quiet for so long that Lizzie and Simon moved away and went to dig in the sand.

'Don't worry about it, son,' said Flora, touching George's hair with a gentle hand. 'Let's have a drink and something to eat.'

Abruptly George's face crumpled and he seized his mother's hand and placed it against his cheek. 'I'm sorry, Mam,' he said in a choking voice. 'I shouldn't be whingeing like a stupid baby! But it was just like it was when it was Rosie . . . I couldn't save Jackie!'

'Hush now! Hush!' Flora stroked his face. 'From what Viv told me, you were lucky to save yourself.'

'I tried to save her. We'd managed to cling to a table when the floods came. We didn't know it was the dam that burst. It had been raining so hard we just thought a river had burst its banks. The mill started to disintegrate and everything began to collapse and float away. It sounds like something out of a book but it really happened . . .' His voice broke and he pressed his face against her shoulder.

Viv's eyes met Flora's over his head and she said, 'I read in the *Echo* about a woman of eighty surviving for hours on a dressing table.'

George lifted his head and swallowed. 'We were flung against a tree and lost our grip on the table. I managed to hold on to a branch but as I reached down with my free hand to

261

help Jackie . . .' He stopped and the muscles in his face twitched. His eyes were staring, staring at something that still frightened him.

'It's all right, George!' His mother folded him in her arms. 'You did your best. We can all only do our best. You saved Viv.'

'Viv!' he cried, and thrust out a hand.

She gripped it tightly. 'I'm here, George.'

'You won't go away?'

'Not yet.'

There was silence then he said, 'I missed you, Viv. All those months in France, not a day went by when I didn't think about you.'

'I thought about you too.'

He lifted his head. 'You're not really going to marry Nick Bryce?'

'I'm sure you know I am, George,' she replied gently. 'But I wouldn't be if you hadn't saved my life.'

He made a disgusted sound in his throat. 'He's not bloody good enough for you! I'd marry you, Viv.'

'That's enough of that, son. Viv's marrying Nick,' said Flora. 'You can't expect to keep her with us forever.' There was a sad expression on her face as she stood up. 'Let's go and have that champagne. It'll cheer us all up.'

Later, much later, after they had drunk the champagne, had a barbecue, and George and Mike had dozed off after the excitement of the day, Flora asked Viv to go for a walk along the moonlit beach. For a while they were quiet and it was restful. Then Flora said, 'I feel I have to say something that you mightn't like, Viv.'

'You want me to go away?'

Flora slipped an arm through hers. 'Of course I don't! What I would like is for you to stay forever but I know that's impossible.' She hesitated. 'It's you and George . . . I can see that as soon as he's feeling better, your engagement to Nick is going to add spice to the way he feels about you. I know he's my son but I have to say I wouldn't put it past him to try and come between you. I can't see him staying with us indefinitely. He'll get bored and then he'll go off looking for a bit of excitement.'

'Perhaps he'll want to stay in America to be near you?'

Flora smiled sadly. 'I'd like to believe it, Viv, but George is a townie – and a Liverpudlian one to boot. He'll head home.'

'I think you're wrong. You were a Liverpudlian townie,' said Viv. 'Now you've taken to all this like a fish to water.' She waved a hand to encompass the rolling sea, the beach and the sky. 'It's beautiful and so is the vinery. You can't miss Liverpool now.'

'Of course I miss it!' exclaimed Flora. 'Liverpool will always be part of me, in my mind and in my heart. I miss the people, the familiar streets. I miss the river and the ships. But I've got Mike and the children. I'm loved, Viv, by a kind and thoughtful man.' She paused. 'I'm glad you're going to marry Nick. I remember him as a boy who hardly ever showed his feelings, but that doesn't mean to say he never felt things deeply. In fact, he probably feels things *more* deeply. When we're young our emotions feel like they're made of glass balls about to break and that can be frightening. Thank God, when we get older they're more like indian rubber. We don't break so easily.'

Viv said abruptly, 'You know who my father is, don't you?'

'I guessed, just the same as you. We're intelligent women, Viv.' She chuckled. 'Don't hurt for me so much. It doesn't hurt me any more.' Her eyes gleamed with the moon's reflection off the sea. 'But the truth would hurt George. Although he doesn't remember much about his father, he reveres what he remembers. He sees him as a hero, which he wasn't always.'

'You mean you don't want George ever to know?'

'You've got to be the strong one if he ever comes trying it on. I know you won't find it easy being hard but – '

'My mother's caused a hell of a lot of trouble, hasn't she?' interrupted Viv.

'But she's suffering for it now,' said Flora hurriedly. 'She said that Stephen asked her to marry him.'

'And you believe her?'

'Yes. When he was courting me I thought at one time they could have made a match of it. She would bring him out of himself and he would give her the security and admiration she's always needed.'

'You sound like you've forgiven her?' said Viv, puzzled. 'I'd find it hard to in your position.'

'It didn't happen overnight. I've lived with my suspicion for years. And truthfully, Viv, not forgiving people can make you feel you have a handful of walnuts right where your heart is.'

There was silence.

'You think about it, Viv.'

'I'm thinking,' she said. It was a very telling simile.

'There's an artists' colony up the coast,' murmured Flora. 'Perhaps we can persuade George to have a look at it when it's time for you to go home?'

'So I can sneak away like a thief in the night?' Viv's voice shook. Reaction was setting in.

'Hardly, Viv,' said her aunt. 'We'll all come and wave you off.' Her voice strengthened. 'And you can take a letter back to our Hilda for me.'

'You're going to tell her that I know,' said Viv, startled.

'Oh, no, I think you should do that yourself,' said Flora firmly. 'Let her know you know and take it from there.'

Chapter Twenty-Nine

It was mid-January before Viv returned to Liverpool. Nick had written informing her that the news that she was in America had left her mother almost speechless while her Christmas present had evoked only a mechanical response as if she could not believe that Viv had really bought it. She had expected gratitude and felt hurt.

The taxi stopped outside the house and after paying the driver Viv squared her shoulders and stared at the now red-painted door. The lower window frame was painted blue and white. What was going on? Was the affair with Mr Kelly on or off? Impatient to know, she hammered on the knocker.

Immediately the door was pulled wide and Hilda stood in the doorway. Viv's prepared speech was forgotten and her uppermost feeling was one of dismay. 'What have you been doing to yourself?' she blurted out. 'Where's your make-up? And why are you wearing that awful sacklike dress? It makes you look terrible!'

'Thanks very much,' snapped Hilda, a scowl replacing the hesitant smile.'Is that what you've come home for? Just to insult me!'

'If the cap fits,' said Viv, her eyes sparkling. 'What are you doing letting yourself go? It's not like you!'

'A fat lot you care what I'm like,' said her mother, turning her back and going into the house.

Viv followed her, slamming the door. 'You expect me to care, do you?' She dropped her suitcase with a loud thud. 'Are you going to give me a sob story about how your sister stole your man and you had every right to do what you did to get your revenge on her?'

Hilda flopped on to the sofa. 'I suppose Nick told you?' she whispered.

'Nick?' She had thrown Viv completely. 'How should he know about my father?'

Varying emotions flickered across Hilda's face. She did not answer Viv's question but said instead, 'Our Flo then? She put two and two together.'

'*I* put two and two together,' said Viv, frowning. 'It wasn't so difficult once you told me that Jimmy wasn't my father.' She sank into the rocking chair. 'After I started thinking straight I realised how often Uncle Tom figured on the photographs that Uncle Steve showed me – and more often than not Uncle Tom was standing next to you.'

'Good ol' Stephen.' Her mother's gaze dropped to the carpet. 'I suppose you've told him?' she said dully.

'No! Of course not.' Viv did not add that she felt sure he had guessed. 'Nor did I tell him about Mr Kelly.' She leaned forward. 'What's with the outside being painted red, white and blue? Is the Queen coming to tea or is Mr Kelly?'

'What do you think?' Hilda's voice was lifeless.

'You tell me!' Viv experienced a momentary frustration. 'Come on, Mam! Buck up! Are you still carrying on with him?'

'I told you I wasn't months ago,' muttered her mother. 'He's just being funny – or so he thinks. I painted over the blue he'd painted the door but I couldn't be bothered with the rest. I haven't gone back on what I said. I've felt too off colour for that sort of thing.'

'Off colour?'

Hilda's shoulders twitched. 'Aches and pains and funny feelings.'

There was silence and Viv waited for her to continue, thinking moodily that it wasn't worth having a fight if your opponent was not up to it. 'You haven't seen Stephen then?' she said.

'No,' sighed Hilda. 'You've no idea how miserable I've been while you've been living it up in California. Did you go to Hollywood?'

Viv shook her head. This meeting was not going a bit the way she'd expected and she did not know whether to laugh or scream. 'I suppose you haven't been to see a doctor?'

'And have him tell me I'm dying?' There was a sudden outburst of anger. 'You're joking! I don't want to know if I am!'

'Why should you be dying? It's just that you're depressed. All your aches and pains are probably in your mind . . . and I bet you haven't been eating properly!'

Hilda stared mournfully at her daughter. 'I've missed your cooking and having you to talk to. Everything became too much. Doris doesn't get round often and I even gave up the job I got before Christmas. I had this awful backache and all the upset with you and Stephen has given me a nervous stomach. It turns over and over.'

'I see,' said Viv calmly, determined not to get annoyed. 'We gave you it. It had nothing to do with you – with your own deceit?'

'I loved Tom!' she cried fiercely. 'I loved them both.'

'Love? After what you said about love to me, how can you make that your excuse? And which "both" are you supposed to have loved?'

'Tom and our Flora, of course,' said her mother with more of her old spirit. 'And I loved Jimmy a bit.'

Viv stared at her. 'Oh, come off it, Mother! How can you say you loved Aunt Flo and yet do what you did to her? If you love someone you don't deliberately set out to hurt them.'

'I didn't do it deliberately,' protested Hilda. 'There was a war on and Tom was going away. I thought I might never see him again. Our Flo wasn't up to satisfying his needs because she was pregnant and sick, and I thought she'd never know.'

'So you *thought* that made it all right for you to have sex with Tom?' Viv could not conceal her anger and disgust.

'I didn't think whether it was right or wrong at the time. It just happened! We met by accident in town. I'd been seeing Jimmy off at Lime Street and Tom's train had just come in.' The words so long battened down spilt out now. 'It was like old times. We went for a meal and had a few expensive drinks that he really shouldn't have bought and then we went to a hotel.'

267

Viv swore.

'I know!' cried her mother. 'The money should have been spent on our Flo and George! But I wasn't thinking about them at the time. I was thinking of how Tom had been mine once and how this could be the last time.' She stared at Viv and there was a tiny sparkle in her eyes. 'He was very good-looking, you know! But, bloody hell, he knew it – just the same as George! He knows he's got something the girls like. You've felt it, Viv. Don't deny it.'

'I'm not denying it,' she muttered in vexed tones. 'But he does have Aunt Flo's blood flowing in his veins as well. You should have told me earlier. What if anything had happened? Hell, Mam, he's my half-brother *and* my cousin!'

There was silence.

'Does he know?' asked Hilda eventually.

'No! And Aunt Flo doesn't want him knowing. Which is difficult because he's got a pash on me at the moment and doesn't like the idea of Nick and me getting married.'

'He's got his voice back?'

'Yes.' Viv gnawed on her lip, her gaze on her mother's face. 'What did you mean earlier about Nick telling me?'

'It doesn't matter. I could have been mistaken all along about him.'

Viv made an exasperated noise. 'You don't believe that, do you? You never have. Now you're wishing you'd kept your mouth shut about Jimmy not being my father and writing to Aunt Flo. Who, by the way, gave me a letter for you.' She delved into her handbag and handed an envelope to her mother.

Hilda turned it over in her hands. 'I can guess what it says.'

'You believe it says "Never darken my doors again!"' She smiled grimly. 'Can you see Aunt Flo writing something like that? She's so much nicer and more forgiving than you'll ever deserve, Mother.'

'You don't have to rub it in,' said Hilda with a touch of anger. 'It's not my fault I was born the way I am!'

Viv gave her a look. 'What's that radio programme where they play "Such is life! Life is what you make it!"?'

'That's only partly true. We're all born with certain traits that make us behave in a certain way.'

'Don't be putting all the blame for your behaviour on your ancestors. You knew what you were doing and so did my father, damn him!' she said, not succeeding in sounding dispassionate enough.

'He didn't want to know about you.'

'Does that surprise you? Married man and all that.' Her voice was icy.

Hilda shrugged. 'Surprisingly, I did expect something different from the cold shoulder I got. I think he realised which side his bread was buttered on.'

'And Aunt Flo was best butter.' Her mother winced and Viv regretted her words, feeling sudden pity. 'But you were never just margarine, Mam,' she said softly. 'You still aren't, so, why let yourself go?' She got to her feet.

Hilda looked up at her and there was panic in her eyes. 'I suppose you're going now and won't be back?'

Viv laughed. 'No. I'm going to make my own cup of tea, seeing as how you haven't offered me one.'

The panic faded from her mother's eyes but Viv could still see it as she made the tea and hunted for the biscuits. She remembered the glamorous mother who had come over from America and compared her with the blown up, out of focus copy that was in the other room and almost wished the old one back. She also noticed that the kitchen was untidy.

She took in the tea. Hilda was standing by the window, a sheet of paper in her hand.

'Dare I ask what she's written?' murmured Viv, placing the tray on the table.

Hilda folded the letter with trembling fingers. 'It's private but it's not likely that I'll ever set foot in America again.'

'You mean she really did say "Don't darken my doors"?' said Viv incredulously.

'No!' Hilda laughed shortly. 'I almost wish she had.'

'Mam, tell us what she says?'

Hilda shook her head. Exasperated Viv did what her mother would have done in her place and snatched the letter out of her hand. She read it, then laughed. 'She never gives up, does she? She's still trying to forge a bond between us!'

'She doesn't say anything like that,' muttered Hilda.

'She says "Take care of each other!" It's almost the same thing.'

'I suppose it is.'

'Well, she's asking the impossible, isn't she?' said Viv irritably. 'You wouldn't know how to take care of the cat!'

She poured out the tea, her thoughts churning. Once she had believed that when she knew who her father was, she would understand her mother better. Well, she did! But it also meant that she couldn't just leave her in the state she was now. Her mother had warned her to leave the past alone. So had her aunt in her letter, and Nick. Her brows puckered. Why should her mother think that Nick had told her about her father? One thing was for sure: in her search for the truth she had hurt other people. It was impossible for her to walk away and leave them still hurting if she could do anything about it. She considered carefully then drained her cup. 'I'll be going now.'

Hilda struggled to her feet. 'I'll see you to the door.'

Again Viv felt that debilitating sense of compassion. 'I know where the door is. I used to live here, you know.' She tried to infuse humour into the words as she bent to pick up her suitcase.

'You could leave that,' said her mother hurriedly. 'I mean – you could stay here. I mean – you're not going to marry Nick yet are you? And this is your home.'

Viv dropped the suitcase. 'I'll see you later then.' She closed the door, thinking that she had not said definitely she would stay. Now she wanted to see Stephen.

'Viv, you're back!' There was no mistaking the warmth in Stephen's voice.

'Did you think I wouldn't be?' She kissed him and then stepped back and smiled. He looked almost as worse for wear as her mother did. There was a hole in his sweater and he hadn't shaved properly. She would have to do something. 'I've been to see Mam,' she said quietly, sitting down at the other side of the desk.

'You've what?' He paled.

'I had a letter for her from Aunt Flo. I had to go. I promised. Flo said it was important,' she explained hurriedly.

270

Stephen stared at her and said with deliberation, 'And what did your mother have to say when she saw you?'

'The usual thing when you haven't seen anyone for a while.' She smiled brightly. 'Then she asked if you were keeping well since last she saw you.'

He cleared his throat. 'And what did you tell her?'

'I said you were very well.' She touched his hand. 'I thought that was what you'd want me to say.'

'Of course it was.' He avoided her eyes and toyed with a ruler. Viv hoped he wouldn't break it. 'I suppose she's all right?' he murmured.

'She's as all right as you are,' said Viv promptly.

Stephen looked up at her and she stared back without expression. 'That well, is she?' he muttered.

Viv nodded, bit her lip and looked anxious. 'Her chest is bad – but then it always is at this time of year.'

He frowned. 'Do you think she needs a doctor?'

'She won't see one.'

'Perhaps you should make her?'

Viv's eyebrows rose. 'Can you see Mam letting anyone make her do anything? Even so I don't want her dropping dead and people saying I didn't do anything so I might go and stay with her for a while– until Nick and I get married. I don't want her on my conscience.'

'That sounds sensible,' said Stephen soberly. 'I liked Nick. He came to see me when he got back from America. We had a good talk. I might be able to put some work his way.'

Viv smiled. 'I'm really glad you like each other.'

He hesitated. 'How's George?'

'Poor George.' She sighed. 'It's a good job he's staying in America or he'd feel like his nose was really getting pushed out of joint. Jealously is such a wasteful emotion.'

'George is probably like his father, a woman's man,' said Stephen, his mouth tightening.

Viv's heart sank. He did know who her father was. Now she knew just how difficult the future might be. She changed the subject and asked when she could come back to work. Stephen said Monday. The married woman he had got in had not really wanted full-time and did not always turn in.

Soon after that Viv left to catch a bus to the Pierhead. She

271

determined not to think of her mother and Stephen for the next few hours. From her handbag she took out the letter with Nick's address and considered instead Ursula.

Viv's eyes narrowed as she took in the stunning outfit patterned with black outlines of diamond-shaped blocks of colour worn by the girl standing in the doorway. Her face was animated and she had beautiful violet eyes.

'You must be Ursula,' she said with a smile, feeling as jealous as hell but not about to make the same mistakes as her mother. Holding out her hand she said warmly, 'Nick's told me all about you but I didn't know you were staying here as well.'

'I'm not,' said Ursula, her smile widening. 'But I drop in quite often. I'm an old family friend while you are the intruder.'

'I beg your pardon?' It took Viv all her will-power not to scream the words.

'You've got a job on your hands, love,' Ursula said in a conspiratorial whisper, her violet eyes sparkling. 'Celia's out to be rid of you and put me in your place. I belong, you see.'

Viv stared at her in astonishment. 'I can believe it, but why are you telling me?'

'Just warning you.' She grinned.

'Thanks,' said Viv dryly, not sure how to react. 'Where's Nick?'

'On site still.' She sighed. 'He's very keen. One of the workers of the world. I'm just a drone.'

Viv shook her head, puzzled. 'Do you know where the site is?.

'Sure. Sometimes I go and watch him play with his building bricks.' She beamed. 'How was America?'

'They build bricks higher there than anywhere else. Perhaps you should go and watch them,' said Viv slowly.

'Want to be rid of me?' Ursula sighed and closed the door. 'Perhaps I will go. I'll show you the site,' she said, further surprising Viv by leading her to a sports car parked in the lane.

Viv could not believe this was happening. 'Why are you taking me to Nick?' she asked with a slight laugh. 'I thought

. . .' She clutched her seat as the car roared up the narrow lane.

'I can guess what you thought,' said Ursula, picking up the conversation as she took a bend smoothly. 'How's your cousin? Nick told me he was caught up in those terrible floods in France. I was there in the summer. Awful thing to happen.'

'Yes. He's much better now.' Viv decided to take the conversation as it came. 'He's painting again which is the right thing for him.'

'Is he any good?'

Viv considered. 'I don't always understand his pictures,' she murmured. 'They're not how I see things.'

'You're not an artist,' said Ursula bluntly.

'Too right,' murmured Viv. 'I like a person to look like a person and a tree to be a tree.' As the car drew up near an estate of completed and half-finished houses she added, 'This is it?'

'Too right,' said Ursula, grinning. 'Do you want me to find Nick for you?'

'Don't bother yourself. Thanks for the lift.'

'My pleasure. Fight the good fight and I'll see you around, no doubt?'

'No doubt about it,' said Viv with a puzzled frown as Ursula drove off.

Viv found Nick on his haunches looking at drains. 'Anything interesting in there?' she said.

He put out a hand to steady himself and his blue eyes gazed into hers with such warmth that she cast aside any doubts she might have had, and, kneeling in the mud, kissed him long and deep.

'How did you get here?' he said when he could finally speak.

'Ursula!' She shook her head. 'I don't dig her and she's too attractive for my peace of mind but there's something about her . . . You don't really fancy her, do you? If you do I'll find a deep hole and put her in it.'

Nick laughed. 'How's George?'

'Safely the other side of the Atlantic. Now pull me up or I'm going to sink in the mud.'

He pulled her to her feet and kissed her again. 'Tell me I'm not dreaming.'

'You're not dreaming.' She smiled into his eyes. 'Now show me the house that you did dream up.'

He laughed and swept her up into his arms before she could protest. Several of the workmen wolf whistled and she waved to them as Nick carried her across the mud. They toured the house and she said all the right things, proud of his achievement.

Then she told him about going to see her mother. 'I'm worried, Nick. She's a mess. I never thought I'd see the day when she'd let anybody find her like that.'

Nick nodded. 'I thought the same at Christmas.'

'She's given up. Stephen hasn't called and her confidence has taken a knock.' She added hesitantly, 'I know who my father is, Nick, and the strange thing is that Mam seemed to think you might have told me. Did she tell you the truth about him at Christmas?'

'No.' He pulled Viv against him and said against her ear, 'I've known for ages.' She stiffened but he kept tight hold of her. 'I guess that most of your mother's antagonism towards me was because she had a fair idea I knew and was scared that I might tell you.'

Viv struggled in his arms and he released her. They gazed at each other. 'How did you know? And why didn't you tell me?' she cried. 'You knew how important it was to me.'

'Because I knew you'd be hurt,' he said fiercely. 'We lived next-door. I overheard your Mam and your Uncle Tom talking. He was cruel to her! Laid all the blame at her door. I'd heard enough of that kind of talk from my father not to know what they were talking about!.

'I see,' said Viv quietly. 'Such a simple answer.'

'The truth *has* hurt you, hasn't it? You wanted him to be a super hero but most men aren't, and most women are only human too.'

There was a long silence while Viv digested all that he had said. Then she pressed herself against him and said in a muffled voice, 'You could have threatened her with telling me but you didn't. That isn't your way is it, Nick?'

'Even when she irritated me, I felt sorry for her,' he said slowly. 'We all make mistakes, Viv. We all get scared.'

She nodded. 'I was scared earlier. Of Ursula. But I don't think she's a threat, really.'

'Of course she isn't.' He hugged her and stepping outside the dream house, said, 'What are we going to do about your mother?'

'Aunt Flo told me that Mam said Stephen had asked her to marry him.'

'She must have said no,' said Nick, frowning. 'I wonder why?'

'It's no use wondering why,' said Viv. 'Stephen's the answer to Mam's problems. He's proud, though, and still hurting from their last meeting.'

'Work on him,' said Nick. 'I'm sure you can do it.'

She raised her eyebrows. 'I never thought I'd hear you say that.'

He smiled. 'I trust you – and him.'

She nodded absently. 'I'll have to go carefully – and I think it would be a good thing to get to work on Mam first. He wouldn't want her the way she looks at the moment.'

Then get to work right away,' said Nick firmly. 'She's slipped pretty far.'

'Let's go and see her now then,' said Viv.

Hilda appeared to have combed her hair when she opened the door to Viv and Nick.'I wasn't sure you'd be back tonight.' Her voice was flurried. 'I was just thinking of going back to bed.'

'Come off it, Mam! It's only nine o'clock,' said Viv in chivvying tones.'We've got some fish and chips and Nick bought a bottle of champagne to celebrate.

Hilda made way for them. 'To celebrate what?'

'Our engagement, of course! You go and get the glasses,' she ordered.

'Oh, that,' said Hilda, plumping herself down in the rocking chair. She sighed.

Viv felt like hitting her. 'Mam! You could be happy for us,' she hissed.

'Why?' She folded her arms across her stomach.

'I'll get some glasses,' murmured Nick, and left the pair of them to it.

'I had thought of staying here like you said,' said Viv, determinedly controlling her anger as she placed the fish and

275

chips on the table and opening the newspaper wrappings.

Hilda pushed herself up from the chair and came to stand behind her daughter. 'What do you mean, you thought?'

'What I said. It depends if you're going to buck your ideas up. I don't want a miserable face round me all the time.'

Hilda cleared her throat. 'People do get miserable when they're on their own, but if you're here I won't feel so bad.'

'Well, we'll try it then,' said Viv, burning her boats. 'Now how about some chips?'

'They smell good. But I shouldn't really eat them. I'll just put on more weight.'

'Are you hungry?' said Viv insistently, waving a chip under her nose.

'Starving!' Hilda snatched at the chip and ate it.

'We'll both go on a diet tomorrow,' said Viv, watching her. 'I've put on some weight while I've been away.'

Hilda began to tuck in, saying with her mouth almost full, 'You look all right. I wouldn't lose too much, honey.'

Viv smiled. 'You just want me as fat as you.'

'No, I don't!' she said earnestly. 'It's uncomfortable being like this. Friends told me that the weight piled on easier when you got round forty but I didn't believe them. Hardly any of my clothes fit properly and I've got some lovely things that Steve . . ' A sigh escaped her. 'No man would look at me now.' She looked depressed and Viv found herself feeling irritated once more. She struggled for words of encouragement.

Nick entered the room and Viv said, 'Tell Mam she's still got what it takes, love.'

'Of course she has,' he said positively. 'She always has had. Some new clothes, Hilda, that's what you need. And get your hair done.'

'We'll go shopping,' said Viv, watching Nick's deft fingers working on the champagne cork and remembering how they had worked on her last summer and how wonderful it had been.

Hilda flushed. 'No shopping until I've lost some weight,' she said, her shoulders firming slightly.

The cork shot out of the bottle and bounced off the wall the other side of the room. Hilda walked majestically over to it

276

and with difficulty bent and picked it up. She turned and looked at them both as Nick filled three glasses with foaming golden liquid. 'We'll have another bottle,' she said a mite breathlessly, 'when I get back into a size twelve.' She accepted a glass from Nick. 'Here's to you both.'

Viv raised her glass. 'Thanks, Mam. And I'm sure you'll get rid of that weight. To us, Nick.'

'To us.' His dark head drew closer. They kissed and Viv wished they could marry tonight, tomorrow! But she knew that they would have to wait until they'd sorted out her mother. Let it be soon, though, God, she prayed. Let it be soon!

Chapter Thirty

'How was your Aunt Flora?'

'Fine.' Viv looked up from her typewriter in surprise. It was the first time that Stephen had mentioned her aunt and instinctively she felt wary. It was almost a month since she had come home and things were not moving as swiftly as she would have liked. Her mother was still a frump and there had not been much improvement in Stephen either. He was tidier than he had been that first day but he was still not his normal self. She had needed to remind him about appointments which was not usual with him. She had considered that all to the good in one way, just like his asking how she was getting along with her mother, but it was not enough. And now he was asking about her aunt. She did not like it. 'Why do you ask?'

Stephen put down his pen, cleared his throat, steepled his hands and rested his chin on them. 'You haven't mentioned your father since you came home. Before all that trouble with George it seems as if he was never out of your mind. I just wondered if your aunt had said anything about him?'

Viv was silent. The last thing she wanted was him thinking of her mother's past. 'I didn't mentioned my father,' she lied. 'George was too much on our minds.'

He flushed. 'Of course! Stupid of me.' His hands dropped and he fiddled with a sheet of paper. 'But have you given your father's identity any more thought?'

'Not really,' said Viv, feeling her way. 'My curiosity caused us all so much unhappiness that I think he's best forgotten.'

He stared at her, his brows puckered. 'You really feel like that now?'

'Yes.' She met his gaze squarely. 'It's the present that matters, isn't it? The past actions of our parents have affected Nick and me too much so we're putting them behind us. We've got the future to think about.'

'Yes. That makes sense. You're both young so you can start all over again,' he said with deliberation.

Viv smiled. 'You don't have to be young to do that, Uncle Steve.'

He sighed. 'It's easier. It's very difficult, Viv, when you're older – to accept that someone you love fraternised with the enemy.'

'The enemy! Heck!' She hesitated before saying, 'Who are we talking about?'

'Your mother, of course, and the man I think was your father.' He flushed once more. 'I find it hard to forgive, Viv. He wished me so much ill.'

'If he's dead,' said Viv quietly, 'does it matter now? Why let it blight the rest of your life?'

'It matters to me,' he said stiffly.

Viv waited for him to say more but he did not. She got on with her work but there was a feeling of helplessness inside her. It seemed that even with the best will in the world things were not going to work out for Stephen and her mother.

When Viv arrived home that evening she found Hilda in her dressing gown, reading a magazine, her hand in a bag of jelly babies.

'Mam, what are you doing eating sweets?' she said irritably, snatching the paper bag from her and placing it on the table.

Hilda gazed at her with frustrated and worried eyes. 'What's the point, Viv? I haven't lost any weight worth mentioning. I might as well give up.'

Viv scowled. 'Don't be so defeatist. Stephen mentioned you today. He and my father didn't get on, did they?'

'Not so you'd notice.' Hilda sighed. 'Mutual dislike. Of course, that could have been down to me. Steve was that bit younger and so believed himself out of the reckoning.'

'I see.' Viv took off her coat and sat in the rocking chair. 'I think he suspects the truth.'

Hilda's smile faded. 'I thought he might. You didn't tell him, though?'

Viv shook her head then stifled a yawn. 'Any post?' she murmured.

Her mother nodded and lumbered to her feet. 'A letter from our Flo for you. I didn't open it.'

Viv smiled and opened the letter. After a few seconds she lifted her head. 'George is on his way back to Liverpool. Damn! I was hoping he'd stay away longer.'

'What are you going to do?' murmured Hilda, picking up the bag of jelly babies.

'I'll have to think.' Nick was not going to like it. 'He'll probably come here.'

'Probably. He's like his father – stubborn,' said Hilda, biting the legs off a green jelly baby.

'Oh, shut up, Mam, about him being like our father,' Viv said crossly. 'Our father must have had some good points or you wouldn't have loved him.' She took the bag out of her mother's hand and bit into a jelly baby herself. 'Now go and boil an egg and have it with dry toast.'

Hilda groaned, and with a hand pressed against the small of her back said she wished she'd never been born.

Saturday morning George came home.

'And where do you think you're going to sleep?' said Hilda, as she held the door open.

His brown eyes widened. 'Good God, Auntie Hilda, you've put a bit of weight on! Bread and water, that's what you need,' he said, dumping his rucksack and painting paraphernalia on the floor and looking round him. 'Not bad,' he said. 'Where's Viv?'

'Upstairs.'

'I'll go up,' he said, starting across the room.

'No, you won't,' she cried, moving as quickly as she could after him. 'Let her sleep!' But it was too late, he was gone. Hilda groaned and sat down, holding her belly. She had that funny pain again. The things a woman had to suffer. Periods or the Change, it was all one. Still, she would wish her periods back if she could be young again.

George entered Viv's room like a whirlwind but if he had

been hoping to surprise her he was disappointed. She was already awake and dressed in jeans and a thick green sweater with a pattern of white hearts across it. He hair was twisted on top of her head in a chignon. He stopped and stared at her.

'Hello, George. I didn't expect to see you so soon.'

'I thought I'd surprise you.'

Viv nodded. 'What brings you home?'

He hesitated. 'I never did get round to thanking you for coming to look for me in France – and for taking me to America.' He made to put his arms round her.

Viv immediately backed away. 'You're family. What did you expect me to do? What are you going to do with yourself now, George? Will you be off on your travels, again or are you planning on staying in Liverpool?'

He stared at her, a slight pucker between his brows. 'Stay a while, if that's all right with you?'

She nodded. 'You'll have to sleep on the campbed downstairs.'

'That's OK.' He hesitated. 'How are you and your mam getting on?'

'Fine.' She made towards the door.

He followed her. 'She's changed.'

'Yes. Come and have some breakfast.'

He had hoped for more time alone with her but had no choice but to follow her downstairs.

Hilda glanced up as they entered the kitchen. 'Well, is George staying?''

'For now,' said Viv, frowning.She was not finding it easy to keep him at a distance.

George went over to his aunt and hugged her. 'You don't mind putting him with me, do you, Aunt Hilda? This house is big enough for all of us.' He kissed the top of her head.

Hilda said, 'You don't have to be coming your tricks with me, George. Sit down. Our Viv'll make you a cup of tea.'

He grinned and glanced at Viv. 'Hear that?'

'I heard. Do as you're told and I'll bring you a cup of tea.'

Five minutes later the two women were listening to George talking about some of the people he had met in the art colony. 'They've kicked over the traces more than I ever did,' he murmured. 'They're on some kind of drug. Makes some of

281

them real weird – violent in some cases, all lovely dovey in others.'

'It's a good job you've come home then,' said Viv.

'I could handle it.' He hesitated. 'What are you doing with yourself today?'

'I'm seeing Nick. Sorry. What'll you do?'

'Still going to marry him?' He looked grim when she nodded. 'I'll have a look round Liverpool alone then, I guess.'

Viv felt irritated and guilty at the same time. 'You could take your drawing stuff. Try and capture some of the old Liverpool before it disappears altogether.'

His expression brightened. 'That's not a bad idea!'

Hilda decided to join in the conversation. 'It's a good idea. Your father was a dab hand with a paint brush.'

'I know.' George grinned and got to his feet. 'I'll do that then.'

After he had gone Viv cleared the table.

'He is like his father,' murmured Hilda.

'Yes.' She glanced at her mother. 'Don't forget he doesn't know.'

'Well, I'm not going to tell him.' She wriggled uncomfortably. 'I've got enough worries without him knowing. Are you going to the shops?'

Viv nodded. 'Did you want something?'

'Something for this pain. Probably constipation.' She groaned. 'I just can't seem to get rid of it today.'

'You eat too many sweets still, Mam. And you don't get enough exercise. Did you go out yesterday?'

'Have a heart, Viv! My back's killing me,' said Hilda indignantly. 'When my mother was ill lying on that sofa . . .'

'We got rid of the old sofa, remember.' Viv shrugged on a coat. 'You'll have to change your story. Make it more heartrending.' She struck a dramatic pose with one hand on her heart and spoke in a hollow voice. 'When I was a girl we didn't have a sofa. My mother was dying and lay on the floor on a heap of old rags. There was no coal in the grate and the snow was ten feet deep past the windowsill.'

Hilda smiled. 'Go and do your shopping. You don't know you're born. You've no idea what it was like for me with Father away. And Mam *was* dying, only I didn't realise it.'

She eased her position and groaned again. 'Don't be away long. Perhaps some syrup of figs, honey?'

Viv made no answer. She was not rushing back. She would go to the library and enjoy a stroll round the shops.

For a long time after her daughter had left Hilda did not move but lay staring at the blank television screen. Then she made coffee, dipping a couple of chocolate fingers in the steamy liquid and sucking them. The pain did not abate and she began to feel restless. She switched on the radio and the D.J. played an Ivor Novello number. Ivor. Welsh. Tom had Welsh blood. She thought about Stephen losing his sisters and mother in that air raid in November when she had conceived Viv. Did he miss her and the fun they had had? He had become a good lover as well as being kind and thoughtful. How she missed him!

The pain struck again, causing her to cry out and clutch her belly. After it passed she stumbled to her feet. The pain had been so sharp, so fierce, that it frightened her. She did not want to be in the house alone. She wanted people. Why had Viv chosen to go out now? she thought unreasonably. She went to the front door, automatically trying to tighten the belt of her dressing gown but she had put on too much weight and it gaped open.

She looked down the row of yellowbrick houses. For once it was not raining and there were a couple of kids playing on bikes further up the road and Joe Kelly cleaning his car outside their door. The pain came again. 'Ouch!' She bent over awkwardly, clinging to the doorjamb with one hand.

Joe looked her way and dropped his chamois leather on the pavement. 'Hey, are yer all right, Mrs Murray?'

'Pain,' she gasped. 'Terrible pain.' Her face was drained of colour.

'I'll get me mam. You go inside and sit down.'

Hilda said nothing, made no move, only breathed deeply of the chill February air.

Joe gave her an indecisive, worried look and yelled, 'Mam! Mam!' Nobody came and after several more groans from Hilda he dived into the house.

The pain passed and Hilda eased herself up. She leaned against the doorjamb, gripping it with a trembling hand. She wanted Viv. Why didn't she come? She groaned and suddenly felt herself damp underneath. What was happening to her? It couldn't be? No, not at her age! It couldn't be! Oh God!

'What's up?' George had appeared and was gazing down at her even as Mrs Kelly came out of her house next-door.

'Is she all right?' said Mrs Kelly, her eyes alight with ghoulish interest. 'She looks awful!'

'Go away,' snapped Hilda. 'I don't need your help. I want Viv!' The pain came again and she bit on her lip to stop herself crying out, not wanting that woman next-door to guess what was up with her. But she could not disguise the effort it took as her teeth drew blood.

'Aunt Hilda, should I phone the doctor?' said George worriedly. Several of the neighbours had come out and were watching.

'Perhaps,' she gasped. 'But I don't know if it'll be any good. I need . . . where's Viv?'

George stood up and glanced up the street. 'No sign of her,' he said, watching a Land Rover approach.

Hilda's gaze followed his. 'That's Nick. He's early. Maybe he'll go and find her?'

The Land Rover came to a halt and the door opened. Viv stepped out. 'I met Nick down the road,' she began. 'What's going on?' She frowned down at Hilda. 'Mam, what are you doing out here not dressed?'

Hilda clutched at the hem of Viv's coat. 'I'm in pain, Viv. I need help!'

She placed the shopping bags on the pavement, her expression uncompromising. 'Not that again, Mam. Come on, get up. I'll help you into the house.'

'I'll get her up,' said Nick, shooting George a swift glance.

'No!' Hilda clung on to Viv's coat. 'I'm ill. I'm ill, Viv. Help me.' She groaned as another contraction made itself felt.

Viv thought, Why does she have to do this to me? She gripped her mother's arm. 'Come on, get up!'

'I can't! I can't,' gasped Hilda.

'You can!' cried Viv. Then her eyes met her mother's and she felt a sudden chill. She *was* in pain and she was scared. Crouching down beside her, Viv said, 'Where's the pain, Mam?'

'In my bloody belly,' she whispered. 'I'll have to go to hospital!' The pain slackened and she gave a quivering breath.

Mrs Kelly said conversationally, 'Perhaps it's appendicitis? They'll cut her open.'

'Oh, shut up,' snarled Viv, her hear drawing close to her mother's. 'Don't worry, Mam. You'll be okay.'

'It's not appendicitis, Viv,' whispered Hilda. 'Oh God help me! You'll hate me all over again now. It's worse than that.'

Viv could only think of one thing worse and that was cancer. 'You mean . . .' The word stuck in her throat.

Hilda yelped, gasped, panted. 'Get an ambulance! Get me to the hospital!'

Viv gripped her hand tightly. 'We'll get you dressed first, Mam. Nick! George! Help me get her up.'

They both moved forward. Nick, his eyes on Hilda, said, 'I think it would be best if we took your mam to the hospital as she says, right now!'

'What do you mean?' Viv stared at him.

'Don't ask questions. Just do it,' he said grimly. 'Come on, love,' he addressed Hilda. 'Take it easy. Lift, George!'

George did as he was told and somehow they managed to get Hilda up into the Land Rover.

'Which hospital?' said Viv, climbing in and shutting the door, her worried eyes on her mother's huddled figure.

'Mill Road,' whispered Hilda.

George's eyes met Viv's. 'Does she mean . . .?'

Viv groaned and dropped her head in her hands as she said in a muffled voice, 'I don't believe this. Nick, get us out of here!'

'Oh God,' moaned her mother.

The Land Rover shot off in a jerky fashion. Viv sat in stunned silence. Her mother's hand grasped hers, the nails biting into her cold fingers as she deep breathed her way through another contraction. Viv offered no words of comfort. She could not have said anything to save her life. All she could think was that her mother might die at her age, having a baby. She had nearly died having Viv.

'This is crazy,' said George, looking stunned. 'How? Who's?'

Nobody answered and he subsided into silence until the Land Rover came to a screeching halt in front of the hospital. By that time the pains were coming so close that Hilda was a trembling, writhing wreck.

'Well?' said George nervously. 'What next?'

'Get her out,' screamed Viv, all her pent up anxiety bursting forth. 'Do you want her to have the bloody baby her, you idiot!'

He jumped out immediately and so did Nick. They both lifted Hilda down but as soon as they released her she collapsed like a concertina on to the ground, writhing and whimpering.

'Nick, pick her up,' cried Viv.

Between them Nick and George picked up Hilda while Viv fled before them into the hospital.

'You've got a sister,' said the nurse, smiling gravely.

It was two hours later. 'My mother?' Viv's voice was thick with emotion.

'She's had a difficult time and is very tired but she'll be all right.'

Viv sagged against Nick's shoulder. 'And the baby? Is she all right?'

'Small but she's all there. Your mother's a very lucky woman.'

'Good.' Viv cleared her throat. 'Can I see them?'

The nurse nodded. 'Your mother's anxious to speak to you. We can allow you a few minutes so that you can reassure each other.'

Viv looked at Nick and then George. 'I won't be long.'

'You take all the time you want,' murmured Nick, and kissed her briefly.

George raised his eyebrows and lit a cigarette.

As Viv walked up the corridor the nurse said, 'It's been a big shock for you, dear.'

'I had no idea.'

'I think that perhaps your mother did but didn't want to believe it. Too good to be true, I suppose.' She chuckled. 'The baby'll be a nice remainder of her dead husband.'

So that's what she'd told them, thought Viv, following the

nurse through swing doors into the ward, trying to convince herself that it was all a dream.

Her mother lay unmoving in a high bed but her head turned as Viv approached. Her first thought was that her mother looked old, much too old to have just given birth. Her eyes were twin circles of a startling blue in her drained features.

The nurse murmured, 'Just a couple of minutes. She must rest.' The she left them alone.

'Well, that was a turn up for the book,' whispered Hilda.

'You're crazy, Mam,' said Viv, her body quivering with a surfeit of emotion. 'How could you be so stupid?'

Hilda's hesitant smile evaporated. 'Don't criticise me, honey,' she said wearily. 'All those years married to Charlie and never a slip up. I just didn't expect it to happen at my age. I thought it was the Change.'

'The Change?' A sharp laugh escaped her. 'Some Change! Whose baby is it, Mam?'

Hilda frowned. 'Whose do you think? Steve's, of course! Dom always took precautions, and honestly I've had nothing to do with him since I went with Steve.'

Viv believed her because Mr Kelly hadn't been near since she'd been back 'OK, it's Uncle Steve's.'

'What am I going to do, Viv? You won't give up on me now will you? I mean, you and Nick will help me?'

Viv suddenly had a vision of Nick and herself slaving away, caring for her mother *and* the baby. 'We'll have to tell Stephen,' she said.

Hilda's throat moved. 'He won't believe it's his. He doesn't trust me.'

'The pair of you made love so there's a fair chance he will,' said Viv positively. 'He's a very moral person deep down. He'd want to do what's right by you and his baby. He's got a right to decide anyway.'

Hilda's eyes brightened slightly. 'I suppose he has. Will you tell him?'

Viv had known as soon as she mentioned Stephen's name it would come to this. 'I suppose I'll have to,' she muttered. 'There's nobody else, is there?'

'No,' said her mother. 'But if there was, I don't think they could handle him better than you.'

'Best soft soap, Mam,' said Viv, smiling slightly. 'I wish I could be so sure . . .' She gazed down at her half-sister in the cot, noting her mass of dark curls and blue eyes. Her smile widened. She was Stephen's all right!

Chapter Thirty-One

'I don't believe it!' Stephen's face wore a stunned expression.

'Why not?' said Viv, perching sideways on the arm of a chair. 'You slept with her for months on and off, didn't you?'

'Yes, but . . . ' He flushed. 'Are you sure she's mine, Viv?'

'She looks like you except for the nose,' murmured Viv. 'Hers isn't broken. She's lovely, Uncle Steve. A picture. Wait till you see her.'

He cleared his throat and dug his hands into his pockets. 'Whose idea was it, Viv, that you tell me? Yours or Hilda's?'

'Mine. Mam believes you won't want anything to do with her. She's been miserable for months believing that. Like you've been miserable, staying away from her.'

'You know why I stayed away. And I still can't bear the thought of her with him. I don't know if our getting married would work. Viv.'

'Why not? And who is *he*?' demanded Viv, leaning forward. 'You tell me, Uncle Steve, who you believe my father was and I'll tell you what I believe.'

He stared at her, hesitated, then muttered, 'Your Uncle Tom. They were in love. They were engaged once.'

She allowed a small silence before saying, 'I see how your mind's worked. I though that once because of the photographs but I've thought again since,' she lied. 'Mam told me that she broke off her engagement to him because she realised she was wrong about him. That he liked himself too much.'

'She told you that?' He raked his fingers through his curling hair. 'Even so, Viv, she might not have been telling the truth.'

She threw down her other card. 'She mightn't have been

289

telling the truth when she said your brother *wasn't* my father. She might have said it just to hurt us because she was so jealous. When you see her and the baby ask her if my Uncle Tom was my father or whether Jimmy was after all?'

'You mean, go and see her in hospital?' He reddened. 'But they'll all know then.'

'No, they won't,' said Viv. 'She's told them the baby's father is her dead husband.' She giggled suddenly at the thought.

'It's not funny, Viv,' said Stephen, his expression harassed. 'What are people who know he's been dead for two years going to say? There'll be gossip.'

'My mother's always set the tongues wagging.' She giggled again. 'Not that I'm going to let our neighbours know the truth. I've told George – who's home, by the way, and a problem – that he's not to breathe a whisper about a baby. I haven't even told him who the father is yet.'

Stephen shook his head at her. 'I think you're a touch hysterical, Viv. But I will go and see Hilda. If the baby's mine, I'll have to support her at least.'

Viv sobered. 'You do that, Uncle Steve. But not today. Go tomorrow. Mam's got to rest. She didn't have an easy time of it, you know.' She got up and kissed him.

He nodded and saw her out.

Viv freed a long breath and then ran to the bottom of the avenue where Nick was parked. 'Well?' he said, putting down his magazine.

'He's going to see her tomorrow. I'll have to see her tonight and take in her make-up and one of her glam nighties. If he see her like she is now he won't want her.'

'That's unkind,' said Nick.

'But the truth.' She grimaced. 'I told him a whopping lie, though.'

Nick stared at her. 'Tell, Viv.'

She told him. 'Tonight I'll have to tell Mam what I've done and it's up to her what she does then. He's really got a thing about my father, just like you have about George.'

'What about George?'

She looked at him. 'What about him?'

'Are you going to tell him the truth?'

290

Viv's mouth set stubbornly. 'Start the engine, Nick. I've got a lot to do.'

'Viv!'

'Not now, Nick. Don't you think I've had a hell of a day already without you going on about George? I wonder what made him come back so soon?' She slumped in the seat and closed her eyes. 'Anyway, he knows we're getting married so isn't that enough?'

'He's staying at your house and tonight your mother's not going to be there. I don't like it, Viv,' he said quietly, starting the engine.

'Later, Nick,' she murmured. 'I'm tired.'

'Later then,' he said.

That evening she went into the hospital carrying a laden shopping bag. Her mother looked a little better but the rough cotton hospital nightdress did nothing for her. 'I've brought you a few things. Your make-up and that.'

'Did you see Steve?' asked Hilda anxiously.

'Yes.' Viv took a peek at her sleeping sister and marvelled at her beautiful skin. 'I hope she opens her eyes for him.'

'He's going to come?' Hilda attempted to sit up straight and looked towards the swing doors.

'Not tonight,' murmured Viv. 'Tomorrow. I told him you had to rest. I though you needed some time to put on your glam act.' She started to unpack her bag. 'Grapes, a nightie – the satin and lace one – a hairbrush and mirror, some what-sies, make-up, a couple of magazines from Mrs Kelly, orange juice.'

'Magazines from her next-door!' Hilda looked startled. 'What have you told them all?'

Viv sat on the chair beside the bed. 'At first I thought of telling them you were dead but decided that was a bit drastic. Besides, they'd expect a funeral.'

'Very funny.' said her mother. 'What did you tell them?'

'That you'd had gallstones taken out. I don't want a whiff of a baby to get back to Mr or Mrs Kelly. If Stephen ever got to know about your affair with him, Mam, that would be the end.'

Hilda's mouth drooped and she rested her head against the pillows and said miserably, 'He won't marry me.'

291

'He will if you play your cards right.' Viv told her mother what had taken place between her and Stephen and eventually a smile began to play about Hilda's lips.

'You know, Viv, you *do* take after me.'

'You mean I'm a prize liar? I don't think that's anything to be proud of.'

'No. I'll have to go to church and confess all my sins.'

'Me too,' said Viv. 'In the meantime you can dolly yourself up and persuade Stephen that Uncle Tom wasn't my father and marry him double quick so you don't have to take the baby back to our street.'

Her mother's smile faded but there was a sparkle in her eyes. 'I'll do my very best.'

'You do that.' Viv bit into a grape, kissed her sister's cheek, told her mother that she'd be seeing her and left to meet Nick, who was taking her out to dinner.

'You can stay the night,' she said across the restaurant table.

'That's your answer to telling George?'

'What's wrong with it? I thought you'd jump at the idea.'

'Can I sleep in your bed?' There was a hint of a smile in his voice.

'What do you think George would say to that?' She forked some curry and rice into her mouth.

'He'd probably stand guard in front of your bedroom door.'

Viv stared at him and suddenly was conscious of the smouldering sexual undercurrent that had been between them since her return from America. 'You could always walk over him, sword in hand,' she said unevenly.

'You still fantasising about knights?' Nick's fingers curled about hers. 'I wish we could get married right away.'

'I wish you and George could be friends. I don't want the pair of you fighting for ever.'

Nick said firmly, 'I don't want to be his enemy but I can see that vendetta you once talked about carrying on forever if he's not told.'

'I don't know why you should think that!' Her fingers twisted in his. 'If Mam marries Steve she'll be moving out. We could marry and you could move in with me.'

'With George there? Some beginning! He came home to

292

try and stop you marrying me. He told me so when you went in to see your mam. Fortunately he didn't make any cracks about my mother because then I would have spilt the beans about his precious father.'

Viv groaned. 'He actually said all that to you?'

Nick raised his eyebrows. 'I don't know why you should be so surprised. You're a beauty, Viv. Even more tasty than you were just over a year ago.' He kissed her fingers. 'Now you see why he should know about his father.'

'I can't tell him, Nick,' she said urgently. 'I promised Aunt Flo. Once I get Mam and Stephen sorted out then I'll do something, trust me.'

'I do, but not George. Anyway, for now I'll stay the night.'

When they got home it was obvious to both of them that George knew exactly why Nick was there. 'Don't think you're sleeping upstairs,' he growled. 'There must have been enough creeping about going on in this house for Aunt Hilda to get pregnant.'

'He never came here,' said Viv swiftly. She still had not told George that Stephen had been her mother's lover. Tomorrow, she might tell him tomorrow. 'You'll both sleep down here,' she said, glancing at Nick. 'Unless I can find a chaperon to be with me upstairs.'

'Why not ask Mrs Kelly?' snapped George. 'Come one! Come all!'

Viv stared at him and suddenly had an idea. She told Nick that she was going to use the telephone round the corner and would not be long.

'Who were you phoning?' he said when she returned and was making cocoa in the kitchen.

'Ursula.'

Nick stared at her. 'What on earth for?'

Viv's eyes twinkled. 'To be my chaperon. She said she'd come.'

'She's coming here?' hissed Nick, closing the door into the front room where George was listening to the wireless.

She nodded. 'I explained the situation. She thought it hilarious and can't wait to meet George.'

Nick groaned. 'She's too classy for him.'

'No, she's not,' said Viv indignantly. 'That's Celia speaking. If you've not careful, Nick, you'll lose touch with your roots. Just remember that all men and women are equal in the sight of God. Even the Queen is only flesh and blood.'

'OK, OK!' said Nick, running a hand through his hair. 'But I don't know why you have to protect George from the realities of life. If you'd only tell him the truth about his father being yours we wouldn't have this trouble.'

'He's suffered enough from the realities of life,' she whispered, shoving a cup of cocoa into Nick's hand. 'Besides he's the only brother I've got, and I love him. I think Ursula would be good for him. Unless of course it could be that you like Ursula too much to hand her over to him?'

'That's not a nice thing to say about Ursula,' said Nick angrily. 'Perhaps we should pretend that it's true, then George would be bound to take an interest in her just to annoy me?'

Viv's face stilled. 'That's a good idea! We could . . .'

'No, Viv,' he said. 'I was kidding. I'm not playing games like that. I'm surprised at you.' He pulled her into his arms and made to kiss her mouth but she averted her face.

'Why don't you think it's a good idea?' she asked.

'Because it's the kind of game your mother played and it didn't come off.' He covered her face with kisses.

'Drink your cocoa,' she whispered. 'You're making my legs go all funny.'

'I don't want to drink my cocoa,' said Nick. 'What did you mean about loving George? Who do you love the most? Is it your brother or me?'

'Be quiet,' she muttered. 'He'll hear.'

'Good!' His mouth swooped on hers but she responded angrily, turning the kiss into a fierce battle of wills that aroused them both as they tussled and ended with them on the floor. She was certain Nick allowed her to win because she was on top of him. 'Well, Viv?' he said breathlessly.

'You ask the most stupid questions,' she panted. 'I could hit you.'

He laughed. 'Make love to me instead.'

She put a hand to his pants but he caught hold of her fingers and kissed them. 'Say it, Viv? Brother George or me?'

It was at that moment that George entered the room with a

294

thunderous expression. 'There's some girl at the door saying she's your chaperon, Viv! By the look of it you bloody need one.' He marched past them and took his jacket from a hook on the wall, picked up his rucksack and went out of the back door.

'He must have heard,' cried Viv, scrambling to her feet and making to go after him.

Nick stopped her. 'I'll go! You talk to Ursula.'

'Nick, you won't . . .'

'Trust me,' said Nick and was gone.

He caught up with George halfway down the darkened entry which smelt of cats and bits of rubbish left behind by the binmen. 'Where are you going, mate?'

'I'm no mate of yours,' snapped George, quickening his pace. 'Go back to her and leave me alone.'

'Running away, are you? You were always good at that, Cookie.'

George slowed down, scowling at him. 'You'll take that bloody back. I can face up to the truth but I've got to get away.'

'I take it bloody back,' said Nick softly. 'But stop and think, George, about what you're doing to Viv. Nothing would make me happier than for you to carry on going and stay out of my life but she happens to care about what happens to you. It's not what I like but that doesn't matter at the moment. What matters is Viv being happy and she won't be if you disappear.'

'I'll send her a postcard.'

'Like you did when you went to France?' Nick's voice was scornful as he kept pace with him. 'She worried then about you. I think she's a fool but that's Viv. Your mother brought her up so you should know better than anyone how she feels about family.'

'More fool her! Mam should never have taken her on. She should have told Aunt Hilda to go to hell!' George glanced about him wildly as they came out of the entry. 'I was always having to look after her. Even after Rosie it was like having another sister –' His voice tailed off.

Nick took a deep breath. 'That's how your mother brought you up. Perhaps she knew what she was doing all those years ago? You lost a sister. She gave you another one.'

George stopped and stared at Nick and there was a glitter of tears in his eyes. 'It is true then? I've often wondered who it was. How could they do that to Mam? *How could they?*'

Nick thrust his hands into his trouser pockets. 'A moment of madness?' he said carefully. 'We all do daft things without thinking of the consequences. I've done it. You're doing it now.'

There was silence.

Then George said in a low voice, staring up the lamplit road, 'Kathleen Murphy became a nun. I didn't realise just how much a part of my life she was until she wrote and told me that she was marrying Jesus. I felt like I'd been stabbed in the back, betrayed.' He swallowed and his voice was husky when he continued, 'I treated her like a little lap dog when we were kids. She'd follow me around, worshipping me. I took it for granted that our life would go on like that.' He stared down at the ground.

'Viv did pretty much the same thing, didn't she?' murmured Nick. 'So you transferred some of your feelings for Kathleen to Viv. Except she wasn't Kathleen. Even so, when she fell in love with me you felt betrayed. But she didn't stop loving you, George.'

'She loves you more.' He kicked at a paving stone.

'I should hope she does because it's me she's marrying, never you,' said Nick frankly, hunching inside his sweater.

George glared at him, balling his fist. 'I don't want it to be true!'

'Perhaps not. But it is. Take a swing at me if you like, I think a punch up would probably do us good, but Viv wouldn't like it if we go back all messed up.'

'You're a right smart arse, Brycie,' said George, relaxing his fists and hitching his rucksack higher. 'But I'm not going back. You can tell Viv –' He paused, swallowed. 'You can tell her I'm OK. That I will be back – when I'm ready. Tell her I'm going to see Jackie's parents. I liked her. Viv'll know who I mean.' Without another word he turned and walked away.

Nick watched him until he was out of sight, then knowing he was in trouble with Viv, strolled back to the house.

She had the door open as soon as he knocked. 'Where is he?' she demanded.

'He's gone. But he'll be back,' replied Nick, nodding at Ursula who was rocking herself in the chair and nursing the cat.

'What a drag,' she said with a sigh. 'I'd looked forward to stealing him away for an hour's raucous merriment at The Iron Door. Now I'll just have to play at strawberries.'

'You mean gooseberries,' said Nick, moving further into the room and warming his hands by the fire.

'Gooseberries?' Ursula looked pensive. 'They're prickly. You can imagine one of them keeping people apart.'

Viv said exasperatedly, 'Do you two mind shutting up about stupid fruits? Nick, what did you say to him? Where's he gone?'

'I said nothing that you'd have disagreed with.' He crossed his fingers. 'And he's gone to see someone called Jackie's parents.'

'Jackie?' Viv frowned then enlightenment dawned. 'She was the one he tried to save when the dam burst. He was racked with guilt about her.'

'Was he the last one to see her alive?' said Ursula, interested. 'If he was he's probably felt deep down inside for some time that he should speak to them.'

'Yes. That'll be it,' said Viv slowly.

'It might even be the real reason he came home,' said Ursula.

'Right,' said Nick, rubbing his hands and thinking things were looking up. 'Now we've got that sorted out perhaps I can have my cocoa, love? I'm freezing.'

'Cocoa? Viv stared at him, still looking worried. 'Go and make your own. I'm too upset!'

He grimaced and did as he was told.

That night as Viv lay in her mother's bed beside Ursula, who was reading one of Hilda's *True Confession* magazines, she wondered just what George had heard of hers and Nick's conversation, and what he had made of it, and what Nick had said to him and what else George had said. It had been a bit difficult to ask with Ursula there. But perhaps she was right about George's reasons for coming home and she and Nick had had it wrong all the time? Maybe they were all right?

She sighed, hoping that George would not do anything

297

stupid. Perhaps she was an idiot to have got all worked up about him knowing? Nick was right. Why should he be protected? He was a grown man! Even so she hoped he would be all right. And that nothing else would go wrong.

She thought of her mother and the baby and suddenly things fell into perspective. She prayed that Stephen would do the gentlemanly thing and that everything would come right for them.

Stephen gazed into the cot and then lifted his eyes and stared at Hilda who looked better than he had expected for a woman of over forty who'd just given birth. She was wearing the satin nightdress that he had bought her for a birthday and her breasts filled it beautifully. He cleared his throat. 'Is she mine, Hilda?'

'I don't know how you could ask,' she said with the slightest tremor in her voice. 'Have you forgotten how many times we made love? Real love, Steve.'

He flushed and glanced about him but the father at the next bed had his head close to that of the young woman whose hand he was holding. 'Viv thinks she looks like me.'

Hilda smiled. 'She's got your hair. Natural curls. She'll thank you for that when she's older.' Her fingers slid along the back of the seat next to the bed and patted it. 'Come and sit down. It's easier to talk that way.'

Stephen sat and immediately could smell her perfume. It was light, flowery, and evoked memories of the Lake District. He longed to touch her but instead clasped his hands tightly together. 'What about Viv's father?'

Hilda's expression sobered and she began to pleat the fold of the sheet at her waist. 'I lied to her, Steve. That night when she came home with that Norwegian sailor, I lied to her. I told her that Jimmy wasn't her father when he was. I wanted to split you up because the pair of you were living in that house together and I'd been excluded.'

'But I asked you to marry me,' he said carefully. 'The three of us could have lived together!'

A small laugh escaped from her rouged lips. 'I know.' She touched one of his hands. 'But I was hurt. And so angry and jealous that I cut off my nose to spite my face. But I paid for it afterwards! You don't know how many time I wished I'd kept my mouth shut, but it was too late. Neither of you wanted to see or speak to me and I – I was too proud to come to you. I never thought that I could be having a baby. Your baby, Steve.' Her fingers stroked the back of his hand. 'Viv's so embarrassed you know what she's done? Told the neighbours that I've had gallstones removed! I don't know how I'm going to face them all. It was bad enough when I had Viv and I was younger. At my age they'll think it's a hoot.'

His fingers caught hers. 'You don't have to lay it on with a trowel, Hilda,' he said. 'I believe the baby's mine. We'll get married. I'll get a special licence.'

Relief flooded her face. 'Thanks, Steve.' She leaned forward and, putting a hand to the back of his head, kissed him. All the banked down passion of the last months and all her gratitude was in that the gesture so that he came out of the embrace convinced he was doing the right thing.

'There's one thing that bothers me, Hilda,' he murmured.

'What's that?' Her voice was anxious and she realised that she was holding her breath.

'The gossip in my avenue when you turn up with a baby. I know we'll have to put up with it for a while but I'd like to move away. We'll have a new house . . . a bigger one. I thought of it months ago before we split up. I still think of that house as belonging to my uncle but it never seemed worthwhile making the move. Now . . .'

'Are you thinking of a brand new house?' said Hilda, her eyes gleaming. 'Because if you are you could ask Nick's advice. Perhaps he could design us one? He won an award, you know.'

He smiled. 'I know. I'll do that.'

They fell silent.

She murmured, 'How d'you feel about Viv marrying him?'

'As long as he makes her happy, that's all I care about.'

'Her real father couldn't have wished her anything better,' she said softly.

'He never was a real bloody father to her, though, was he, Hilda?' His blue eyes blazed into hers. 'Not as much as I've been! So let's forget him forever and consider instead what we're going to call our daughter.'

Hilda was struck dumb but swiftly rallied. 'I thought Melanie.'

'Never heard of it.' He tried it on his tongue and thought it sounded like music.

'She was a character in a book – and maybe we could have you mother's name as well?'

'It would be two Ms,' he said gruffly. 'And Mabel's a bit old-fashioned.'

'Perhaps we could call her Melanie Stephanie then?' She smiled at him. He covered her hand with his and consigned Tom and Jimmy to oblivion.

'They're getting married,' said Viv, smiling as she opened the front door to Nick on Monday evening. She was feeling much better about everything.

'I know. Stephen phoned me about designing them a house.' He kissed her.

'He didn't tell me!' She reached for her coat. 'He didn't tell me what Mam said about my father either.'

'Perhaps he wants to forget all that?' Nick turned her round and did up her buttons and kissed the tip of her nose.

She nodded. 'I'll find out from Mam. Will you take me to the hospital?'

'Sure. Heard anything from George?'

'No.' She sighed. 'I'm not going to worry about him. Let's get going to the hospital.'

When Viv came out Nick took one look of her face and grinned. 'Come on – what did she say?'

'My mother is the most terrible liar!' said Viv in severe tones. 'Apparently Jimmy was my father after all, or so she's told Stephen.' She smiled innocently.

'As if you didn't know she was going to say that,' murmured Nick. 'And you think he believed her?'

'Obviously.' She shrugged. 'Although I don't know why he couldn't have told me so.'

'Perhaps not so obviously,' said Nick dryly.

Viv stared at him. 'You mean he didn't believe her but pretended to?'

He raised his eyebrows in a very speaking way. 'People go around pretending all sorts of things all the time. Maybe he

300

chose to believe her because it was what he wanted to believe. What does it matter? They've got a child to consider.'

'They're going to call the baby Melanie. It's out of *Gone With the Wind*. She was a nice character, understanding and forgiving. A lot of the time in the book Scarlett O'Hara believed herself in love with Melanie's husband.'

'I know. I saw the film. And all the time she was really in love with the rogue with the heart of gold, Rhett Butler,' murmured Nick. 'There's a moral there. Women! They never know their own minds. How do you really feel about George?'

'He's a grown man,' said Viv, taking a deep breath. 'I'm not his keeper. I'm not going to worry about him.' She went into his arms. It was a lie of course but she was not going to let her feelings about George show. She smiled up at Nick. 'I know my mind. Now when's our wedding going to be?'

Chapter Thirty-Two

Viv stood before the long mirror, barely able to believe in the vision in ivory satin that was reflected there. The dress had a boat neck and a bell-shaped skirt dipping at the front with a train falling in folds from the back. Ursula had designed it but Viv had another costume for later that she had made herself. The thought of tonight made her smile. She was going to surprise Nick.

Hilda adjusted the short bouffant veil yet once more. 'Mam, you're fussing,' cried Viv.

'I'm allowed to fuss on my daughter's wedding day,' muttered Hilda. 'I want you to bowl them all over when they see you.'

'I want Nick dumbstruck but not speechless,' said Viv dreamily. 'I don't care about the rest.'

Hilda smiled and shook her head. 'What about George? Just like him to turn up out of the blue.'

Happiness flooded Viv's features. 'I was so glad to see him, Mam! And to hear his news. Wasn't it great about that girl not being dead but having been rescued further down the valley? It's made such a difference to him.'

'Lovely,' said her mother dryly.

Viv grinned. 'How about Aunt Flora, Mike and the kids? Weren't you thrilled to see them?'

'Of course!'

Viv turned her head and reached for the bouquet of yellow roses and white carnations. 'Has she said anything to you?'

'I take it you mean about Tom?'

Viv nodded and Hilda moaned, 'Don't move your head like

302

that! You've disturbed your veil and I had it just right.'

'Mam! You do realise that you're doing the bridesmaids' job?' said Viv, exasperated. 'Where *are* Dot and Ingrid and Ursula?' She rustled over to the door.

Hilda hurried after her. She was wearing a cerise-coloured suit made of wild silk. 'Where d'you think you're going? We don't want anyone seeing you yet. Not until you make your big entrance in church.'

'I want to see Dot.'

'You'll see her in a minute. They're getting ready in the other room. Our Flo's in there as well as Lizzie. She's got you a lucky black cat. Now relax. I'll get us both a sherry.'

Viv raised her eyes to the newly whitewashed ceiling. 'You'll have me falling up the aisle!'

'It won't do you any harm. It'll calm your nerves,' said her mother.

'I haven't got any nerves.' Viv did a little jig round the bedroom. George had called her 'Sis'. She had hugged him and told him that he was never to do so again. The fewer people who knew the truth the better. 'I'm happy,' she said.

Hilda shook her head at her. 'We all have nerves on our wedding day. I had nerves and it was my third wedding. I just wasn't sure that Stephen would go through with it after all.'

'He's a hero is my step-daddy,' said Viv. 'I just hope he has no regrets – ever!'

'Three females who spoil him soft – why should he have regrets?' said Hilda, delicately arching her pencilled eyebrows.

Viv glanced about the bedroom in what had been Stephen's house. While Stephen's and Hilda's new house was being finished they were going to America on a belated honeymoon so that at last Hilda could visit Hollywood. Nick and Viv had taken out a small mortgage on this house. Stephen had asked much less than it was worth. In two years or so they hoped to be able to buy land and build their own. 'What about that drink?' she said to her mother suddenly. 'I'd like us to toast each other while we're on our own.'

'We've got a lot to be thankful for,' said Hilda, her face brightening.

Viv leaned against the dressing table and scrutinised her

mother's face. She said in mischievous tones, 'Are you getting all sentimental on me, Mam?'

'Me! I haven't a sentimental bone in my body,' said Hilda in scandalised tones, and whisked herself out of the bedroom.

Viv shrugged and went over to the window. Already a small crowd had gathered outside. Tonight, tonight! she thought. There was a knock on the door. 'Enter,' she said, considering the occasion demanded a grand word.

Her Aunt Flora entered, her hazel eyes alight with admiration and affection. 'You look beautiful, love. I just came to see if you needed any help from your bridesmaids?'

'Not yet. Shut the door, Aunt Flo. Mam's just gone to get us a drink. She said I'm nervy but it's her who's got the nerves.'

'She's only had you for a short while,' said Flora softly, 'and now she's losing you. It's a moving moment.' She looked about her. 'It feels strange to be here in such circumstances. To think I could have lived here . . .'

'Well, you didn't. And thank God you didn't,' said Viv, sitting beside her and putting a hand through the crook of her arm. 'Stephen's right for Mam.' She hesitated. 'How are you and Mam now?'

Flora murmured, 'Just the same as we've always been. We give and we take what we need from each other, and that's how it's always been with us. Nothing's going to spoil your wedding. This is your day so don't worry.'

'What about George? Has he said anything – '

'Not a thing.' Flora patted her hand. 'I think I worried unduly. After all, he barely knew his father.' She pulled a face. 'Anyway he's flirting with all the bridesmaids if that's any consolation to you, but especially that Ursula. What do you think of her?'

Before Viv could answer there was a knock on the door and Flora got up and opened it to her sister. They stared at each other. 'Perhaps I should get another glass?' said Hilda.

'No,' said Flora, smiling. 'You have your moment with Viv. I'll see you later.'

With her colour slightly high, Hilda handed a glass to her daughter. 'Here's to you, Viv. I hope he won't disappoint you.'

'Mam! What a thing to say,' she chided, placing her bouquet on the bed.

Hilda pulled a face. 'Well, you accused me of going soft on you before so I couldn't have that.'

Viv smiled and raised the glass. 'I hope you'll be content in your new house, Mam, and that you find a hard-working daily to take my place.'

'I'll see to it, don't you worry.' Hilda smiled and drank the toast. 'I'd better go and take Melly off Steve. He'll have to get ready for you.'

Viv nodded, then just as Hilda made to go she leaned forward and kissed her. Her mother stilled and stared at her, her eyes suddenly moist. Then she reached out scarlet-tipped fingers and touched Viv's cheek gently. 'You both deserve to be happy,' she said quietly. 'I don't know what I'd have done without you both. Tell Nick I said that when you're alone and faraway or he'll think I've gone soft.'

'I'll tell him,' whispered Viv, moved almost beyond words.

Epilogue

Viv gazed at herself in the bathroom mirror and adjusted her veil, humming a song from *Kismet*. She had left Nick undressing in the bedroom that overlooked the sea.

'Are you ready yet?' he called.

'Are you?'

'Ready and waiting.'

She smiled and took one last look at herself in the brief chiffon bodice and the skirt that she had made from several lengths of sheer material. Unexpectedly nerves fluttered in her stomach. She told herself firmly not to be so daft. It wasn't as if she was a Victorian virgin bride who knew nothing about sex and had never seen a man without his clothes on before.

She walked slowly into the bedroom and then stopped and drew an unsteady breath.

Nick lay naked on the bed – that was, naked except for the knight's helmet. 'I thought the full suit would be inappropriate so I . . .' His voice trailed off.

Viv's hands fluttered in the air like butterflies caught up in a courtship dance. 'The Seven Veils, sir? Or would you like me to peel you some grapes?'

'Where did you get it?' he murmured.

'I made it with my own dainty little fingers,' she answered. 'Where did you get the helmet?'

'I made that too. It's cardboard.' He took it off and slung it across the room. 'Come here.' His voice had deepened with emotion. 'I think we've put off this moment long enough.' Slowly she went to him and he pulled her down on to the bed.

'Mam said that I was to tell you that we deserve to be

306

happy,' said Viv, stroking his chest. 'That she wouldn't have known what to do without us.'

'That was big of her,' said Nick, removing her bodice. 'I'm sure we will be happy.'

'As happy as anyone can be.' Her fingers travelled downwards.

'How much do I love you?' he whispered.

'You could show me a number of ways, I reckon.' She smiled into his eyes.

'This time nobody and nothing is going to stop us,' said Nick, and slowly removed the first veil and began to show her just how much he really did love her.

You have been reading a novel published by Piatkus Books. We hope you have enjoyed it and that you would like to read more of our titles. Please ask for them in your local library or bookshop.

If you would like to be put on our mailing list to receive details of new publications, please send a large stamped addressed envelope (UK only) to:

Piatkus Books: 5 Windmill Street
London W1P 1HF

PIATKUS

The sign of a good book